FRACTURED SEA

PRESENTED BY FAIRY TALE INK

D1713921

JO SCHNEIDER - ADRIENNE MONSON - TERI HARMAN

LEHUA PARKER - ANGELA BRIMHALL

TORK MEDIA

BOB HOUSTON eBOOK FORMATTING

CONTENTS

INTRODUCTION

Fairy Tale Ink is a group of independent authors who write in different genres. But we have a couple of things in common: we love fairy tales and have always wanted to write our own retold versions. Since our desires lined up perfectly, we decided to do a series of anthologies. That way, readers can find one set of their favorite fairy tale, and read a few different versions of it.

We look forward to retelling more classic fairy tales and would love to hear what you think of the stories we have published so far. Please post reviews on any channel you frequent. If you'd like to learn more about the authors and their other works, or would like to see more information on our other anthologies releasing soon, please visit our site www.FairyTaleInkBooks.com.

THE ACADEMY

Young Adult Fantasy

By

Jo Schneider

The Academy
Copyright © 2018 by Jo Schneider
All Rights Reserved

First Edition: 2018

CHAPTER 1

*R*i's eyes slid past her father's palace and beyond the forest of seaweed. Above, a school of fish turned in unison and shot toward the top of the ocean. Sunlight sparkled and twisted on the surface, waning as it descended until it crested the coral palace's top spires.

"Are you even listening to me?"

Ri blinked, returning her attention to her grandmother. "Uh, yes?"

The older mermaid shook her head, her long gray hair slowly following the motion through the water. "It's like you've already got your land legs."

"Grandmother." Ri flicked her tail, moving closer. She reached a slender hand out to touch her mother's, mother's shoulder. "I'm ready for this. You've been preparing me for months." Ri lowered her voice, speaking in a familiar cadence. "'Pay attention in class.' 'Don't commit to anything on the first day.' 'Keep your options open.' 'Try not to provoke the orcs, watch out for the faerie folk, and be nice to your roommate.' 'Don't flaunt your beauty, because your sisters won't like it.'" Ri threw her most dazzling smile. "See, I listen."

"Child, you are going to be the death of me," Ri's grandmother muttered.

Ri opened her mouth to retort, but spotted her father and his foreign diplomatic advisor—Ri's oldest sister's husband—over her grandmother's shoulder.

Her father, Triton, swam straight and tall. His shoulders reached an impressive spread for a merman his age. A golden crown sat atop his brow, and streaks of white shot from his temples and through his mane of hair.

People always said that Ri's hair was an even more beautiful shade of red.

Triton's tail shimmered as he approached, catching the light from above and sending a rainbow of colors off his scales. Even the oysters attached to his caudal fin shimmered. Ri knew he'd trained himself to reflect the light while he swam. It had taken her a year to master it.

Next to Triton, her sister's husband looked scrawny. Instead of wide, he was tall. He cut a fine figure, but in a slender way. He'd drawn his dark hair into a piece of seaweed at the base of his neck. The scales on his tail reflected a dark red. Unusual, and very fashionable right now.

The two mermen inclined their heads together, talking.

Ri leaned around her grandmother, willing her ears to catch their conversation.

"The humans have always been reluctant to meet with us," Karel said to the king.

"I must speak with their king," Ri's father said.

"I have asked multiple times, but they either do not respond, or they tell me their king is out of the capital."

Triton snorted. "We know where he's been."

Karel held up a finger. "We *think* we know where he's been." He leaned closer. "Perhaps one of your daughters could speak with the prince at the school."

"They don't like him," Triton said. "You know that."

Ri's eyes narrowed. The *human* prince? He was a student at the Academy? Neither of her sisters had said a word about him.

A peal of laughter sounded behind the two mermen, and a tiny, red-tailed mermaid shot between them, leaving a trail of bubbles leading right to Ri.

"Auntie Ri!" The young blonde-haired, blue-eyed mermaid approached with her arms out. The blue eyes went wide when she discovered she was headed for Grandmother.

Ri smiled, moving to catch her niece. The little mermaid's hands closed around Ri's neck, and Ri turned in a circle to slow her down.

Karel sighed.

Triton grinned.

Ri held her niece out where she could see her. "What are you doing, Gail?"

Gail's entire round face pouted. "You're leaving."

"Just for a little while."

"For a long while."

Ri patted Gail on the shoulder. "I'm going to school. Just like you have classes."

"But they're on land." Gail scrunched her nose. "It smells funny up there."

Ri laughed. "Yes it does, but if I want to be a real princess then I need to know as much as I can." She looked hard at Gail. "You know you're going to be a princess too, right?"

Gail nodded.

"Well then, you'd better keep track of things down here for me."

The blue eyes went wide. "Really?"

Ri leaned in. "Someone has to watch out for Grandpa, Great-Grandma, and your parents. You know how adults are—they get too serious."

Gail's head bobbed up and down.

"Don't let that happen." Ri poked Gail in the stomach, which drew a giggle.

"Gail," Karel said in a stern voice, "you're supposed to be with your mother."

"I was," Gail said, "but I escaped."

"That's my girl," Triton said with a wink. Then he turned his eyes on Ri.

Ri braced herself.

One of the king's eyebrows rose as his gaze traveled to Ri's fin. "Interesting choice in oysters."

She had attached eight oysters to the end of her fin, four on each side. It was tradition that the royal family wear them, and Ri had spent hours picking these out. They would, in time, produce unique and valuable pearls that would go to her children when she died. She rose and flapped her tail. "Do you like them?"

"They're a bit showy."

"Daddy," Ri said before he could get going, "I'm the princess. Aren't I allowed to be a little showy?"

Triton's eyes traveled to her torso. "And you'd better be wearing more than that when you transform."

The form-fitting—and even, Ri had to admit, slightly revealing—top had been her latest purchase from the market. It fit her perfectly. The blue-green color matched her eyes and complemented her hair. It clashed a little with her orange and green tail, but once she had legs, no one on land would know.

"It rolls down into a dress," she said.

"And a jacket?"

Ri was surprised her father knew what a jacket was. It wasn't like they ever needed them in the ocean. "Of course."

Technically she was telling the truth. She had a jacket, just not one she was going to put on after she transformed.

The look on her father's face told her he knew as much, but she smiled and swam toward him. "Oh Daddy, I'm so excited." She turned on her big eyes and her best expression of wonder. "You know I've wanted to go to the Academy since I was Gail's age." Ri reached out, and her father sighed and took her hands. Ri bent down and kissed his ring. "I promise to make you proud."

"All my girls make me proud."

Gail, who had gone to Grandmother, squealed. Triton gave her another wink, then turned back to Ri. "Remember, you're a princess of the merpeople. My daughter. Your duty is to bring honor to our name, learn everything you can, make friends, and do not make me come up there for any reason."

"Of course!" Ri said.

"And don't forget: two of your sisters are already there. Do not be afraid to ask them for help."

Ri waved her hand. "I won't need any help from them."

"You might."

"I won't."

The deep vibration of a horn thrummed in the water.

A thrill ran from the tip of Ri's tail up through the top of her head. Her insides churned, but her smile grew wider. "It's time."

"My baby, going off to school," Triton said.

"Please don't cry, Dad," Ri said. "You promised."

When her father—the king—spoke, his voice caught in his throat. "Your mother would be so proud."

Ri had to keep from rolling her eyes. She moved forward and embraced her father. His strong arms wrapped around her, and for a moment panic pushed at her calm. He'd always been there, just a short swim away. And now she wouldn't see him for many moon cycles.

But she couldn't show weakness. If she did, he might change his mind and keep her under the sea for another year.

She pulled away, shooting a grin at Kalel. "Take care of him while I'm gone."

"We'll do our best. Shiari said to wish you luck. She's struggling."

"That's what happens when you two go at it all the time." Ri winked.

Kalel had the decency to blush, but then he grinned. "Good luck."

"You too. Send me a message when Gail has a little sister."

"Or brother."

"With our family's luck? It's a girl for sure." Ri gave her grandmother one last hug, showered Gail with a flurry of kisses, then turned her attention upward.

A dark shadow had moved right over them.

"Are you ready?" Grandmother asked.

"I'm ready." Ri squared her shoulders and rose.

"Bye!" Gail said.

"I love you, Ariel," Triton said. "Remember who you are."

"I love you, too," Ri said over her shoulder, and without another look back, she rose to the water's surface.

CHAPTER 2

She'd been to the surface hundreds of times, but always
with the threat of death in the back of her mind. A
mermaid or merman could live outside the ocean for a
little while, but without a spell to alter their lungs, they would
only last an hour or two. Any more than that and important
things would wilt and die.

Right before she breached, Ri shook her head to make sure
her long hair streamed behind her. She'd wanted to jump out of
the water and make a big show, but her oldest sister had talked
her out of it. *"Be a bit mysterious. People will take you more seriously."*

So she came out of the water head first, her hair trailing
behind in a manner she'd practiced for a week. She flicked her
tail, which pushed her top half into the air.

A tall, thin ship rose before her. Twin sails billowed in the
wind, and the wood creaked as the water moved under it. A
smaller boat swung from ropes securing it to the ship's side.

The sunshine warmed Ri's skin. The smells—so disgusting to Gail—filled Ri's nose, and she breathed every one of them in. The salty air. The ocean. The wood of the ship. The canvas of the sails.

"Mermaid!" a man's voice bellowed. "Port side."

Ri glanced up at the deck and found two sailors and one woman looking over the rail. A neat hat perched atop the woman's head, and a fitted, black blouse with white lace trim covered what Ri could see of her.

"Do you have your things?" the woman asked.

As if on cue, three large bubbles with ropes trailing behind them surfaced next to Ri.

She pointed.

One of the men poked his head back over the side. "We're going to lower the small boat."

Ri nodded. She grabbed the three ropes and pulled her luggage away from the ship.

The smaller boat began to move immediately. It hit the water with a splash, and Ri saw two more men in it.

Only these were younger. Maybe her age.

One of them was short and stout, with darker skin and black hair. The other sat a head taller than the first, his light skin a nice contrast to his companion. Neither wore shirts, and both obviously took the time to take care of their bodies.

"Can you swim over here?" the taller one asked.

Ri almost snorted, but remembered that these boys had probably never seen a mermaid before.

Well then, she could give them a little show.

Ri kept the ropes in one hand, and swam forward. She let them have a good view of her back before she dove under the water, allowing her tail to catch the sun.

Swimming right below the surface of the ocean always brought Ri a surge of delight. The sun's warmth hit her skin and her tail. The light played games with the water, providing a tantalizing array of colors and shadows. She stayed there until she got close to the smaller boat, then she came back up, once again rising out to the top of her tail before sinking back down.

The looks on the boys' faces gave her an immense amount of satisfaction.

The shorter one recovered first. He stood, keeping perfect balance in the boat, and gestured toward her luggage. "Can I take that for you?"

In the water the bags weighed almost nothing; out of it, they would be heavy. Ri pulled them next to the boat, and the boys hauled them in. Neither one complained.

Once they got the bags settled, the boys turned back to her. For a moment the short one said nothing, just stared into her eyes.

The taller one cleared his throat. "I'm Sam, and this is Tayle. We're here from the Academy."

Ri smiled.

Sam frowned as though he was offended.

Tayle shot Sam a look of irritation. "She can't talk out of the water."

Sam shrugged. "Are you ready to come in?"

Ri nodded. She unhooked her skirt and let it fall to the middle of her tail.

Both boys held out a hand, but Ri swam to the little boat, grasped the edge and gave a great flap with her tail. Both boys moved to the other side to stabilize it as she turned and, as gracefully as she could, slid her tail over the edge and into the boat.

They had a wet blanket lining the wooden surface.

"Here you go," Tayle said as he gently set another on her tail. "Hopefully that will be more comfortable."

She smiled.

He smiled back.

His dark eyes danced, and his skin shone in the sunlight. His broad shoulders reminded her of her father.

"We'll get you up there fast," Sam said, setting a hand on her bare shoulder.

Tayle almost rolled his eyes before he sat down.

A few minutes later they were in position. The little boat lifted off the water. Sweat broke out on both boys' faces and chests as they pulled on the ropes.

This was it.

They rose to the ship's rail. Six sailors stood ready to assist her. The woman and two robed figures—wizards—hovered nearby. Next to them, a strange circle had been burned into the deck. Geometric patterns ran through the middle of it.

As soon as her escorts had stopped tugging, the other sailors rushed forward.

"They'll take you for the spell," Tayle said. "Let them help you."

Ri forced a smiled. Each breath took a little more moisture out of her lungs, and a tickle had started in her throat.

It felt strange to have humans putting their arms under her. Each touch sent tingles through her body, and the warmth of their skin sent shivers racing up her spine.

"Easy does it. Make sure you've got that tail," one man said. "Don't let the end hit the ground. Those oysters'll put a hole in the deck."

He must have been an experienced seaman.

"That's right, lift her out of there. Move together. Get her into the middle."

The two wizards moved to opposite sides of the circle and squatted down. They put their palms onto the wood.

Tayle gave her nod of encouragement.

Sam winked at her.

The sailors lowered her to the deck, right in the middle of the circle, and then everyone except for the wizards moved back.

Ri's mind screamed at her to jump over the rail and back into the sea.

The woman with the black blouse stepped forward. "Ariel, I'm Miss Telly from the Academy. These wizards are going to perform the spell to turn your tail into legs, and then they'll give you an enchanted amulet so you can speak."

Ri nodded, sitting up straight and tall just as her father did.

"If you are ready, we will begin," Miss Telly said.

CHAPTER 3

R i kept her head up and nodded again.

The wizards began to chant, and the circle beneath Ri started to glow. She had expected it to be hot, but instead the wood turned cool beneath her.

She'd never done this before, but all six of her sisters had. They'd all said that the only thing that hurt worse than the actual spell was the first day after the transformation, when every step felt like walking on sharp stones.

The cold seeped through Ri's scales and into her core. A shiver ran through her body. The air around her constricted, and Ri had to clamp her teeth together to keep from crying out.

Once, Ri and her sisters had played so rough that their game had caused a minor rockslide. The others had been old and wise enough to get out of the way, but little Ariel had not. The initial sensation had hurt, which made sense because her tail was being smashed. Then adrenaline kicked in and her tail had gone numb, but in the strangest way. Somehow her mind had sent the pain elsewhere, but Ri had known that there was something terribly wrong. She'd cried and cried until her father and his guards had come and moved the rocks.

The doctors had done their best to stitch Ri's tail back together, but there had always been a tiny piece missing. It was a reminder to steer clear of rockslides, or to learn to swim faster. She'd always covered the scar with an oyster.

The cold continued to numb Ri's tail, and even though she shouldn't have felt the tear when her tail separated into legs, she did. Not pain, but pressure. And panic.

Ri fought to keep her breathing steady as part of her ripped in half and transformed into something else.

At some point she had closed her eyes. Now Ri forced them open and looked down at her body. Her tail had shrunk, and sat in two pieces. The scales sank from the surface, giving way to…legs.

The transformation continued. Ri knew she should close her mouth, but she couldn't. She watched as thighs appeared, then knees, knobby and somewhere between hideous and beautiful. Then calves, and then feet.

The bones—still numb—changed, fusing into a new configuration. The oysters at the end of her tail shrunk, and toes appeared. Four on each foot.

As her sisters had warned, the cold wore off, replaced by a searing pain that reached from her newly formed toes up into her spine. Ri wanted to scream, but settled for a little moan.

Then people were around her. Someone put a blanket over her, while another spoke softly. "It's okay. It'll pass."

Ri had expected it to be the woman, but it was Sam. She opened her eyes and saw the young man kneeling next to her with his hand on her back.

Her unwavering sense of pride kicked in, and despite the pain, Ri lifted herself and sat up.

The shorter wizard approached and knelt. She held an orangeish, twisted seashell dangling from a strip of leather.

"Now that your lungs have changed, I'm going to put this on you."

Ri nodded.

The wizard leaned forward and put her hands behind Ri's neck. She whispered a few words before she clasped the necklace and let the shell drop. It hit right where Ri's collarbones met. Heat pulsed from the shell, and it began to glow. Something in her throat changed. The orange light faded, but did not disappear.

"Can you speak?" the wizard asked.

Ri swallowed, then cleared her throat. A noise came out. It sounded rough. Raw. Nothing like her voice under the water.

Ri took a breath and answered the question. "Yes."

"Say a few sentences."

Ri looked the woman in the eye. "Thank you for performing the spell. I can breathe and speak."

"What's your name?" Sam asked.

"Ariel, but everyone calls me Ri."

"Ri." He said the name as if trying it out. "It's good to meet you."

"Thank you."

Miss Telly stepped forward, beaming. "Welcome to the surface, Ariel. We are here to escort you to the Academy, where you will spend the next four years getting an education."

"It is nice to meet you, Miss Telly."

The woman shooed the others away. "Leave us."

Sam gave Ri a crooked grin before he went below deck. Tayle followed, his smile replaced by a frown.

Miss Telly watched until all the sailors, the wizards, and the two boys had left for other parts of the ship. Then she moved to Ri, offering her both hands. "Can you stand?"

Moving her tail came naturally—all merpeople could swim from the moment they were born—but these legs felt alien. She flexed the muscles that had controlled her tail. Each leg moved, but not exactly as she had pictured.

"Get your feet underneath you," Miss Telly said unhelpfully.

It took Ri a few seconds of concentration to get her legs to cooperate. Each bend of her knees sent a dull throbbing through her body, and each turn of her ankles felt like seashells crunching together. She grit her teeth and did as Miss Telly had said. Then the woman reached down, grasped both of Ri's hands, and pulled.

Ri rose. Her legs scrambled to keep up, and a moment later, Ri was looking at the world as a land-dweller. Both of her legs shook, but they held. Ri had to let go of Miss Telly with one hand to keep the blanket around her shoulders.

"Come inside," Miss Telly said. "You can change. By the time you are finished, we will be at the dock where your sisters are waiting."

Ri took a tentative step. Then another. Her sisters had not exaggerated. Each time her smooth feet made contact with the rough wood, it felt as if she were walking over sharpened obsidian. The sensation ricocheted up through her knees to her waist and ended where her tail used to start.

The pain took her breath away, and Ri was grateful that Miss Telly didn't require her to speak. They slowly made their way to a nearby door leading to a small cabin. Inside sat a chair, a bed, and a table. A little oval mirror with a wavy surface hung on the wall. Light poured in from a slit of a window. Someone had stacked her bags in one corner.

"Do you need help with your clothes?" Miss Telly asked.

Ri shook her head. "I'm fine, thank you."

"Excellent. Then I shall be waiting right outside. Knock or call out if you need anything."

"I will."

The moment the door closed, Ri moved to the bed and sat. She wiped moisture from her brow. Sweat.

She gave herself a moment before standing again. The pain didn't wane, but this time she was prepared. She moved to her bag, retrieved the outfit she wanted to wear, and changed into it. Putting one leg at a time through the skirt proved more challenging than expected, especially since the ship chose that moment to roll to one side and then back.

Once Ri had finished with the clothes, she surveyed herself in the mirror. Her skin looked paler than she would have thought, but it did contrast nicely with her deep red hair. Ri reached up and touched a section of her hair that had begun to dry. It felt strange. Fuzzy.

Here again she'd been practicing, and she had a plan. It took a few minutes, but when she stepped from the cabin, her hair lay in rolling layers held up by pearl hair pins.

"Ready?" asked Miss Telly, who had been standing like a sentinel outside the door.

"Yes. Should I bring my bags?"

"Someone else will do that. Come."

Ri followed Miss Telly up a set of stairs and found herself staring at the harbor. Small and large ships bustled back and forth. Men shouted, and a strange contraption sat on one dock, lifting crates of goods off the largest ship.

They had pulled up along the pier, and the sailors were just setting the gangway in place.

Ri squinted against the light. Two tall, slender figures waved from the end of the wooden dock.

Her sisters.

"How are you feeling?" Sam asked.

Ri turned and found the young man dressed in a fine set of trousers and a silk shirt. She raised her eyebrows.

"What?" he asked. "You don't think I go to school like that, do you?"

"I guess not," Ri said.

"You look great, by the way," Sam said.

Tayle appeared. He'd also changed his clothes. His finery did not match Sam's, but his shoulders filled out his shirt in a pleasing manner. "How are you feeling?" Tayle asked.

"It's going to take a little getting used to," Ri said. "But I'm looking forward to it."

The sailors finished with the gangway, and Sam stepped forward and offered Ri his arm. "May I?"

A strange heat rose up Ri's neck and to her cheeks. At this moment, she was grateful her father had forced her to learn as much as she could about the land-dwellers. She linked her arm with Sam's and put her other hand on his arm. "Thank you."

Tayle turned away to speak with one of the sailors as Sam led Ri down to the dock.

"You're going to love it here," Sam said.

"You think so?"

"Well, I hope you love it. I love it." He smiled at her again.

Ri fought to keep her expression neutral. "I'm excited to see and do as much as possible."

"I'm so glad."

Ri cleared her throat. "So you go to the Academy?"

"Sure do," he said with a twinkle in his eye.

Ri wanted to keep watching him, but had to concentrate on putting her feet in the right places. Each time she faltered or leaned, Sam tightened his grip.

"Your sisters are here," Sam said.

Ri risked a glance up, and saw her sisters at the end of the gangplank.

Marian, the older of the two, looked as if a strong breeze would pick her up and carry her away. Long, blonde hair cascaded down her back to her waist. The knee-length blue skirt hugged her slender curves, and the white blouse cut low, but not too low. A flat, pink shell on a silver strand sat at the base of her throat. She gave Ri a little wave.

Kyla, the sister two years older than Ariel, had pulled her light red hair up into a bun. A few tendrils had come loose, giving it a messy look. Unlike Marian's conservative garb, Kyla wore a bright yellow blouse that their father would be furious about. And instead of a skirt, tight blue trousers covered Kyla's legs. A green shell hung around her neck. Ri felt Kyla give her outfit the once-over. Then her eyes landed on Sam, and they widened.

"Ladies," Sam said as they approached, "I believe this delightful creature is your sister."

Marian's eyebrows drew together, and Kyla's expression went cold.

Marian recovered first. She smiled—she had the best smile of all the sisters—and gave a little bow. "Yes, Your Majesty. Thank you for going out to meet her."

Sam laughed. "It was my pleasure."

Ri glanced back and forth between them. Your Majesty? Who *was* Sam?

Two men armed with spears and dressed in uniform approached. They bowed to Sam. One of them spoke. "Your Majesty, your father requests your presence."

Sam sighed and turned to Ri. "Thank you for allowing me to help you. I look forward to seeing you at the Academy." He gently let go of her arm.

"The pleasure has been, and will be, mine." Ri bowed as low as her sisters had.

That glint hit Sam's eye again, and he gave her a wink before turning and leading the guards away.

Kyla stepped close and took Ri's arm. "What are you doing?"

"What? Is the skirt too short?"

Kyla snorted. "No. I mean what are you doing with *him*?"

"Him who?"

Marian crossed to Ri's other side. "That's Prince Samuel."

Ri's breath caught in her throat. "*The* Prince Samuel?"

"That's him."

"He's not the nicest person," Marian said.

"That's the understatement of the year," Kyla said.

"He seems nice," Ri said.

"Stay away from him," Kyla said. "He's trouble."

CHAPTER 4

*R*i's sisters spent the ride to the Academy asking Ri about home. Ri answered as best she could, but each turn they took through the city showed her more wonders. Buildings soared above her head, and she saw more people than she thought possible. They passed vendors selling their wares, and the tantalizing smells of new spices. She wanted to take it all in.

They followed the prince's carriage until it turned just before the city wall, and then went through the gate and out into the countryside.

Rolling hills of yellow and green spread as far as the eye could see. A windmill sat in the distance, just like a painting Ri had once seen.

The carriage went over a bump, and Ri grimaced.

"The pain will go away in a day or two," Marian said.

They spent the rest of the time talking about family and friends. By the time she was thirteen, Ri had asked her sisters every question about the Academy she could think of, so there was no need to pester them.

The ride didn't last long, and Ri recognized the Academy's tower as soon as it came into view. Tall and round, it rose from the earth like a living thing. It stood sentinel over the rest of the campus, which consisted of half a dozen low buildings for classes, one larger gymnasium and performance stage, and a row of dormitories.

She would be in the dorm farthest from the school, which was the first of many punishments for being a first-year.

"Are you excited?" Marian asked as the coach took them through the spindly gates shaped like birds.

"You know I am," Ri said.

Kyla glared at Ri's legs. "Your skirt is too short."

"Not too short for school code," Ri said. "I checked."

"Father had no idea you were going to wear that, did he?"

Ri met her sister's gaze. "Does he know that you wear pants?"

"I can wear whatever I want," Kyla said.

"Then so can I."

Marian shook her head. "Will the two of you stop?"

"No," they said together.

The carriage turned toward the dorms. As they approached the last one, Kyla looked hard at Ri.

"What?" Ri asked.

"Just wondering how much I need to remind you about being a princess."

Ri rolled her eyes. "Please, Grandmother just lectured me for an hour."

"Well, remember it. You not only represent yourself here, but more importantly, you represent the entire kingdom."

"I know, I know," Ri said, waving a hand. "And anything I do could be taken as an affront by someone from another kingdom. I do listen."

Kyla continued glaring. "Well, put some effort into actually doing it, will you?"

Ri sat up as straight as she could. "Oh don't worry, I won't be an embarrassment to you, if that's what you're worried about."

Marian interrupted. "I found out who your roommate is. Her name is Su'la. She's human, and a gifted spell caster."

"My roommate is a wizard?" Ri asked.

"She is. Her family is fairly prominent in the kingdom, so don't offend her."

Ri gave Marian a flat look. "Do you think I'm going to go around offending everyone?"

The carriage stopped.

Marian sighed. "Just try to behave like a lady."

Ri didn't bother to answer as she allowed the coachman to help her out. Two others were already unloading her bags.

Another woman dressed like Miss Telly appeared. "Ariel, so glad to have you here. I will show you to your room."

Ri gave her sisters one last wave—although it may have been construed as a shooing motion—and followed the woman inside.

Behave like a lady? What did her sisters think she was going to do? They were obviously jealous that the prince had come to meet her.

Why *had* he come to meet her?

The woman led Ri up one flight of stairs to her room. "Your roommate is Su'la. She is new as well. Your schedule is on your bed, along with a map. Your room has been specially hydrated, so you shouldn't feel dry as long as you sleep here each night. If you do feel dry, please contact the campus doctor. He can help you with whatever you need."

The woman stopped and pointed to a closed door. "This is it."

"Thank you," Ri said in her most respectful voice.

"You are welcome. Now I have three more students coming. Please, make yourself at home. Orientation begins in a few hours, and you'll need to be at the auditorium five minutes before."

"I will."

And she was gone.

Ri turned to her new home. An uninteresting wooden door barred her way. The tarnished knob felt smooth beneath her fingers, and it turned with a quiet click. Ri pushed the door open. It let out a light squeak, and she peered inside.

A small hallway led to the room, which was larger than she had expected. A bed sat on the wall to her right, and another on her left. Modest dressers stood at the head of each bed, and desks occupied the space at the foot. A large window made up most of the far wall. The curtains were open, giving her an unobstructed view of the beautiful countryside.

The right half of the room was already occupied. Books covered the desk, and potion jars filled the shelf above. Clothes and blankets lay heaped upon the bed, and two other chests sat with their lids open, ready to spew forth even more stuff.

A clunk sounded from the closet, and Ri jumped.

"Hello?" a voice asked.

"Hi," Ri said, looking around the corner.

A short human girl with dark skin, spiky black hair, and a little extra weight on her frame stood trying to push a wooden box onto the top shelf of the closet. Despite her curves, the girl had excellent taste in clothes. A dark shirt clung in all the right places, and her long black skirt left little to the imagination.

"Here," Ri said, "let me help."

The short girl turned and held up a single finger, her other hand still trying to get the box to her goal. Her almost-black eyes glittered. "Do *not* touch my stuff."

"Uh, okay," Ri said, taking a step back and holding her hands out.

"I use all these things for spells. If they are tampered with in any way, I will know."

"Will anything turn me into a toad?"

"It depends on my mood."

"No touching your stuff. Got it." This was not going as planned. "I'm Ri."

"Su'la," the other girl said as she jumped and finally got the teetering box far enough over the shelf's edge to stay. She eyed it for a moment, as if daring it to come back down, before returning her attention to Ri. Her eyes traveled from Ri's head, pausing at the shell necklace, down to her toes and back up.

It didn't feel the same as when Sam had done it. Not at all.

"Siren?"

"Excuse me?" Ri asked.

"Are you a siren?"

"Mermaid," Ri said between clenched teeth.

"Ah, that explains the four toes and the voice box."

"Are you always this cordial?"

Su'la took a breath and closed her eyes for a moment. When she reopened them, she spoke in a voice that Ri knew all too well, only it usually came from her frustrated grandmother. "Look, I'm here to learn as much as I can. I'm not here to make friends or to party."

"Okay," Ri said. "Can I at least ask you a few questions?"

The expression on Su'la's face told Ri she wanted to say no. "Go for it."

"Where are you from?"

"My family lives a few hours from here."

"Do you have brothers and sisters?"

"Yes. Do you want to know my favorite color?"

"Black?" Ri ventured.

"Purple. Anything else?"

"Not yet."

Su'la turned away. "I keep strange hours. Just to warn you."

"I consider myself warned."

Ri spent the hours before orientation unpacking, and most of that went to organizing the closet. She caught Su'la's disapproving look over the amount of clothes she'd brought, but ignored it. Ri loved clothes, and had been collecting them for years just for school. She'd dreamt about the day she would be able to do more than just cover her breasts. This land body gave her so many more possibilities.

The time for orientation came, and Su'la reluctantly agreed to walk over with Ri.

They passed through the center of campus, where most of the students were lounging. In one corner of the middle green, a group of centaurs played a game with a ball and bats. Three petite girls splashed in the main fountain, and a mixed group of satyrs, an orc, and several humans sat at a table, talking and laughing.

The satyrs watched as Ri and Su'la passed, their eyes following the two girls. Ri smiled and gave one of them a wink.

"Don't encourage them," Su'la said. "They'll be after you all year."

"Would that be so bad?"

"Have you heard how they court?"

"Uh, a little."

"Trust me, just stay away."

Ri made a mental note to learn more about satyrs.

As they approached the auditorium, Ri slowed. With each step pain shot up her legs, and she eyed the stairs with dread. Until she saw a familiar figure.

Sam—Prince Samuel, Ri corrected herself—stood outside the main doors, greeting the first-years as they entered. He spotted her and gave her a huge smile.

"Ri." He spread his arms and walked down a couple of steps. "How are you? Did they get you settled in?"

"Yes. Thank you, Your Majesty." One side of Ri's lips twitched.

"Someone ratted me out, eh?"

"My sisters."

Sam laughed. "I'm sure." He reached out and patted her on the shoulder. "Go find a seat. We're going to start in a few minutes."

She nodded.

Sam's expression faded. "Su'la. Good to see you."

"Your Majesty," she said in a tone that would have turned the fountain into an ice cube. She pushed past Ri and went into the building.

"What's that about?" Ri asked.

"She's an old family friend," Sam said.

"Doesn't sound like it," Ri said.

"It's complicated," Sam said. He stepped closer. "She had a little crush on me when we were kids. I think she's embarrassed about it."

"Ah," Ri said.

"Don't tell her I told you."

Ri put a finger to her lips. "Your secret is safe with me."

"Good." Sam took her fingers, raised them to his lips and kissed the back of her hand. His blue eyes bored into hers. "I hope to see you later."

Ri's heart beat wildly in her chest. The warmth from Sam's lips lingered as she climbed the rest of the stairs and followed Su'la into the auditorium.

The picture of the auditorium in Ri's mind had been spot on. Rows of chairs—some modified for centaurs, satyrs, and others with unusual limbs—fell away from the back door toward a wooden stage. Pillars carved with vines and flowers rose from each side of the stage up to the ceiling far above. Iron chandeliers—probably enchanted—let out more light than their few candles should have. Rich red curtains hung closed.

"Please go to the front," an usher said. His voice hissed, and Ri wasn't surprised to find one of the undead standing well away from the sunlight.

Ri followed his instructions, making her way forward. She wanted to grimace with each step, but she kept her head high and her eyes open.

Older students occupied the first two rows. They craned their necks to watch the first-years come in.

Ri decided to sit in the fourth row. Not too ambitious, but not in the back. Su'la had positioned herself as far away from the stage as she could get without looking stupid. Ri sat between two elves. They said hello, but not much else. That was fine; Ri was more interested in Sam, who was making his way up onto the stage with a short—but somehow handsome—goblin. Sam leaned down to speak to the smaller creature, and they both laughed.

"Who's that?" Ri asked the elf on her right.

"Prince Samuel?" he asked.

"No, the other one."

"Rakar. Last year's student body president." He must have correctly interpreted the confused expression on her face, so he went on. "Prince Samuel will take over for him in a week's time, at the ball."

"Ah," Ri said. Maybe she should have tapped her sisters for information before orientation.

The goblin, Rakar, gave a wave. "Greetings."

The older students waved back and said, "Greetings."

"I said *greetings!*" Rakar said more loudly.

The first-years repeated it, and Rakar nodded. "Good."

Ri's eyes slid from Rakar to Sam, and she found him watching her. He wiggled his eyebrows once. Ri looked away.

Rakar went on, talking about how happy he was to have them all there, and about the great opportunities that lay before them.

Ri tuned him out. Instead, she thought about Sam. The prince.

Sure, he was older, but only two years. He'd already shown some interest in her, and she had to be honest: it wouldn't be at all painful to get to know him better. She didn't understand what her sisters' problem was, and she didn't care. He was obviously interested, and she was going to explore that. If she could get an in with Prince Samuel, then maybe she could convince Sam to convince his father to meet with her father.

"Ariel."

Ri blinked, turning her attention to Rakar.

Rakar squinted into the crowed. "Ariel? Are you here?"

Sam pointed. "She's right there. Come meet your mentor."

Mentor? How long had she been daydreaming? A quick glance around showed others moving toward the front, so she rose from her seat and made her way to the aisle. The slope threw her balance off, and she gained more speed than she had planned. The stage grew closer, the slope grew steeper, and her top half began to outdistance her clumsy legs.

Ri winced. Face-planting in front of all the mentors and first-years had not been on her to do list.

CHAPTER 5

S o it was a good thing that Tayle was there to catch her. He stepped out from the rows of older students, turned and put his hands on her arms to stop her momentum. "Easy."

"Tayle," Ri said.

His touch sent a shiver through Ri. He looked into her eyes and grinned. "You okay?"

She caught her breath. "Where did you come from?"

"Right there," he said, pointing. "Come on." He steered her by the elbow.

"Where are we going?"

"I'm your mentor."

"You are?"

"Weren't you listening?"

"Uh…"

"Never mind. They're pairing one of us with one of you. We're going to show you around campus and answer any questions you have."

"Oh. Right."

Tayle laughed. "You weren't listening."

"I got distracted." Ri's eyes flicked to Sam, who stood above them on stage.

"Ah, I see." Tayle's expression fell.

"What?"

"Don't worry, I'm used to it," Tayle said. "You're not the first girl to be completely distracted by him."

"What? No, it's not like that."

Tayle waved a hand. "Come on, I'll show you around."

They followed other pairs through the side door and back outside. The clouds had grown heavy, looking as if they would burst any minute.

"What do you mean you're used to it?" Ri asked.

"The prince and I...grew up together. People always pay attention to him."

"You grew up together?"

"Sure did."

"What was that like?"

"It's pretty hard to get into trouble with guards around you all the time."

So Tayle and the prince were lifelong friends. Good to know.

"This is the arts building," Tayle said. "We do painting, sculpting, music, and a few things I can't pronounce."

"Do you do any art?" Ri asked.

"I sculpt. What about you?"

"Not really."

"Your sisters sing," Tayle said.

"Believe me, I know."

"No, I mean they sing up here."

"They do?"

"Yeah, they're set to sing at the ball at the end of the week."

"They never told me that."

"Maybe it's a surprise. Don't tell Kyla I told you—she'll skin me alive."

Ri snorted. "It sounds like you know her a little."

"We've had some classes together."

They walked through the arts building and into the language building.

"With so many different kingdoms here, they have us learn the basics of everyone's language," Tayle said. "With the exception of a few."

"Like mine."

"Pretty hard for us to speak underwater."

Ri waved a hand. "Now you're just making excuses."

"Yeah, that's it."

"And how many have you mastered?"

Tayle looked at her. "All of them."

He put his hand on her back when they went around corners and through doors. A flutter began, and Ri felt like eels were swimming in her stomach.

He led her into the next building. "This is where your history class will be. You'll attend every morning, first thing." Tayle opened his mouth to say something, but closed it again.

"What?" Ri asked, slowing.

"I should probably warn you that the history teacher can be a bit blunt."

"Blunt how?" Ri had only heard whispered rumors about history class.

Tayle scratched the back of his head. "Well, last year we talked about the Bloody War."

"The war between the humans and almost everyone else?"

He raised his eyebrows. "That's the one."

"So you talked about it. So what?"

"Well, the teacher went into horrible, graphic detail about what the humans did to prisoners during that war."

Ri wrinkled her nose. "Trying to cure them of their magical ailments, if I remember right. Ripping off wings, cutting centaurs in half."

"We went through it all."

"Okay, that's gruesome. But it's history."

Tayle cleared his throat. "The prince's great-grandfather started the war. My grandfather was his master-at-arms, and my grandmother a witch, which means he did most of the heavy torturing."

They kept walking down the hall. Ri waited.

"The teacher told everyone in class. Not to be cruel. There were plenty of times that others had their ancestors or their races called out for something horrible they'd done." Tayle forced a smile. "Just know that she doesn't hold back."

They exited the building and walked into the sunshine.

It took a strong person not to balk at something like that being told to everyone. There were plenty of conflicts in the merpeople's past that had started or ended with her family spilling blood. And they'd sunk plenty of ships from the other races over the years. Ri's father was trying to make sure it didn't happen again, which was why he needed to speak with the human king.

"Every race has a checkered past," Ri said. "The question is, what are you going to do differently?"

Tayle looked at Ri, his dark eyes searching hers.

"The races have lived in relative peace for over fifty years," she said. "There has been some strife here and there, but nothing that couldn't be resolved with open talks. As a human, do you plan to keep it that way?"

"Of course," Tayle said. "War is a necessary evil, but it is a last resort. A peaceful solution is always preferable."

Ri was surprised he'd answered. So many her age hated to talk politics. Ri loved it. "Says the warmongering human," Ri said, giving him a little push.

Tayle raised his eyebrows. "And how would you answer your own question, my little mermaid?"

Ri sighed and twirled a red curl around her finger. "My father is trying to cultivate peace with all the races. Obviously we have a much stronger presence in the sea than most, and we're by far the most powerful race in the ocean, but my sisters coming to the

Academy opened their eyes, and therefore opened my father's eyes." She looked at Tayle. "I believe we are stronger together. Always."

Tayle grinned. "Well said." He winked. "For a girl."

Ri gave him her most predatory gaze. "They'll never see me coming."

Tayle laughed.

They'd walked quite a ways, and Ri's legs were beginning to tire.

"You want to sit before we go back?"

"I'm okay," Ri said.

"Your sisters made me promise to be nice." He gestured to a stone bench facing the fountain.

She opened her mouth to protest.

Tayle sat. "Well, I'm tired." He held out his hand.

Ri took it and settled in next to Tayle. "If you insist."

"I do," he said. He let go of her hand, but their shoulders touched. An electricity she'd never felt with any merman jolted through her.

Ri looked around. "Where did everyone go?"

"They're getting ready for the parties tonight."

"Parties?"

"Sports teams, art clubs, science clubs, and even a few more prestigious parties. It's a good way to reconnect after the summer."

"What about first-years?"

Tayle looked at her. "First-years have to be invited by third- or fourth-years."

"Ah, so we're expected to sit in our dorms and go to sleep?"

"It's good for you to be rested before classes start tomorrow."

"Right. Rested."

Tayle scratched his cheek. "But if that doesn't sound like fun to you, you could come with me."

Ri's heart skipped a beat. "With you?"

"Sure, to the prince's party."

Ri sat up. "Are you serious?" She could get to know more about Tayle and spy on the prince at the same time.

"I'm serious. If I go alone I'll never hear the end of it."

"You? Going alone?"

"It's hard to catch most girls' attention with the prince around."

"Then I'd love to come."

He blinked. "Really?"

"Yes."

"Great. It doesn't start until late. Can I pick you up at nine?"

"What should I wear?"

"Something fun."

"I can do fun."

CHAPTER 6

*I*t took Ri four outfit changes to find just the right thing. In the end, she settled for a blue-green, off-the-shoulder top that accentuated everything good about her upper half, and a knee-length, off-white skirt that flared like a flower when she turned a circle.

Su'la came to the room to pick up a bag of spell items and then left. She barely looked at Ri.

Ri's sisters had all gotten good roommates. It figured that she would end up with the grouchy one.

By the time Tayle arrived, Ri had been ready for an hour.

When Tayle knocked, Ri smoothed her blouse before opening the door.

Tayle wore a relaxed fit, button-down orange top with blue pants. A couple of the buttons on the shirt were open, revealing a hint of what Ri had seen on the boat.

"Hey," he said.

"Hi."

"You look nice," he said, motioning her into the hall.

"You too."

He offered her his arm, which she gladly took. The warmth of his body relaxed Ri, and he kept the pace slow for her.

Ri asked about the other races, and Tayle kept up a steady stream of interesting information. A few others were headed in the same direction, and most of them said hello to Tayle. He introduced Ri, and often referred to her as Kyla's sister.

"You're going to make everyone afraid of me," Ri said.

"You'll thank me."

The far dormitory was larger than the others; the entryway took up at least a third of the bottom floor. A row of tables laden with food sat on one side of the room. Chairs occupied on the far end, grouped together so people could talk. The middle lay open, and a band was almost ready to go in the corner.

The place was already packed. Students from every realm were there, including a siren. A few people said hello to Tayle as he came in, and more than one took a second look at Ri.

She smiled. She'd totally picked the right outfit.

Her smile widened when she spotted Sam. He stood at the far end of the dance floor, talking to Rakar and a group of other students. Instead of his formal silk outfit, he wore a more casual ensemble, one that drew out the blue of his eyes and accentuated the taper of his shoulders into his waist.

"Come on," Tayle said. "Let's get some food." He looked at her. "You do eat, right?"

"I'm starving," Ri said.

Tayle led her to the tables and handed her a heavy white plate with a golden border. The spread of food was impressive, to say the least. It started with breads and cheese, progressed to little rolls of meat, and then to delicious-looking sweets. Ri had only tasted samples of human food, and she had been looking forward to this.

"Where do I start?" she asked.

"I usually start at the other end."

Ri's heart leapt, and she turned to find Sam standing next to her.

"Thanks for getting her here, Tayle."

Ri glanced over at Tayle, who gave her a sheepish grin.

"See you guys later." Tayle gave Ri a little wink. "Hopefully we can continue our discussion about politics another time." With that, he walked away.

A tiny bit of Ri panicked. Tayle had brought her here and now he was leaving her? With the prince? She'd had one idea about the evening, and now she'd need to change it. "What is this about?" Ri asked.

"I asked Tayle to invite you. I thought we could spend a few minutes together." Sam took her plate in one hand and set the other on her back. "Come on, this is the best part."

He propelled her toward the far end of the table, and began stacking desserts on her plate.

So he wanted to spend some time together. Ri adjusted her expectations. "I could use something besides sweets."

Sam raised his eyebrows. "Oh, so you know what these are."

"Some of them."

"Fine." He stopped and narrowed his eyes. "This might be an offensive question, so please don't call the dean on me, but do you eat fish?"

Ri laughed. "I live in the ocean, and we're not what you would call vegetarian. So yes, I eat fish. It's not like they hang around and talk to us."

"Well, this is the best." Sam continued to fill the plate. When he was finished, he nodded at the chairs. "Let's go sit."

"Okay." Ri's stomach did a little flip. She was pretty sure it wasn't a hunger pang.

Once again, Sam put his hand on her lower back and gently guided her through the crowd. Like Tayle, but differently. A thrill ran up her spine, and she shivered.

"Are you cold?" Sam asked as they got to the chairs. He gestured for her to sit.

"No. I'm fine." She frowned. "This might be a dumb question, but am I supposed to wait for you to sit?"

"No," Sam said. "A human should, yes, but not you. You're a princess—you hold the same rank as I do." He sat after he was satisfied she was comfortable. "Besides, much of that blurs here. We're all friends." He waved his hand at the swelling crowd.

Sam handed her the plate.

"What should I try first?"

"Do you want sweet or salty?"

"Um, salty."

"Okay, bread or meat?"

"Uh…"

Before she could decide, Sam retrieved one of the small pieces of rolled up meat and held it out toward her lips. "Try this."

She eyed him.

"I'm serious. Try it." Sam inched the meat closer.

"Okay," Ri said. Her stomach flipped again, and she leaned forward and gently nibbled the end off the meat.

An explosion of flavor erupted in her mouth. The salty brine hit first, but was quickly overcome by a smoky undertone. Spices she had never tasted before tantalized her tongue, and she closed her eyes as she chewed and then swallowed.

"You like it?" Sam asked.

Ri slowly opened her eyes. "Delicious. Is it chicken?"

"You got it." Sam popped the other half in his mouth. "One of my favorites. Now, what about bread?"

"Any of them," Ri said. "I've only had bread once."

"We'll start with this one." Sam once again offered it to her.

With a quick glance around, Ri noticed a couple others looking at them with disapproval. So she reached out and took the bread from Sam's hand, ensuring that their fingers touched.

Sam watched her every move as she took a bite. "Well?"

"Mmm," Ri said, savoring the almost-sour flavor. "I like it."

"Good."

They continued on, working their way through the plate. Ri kept her eyes moving; more people were taking notice of them. "This is your party. Shouldn't you be hosting?"

Sam sighed. "You're probably right. I don't know if anyone told you, but I'll be student body president this year. My reign, if you could call it that, starts in a week. I'm trying to avoid extra responsibility until then."

"I heard. That's great." Ri jerked her head at the crowd. "Go mingle."

"You'll be okay?"

"I'll be fine."

Sam leaned forward and put a hand on Ri's knee. "I'd like to see you again. Soon."

"Would you?"

"Very much." He stood. "If you're available tomorrow night, I'm going to head back into the city to get a few things at the market. Would you like to join me?"

"The market?"

"Yes. For food, clothes, and other wares."

Ri did her best to hide the excitement on her face. However, the expression faded when a figure appeared behind the prince.

"Your Majesty," Kyla said in a cold voice.

Sam kept his eyes on Ri. "Well?"

Kyla turned her glare on Ri.

Ri swiveled her attention back to Sam. "I'd love to."

"Wonderful," Sam said. "I'll pick you up at six."

"Great."

To her surprise, Sam reached out and brought her fingers to his lips again. As he lowered her hand, his eyes bored into hers. "Until then."

"Until then."

Sam turned. "Kyla, thank you for coming. It's always an honor to have the mer-princesses attend my little parties."

Kyla let out a *humph*.

Sam gave her a nod and moved into the crowd.

Ri braced herself and looked at Kyla. "What?"

Kyla sat down, picked half a brownie off the plate and ate it. "Look little sister, you're in over your head with that guy."

"I have no idea what you're talking about."

"What's he asking about?"

"Nothing."

"What's he picking you up for?"

"We're going to the market."

"Why?"

Ri leaned forward. "Why do you care?"

"I care because he is not a nice guy. He dated an elf girl all last year, then dumped her in front of half the school."

"Do you know why?"

"Because he's a jerk."

"So you say, but I say different. He's been nothing but a gentleman."

Kyla opened her mouth to argue, but Ri stood. "I know the mermen think you're all that and a bundle of coral, so it must kill you to think that some guy might pick me instead of you, but you'd better get over it."

"Ri, this isn't about before," Kyla said. "Listen to me."

"No. Not this time," Ri said. She took a step toward Kyla and lowered her voice. "Stay out of my business." Before her sister could retaliate, Ri sped away her and walked back into the night.

CHAPTER 7

The next morning, Ri woke to the first rays of the sun. She rose on wobbly legs and moved to the window. To her satisfaction, walking now felt like stepping on gravel instead of spears. When she reached the curtains, she pulled them back.

Orange and red streamed across the low clouds, and sunlight raced from the horizon through the window and onto Ri's skin.

The fight with her sister from the night before was forgotten. Warmth filled her, and she laughed.

"What are you doing?" Su'la demanded as she threw the covers over her head.

"Enjoying the sunrise."

"No one enjoys the sunrise. Go back to sleep."

But Ri couldn't; energy like she'd never felt before coursed through her. Excitement. Anticipation. Joy. It was all of those and more. It overflowed and bubbled out, and Ri began twirling in circles, flinging her arms wide.

"There is seriously something wrong with you," Su'la said.

The space between buildings quickly filled with students. Ri kept glancing out the window, amazed to see how many races sent their children here to be educated. Ri took her time in the shower—a device she quickly decided might be her favorite— and then got ready.

Su'la had rolled out of bed and gotten dressed in the time it took Ri to do her hair.

"Where were you last night?" Ri asked as she pushed the last pin into her hair.

"None of your business."

"I'm just trying to be friendly," Ri said.

"Try less."

Kyla had given her plenty of experience with grouchy people. Ri knew just where to poke them. "We should walk together this morning."

"Why?" Su'la asked in a cold voice.

"Because we have our first class together." Ri smiled sweetly. "It'll be fun."

"I highly doubt that," Su'la muttered.

"Oh come on, at least try to be civil."

"I am trying."

"Try harder."

"You are really obnoxious."

Ri grinned. "Oh, I know."

In the end, Su'la relented, and the two of them walked across campus together. Ri kept up an unending stream of question, and Su'la finally started answering some of them.

"What kind of magic do you use?" Ri asked as they passed the science building.

Su'la sighed. "Earth magic."

"So ley lines, potions…stuff like that?"

"That is correct."

"Do you have any brothers or sisters?"

"I have two brothers. Both older."

Ri concealed the triumph she felt as Su'la gave her more information than she had asked for. "Have they attended the Academy?" Ri asked.

"Yes, both of them."

"What do you hope to do with your spell casting?"

Su'la frowned. "What do you mean?"

"Well, earth wizards can do all sorts of things. They work for the king, or private companies, or freelance for the highest bidder."

"You seem to know a lot about wizards."

"I didn't want to come up here unprepared. I learned as much as I could."

For the first time since they'd met, Su'la looked impressed. "What about you? What do you hope to become, since you're the sixth daughter of the king?"

Ri blew air out of her mouth. "Well, I'm thinking about going into our ministry. Maybe trade or relations with the other races."

"Oh?" Su'la raised one slender eyebrow.

"Sure. I'm good with people, and my father needs someone he can trust. Kyla is uh…a little too much, and Marian is too timid for negotiations."

"What about the others?"

"Well, the oldest will rule, along with her husband. The other two are both working with my father on internal policy. Keeping the kingdom from collapsing in on itself."

There was much more to it, but Ri kept it simple. For instance, if Su'la—a spell caster—found out that Ri's middle sisters had found a way to keep most of those who manifested sea witch powers from going crazy, she might not like it. Most people distrusted sea witches more than any other kind of spell casters, because no matter their original race, their eventual transformation into a sea creature almost always left their minds scarred and unstable.

Su'la let out a *humph*.

They reached the history building and followed a handful of others inside. The elf from the day before walked perfectly straight, his gaze studiously forward. A gnome had to jump out of his way as he went by.

Ri led them to the classroom and dragged a protesting Su'la up to the second row of desks. There was one centaur with a clear space and a tall desk in the back, a couple of gnomes, and three tiny faeries that settled into miniature desks at the front.

Ri pulled some blank parchment and a pencil from her bag and set it in front of her.

Su'la shook her head and slumped back in her chair.

Just as the last goblin arrived, their teacher walked through the door. The woman—an elf—stood at least a head taller than Ri, and walked as if gliding on water. Her long blonde hair drifted out behind her and framed her oval face, drawing attention to her almost-lavender eyes.

"Good morning," the elf said. "I am Bo'ab, your history teacher. Some of the other teachers will have an orientation today, but we're getting right into it." She eyed those who weren't ready to take notes. Suddenly there was a flurry of activity, and a lot more desks had parchment on them. Even Su'la pulled out paper and a quill.

"We're going to start with today, and work backward," Bo'ab said. "Who can tell me why we have this Academy?"

One of the human boys raised his hand. "Because the realms are trying to cultivate peace and understanding instead of war."

"A memorized answer, but adequate."

Su'la rolled her eyes.

"You have a different answer, spell caster?" Bo'ab asked her.

Su'la didn't bother to sit up. "We're here because our parents want us to get to know one another. They're counting on that personal knowledge to keep us from going to war."

"Isn't that what he said?" Bo'ab asked.

"Sure, I guess."

"But?"

Su'la shifted in her seat. "We're also here to spy on one another. To find out little things about the other races. Dig for weaknesses. So that if war does come, we have more information for either fighting or negotiations."

Ri couldn't have said it better herself.

Bo'ab raised her slender eyebrows. "Very astute." She turned her gaze onto the rest of the class. "Would anyone disagree?"

A dead silence answered. Bo'ab waited until it was uncomfortable before she spoke. "Good, then my job isn't going to be as difficult as it was last year." She began to pace back and forth. "What year was the school founded?"

Ri began scribbling notes. Most of this she already knew, but it was interesting to get a fresh perspective. Tayle had been right about this teacher.

The rest of the day went by in a blur of classes and new people. Ri made an effort to introduce herself to as many other first-years as possible. She started making connections in her mind about the alliances their families had, and how they intertwined with the other kingdoms, and most importantly with hers.

By the time she was finished, Ri's mind swirled with new ideas and possibilities, but it still wasn't enough to keep her from thinking about Sam and his promise to pick her up at six. She had to turn down three dinner invitations with other students because of it. She hoped she'd made adequate excuses and hadn't closed any proverbial doors.

Ri rushed back to her room where Su'la had laid an array of crystals on her bed. The largest measured the size of Ri's hand, and the smallest a single digit of her little finger. The colors ranged from clear to red, blue, pink, orange, and everything in between.

"Those are pretty," Ri said. "Especially that heart-shaped pink one."

"Touch any one of them and I won't be responsible for what happens to you," Su'la said.

"Duly noted," Ri said. She got to work changing her clothes and fixing her hair. She could feel Su'la's eyes on her.

"What are you doing?"

"Changing."

"I can see that. Why?"

Ri turned and let loose her brightest smile. "Because I have a date."

"A date?"

"That's right."

"It's the first day of school."

"He asked me last night."

Su'la made a face. "Who is he?"

"Prince Samuel."

Ri had already seen Su'la's irritated expression, and perhaps her mildly angry expression. This was different. Su'la's eyes went hard, and her lips drew into a tight line. The air around her seemed to cringe back, and a dark aura filled the room. "Prince Samuel?"

"Yes. Is there a problem?"

As fast as it had come, the change in Su'la departed. The other girl shook her head and turned back to her crystals. "No, of course not. Have fun."

"Don't you even want to know what we're doing?"

"No."

There was a finality to the words that kept Ri's mouth shut. Apparently Su'la did have some sort of quarrel with the prince. Ri checked her hair one last time, took a small bag with money and a scarf, and went out the door.

Su'la said nothing as she left.

Stairs—of which she had two flights to contend with—were still painful, and Ri grasped the rail as she descended. Once she reached the bottom, she took a deep breath of relief and started toward one of the couches.

Ri stopped in her tracks when she saw Sam already sitting there. He was back to a silk shirt and dark trousers. Tall boots rose to his knees.

He stood as if the couch had bucked him off. His eyes fastened on Ri, and he smiled. "Hey."

Ri's legs threatened to turn to jelly. "Hey. You're uh, early."

CHAPTER 8

"*J* know," Sam said. He held a cap in his hand. "I uh, got here early."

The notion of the prince of the human realm being nervous around her brought a smile to Ri's face. "Does that mean we get to leave early?"

"We can go now." Sam came forward and offered his arm.

Ri took it, grateful for the extra balance, and followed as he led the way outside and into a small carriage. A coachman held the door, while two guards stood nearby.

"We're trying not to draw too much attention today," Sam said as he helped her up.

"What do you usually ride in?" Ri asked as she settled in. Dark leather lined the seats, and rich curtains had been pulled back from the windows. Sam took the bench across from her, and the footman closed the door behind them.

"A much bigger carriage, along with six or more guards."

Ri stared at him.

"What?" Sam asked.

"It's just strange. My father always has guards, but no one else."

"You mean you can just go where you want?" Sam asked. They both leaned as the carriage moved forward.

"Yeah, I guess. I mean, there are places we aren't allowed to go, but that's because of the other things that live there, not the merpeople."

"Other things? Like kelpies? Or the Kraken?"

Ri waved a hand. "Kelpies don't bother us. They only like human blood. The Kraken, however, is dangerous."

"From what I understand, his domain is huge. And treacherous."

"Yes." The Kraken was the one thing even Kyla was afraid of.

The thought of Kyla brought Ri back to the night before. To her accusations that the prince was only using Ri.

"I heard a rumor that a ship had to have mermaid blood on the hull to get through the Kraken's waters." Sam's face oozed innocence.

Ri narrowed her eyes. "Those rumors are highly exaggerated."

Sam let out a single laugh. "I thought so, but we still go around. Our sailors are terrified of the Kraken's waters." He gestured out the window. "How do you like our countryside?"

Ri breathed a sigh of relief at the change of subject. "It's beautiful. I love the bright colors."

"Don't you have bright colors under the sea?"

"Of course, but it's different. Everything here seems crisp around the edges."

Sam laughed. "I think it would be wonderful to see your world. I bet it is soft and beautiful." He leaned forward. "Mysterious, even."

"It is beautiful, but I may be biased."

"As am I about my country."

Ri took the opportunity to press him a little. "I'm dying to know more about your country. I know my father has had some communication with your father, but he's always tight-lipped about that sort of thing."

Sam waved a hand. "I try not to get involved. Foreign policy is something I'm going to have to deal with every day for the rest of my life after I get out of the Academy. The last thing I want to do is waste what little freedom I have left worrying about something I have no control over."

Ri shot him a dazzling smile. "I can understand that." She looked out the window. "Why do some of the trees have green leaves and some have red?"

"You ask such difficult questions," Sam said.

"Okay. Well then, tell me about your court. Do you have musicians?"

Sam warmed up to that topic, and they spent the rest of the journey talking about the differences between their two worlds.

Once inside the walls of the city, the carriage only took a few turns before halting between two buildings. All Ri could see were stone walls.

"Here we are," Sam said.

The footman opened the door, and Sam got out first and offered her his hand as she traversed the swaying steps.

A tingle of pleasure rushed from Ri's fingers into her stomach.

Sam bowed, still holding her hand. "Princess Ariel, please allow me to show you our market."

Ri bowed back. "I would be honored, Prince Samuel."

Sam once again took her arm and led her to the end of the alley.

How one wall could hold back so much noise and bustle Ri would never know. The moment they rounded the corner it hit her like a blast of bubbles from a dying ship.

The smells came first: exotic spices, and the almost-sour odor of too many bodies in the same place. Then Ri blinked, and she tried to look at everything at once.

Rows and rows of wooden stalls filled with all manner of things led away from the alley. Food—most of which she could not identify—and dishes, and lace, and cloth, and ribbons, and more things than she had ever imagined could be in one place at one time. People shouted and laughed and talked. The whole scene felt more alive than anything Ri had ever seen or felt.

Sam leaned down and whispered in her ear. "Do you like it?" His breath tickled the hair on her neck.

She looked at him. "I love it. Can we see everything?"

Sam threw back his head and laughed. And for a moment, Ri saw the real Sam. She knew a little something about being royalty—no matter how much you tried to be yourself, duty and protocol always seemed to hide the parts of you that were you.

Sam was no different, and the brief glimpse into his inner self left Ri feeling lighter.

"We only have a few hours until it gets dark. So no, we won't be able to see everything. But if you tell me what you like, I'll make sure we see it."

"I have to choose?" Ri stuck out her bottom lip.

"I'm afraid so."

Ri thought about it. "Clothes, jewelry, and food."

"In that order?"

"Order doesn't matter."

"Then this way."

Sam led her into the marketplace. The two guards flanked them, with another out front. A few vendors waved in greeting, and Sam addressed each of them by name. The crowd parted for them, and soon they stood in front of a booth that looked as if a cloth explosion had occurred inside. Ri wasn't sure how they kept the bright colors clean until she saw a magical crystal hanging from the center of the booth. The green gem glowed slightly, and Ri watched as a speck of dirt that settled on the cloth disappeared.

"Prince Samuel!" a round, dark-haired woman said from the bowels of the booth. She curtsied. "We are grateful for your presence."

"Sally, stop." Sam waved for her to stand. "Don't make a fuss."

The woman looked at Ri and winked. "One must make a fuss over a prince."

A sly look entered Sam's eyes. "Sally, this is Princess Ariel of the merpeople."

Suddenly the woman's intense, searching gaze swept right through Ri. She curtsied again. "Your Majesty, so pleased to meet you."

Ri bowed in return. "The pleasure is mine."

"Oh, I like her," Sally said to Sam. "What can I do for you?"

"Ri has never been to the market before, and she asked about cloth. And since you're the best vendor in the kingdom, I thought I would bring her here."

"Dear child," Sally said, "you do know how to flatter an old woman."

"It's not hard when you're the best," Sam said.

Sally cackled and turned to Ri. "Watch out for this one. He's got a silver tongue." She rubbed her hands together. "Now, what do you want to see?"

Hours later, after the guards had been laden down with several bolts of fabric, two new tops, three pairs of shoes, and after Ri could barely walk for having eaten so much, she and Sam made their way back to the carriage.

"I thought that man at the fish shop was going to fall apart when I said you were a mermaid," Sam said.

Ri laughed. "As I tried to tell him, it would be like you eating chicken."

Sam chuckled. "Still, I thought he was going to apologize until he fainted."

"And he wouldn't take my money."

"You mean *my* money."

"Either of ours."

"Don't worry, I'll make sure someone compensates him tomorrow."

When they got back into the carriage, Ri sat on her own side. Sam had been holding her arm the entire evening, and she felt suddenly vulnerable without his warmth next to her.

Much to her delight, when Sam got in he pointed next to her. "May I?"

"You may." Ri slid over.

Sam sat, and took her hand. He raised her fingers and gently pressed his lips against the back of her hand, a gesture she was beginning to like. Then he looked into her eyes. "I had a lovely evening."

"I did, too. Thank you for bringing me here."

Kyla's words once again plagued Ri's thoughts. She opened her mouth, then shut it again.

"What is it? Did we miss something you wanted to see?" Sam asked.

"No, nothing like that." Ri steeled herself. She may as well be honest. What did she have to lose at this point? She looked into Sam's eyes and said, "Can I ask you a personal question?"

Ri recognized the veil of wariness that fell over Sam's face. "I suppose."

She swallowed. "My—my sisters warned me away from you. Kyla said you dumped an elf you had been dating in front of everyone at the end of last year."

Sam's lips pressed together. "Did she?"

"She also said you were likely using me."

Irritation shot through Sam's eyes. He sighed and shook his head. "She would say that."

"What do you mean?"

Sam once again started to stroke Ri's hand. "I did date an elf girl last year. I thought I loved her…until I figured out she was using me to get to my father."

Ri's stomach tightened. "Using you how?"

"The elves wanted a new trading contract, and she lured me in until I wouldn't say no to her. By the time I figured out what was going on, I was furious." He lowered his eyes. "So yes, I did dump her. In front of a lot of people. She hurt me, and I was angry."

The pain in his voice caused Ri to wrap her hands around his. "I'm sorry, I shouldn't have brought it up."

"No, it's okay." Sam met her gaze and gave her a small smile. "I'm a little ashamed of it. Kyla and the elf girl were friends. I can see why she would warn you away from me. I understand if you don't want to see me anymore."

"I didn't say that," Ri said. "I'm sorry to bring up a bad memory. I just wanted to know."

"Better to have things open between us. Yes?"

Ri sighed in relief. "Yes."

"Good." Sam settled back in the seat. "How are your legs?"

"Tired."

"What about your neck?"

"Why would my neck be tired?"

"After all that time spent looking at things, I thought you might want to rest it on my shoulder."

Ri's heart began to gallop, and she swallowed. "Maybe it is a little tired."

"You'd better rest for a bit."

"Good idea." Ri snuggled in, and Sam drew her closer. She lay her head in the crook of his shoulder, and to her delight, they were a perfect fit. Her ear pressed against his chest, and she could hear the beating of his heart.

Sam rubbed her arm.

Ri had been interested in a few mermen. She'd even dated one for a while, but in the end they hadn't been the right fit. Some couldn't handle that she would always have a higher rank than them. Others only wanted to get close to her because of her rank.

Sam was different. He was the crowned prince, and she a sixth daughter. But none of that mattered as she listened to the beating of his heart and thought about what a nice time they'd had together. And he'd been honest with her. No pressures of court. No talk of trade or treaties or anything else. Just two young people getting to know one another.

Could this be more than her wanting to help her father?

The carriage slowed as they got to campus, and long before Ri was ready, they pulled up in front of her dorm. She was loath to sit up, but did so anyway. She found Sam grinning down at her. He helped her out of the carriage and walked her to the door. The guards followed, carrying all the things she had bought.

Sam took both of her hands in his. "I want to see you again."

"I'd like that."

"Soon. What about tomorrow?"

Ri made a face. "I have extra classes tomorrow. What about the next day?"

"Done." Sam stepped forward. "Thank you for this evening."

"What do you mean?" Ri asked.

"I mean I feel like I can be myself around you. It's refreshing." Ri nodded.

Sam stepped in again. He stood mere inches from Ri. Her breathing sped up.

He looked down at her with fire in his eyes. "Ariel, if it's not too forward, I'd like to kiss you."

"Hmm," Ri said. She reached up and laced her hand around his neck and into his thick, blond hair. She stepped forward and the space between them disappeared. He wrapped his arms around her, and slowly bent his head until their lips met.

It felt like a thousand fish brushing at every part of Ri's body. She softened her lips and stood on tiptoe. If not for gravity, she surely would have floated off the ground. Ri thought—and hoped—that the moment would never end. But someone behind her cleared their throat.

Ri and Sam jumped apart as if their mothers had caught them doing something naughty, and looked away from one another.

"Can I get by?" Su'la asked with venom in her voice.

"Oh, sorry," Ri said as she moved aside.

Su'la gave the prince a look that would have melted an iceberg, then walked through the doors.

Ri looked at Sam, who scratched his head.

"Uh, I should be going."

"Yeah," she said.

"Listen, there's a big ball at the end of the week. It's when I take over as student body president. I was wondering if you would accompany me."

"Me?"

"Well, we did just kiss."

An uncontrolled giggle escaped Ri. She stifled the rest and swallowed. "Yes, of course. I would love to."

"Wonderful. You'll need a gown."

"With this fabric, I think I can make that happen."

"Good." Sam took her hand and kissed it one more time before he ushered her inside, had the guards take her purchased items to her room, and then left.

Ri watched the carriage until it was out of sight. Her fingers brushed her lips, and she wondered if her plan to get close to the price for political purposes had just taken a drastic, though not entirely unwelcome, turn.

CHAPTER 9

The next two days of school dragged by like a sea snail crawling along the edge of a reef. By the time Wednesday afternoon arrived, Ri had been to all her classes and met all the other students her age. She'd been to lunch with a handful of them, and had learned things like how strawberries made male faeries a little bit frisky, and that every centaur loved a good joke.

Wednesday night Sam took her to a nearby village where they ate in a pub, walked along a river, and saw a dozen kinds of birds Ri had never seen before. Ri's skin still burned when she thought of Sam's hands gently caressing her back, and his lips on hers.

With thoughts of Sam filling her mind, classes proved more difficult than they should have been.

Bo'ab's history class, which Ri had every morning, turned out to be her favorite. She found she loved learning about what had happened to make things like they were now. Tayle had been right about her blunt manner: she spoke of wars, massacres and other unsavory topics as if discussing the weather. More than one student had squirmed at their desk as Bo'ab described some horrible thing their people had done in the past.

Sculpture, her art class for the first half of the year, had opened her eyes to a whole new world. The teacher had taught her how to find the figure in the medium instead of forcing her ideas into the material.

The first day they'd started with a bar of soap, which had dried Ri's hands out so badly they'd had to find her some gloves. She'd studied the fist-sized block and had found within its depths a shell. And while many in the class had more recognizable objects, hers felt special, like a part of her she'd just discovered.

Between that and thoughts of Sam, Ri had a difficult time concentrating in science and math.

Thursday, her fourth day of sculpture, she found a nice surprise. Instead of their teacher, Tayle sat at the front of the class. She'd only seen him in passing since the party.

She walked up to him and folded her arms across her stomach. "So, you flirt with me, get me to go to a party with you, and then ditch me?"

Tayle scratched the back of his head. His dark eyes pleaded for forgiveness. "Yeah, sorry about that. The prince asked me to get you there, so I did."

"You guys are friends?" Sam hadn't mentioned Tayle.

Tayle held up a finger. "We grew up together. He's my ruler. I never said we were friends."

Ri's stomach did a little twist. "Oh, sorry."

"Besides, once you were with him, you didn't look too sorry to see me go." His eyes sparkled as he spoke.

Ri put a hand on the table and leaned forward. "Every girl wants a prince charming, right?"

Tayle put both of his hands out, palms up. "And here I am, helping you out. What a guy."

"What a guy," Ri repeated.

She'd seen a few moments of the real Sam at the market, but it seemed that Tayle was genuine all the time. He certainly brought her more feisty side out. She liked it.

"So are you our teacher today?"

"That's right." He wiggled his eyebrows. A deep dimple creased one cheek. "You have to do what I say today."

Ri leaned forward until their faces were only a few inches apart. "I'm looking forward to it."

Tayle's eyes danced, but he broke the gaze and stood. "Good morning, everyone."

A murmur of greetings answered. Ri heard a couple of girls giggle as she took her seat at the front.

"My name is Tayle. I'm the senior sculpture student. Today your instructor has left me in charge." Tayle's eyes returned to Ri. "Does everyone have their soap blocks from last time?"

Ri retrieved hers from her bag and set it on the table. Even the next day it didn't fail to amaze her that she had made this thing, discovered it in the soap.

"Good," Tayle said as he stood and looked over Ri's head at the others. He walked to the table behind him and swept off the cover. Underneath sat two rows of soap blocks twice as big as the day before.

"Same exercise: come pick a block and sculpt. Don't forget to use the techniques you've learned. I'm going to come around and talk to each one of you." He clapped his hands together. "Get to it."

Ri rose and got to the table first.

"How are your legs?" Tayle asked quietly.

"Fine now, thank you," Ri said as she weighed the options before her.

"Good. Which one are you thinking?"

Ri's hand hovered over a chunky pink block, but her eye was drawn to the yellow one next to it. She didn't even like yellow, but her fingers closed around it, and she hefted it off the table.

"Interesting choice. What do you have in mind?"

Ri closed one eye and tilted her head. "Not sure."

"Good girl," Tayle said, patting her on the shoulder. "Let those creative juices flow."

Ri took the block back to her table. She donned her thin gloves and picked up her tools.

First off, it was too thick. It need to be thin and tall, so Ri slowly cut away the outside layer. Soap shavings curled and dropped to the table as she worked. They were pretty in and of themselves, but Ri kept her attention on whatever was inside, waiting to be freed.

Once the width felt right, Ri began to draw a shape out. Curvy, like an hourglass, but with a slender bottom half.

Symmetrical, unlike the shell. She smiled when she realized what it was.

"And why are you smiling, my young mermaid?"

Tayle's voice made Ri jump. She glared up at him. "You're lucky I wasn't cutting."

Tayle crossed his arms over his chest and grinned. "Oh?"

"My father wouldn't want the top spire of his palace maimed."

"That's what you're sculpting?" He leaned down and studied it.

"That's what's in there."

Tayle turned his attention back to Ri. "I wish I could help you, but I've never seen the merman palace."

"Not many have."

Tayle pulled up an empty chair and sat. "What do you miss about it?"

Ri shrugged one shoulder. "Sometimes everything. Other times nothing." She shaved off a bit of soap before continuing. "I do miss my father, but don't tell him that."

"What about your other sisters?"

"Them too. And my niece—she's adorable."

"How old is she?"

"We reckon time differently under the sea, but she's about four years old by your standards."

"I can tell you really love this place," Tayle said.

"How?"

"Because you're barely looking at it while you sculpt."

Ri blinked. He was right.

"That's the sign of a real sculptor. However, you're using that tool like a peeler. It's more than that. Let me show you."

Tayle reached over and took her hand in his.

Tingles raced up Ri's arm.

"Put your fingers like this." He manipulated her hand until he nodded. He did not let go. Instead, he stood and came around behind her. She could feel his breath on the side of her neck and the heat of his chest on her back.

The tingles whirled inside Ri like a school of crazed krill. Unlike the blatant attention that Sam gave her, this felt different. Somehow more personal.

"Use your wrist to control it, and then your fingers at the end." Tayle guided her hand through the motion, shaving a line of soap so thin that it barely had substance. "Can you feel that?"

"Yes." The word barely came out, a reverent whisper.

"Good. Keep going."

"What's this?" an amused voice asked.

Ri felt Tayle tense. He let go of her hand and straightened. "What are you doing here?"

Ri turned and found Sam standing behind her.

"Hi." She smiled. "Look what I made."

Sam's eyes flicked to the sculpture, then back to Tayle. "Where's your instructor?"

"I'm the instructor today."

Sam glared.

The muscles in Tayle's jaw jumped before he added, "Your Majesty."

"Where is the instructor?" Sam asked again.

"He's not on campus."

"I need to leave a note for him."

Tayle pointed. "You can leave it on his desk. I'll be sure he gets it."

Sam shot Tayle a smug look. "Get me parchment and pen."

Tayle ducked his head once before retrieving both items for the prince.

Sam sat and began scribbling a note.

Tayle gave him one last tight-lipped look before he moved to the next student.

Ri swallowed, and her eyes darted to Sam. He didn't look up, so she went back to her sculpting. Only now her hands were shaking, so she closed her eyes and took a couple breaths.

The chair beside her screeched as Sam stood. A hand brushed hers and deposited a small piece of folded paper into her palm.

Ri waited until Sam had left the room before she pulled the paper to her chest and opened it. There were only four words on the page.

Can't wait until the ball.

Footsteps sounded, coming toward her. Ri re-folded the paper and tucked it into her bag.

Tayle walked by. He didn't look at her, and he didn't say anything else to her through the rest of class. When the chime sounded, Ri put her mostly finished sculpture back on the table with the rest. She tried to catch Tayle's eye as she left, but he refused to look at her.

A strange tightness settled into her chest.

It got worse when she saw both of her sisters leaning against the wall outside the door.

"Hi," Marian said, forcing a friendly smile.

Ri grit her teeth. "Hi."

"How has your first week been?"

Ri's eyes darted to Kyla, who stood with her arms crossed over her chest and a frown on her face. "What do you two want?"

Marian's normally serene face contorted into an expression of concern. "We're just checking on you."

"No you're not," Ri said as she kept walking.

Her sisters followed. She could practically hear the silent conversation that passed between them.

They almost got to the doors that led outside before Kyla grabbed Ri. "Fine, you want it straight?"

Ri turned, jerking her arm away. But Kyla stood directly in front of her, and kept coming until Ri's back was up against the wall.

"Kyla," Marian said in a low voice.

Kyla leaned down to look into Ri's eyes. "No, she wants it quick and dirty. So here we go." Kyla held up a finger. "Stay away from Prince Samuel."

"Why?" Ri asked. "Just because he doesn't like you?"

"No, because he's not paying attention to you because he likes you. There's some other reason."

A flash of anger washed over Ri. "Is this about your friend the elf? Because I asked him about that, and he told me the truth."

Kyla flushed. "He's always got an angle. He's using you."

Ri pushed Kyla away and stepped away from the wall. "You don't know him."

Marian stepped in. "No, Ri. Listen, she's right. He's not...good."

Ri pointed at Kyla. "He's been kind to me. He was there when they pulled me out of the water. He's made sure I have everything I need. We've been out a few times. Just because a boy doesn't like your friend because she was manipulating him, or pays more attention to me than you or Marian, doesn't make him evil."

Kyla opened her mouth to retort, but Ri pushed her aside. "I don't want to hear it."

With that she joined the remains of her class as they walked outside.

Once again, Ri's hands were shaking. Her insides felt hot and cold at the same time, and all she wanted to do was scream.

Their father had always been overprotective of Ri. Her mother had died when she was little, and he'd never fully gotten over it. Instead, he'd taken it as his personal duty to make sure Ri was a good girl. That she got everything she needed. Her sisters had always been jealous of his attention toward her.

Ri had been hoping that the Academy would be different. That she could become one of them. But obviously that wasn't going to happen.

They hadn't told her they were in a band. They kept telling her not to see the prince. What did they know? They hadn't even bothered to ask what her plan was. That yes, she liked the prince, but she'd started seeing him to strengthen the relationship between kingdoms. Apparently they'd built some sort of wall that Ri might not ever be able to break down.

The world blurred, and Ri blinked. A single tear ran down her cheek. Ri wiped it away and shook her head. Now was not the time to cry.

"Hey," a voice said from behind.

Ri took a steadying breath, wiped her eyes again and turned to see Tayle jogging after her.

He saw her face and frowned. "What's wrong?"

"Nothing," Ri said. "What do you need?"

"Uh, well, I saw your sisters talking to you." He reached up and scratched his head again. "Actually, I heard what they told you."

Ri grit her teeth. "And?"

He softened his voice and put his hands on her shoulders. "They're right."

"Are they?"

"About the prince. You should stay away from him."

Anger flared to life. "You're the one who brought me to his party and left me with him."

"Yeah, because I thought he wanted to get back at Kyla."

Ri shrugged out of Tayle's grasp and stepped back. "So now you're not only out to put me in a bad spot, but my sisters, too?"

Tayle let out a huff. "Look Ri, I like you, and I don't want to see you get hurt."

"Is Prince Samuel into hurting girls?"

"Well no, but he's—"

Ri slashed the air with her hand. "I'm not sure what position you're trying to play here, but stay out from between Sam and me."

Tayle's face darkened. "Why, because he took you to the market and spent money on you?"

A growl almost escaped Ri's throat. She sneered. "No, because if you cared in the first place you wouldn't have left me with him at the party. You missed your chance."

A look of hurt crossed Tayle's face.

"Go back to your rocks, Tayle. Leave me alone."

CHAPTER 10

Ri didn't talk to her sisters or Tayle for the rest of the week. When they passed in the halls or on campus, Ri kept her eyes forward. Sam slipped her two more notes, coming into classes for other things. She had all three in her pocket, and whenever she felt like she was going to fall apart, she would caress the paper with her fingers and remind herself that she was going to the ball with the prince. Didn't every girl want that?

She'd found a seamstress on campus who had made her a beautiful gown in green and blue with shells and pearls. It had cost her a fortune, but Ri didn't care. Her father had given her plenty of money; she might as well use it.

The cut of the gown was in fact called the "mermaid style." It stayed tight until just below her hips, where it flared out like a mermaid's tail. Her back, neck, and shoulders were bare. Shells and pearls garnished the top section in a crisscrossing pattern.

The shimmering skirt billowed as she walked. The color of the dress made the shell around her neck look striking. Ri twirled once in front of the mirror to get the full effect.

Sam was coming to pick her up early so they could dine before the ball. He was afraid that, once his position was official, they wouldn't get to spend any time together at the party.

Su'la, who had been eerily quiet all week, looked at her and said, "Nice dress."

"Thanks."

"Have a good time."

Ri narrowed her eyes. "Why are you being nice to me?"

"My brother said I should try to make friends."

"Got it."

"You're going with the prince?"

"That's right."

Su'la opened her mouth, closed it and cleared her throat. "Don't stay out past midnight."

"Why?"

Su'la shrugged. "It's a fairy tale thing."

"I don't know that one."

"You'll have to read it."

Ri checked her hair one last time. A knock came at the door, causing her pulse to quicken. She grabbed a shawl and threw it over her shoulders.

"Have fun," Su'la said again.

"Thanks." Ri straightened everything and moved to the door. She opened it and found Sam on the other side.

Whoever had picked his wardrobe had been spot-on. He wore an off-white jacket with a blue shirt and a green vest. Black trousers hugged him in all the right places, and instead of boots, he wore soft leather shoes.

Ri looked at him and found his jaw hanging open.

"Hi," she said.

His lips moved, but nothing came out, so he shut his mouth, swallowed and tried again. "Uh, hi." Then he stared some more.

"I'm ready to go."

Sam shook his head. "Oh, right. Yeah. Great." He gestured for her to go first through the narrow hall and then down the stairs. As soon as they got outside, he offered her his arm.

He had a carriage waiting.

"You really look beautiful," he said as he helped her inside.

"Thank you. You look very nice as well, your Majesty."

"Stop that," he said as he ducked his head and climbed in.

Ri's heart skipped a beat when he sat next to her and took her hand.

"I hope you're looking forward to this as much as I am," Sam said.

"How could I not be?"

Sam smiled. It wasn't like his other smiles. This one was different: not quite his true self, but not the man around campus. No, there was more to it. Triumph.

A moment later, Ri understood why. He took her chin in his fingers and drew her to him. Their lips met, and Ri's mind reeled. He tasted like fruit. One hand stayed at the base of her neck, causing pinpricks of excitement, and the other moved to rub her bare back. Sam's fingers pushed the edges of her dress as if he wanted to explore.

Ri parted her lips and drunk him in. Sam stiffened, then pulled her closer.

Reality left, and Ri felt as if she were flying like the birds she had spent hours watching as a child. Free, gliding, weightless.

Then the carriage lurched into motion, and they almost fell off the seat.

They broke apart, and Ri laughed. It felt good to laugh. After the past few days, she needed to be herself, needed someone to support her. Love her.

Ri looked at Sam, expecting to find him smiling or coming in for another kiss—which was her preferred of the two—but instead she found his eyes darting around her face, his lips pressed into a tight line.

"Sam?" Ri asked.

"Are you feeling all right?"

"I'm fine."

"You look a little pale."

Ri laughed. "Your kiss wasn't *that* good."

Sam didn't smile.

At that moment, a weight formed in Ri's head. She blinked, and suddenly the coach shifted. Or the world shifted. Everything spun, and she reached out to Sam.

"Whoa, there we go," he said.

"What's happening?" Ri asked.

"Maybe you should close your eyes," Sam said. "You look like you're going to throw up."

"No, it's not that," Ri said. She shook her head to try to clear it, but some unseen force pressed in from every direction. The air burned her lungs, and her legs began to throb. Had the spell to make her human worn off? Maybe she hadn't spent enough time in her room. "I think I need to go to the doctor."

"Of course," Sam said. "We'll go there right away."

The carriage slowed.

How had they gotten to the doctor so quickly?

Dark splotches formed in Ri's vision. She blinked, but they didn't go away. "Sam?"

"Lay down," he said.

"But."

"Just lay down." His voice had lost its usual kindness; he sounded as though he was ordering her like a pet.

Ri fought to stay upright, but pain shot through her abdomen. Something inside her rippled, and Ri cried out.

"Shh," Sam said. "We can't have anyone hearing us."

To Ri's horror, Sam reached out and pulled the shell from her neck.

Ri tried to grab the necklace, but Sam held it out of reach. She tried to talk, but nothing but raspy, hissing noises came out.

"Don't worry—once I have what I want, everything will be fine."

More pain churned, and it felt as if Ri's legs were on fire. She looked down and saw that her shoes had come off. Her feet were changing. Elongating. Thinning. Turning back into a tail.

Ri's eyes shot to Sam.

He smiled. "I need something, and you're going to give it to me."

Ri tried to push herself away, but pain sapped the strength from her limbs.

The door of the carriage opened behind Ri, and before she could turn, something hit her on the back of the head. The dark splotches combined, and she passed out.

CHAPTER 11

The cold woke Ri. A hard surface without warmth lay beneath her. The air bit at her skin. And her tail.

Ri forced her eyes open. She lay on a tile floor. The pain from her legs had ceased, but a single glance told her that she was once again a full-fledged mermaid—still wearing a mermaid dress. Her orange and blue scales looked lackluster, and the edges of her fin were already wilting.

How long had she been here? She forced herself onto her hands. She lay in a square room made of white stone. A single door without a handle stood along one wall. There was no light source, and yet she could see. The room must be enchanted.

What little strength she had waned, and Ri collapsed. Her tail barely twitched when she commanded it to, and her body felt like rocks.

She opened her mouth to cry for help. When nothing came out, her hand rushed to her throat.

Sam.

The prince.

He'd done this.

But why? Was it a sick joke? Something the human prince played on a first-year? Would he show her to all his friends?

No, that didn't seem right. But neither did the alternative: that he'd turned her back into a mermaid and left her here to die.

His lips had tasted like fruit, a common cover for poison.

The question was, why?

Ri wracked her brain. She went over every moment she and the prince had been together. Had he given her any indication of betrayal?

Surely he knew that her death by his hand would mean war between their kingdoms. And surely he knew that while her father would be angry, she was not his sole heir. Killing the sixth daughter didn't seem like a political play.

Tears formed and pooled in the corners of Ri's eyes. She blinked them away and wiped her cheeks. She did not have moisture to spare.

People would notice if she just disappeared. Su'la knew that Ri had a date with the prince. So unless Su'la was with him, or he'd somehow silenced her, he wasn't planning to kill Ri.

However, as the dry air leeched her lungs and her tail continued to wilt, Ri wondered what his plan might be. Why else would he do this?

Ri didn't have to wait long for her answer. A click sounded, and the door swung open. The breeze caused bumps to spring up on her arms. More light poured in, silhouetting the prince.

"Oh good, you're awake," the prince said as he stepped into Ri's prison. He still wore the outfit for the party, which sent a wave of relief through Ri. It hadn't been that long since he'd thrown her in here.

Ri drew on every bit of courage and strength she could muster to straighten and stare him in the eyes. She did her best to convey *"What is the meaning of this?"* without talking.

The familiarity in Sam's face had disappeared, leaving a haughty expression behind. He came and squatted down in front of her. He reached out and patted her on the head. "Don't worry, Princess. This won't take long. I just need a few things, then I'll get you some salt water and you'll forget this ever happened."

The prince stood, and two other humans entered. A sick feeling began in her stomach when she saw one of them was a wizard from the ship that had brought her up. The other's shoulders were almost as broad as Ri's father's.

"Hold her tail still," the prince said to the muscle-bound man.

He came and knelt next to Ri.

Her eyes widened, and she shook her head. The man's large arms reached out and pinned her tail in place. Her scales were thick, so it didn't hurt, but it did feel like she was being smothered.

Normally Ri would have been able to throw him across the room, but now only the tip of her fin twitched. The prince knelt and put his hand on her fin, rendering it useless.

"How many do you want?" the wizard asked.

"Five," the prince said.

The wizard drew a large pair of metal pincers from her robe.

Ri's heart raced. He wanted five of her oysters? All this was for profit? Maybe he'd promised them to a neighboring kingdom in exchange for something more.

The man holding her down grunted as her tail began to respond. Ri tried to pull herself away, but her arms weren't strong enough.

"It will hurt less if you don't struggle," the prince said as he patted her scales.

Ri shot him a withering glare and kept struggling. But she wasn't making progress. Without something to hold on to and her strength, she would not be able to overpower the three humans.

The wizard put the pincers on the oyster second from the end of her fin.

Tears sprung up in her eyes. They rolled down her cheeks when she tried to blink them away.

No! No! No! Ri screamed in her mind, but nothing except a rasp of air came from her lips. Her breathing came in great gasps, and she tried one last time to pull away.

Too late. The pincers fastened around the oyster. The wizard muttered a few words. Heat like Ri had never felt pulsed in her fin and then up into her tail. The wizard yanked.

The heat became burning, and her entire body arched in pain. She fought to keep her eyes open, and watched as the pincers came away with the oyster, along with five of her scales. Mermaid blood—almost clear—flowed from the wound.

Scales. Her eyes darted to the prince, who smiled a sickening smile.

He wanted her scales to get past the Kraken.

He'd known.

He'd used her.

That single thought channeled Ri's blinding pain into fury. She flexed her tail, throwing the man who had been holding it down across the room.

Ri pushed herself up and flung her tail at the wizard. Two of the seven remaining oysters hit her, and bones crunched. The wizard cried out and flew back, hitting the wall hard.

"Ri!" the prince cried out. "Stop."

Ri turned her attention on him.

He was close, just a few feet away. But he didn't look concerned. Instead, he smiled. "If you hurt me, you'll die here." He drew a crystal out of his pocket, and Ri froze.

It was the pink, heart-shaped crystal that Su'la had had on her bed.

Su'la was the only person who knew where Ri was. That she had been with the prince.

Ri grit her teeth and lunged.

But she was clumsy, and he jumped away like a nimble animal. Then he darted in and dropped the crystal around her neck. It dragged her head to the ground like a stone and held her there. What little strength she'd had evaporated, and Ri's body shuddered.

The prince squatted down again. "Now Princess, that crystal is going to keep you from moving until I get back. Don't worry, you won't die. But you're going to be very uncomfortable until I can find another wizard to replace your memories."

Ri glared at him. Her cheek lay pressed to the floor and her arms shook with the effort of trying to rise.

"I see you're still deciding." The prince rose to his full height. "Well, you have some time. I'll be back after the party."

With that he turned and walked out the door. The other two followed, the man helping the wizard who cradled one arm in the other.

They each disappeared, and the door shut behind them with a final thud.

CHAPTER 12

Ri closed her eyes, and the tears broke free. A great sob wracked her body, and Ri pounded the floor with her fist. Of course nothing happened, but it masked the pain throbbing in her tail and the emptiness in her heart.

Her sisters had warned her not to get involved with the prince. So had Tayle. Even Su'la had given Ri the impression that the prince had been up to no good. But in the end, Su'la had been helping him.

And now he had her scales. The oyster was just a bonus for him. He probably already knew there was an abalone pearl inside. Rare, beautiful, and worth more money than some of the kingdoms represented at the Academy. Only royal merpeople produced them.

Maybe the prince thought she was stupid enough to think the pearl was his goal, but she knew better.

Ri snorted and gritted her teeth together.

He was going to pay.

The tears kept coming. And it should have been because she'd just lost a bigger chunk of her tail, but it wasn't. It was because now everyone would know her shame. Everyone would see her mistake. Everyone would know that she'd been duped by a handsome face.

She'd been prideful. An idiot. More absorbed in her own little conquest than willing to listen to the people who loved her.

If she lived through this, Kyla would kill her.

Another sob came from her belly, and she squeezed her eyes shut.

No one was coming for her. She was at the prince's mercy, and from what she'd just seen, there wouldn't be much of that.

Every bit of her body began to dry out. Not to the point of cracking, but to the point of being itchy. The air running through her throat caused her to choke as her gills begged for water. Which they were not going to get.

As the prince had promised. She wasn't going to die, but it felt like it.

Ri forced herself to stop crying. She wasn't sure how long she lay there, shivering and gasping for air. It couldn't have been long enough for the party to be over, so when the door clicked, something between fear and fury sprung to life.

"Ri?"

The voice came garbled to Ri's ears. She tried to push herself up, but the heart-shaped crystal kept her neck pinned to the ground.

"Oh, Ri."

That didn't sound like the prince.

Feet appeared in front of Ri, and she swiveled her eyes up.

Instead of the prince or the muscle man, Ri found Tayle standing there. His gaze traveled from her tail up to her face, and when their eyes met, he fell to his knees.

He reached out and touched the skin on her back. The warmth of his hand sent a shiver of hope through Ri.

Tayle's voice came out as a growl. "I'm going to kill him. Can you move?"

Ri's head barely twitched as she shook it.

"Can you breathe? Blink twice if you can breathe."

Ri did so. She fought back more tears.

Tayle stroked her hair. "Can you talk?"

Ri blinked once.

"Okay, okay," Tayle said as he looked her over again. "Where's the crystal?"

He knew about the crystal? Ri pointed at her neck.

Tayle gently moved her hair, exposing the gem. His fingers left lines of warmth along her skin. "I'm going to get this off you, but it will probably feel like I'm ripping your throat out. It will be fine once it's off. No lasting damage, but it's going to hurt." He studied her eyes. "Are you ready?"

Ri blinked twice.

Tayle didn't wait. Ri felt the strap around her neck move, and then Tayle pulled.

If she thought having her tail split apart had hurt, it didn't compare to this.

It felt like he was trying to rip her spine out through the front of her neck. Muscles burned. Bones groaned. If she could speak, her screams would have been heard in the city.

She'd closed her eyes. Ri forced them open and found Tayle red-faced and leaning away. The muscles in his arms bulged.

He let out a yell of frustration and put one last infusion of strength into it. Finally the leather strap gave way.

Tayle flew back, landing on his butt and almost hitting the wall.

Ri's body arched as what felt like lightning crackled inside her. But as quickly as it had come, the pain dissipated. She rolled onto her back and put both hands over her face.

"Ri?" Tayle said. "Ri, move your hands."

She did, and she found a small vial in Tayle's grasp.

"I need you to drink this. You'll be able to breath and talk. Can you do that?"

Ri nodded. She fought with shaking hands and twitching muscles to get her top half upright.

Tayle moved closer. He put one knee behind her back and knelt on the other. One of his hands cupped the base of her neck. He pressed the vial to Ri's lips, and she took a sip of the thick, cold fluid.

The moment the liquid hit the back of her throat, the muscles in her mouth seized up and she spit it back out.

"Whoa," Tayle said.

Ri doubled over and started to cough.

"Easy," Tayle said. He drew her to him and rubbed her back.

Ri clung to him as convulsions charged through her body. His warmth spread through her, and his steady hands kept her from flying apart.

"It's okay. You're okay," Tayle said. "She said that might happen." Tayle cupped her chin in his hand and drew her eyes to his. "Listen, I'm going to pour it into my mouth, then I'm going to kiss you and give it to you. That should work."

Ri gave him a confused look.

"I know it sounds strange. Will you trust me? Or is kissing me that bad of a prospect?" He tried, and failed, to pull off a lopsided grin.

Ri swallowed, then nodded.

Tayle poured the liquid into his mouth, then he moved his hand to her cheek and leaned down.

Ri's lips rose to meet his. A tingle ran through into her mouth. Magic.

He inhaled through his nose, and then his lips parted.

Ri did the same, pulling the liquid from his mouth to hers.

This time her throat didn't reject the offering, and the fluid ran down. It took two swallows to get it all.

Tayle pulled away, but kept his hand on her cheek. His eyes studied her.

Cold slid through Ri's body. But not just cold. Also moisture. Her lungs stopped burning, and she took a great breath.

"Did it work?" Tayle asked.

Ri swallowed, then cleared her throat. A noise came out. She tried to speak. "I...I think so."

Relief washed over Tayle's face. "Thank goodness." He turned his attention to her tail. "How bad does that hurt?"

She didn't look. "I'll live." In truth, it hurt so bad she wanted to scream.

Tayle shook his head. "This is all my fault. I'm so sorry. He used me to get you to his party. I never suspected he would do something like this."

"No," Ri said. Little by little, moisture filled her body. Her strength returned, the pain ebbing enough to let her think. Her anger boiled. "No, this isn't your fault. I didn't listen to you or to my sisters. This is my fault—I fell for his games. I didn't even see this coming. How long is this spell going to last?"

"A few hours at most. We need to get you to the wizards."

Ri shook her head. "No. One of the wizards who transformed me was here with the prince. I can't trust them."

"Then who?"

Ri bit her lip, but she knew what she had to do. And since Tayle would need a wagon to transport her anywhere, she only had one option left. "I need you to find my sisters. Tell them the prince took my scales, and bring them here."

CHAPTER 13

ayle found a wet blanket and wrapped it around Ri's shoulders. He gave her a peck on the cheek and said, "I'll be back soon."

He left the door open, and while Ri could have moved, she decided to conserve her strength.

Each sound from outside caused Ri to jump, but she did her best to stay calm, and by the time Tayle returned with her sisters, she hadn't cried in at least ten minutes.

Kyla ran in first. She wore a bright blue sequin dress that hugged her body and went halfway to her knees, and crystal heels. She took one look at Ri and said, "That piece of kelp. I'll kill him."

Marian came next. She wore almost the same outfit, and her blonde hair cascaded down her shoulders in large curls. When she saw Ri, her hands flew to her mouth, and tears sprung to her eyes.

Kyla knelt next to Ri. "Are you okay?"

"More or less," Ri said.

"Your tail," Marian said, sinking to her knees next to Kyla.

Ri pushed past the pain to speak. "Prince Samuel took it, but I don't think he was after the oyster. I think he was after my scales."

"So Tayle said," Kyla said with narrowed eyes.

"For the Kraken," Ri said. "At least, that's my guess."

Marian's gaze turned to ice. "That was unwise of him."

"I knew he was a jerk, but I never thought he would do something like this," Kyla said.

Ri looked between her sisters. "I'm sorry I didn't listen to you."

Marian teared up again.

"Apology accepted," Kyla said. "How did he think he was going to get away with this?"

"He said he was going to have a wizard replace my memories."

Marian snorted.

"Where's Tayle?" Ri asked.

"He's gathering a few things for us," Kyla said. "We think Marian can reverse what he did."

Ri blinked and looked at her sister.

Marian ducked her head. "I may have taken a few spell casting classes."

Kyla snorted. "A few?" She leaned toward Ri. "It's more like she's the most powerful wizard in her class."

Ri's jaw hinged open. "Really?"

"I haven't told anyone at home yet."

A clatter from the hall sounded, and both Marian and Kyla stood and turned. Marian's palms began to glow.

"Just me," Tayle said as he came through the door. "Sorry, I dropped some stuff."

Marian moved toward him. "Did you get everything?"

"I got it all, just like you said."

"Perfect. Ri, give me a few minutes. We'll have you back in your land legs in no time."

Ri knew what to expect, but that didn't make the process any less painful. By the time Marian had her up and walking again, Ri wanted to cry at every step. Not only had she lost an oyster, but she'd lost a toe as well. It threw her balance off, and Marian stayed at her side.

Instead of weeping, Ri grit her teeth and kept walking around.

"You okay?" Tayle asked.

"I'll live," Ri said. "What time is it? Has the party started yet?"

"Not yet," Tayle said.

"We should have about thirty minutes," Kyla said. "The band is probably going crazy wondering where we are."

Ri glanced at Kyla. "I think we should go to the party."

"What?" Kyla and Marian said together.

Tayle held up a hand. "That's a terrible idea."

Ri took a breath. Then she told the others how Prince Samuel had threatened her.

Marian's grip tightened around her arm, and a vein pulsed in Tayle's temple. Kyla's expression promised murder.

"People need to know what he did," Ri said.

"Unfortunately, it's his word against yours," Tayle said between clenched teeth. "It will be difficult to persuade everyone else that he's done something wrong. While I know what he is, and your sisters saw through him their first days here, most of the rest of the students love him. Plus, we're in his kingdom."

"I flung mermaid blood on him and both of his lackeys. It doesn't wash off."

Kyla gave her a dazzling, wicked smile. "That's my baby sister."

"What do you mean, doesn't wash off?" Tayle asked.

"No water or soap will remove it," Marian said, nodding her approval. "There are microbes in the ocean that digest it, but nothing else. If it's anywhere on his skin or clothes, we'll be able to see it."

"But no one else can see it," Tayle said.

"The sirens can smell it," Ri said. "How much do they like the prince?"

"They don't like anyone," Kyla said. "They'll back us."

Marian eyed Ri. "I bet you could fit into one of my dresses."

Kyla nodded. "I like where this is going."

"Where is it going?" Ri asked.

Kyla smiled, showing all her teeth. "How would you like to debut with the band tonight?"

"Me?"

"You."

"But I haven't even tried to sing up here."

Marian waved her hand. "It's actually easier. We'll bring you in for one number. You sing a few lines, then you get to sit back and see what the prince does when he sees you."

"I'll make sure he doesn't run," Tayle said.

Ri snapped her fingers. "We need to watch out for Su'la, too."

"Your roommate? Why?" Marian asked.

Tayle took a step back.

"Because she gave the prince the crystal that Tayle pulled off me."

"You're sure?" Kyla asked.

"Positive. I saw it on her bed earlier this week."

"I can take care of her," Marian said. "She's got a lot of talent, but she's not very experienced."

"This is a great plan," Kyla said. "I can't wait to see the look on that bastard's face when he sees you."

Marian gave Ri's arm a squeeze. "Are you up for it?"

"Ready and willing."

CHAPTER 14

*R*i tried to scratch her back where the sequins met her skin.

"Stop fidgeting," Kyla said.

"The dress is a bit tight."

"Marian doesn't have a chest. You can live with it for an hour."

Ri sighed. She could.

Her foot and leg still ached, but thanks to a healing spell from Marian the pain had dulled. She stood backstage with her sisters and their band.

"Rakar is about to go on," the piano player reported from the curtain's edge.

"Get ready," Kyla said. She looked hard at Ri. "Remember, you sing the first couple lines of the second song, then we'll take it from there. You wander out into the audience, and go to the prince. See if you can get him to crack."

"Got it," Ri said.

"Can you handle it?"

"I can handle it."

Marian slipped in the back door and came to them. "The sirens are ready."

Applause broke out as Rakar made his way to the stage.

Ri inched toward the curtain and looked out.

Round tables filled the gym floor. Students dressed in their finest occupied every chair surrounding the tables. The ceiling had been enchanted to look like clouds, and the walls bore windows overlooking a fake landscape. Rakar, the prince, and a handful of others were seated at the table closest to the stage. Tayle had made certain that the sirens were nearby.

Ri leaned farther until she finally caught a glimpse of Prince Samuel.

He must have noticed the blood on his jacket collar, because he'd changed into a black suit with a red shirt underneath. It wouldn't matter—he had blood on his hands and neck. Next to him sat one of the most striking students Ri had seen: pale, perfect skin housed dark eyes and dark hair piled atop her head. Her lean face and pointed ears gave her away as an elf. The gown she wore was cut low, revealing a flat stomach and concealing what had to be very small breasts. A misshapen pendant hung on a gold chain. The muscles of her arms slid under her perfect skin as she plucked her glass off the table and took a drink.

Ri withdrew. "Who's with the prince?"

"Tall? Reed thin? Dark hair?"

Ri nodded.

"Se'wh," Kyla said. "She's the fey king's daughter. She and the prince have been on and off since they started at the Academy, but she didn't get here until yesterday. Something about a cultural ritual."

Rakar's voice boomed through the room. "Greetings."

"Greetings!" the crowd replied with enthusiasm.

"Ladies and gentlemen, beasts and beauties, today I step down as your student body president."

A few disappointed boos sounded.

"Never fear—we've got someone extra special to replace me. I think you all know who it is."

A smattering of clapping preceded an outburst of cheers.

"But before that, we have a couple special treats for you. Here to serenade me off the stage are the mersisters, Kyla and Marian!"

A roar of cheering exploded.

Kyla looked at Ri. "Remember, you come out after this song."

"I've got it," Ri said.

Marian patted her on the shoulder as the rest of the band went on stage. "Good luck."

"Thanks."

Ri leaned on the wall, keeping as much weight as possible off her injured leg.

The crowd continued to applaud and whistle.

Kyla waved her hands, and the audience settled down. "While we're sorry to see Rakar go, we're excited for Prince Samuel to take his place. *Not* replace him, because no one could replace this little guy." Kyla winked at Rakar, who wiggled his huge eyebrows and ears at her.

Kyla snapped a few times, counting backward from three.

The band began to play, and Ri listened. Singing had been a love of hers since she'd been little, but she had given it up after all her sisters made it a focus of their lives. Ri had wanted to be different.

As soon as Kyla began to sing, Ri wished she'd had more time to practice. Her sister's low, alto voice filled the air like a perfect current. The words washed over the crowd, and they swayed to the music.

When Marian joined her, several students jumped to their feet.

Not only were her sisters beautiful, but they held the audience in the palm of their hands.

They sang of leaders and battles and triumph and tragedy. Ri didn't recognize the song, but the students did, and they loved it.

When the music faded, everyone jumped to their feet, the applause thundering like a storm.

Both Kyla and Marian bowed, and they motioned to the band.

Rakar came over and gave Kyla a kiss on each cheek. Kyla had to bend over, but she didn't seem to mind.

Then Rakar hugged Marian before heading for the stairs.

A guitar strum sounded. Ri's cue.

She took a deep breath, trying to keep hands from shaking. Her stomach kept seizing up, and part of Ri wanted to run and hide. But that wasn't going to happen. Not after what the prince had done to her. So she squared her shoulders and walked out on stage.

Kyla came and put her arm around Ri. "Everyone, this is our little sister, Ariel. She's the newest addition to our band. You're going to love her."

To Ri's surprise, she got almost as much applause as her sisters.

The one person who didn't smile was Prince Samuel. He sat ramrod straight with his hands clasped together. His eyes went wide, and then shifted back and forth, as if expecting an attack.

Ri gave the crowd a wave and waited for the moment she was supposed to sing. The words came out easily, just as she'd practiced. She only had the first few lines before she moved to the stairs and walked down them.

Each step burned, but Ri didn't let it show.

Rakar had taken his seat, and Ri went to him, trailing a finger along his shoulder as she passed. He smiled and winked.

Then she moved to the prince.

Kyla took the melody and Ri only had to *ooh*. She put on her best smile as she walked behind the prince.

He sat tense, his eyes following her every move.

Ri trailed her finger along his shoulders, and then draped an arm around him and leaned down to look at him.

The elf next to him seemed amused. She laughed at his discomfort, and clapped when Ri gave the prince a kiss on the cheek.

The prince laughed too, but it was forced.

As Kyla had instructed, Ri pulled the prince to his feet and wove her arm through his. She led him to the stairs and then up.

He leaned over and whispered to her. "What do you hope to accomplish with this?"

"You'll see soon enough."

"Are you threatening me?"

Ri shot him a dazzling smile. "I don't threaten."

The song ended, and Ri led the prince to Kyla, who took his other arm. Ri felt his muscles tense under the black jacket.

"Now, Your Majesty," Kyla said, "we have a few get-to-know-you questions from the audience."

Laughter broke out.

Kyla pulled a stack of small papers from the bodice of her dress, winked at Rakar, and turned back to the prince. "Here's the first one. Prince Samuel, are you seeing anyone?"

Kyla eyed him.

The prince chuckled. "Why yes, I am. That beautiful creature I was seated next to, Se'wh, is my girlfriend."

Kyla let out a tutting nose. "Sorry ladies and gentlemen, he's taken."

A groan sounded.

Rakar climbed on the back of his chair. "But I'm available." He turned to Kyla. "For now."

More laughter.

"Okay, the next one reads, 'Didn't I see you with Princess Ariel at the market earlier this week?'"

The prince took it in stride. "Why yes, you did. I took it upon myself to show Ri around our kingdom. Our merpeople neighbors have always held a special place in our hearts."

"So true," Kyla said. She flipped to the next paper. "What is your stance on forcing someone to do something they don't want to do?"

This time Prince Samuel frowned. "Of course I don't condone that kind of behavior. Even if it's Rakar trying to take the centaurs' beer."

That drew a peal of laughter from the back corner.

Rakar pointed in that general direction.

"What about theft, or bodily harm?" Kyla asked.

"Is that on a card?" the prince asked.

"No, I'm just curious."

"No, of course I don't condone theft. Or bodily harm."

Kyla's smile faded. "Then why did you hurt my sister?"

Silence settled over the crowd.

"Hurt your sister?" the prince asked. "I don't know—"

"You turned her back into a mermaid and ripped off one of her oysters. You left her to die."

The prince unhooked his arms from the girls and stepped back. "I think this joke has gone too far."

Kyla waved the siren forward. "Ri says you have mermaid blood on you. It doesn't wash off."

The siren moved onto the stage like the seductress she was. Every eye rested on her. She approached the prince and circled him once, inhaling and closing her eyes.

Ri clenched her fingers into a fist.

Kyla leaned forward.

The siren's eyes shot open, and she gave Kyla a little shake of the head.

"What?" Kyla asked.

"He's clean."

Prince Samuel sighed. "Security, come get these girls off the stage."

The prince's guards must have been closing in, because a second later strong hands clamped around Ri's upper arms, and they were dragging her down the stairs.

"How did you do it?" she demanded.

"I have no idea what you're talking about," the prince said. "Maybe you've had too much to drink."

The guards continued pulling her, and Ri barely caught a glimpse of Se'wh. Her eyes were drawn to her necklace.

"Wait!" Ri yelled.

The guards paused. Everyone paused.

"Take her," Prince Samuel growled.

"No!" Ri said. "Se'wh, where did you get that pearl?"

The fey's fingers brushed the dark, misshapen pendant. "The prince gave it to me."

Ri grinned. "When?"

"Tonight."

Ri turned back to the prince. "That's from my oyster. Those pearls are rare, and even rarer is one with an orange tint to it. I've only had them on my tail for a few weeks, so the tint hasn't had a chance to penetrate. I can't believe you took it out."

The muscles in the prince's cheeks flexed as he ground his teeth.

Rakar stood. "Prince Samuel, is this true?"

"Of course not."

Kyla shook off the guards. "Of course it's true. Have Ri take off her shoe. She's missing a toe. Yesterday she had all of them."

"This is ridiculous," the prince said. "Take them away."

"No!"

Everyone turned toward the sound of the voice. Tayle stood by the far door. "She's not lying. Take off her shoe."

The guards looked back and forth between the prince and Tayle.

"My father is your commander," Tayle said to the guards. "If I'm wrong, he'll punish me. But if I'm right, this is an international incident, and it needs to be resolved. Now. Your loyalty is to the crown, not the prince."

"Do it," Kyla said.

"Miss, do not move," the guard on Ri's left said. "If you try to run, we will harm you."

"I understand," she said.

The guard let her go and knelt. He slipped her shoe off, and frowned.

"Well?" Rakar asked.

"She is missing a toe," the guard said. "The wound looks fresh."

All eyes, including Ri's, turned toward the prince.

"Why would I harm the princess?"

"To steal my scales," Ri said.

"Why would I need your scales?"

"To get your father's troops past the Kraken and into the faeries' land."

A murmur rose from the faeries.

Se'wh stood, her eyes blazing. A soft, red glow began to gather around her. She reached up and yanked the pearl free. "Explain," she said to the prince.

"I bought it from our royal jeweler." Prince Samuel waved a hand. "I bought the necklace, and I don't have any mermaid blood on me. Someone else did this horrible thing, and we need to find out who."

The murmur grew in volume.

Tayle made his way across the room and stopped a few feet from the prince. He pointed at Ri. His voice shook as he spoke. "I found her in an enchanted room. Alone. Wounded. Dying. You put her there. You did this to her."

Prince Samuel smoothed his face. "You are mistaken. Perhaps someone has put a spell on you."

"No one has, and you know it."

Prince Samuel leaned close. Ri barely made out the words. "Back off now, or I tell the world about your sister."

Tayle's nostrils flared. His hands balled into fists. "Leave her out of this."

A gleam of triumph shone in Prince Samuel's eyes. "Back off. Now."

Tayle's eyes darted from the prince, then to Ri. "Guards, arrest him."

The prince took a step back. "Everyone, Tayle's sister is a sea witch. They concocted this together."

Another gasp ran through the crowd.

Before anyone could stop him, Tayle punched Prince Samuel.

The shock on the prince's face, as well as the blood that spurted from his nose, filled Ri with a sick sort of happiness.

The guards rushed forward and pulled the two boys apart before the prince could retaliate.

"She's a sea witch!" Prince Samuel said again.

"Yeah, yeah," a new voice said.

Su'la walked in, her voice amplified so all could hear. "I've decided that being a sea witch is better than being your slave."

All eyes turned to her.

Su'la's eyes met Ri's. "I'm sorry. He forced me to make the crystal and the poison. I didn't know what his plan was." She turned to Rakar. "He also forced me to take the mermaid blood off him."

"This is ridiculous," the prince said. "Let me go."

The guards didn't budge.

Rakar spoke. "You're not going anywhere."

The prince turned on the goblin. "What are you talking about?"

"This is an Academy incident. Your title means nothing in this case. Neither does anyone else's. You're here until we figure out what happened."

For the first time, anger flashed on Prince Samuel's face. His pale skin turned red, and his nostrils flared. "Rakar, allow me to pass."

"I can't do that."

"This is going to cause an incident," the prince said through clenched teeth.

"It seems we already have an incident. I've summoned the dean, and no one is leaving until we figure out who is responsible for maiming the princess of the merpeople."

"It's my word against theirs."

Rakar waved a hand. "We have quite a few wizards who have been studying truth spells. Either you surrender to one willingly and clear your name, or we throw you in a cell until we prove the accusations true or false."

Kyla turned to Rakar. "We also need Ri's scales back."

Se'wh, who was still glowing, turned on the prince. "My father will hear of this. Your kingdom will suffer." She turned and threw the pearl at Ri, who somehow caught it. "Take it."

Ri understood the flames in the elf's eyes. "Thank you."

Rakar spoke to Prince Samuel. "Looks like you get to spend some time in the cells." He jumped up on to table. "Okay people, let's get to the bottom of this."

CHAPTER 15

Three days later, Prince Samuel had been accused and found guilty of assaulting and almost killing Ri. The other kingdoms were looking into the matter of his father attacking the fey. The prince had been kicked out and stripped of all school titles. Everyone knew what he had done. He would never be a power player in the kingdoms again.

Ri and her sisters, who had become instant celebrities, walked across the courtyard toward the arts building. A group kicking a ball around waved as they passed.

"Here come the faeries again," Kyla muttered.

"I think they're adorable," Marian said.

"Yeah, because they like us."

"Let's keep it that way," Ri said.

The swarm of knee-high students fluttered around the three mermaids, thanking them and complimenting them on their outfits, their hair, and their auras.

Kyla kept Ri and Marian moving, but in the end, it was Tayle who saved them.

"Hey," he said as he approached.

The faeries all giggled—male and female—and flew off.

"I will give you anything you want," Kyla said to him.

Tayle grinned. "Can I have a few minutes alone with your sister?"

"Marian?" Kyla asked, a glimmer in her eye.

"Uh…" Tayle glanced at Ri's blonde sister.

Marian pushed Kyla. "You are so mean." Then Marian smiled at Tayle and dragged Kyla away.

Ri slowed and stopped.

Tayle and Su'la had been heavily involved with the investigation, and Ri had only seen him in passing. As she studied him, she noticed the dark circles under his eyes, and his rumpled clothes.

"You look like you could use a break," Ri said.

Tayle scratched his dark hair. "Yeah. Uh, can I ask you something?"

"Sure."

Tayle started to walk. Ri followed.

"Well, Su'la wants to talk to you, but she's afraid you're going to kill her."

Ri laughed. She'd been angry with Su'la, but as soon as she'd gotten the whole story from Tayle, her anger had melted away. Pity had replaced it. "I'm not going to kill her."

"Well, she did betray you, and she's a sea witch."

Ri glanced around to make sure they were alone. "We don't kill sea witches anymore. We teach them. My father has a whole group of people to help them so their powers don't drive them crazy. It's rare to find a human with the gift, but not unheard of." Ri brushed her long hair behind her ear. "And I feel bad that Prince Samuel manipulated her like he did. No one deserves that."

"No, they don't."

Ri looked at Tayle until he met her eyes. "Not even you."

Tayle snorted. "I was just trying to keep him away from my sister."

"Well, tell her to come back to the room and I promise not to bite, hit, or kick her."

"I'll let her know."

The two of them neared the arts building, and Tayle slowed again. "Can I ask you one more thing?"

"Fine, but just the one, so think carefully."

This drew a chuckle from Tayle. "Okay, then this is my one thing. I asked you out before because the prince ordered me to." His eyes bored into Ri's, and her stomach did a little flip flop. "Now I'd like to ask you on a date. A real date."

"That's not actually a question."

Tayle knit his eyebrows together. "Uh, then, will you come with me to my sculpture unveiling tomorrow night, as my date? Or did I miss my chance?"

Ri made a show of thinking about it. "Well, I just broke up with someone."

"Someone you went on like three dates with."

"Well, we did kiss."

"You did?"

"Your prince is an adequate kisser." She narrowed her eyes. "But you seem promising as well."

"Me?" Tayle had the decency to blush.

"You did kiss me. Or did you forget?"

"No, I didn't forget. I, uh…" He glared. "You're making fun of me."

Ri poked him in the chest. "If you're going to take me on a date, you'll have to lighten up."

"Is that a yes?"

Ri tapped her chin with a finger. "Well, considering you did rescue me from a great deal of pain and possible death, I suppose I could go on one date with you."

"With the negotiations open for more?"

"Why Tayle, did you just try to outmaneuver me?"

"What if I did?"

Ri couldn't help the smile that spread to her lips. "I like it."

ABOUT THE AUTHOR

Jo Schneider grew up in the wild west, and finds mountains helpful in telling which direction she is going. Her lifelong goals include: travel to all seven continents, become a Jedi Knight and receive a death threat from a fan. So far she's been to five continents, has a black belt in Kempo and is still working on the death threat.

Being a geek at heart, Jo has always been drawn to science fiction and fantasy. She writes both and hopes to introduce readers to worlds that wow them and characters they can cheer for.

Stalk Jo at: joannschneider.com

Or on Facebook at:

https://www.facebook.com/JoannSchneiderAuthor/

Sand and Sea

Paranormal Romance

By

Adrienne Monson

CHAPTER 1

*A*ria raced through the waters at her fastest swim, anger and betrayal giving her the energy to keep going. She fled over the coral reefs, sea life scurrying to hide in her wake. Normally, she'd stop and visit with them and play with the little ones, but today she paid no attention to anyone around her. The conversation she'd overheard echoed in her mind. *It couldn't be true.*

And yet, her father had paid a merchant to keep his silence. How many mermen had the king paid off in the past? Was that why she was just now learning about his history, twenty years later? Aria had used the servants' door to enter King Caspian's receiving room. She'd needed to report to him about the meeting she'd had that morning with the advisory board. She hadn't meant to eavesdrop on the conversation. She'd come in quietly, hoping not to disturb the king's meeting that she knew should have been ending at any moment. But when she'd overheard the merchant telling King Caspian that he knew the king had turned human during his sabbatical twenty years ago, the king hadn't denied it. Only asked his price for silence.

Aria turned her head, which shifted her body swiftly in the water. Her oldest sister, Kessida, didn't live far from the palace. She was twelve years older than Aria and had been more mother to her than a sister. She'd know the truth. *And if everything that merchant said is true, then that means Kessida kept it from me all these years as well as Father.*

Given her age, it was easy enough to do the math. That meant that the queen had died *before* Aria was even conceived. She'd heard about the infamous sabbatical her father had taken after her mother's death—*If she's not my mother, who is?* Her entire life, Aria'd grown up believing the queen had died giving birth to her. But after hearing what that merchant had said, it didn't add up. She shared some similarities with her sisters, but her fiery red hair . . . she was the only mermaid with hair this color. And she was more petite than her sisters as well. Every talent, everything that made her unique now whirlpooled through her mind. *What a fool I was to think that I belonged in this family!*

This also meant that her father, the king of the seven seas, was a hypocrite. He'd preached her entire life about staying away from humans, saying how evil they were. If her father really had turned human all those years ago, it also meant that he would have had to ask a mermaid to give in to dark magic to make the transformation. While her father's royal magic had the power to perform such spells, he couldn't use that magic on himself. And the only other magic strong enough to make such a transformation was dark. For a mermaid to give in to such power, she would have to damn her immortal soul. *Prya. It had to have been her.*

Most mermaids didn't live long after giving in to dark magic. Her sisters told her that once a mermaid accepted dark magic, it consumed them to the point that they used it constantly until all of their energy was taken and they couldn't even lift a hand to feed themselves.

"Except for Prya," Kessida had told her. "She was Father's most trusted advisor until she turned to dark magic. I was young, but I remember how shocked everyone was. They said it was because she was heartbroken over Mother's death. But she still lives. Keeps to herself in the cold waters just outside our kingdom."

Trusting her father both as a patriarch and king, she'd never questioned him. Even when she'd ventured to the surface years ago, after she'd played a few times with a boy in the water, she'd known she wouldn't stay with humans. She knew it was just a rebellious stage and that she'd settle down with maturity. But after learning that he'd become human during his sixteen-month sabbatical while he grieved for his dead wife, Aria wondered what else Father had lied to her about.

Growling in her throat, she maneuvered through a school of dolphins, making them squeal in dismay. Her sister's home loomed ahead. Kessida had followed the example of their ancestors and used white magic to keep the large home glowing, even down in the depths of the dark sea. Kessida's home was only a quarter the size of King Caspian's palace, but it was just as regal and inviting.

A servant bowed when Aria approached and slowed her pace. "Princess Aria, if you'll follow me to the receiving room, I'll see if your sister is available."

Clenching her jaw, Aria nodded and followed him into the large receiving room. After swimming so quickly at such a long distance, floating in a room and waiting made her feel antsy. Aria inspected the pearl encrusted chairs and crystal chandelier. Would she ever have a home of her own? What merman would marry her if he knew the truth? She didn't even know the whole truth yet, something she'd hoped Kessida would help her with.

A stinging pain in her tail caught her attention. Looking down, Aria saw blue blood slowly floating into the water from the bottom of her tail. She must have scratched it on some rock or coral during her hasty swim.

Closing her eyes, she cleared her mind and mentally reached out to the white magic that was always deep within, ready to aid her. The dark magic was there too, but she ignored it and focused on the pure whiteness and tapped into it to pull its healing energy into her scratch. Her scales shimmered as the magic seeped toward the bottom of her tail, then stopped at the small wound. Flesh melded together, healing until her tail was whole again. She sighed as she let go of the magic. Not only had it healed the scratch, but it had also calmed her nerves a little.

Giggles sounded down the hall. Hearing her nephews, Aria felt her shoulders relax a notch. She left the room and followed the sounds to the dining hall, where Ragni and Crese swam around and caught bits of floating food into their mouths.

"I'm winning," Ragni exclaimed as he quickly chewed, swallowed, and then rushed to the next piece of fish to eat.

"No fair," Crese whined. "You're bigger than me. I can't swim as fast."

At age five, Ragni was large for his age. He showed potential to be a faster swimmer than Aria. He grinned. "Then I guess you won't get much food today."

Aria glided further into the room. "Ragni," she scolded. "You can't eat all of that without getting sick, and you know it."

They both whirled around, smiles breaking onto their faces. "Aunt Aria!" they said in unison and swam over to her, taking turns to give her hugs.

Aria embraced each child, getting a form of comfort. These two loved her. That wouldn't stop if they found out that she had a different mother, right?

Kessida entered, her belly protruding from under her vest. She'd be giving birth in just a matter of weeks now. Her smile dulled with the confusion tugging at her brow. "I didn't know you were coming for a visit, Aria. Have you eaten supper yet? There's plenty." She waved a delicate hand at the food. "It's pretty late. Are you planning to spend the night?"

Aria's stomach clenched as she watched her oldest sister. Kessida's dark brown hair was loose and floated around her head and shoulders. Even with her large stomach, she held herself erect and regal, as all of the sisters were taught to do from birth.

Her kind, green eyes narrowed as Aria watched her without responding.

"What's wrong?" Kessida asked. She knew Aria better than anyone. Aria had thought them close, but she'd also thought she was close to her father. How could the people she loved and trusted the most lie to her?

"I need to speak with you privately," Aria said. Without waiting for a reply, she moved past her sister and went back into the receiving room.

Kessida followed and had a servant close the doors behind her before putting her hands on her waist. "What's going on, Aria? I've never seen you like this."

Doing her best to tamp down her emotions, Aria tersely explained, "I overheard something this afternoon. Something that leads me to believe my mother is not yours."

"Oh, Aria." Kessida swished her tail to move forward and hugged her.

Aria stiffly accepted the embrace, not ready to forgive her sister but not wanting to push her away either.

"I'm sorry you found out this way, but it's probably time you know the truth."

Pulling away, Aria blinked back tears. "You knew this whole time and didn't tell me?"

"Father forbade it."

Shaking her head, Aria pulled at the hem of her vest so she wouldn't give in to the impulse to hit something. "How did you do it? How did you stay loyal to Father when you knew he became human?" She huffed, bubbles shooting around her face.

"I would have been bitter every time he ranted about how terrible humans are."

"Sister, you're not making sense." Kessida sunk into a chair. "What does any of this have to do with how Father feels about humans?"

Glancing down at her fingers, Aria twisted her lips to the side. "I thought you knew about that other part too."

"What other part?"

"When Father took his sabbatical, he became a human and lived among them."

"What?" Kessida touched her throat in surprise. "He became human? How—" She stopped, her eyes going distant. "Prya. Of course."

Aria sat in the chair opposite her sister. "You told me that she embraced dark magic after Mother—I mean, your mother's death."

"Yes." Rubbing her belly, Kessida turned troubled eyes to Aria. "Why would she do that for him?" She didn't wait for Aria to answer. "You're half human?" She mumbled it as if she struggled to voice the question.

Pausing, Aria frowned. It was a thought she'd been avoiding, trying not to put words to it since she'd overheard that conversation. She didn't want to think that she was half of a race that her father detested. He'd engrained it into her that humans were horrible, evil beings. Aria thought back to the few times she'd played with that human boy in a small lagoon. He hadn't seemed cruel. He'd acted just like all the other merkids she'd grown up with. *Did you lie to me about that too, Father?*

She realized that Kessida was watching her, waiting for a response. "I suppose I could be half human," she said slowly.

Kessida pursed her lips. "I guess Father is the only one who can answer that."

Realization struck, and Aria met her sister's gaze. "Or Prya."

Kessida's eyes widened. "Are you suggesting what I think you are?"

Aria drifted to the window before she answered, bitterness flooding her chest. "Let's be honest, Kessida. Father has kept many secrets from all of us." Her words came out clipped. "Do you really believe he'll tell all if I confront him?"

It was quiet for several seconds before Kessida answered. "You're right, of course." Floating out of the chair, she swam toward the door. "I'll go with you."

"No." Aria glided over and put her hands on Kessida's shoulders. "You shouldn't come in your condition."

"But you can't go by yourself. Prya could be dangerous. She's the only mermaid who's been able to live with her dark magic." Kessida grabbed one of Aria's hands from her shoulder. "I fear what would happen if I'm not with you."

Aria forced a smile. "I'm the fastest swimmer in the sea." When Kessida didn't look convinced, Aria added, "I need answers, Kessida. I can't rest until I have them."

CHAPTER 2

*K*essida was reluctant to let Aria go but finally said goodnight. "Promise that you'll send a spelled shell message to me as soon as you come back, no matter the time."

Aria agreed, then left, racing to the outskirts of the kingdom. The sea life became more and more sparse as she went.

Aria's stomach rumbled with hunger. *I should have grabbed a snack before I left.* There was nothing to be done about it now, so she just kept swimming. She hoped it wasn't too late to visit Prya. Did evil mermaids keep normal hours? She doubted anyone knew the answer to that question.

Arriving at the edge of the kingdom, Aria swallowed. The ground dropped into a dark void, the water colder. She steeled her spine and headed down. Tapping into her white magic, Aria used a spell to help her eyes see in the darkness. The water tasted different as she swam deeper, like it was stale. Perhaps devoid of life was more accurate. Was this Prya's dark magic at work?

Pausing, Aria wondered if it was prudent to continue her journey. Was it worth the risk to get answers? Aria became painfully aware of her unusually petite frame, her red hair. Even when she was a child in school, her favorite subject was the study of humans. Most merkids were bored when their teachers taught about humans. Did others sneak up to the surface like she'd done as a teenager? What *else* was different about her? Father would never tell, and as she thought on it, the stale darkness of the water below seemed an omen of the life of ignorance she faced by not knowing who—or what—she truly was. The thought crashed into her mind.

She closed her eyes and dove. She gave wide berth to a family of electric eels and swam even deeper. Aria wondered if it would take her all night to get to the bottom. Finally, a silvery light shone in the distance. Aria swam to it and saw a dwelling carved out of black rock.

She hesitantly moved to the opening. There was no door or cover, so Aria lightly rapped on the wall. "Hello," she called softly. No response.

Perhaps the vibrations of her voice hadn't carried far enough. "Hello?" she called out louder. "Prya?"

Strange whispers vibrated in the water all around her. Heart pounding, Aria forced herself to swim forward until she reached the end of the cave and entered a dimly lit interior. Shelves lined the inside, holding vases and vials of different sizes and shapes.

There were also flutes, harps, and other items that she recognized from the human world.

Prya was writing in the sand floor with a thin stick, her oval face pinched with concentration. Aria was surprised to see the older mermaid was quite pretty, with full lips and black hair floating around her thin shoulders. Her tail was black, the scales shimmering in the dim, silvery light. Aria had never seen anyone with a black tail before.

Using her white magic, Aria opened her sight to read the mermaid's aura. While it was certainly tainted black, there was also blue, which indicated kindness and loyalty. The red had different shades, which indicated anger and passion. Most surprising was the glowing pink at her heart, which meant that Prya held a very deep love and affection for someone.

All things considered, Prya wasn't nearly as intimidating as Aria had expected. Perhaps merfolk judged the mermaid by the scar running down the side of her face, but even that didn't take away from the witch's striking appearance.

"It wasn't from a fishing hook," Prya said without looking up.

"What?" Aria asked, hoping that the mermaid didn't detect the tremble in her tone.

"Everyone always asked if my scar is from a hook. It's not."

"What is it from then?"

Looking up, Prya smiled bitterly. "I won't say. But your father could tell you."

Aria drifted back. "You know who I am?"

Nodding, Prya continued scrawling as she spoke. "I'd know your face anywhere."

Shaking her head, her brows pulled down. "We've never met. How could you possibly recognize me?"

Dropping the stick, Prya floated up to the ceiling and stretched her arms. "I can see both your mother and father in your face, dear. I never forget faces."

"You knew my mother?" Aria asked with caution.

"Yes," Prya sang slowly. "I met her once. It was she who did this." She pointed to her face.

Aria gasped.

Laughing, Prya waved her hand. "I suppose that's a bit of an exaggeration. She only ordered it. And I wasn't her target."

Chewing her bottom lip, Aria wasn't sure what to think about this story. Could Prya be trusted? If so, was her mother some horrible monster?

"Was she human? My mother?"

Prya floated closer and watched Aria upside down. "Indeed." She smirked as if she were telling a fine joke.

Aria glided further into the room. "Tell me everything."

Sinking back to the floor, Prya used her stick to draw some more. It looked like she was etching runes surrounded by words in a language Aria didn't recognize. "Look around you, Princess. I'm an outcast." She smiled. "One of the biggest perks of my current station is that I take orders from no one, no matter how royal."

"But I must know!" Aria cried.

"'But I must know,'" the older woman mimicked. She dramatically raised a hand to her forehead and arched her back. "Please save me. I'm in such peril."

The mermaid's behavior was so juvenile that it rankled Aria's nerves. "You can't treat me like that," Aria scolded. "I am Aria, daughter to King Caspian, and I will have respect."

Prya giggled, making Aria question the mermaid's sanity. "Very nice, Princess. I'm sure that works on anyone within the kingdom." She grinned. "But you're in my domain now. I treat you however I like." She laughed again. "It's so fun to have company! No one has dared visit me in years."

Aria pulled water through her gills slowly as she did her best to cling to patience. "Prya, please tell me about my mother and father, if you will."

Floating closer, Prya studied Aria's face. "To what purpose? What will you do with the information I give, should I choose to do so?"

Blinking at the question, Aria wasn't sure what to answer. She wanted answers. So many answers. But what would she do with the information? She now knew she was half human. Did she want to track down her mother? But if her mother was as awful as Prya indicated, would Aria even want to know her?

"I thought so." Prya rolled her eyes. "Just like anyone else who ventures down here, you've only thought of your immediate situation. Why can't anyone think further ahead? Can none of you ninnies plan? Visualize your future?"

Aria narrowed her eyes. "Did you, Prya? When you gave in to the dark magic, were you thinking of your future?"

Prya smirked and slyly looked to the side. "Touché, Princess. Perhaps you have more brains in your head than I thought."

She swam down to the in the center of the room. "What will it benefit me to answer your questions?"

This was something Aria knew how to answer. "I brought payment." She reached into a bag on her belt and pulled out three gold coins. "Will this do?"

Prya didn't glance back at her. "Princess, I live completely on my own. You think money holds any value to me?"

"Then what would you consider for payment?"

Swishing her tail, Prya glided closer until her face was mere inches from Aria's. "The blood of a royal half-breed would be payment enough."

The scales on her tail tightened, and her stomach clenched. *I'm a half-breed.* The term made her ill. Tears threatened, but Aria forced them back. She would maintain composure in front of this witch and focus on what was being said. "What would you do with my blood?"

"It would be used to enhance some of my spells, dearie." She drifted back. "What, did you think I would curse you?"

Aria glanced away. It was exactly what she'd thought.

The older mermaid laughed again. "I only curse those who cross me, Princess. And while your manners need work, you haven't done anything to upset me." She paused. "Yet. Let's hope it stays that way." She waved a hand. "Besides, I don't need your blood to curse you."

Aria pursed her lips. "Exactly how much blood do you want?"

Tilting her head, Prya smiled. "Smart girl. You'd be surprised at how many forget to ask that question." She shrugged. "Eight ounces of your blood is my price."

"And if I give you some of my blood, you'll tell me about my mother and father?"

Prya tapped her chin. "As much as I can without breaking my oath."

Aria wrinkled her brow. "What oath?"

"The one I gave your father. He promised to leave me be on the outskirts of his kingdom if I kept his secrets."

"But haven't you already broken it by telling me my mother is human?"

Prya looked at Aria as if she were slow. "I didn't actually tell you that, did I? You asked and I confirmed. Quite different than me blabbering everything I know to you."

"So if I ask the right questions, you can tell me?"

"Now you're using your brain. Did it hurt?" Prya gave her a sarcastic salute. "Are you sure you can think of the right ones? They might give you a headache."

"If anything gives me a headache this night, it'll be you, Prya."

The older mermaid tittered. "You're fun company indeed. Now," she swam to a shelf and grabbed a needle and bottle, "let's get on with it."

She went to Aria and jabbed the large needle into her upper arm.

Pain shot through her entire limb, and Aria bit her lip so she wouldn't cry out.

Completely unrepentant, Prya pulled out the needle and twisted her fingers through the water. "You'll live," she muttered.

The room grew colder. Aria tasted the dark magic in her mouth and felt a chilled tingling on her arm. Her blue blood drifted in a straight line until it went into the bottle Prya held. Then the blood stopped. Aria inspected the wound; it was gone, her skin unbroken. She hadn't even felt the flesh mending like she did when she used white magic to heal herself.

Prya put a stopper in to seal the bottle and took it to the opposite end of the room. She chanted something under her breath and the ground opened up to reveal shelves of thousands of bottles.

Aria tried to inspect them, but Prya shut the compartment with a snap of her fingers. *How much power does this woman hold? Is this how she's stayed alive without the dark magic consuming her?*

"Now then, Princess, ask me your questions."

Blinking, Aria straightened. "Do you know who my mother is?"

"Yes."

"What's her name?"

Prya rolled her eyes. "That, I cannot say. Sworn to secrecy, you know."

Pursing her lips, Aria thought before asking her next question. "Did you give in to dark magic in order to make my father become human?"

"Nice one, Princess. Yes, I did."

Aria studied the older mermaid. "Why would you do that? Give up everything, just to make him human?"

For the first time, Prya's face softened and she turned away. Aria stared at her back, wondering if she'd answer.

"Your father loved the queen very much. Her death devastated everyone in some way. All I can tell you is that in that moment, I would have done anything to help Caspian overcome his grief."

Aria mulled on that for a moment, sympathy tugging at her mind, before moving on. "Why did my father want to become human?"

"That one, I can answer." Prya turned back to Aria and smirked. "He never specified that I couldn't discuss his motives, the foolish crab." She swam to a lounge chair carved out of igneous rock and reclined. "Caspian had always had a fascination with the humans. He used to swim up to the surface and watch them, learn about them. He even spoke of making ourselves known to them and begin trading with them." She chuckled. "Poor Caspian and his naïve, innocent ambitions."

Aria didn't comment. She thought the idea had merit but was shocked that her father would have ever had that inclination.

"Anyway, while he was overwhelmed with his grief, he felt the only way he could move past it was to become human and learn more about that race, first hand. Apparently, what we teach the merfolk about humans in school wasn't enough. He thought his wife would have wanted him to do it. So, he placed his advisors in charge of things while he took a year sabbatical. He told no one where he was going. They all understood how much he was grieving."

"But I heard he was gone for sixteen months, not a year."

"Yes, Aria. He stayed much longer than he should have." Prya frowned. "I wasn't sure if he'd ever come back."

"Do you mean he decided to stay and not come back?"

Her face hardened. "No. He was captured and couldn't escape."

Aria's mouth dropped open. "How could anyone capture Father? No one can rival his magic."

Prya raised her brows. "Our magic only works when we're connected to the sea, Princess. Caspian couldn't even stand on the beach to tap into his powers while he was captive."

Aria drifted closer. "How did he escape?"

Instead of answering, Prya traced the line of her scar.

"You helped him, didn't you?"

Prya sent Aria a sidelong glance of respect. "You *are* smarter than you look."

Drawing her head back, Aria wasn't sure if she should feel insulted or not.

"No more questions?" Prya asked.

"I'm thinking." A thought was niggling at the back of her mind. There was something she was missing. "Wait." She swam closer to Prya. "You insinuated that my mother gave you that scar. And now you're telling me that you got it rescuing my father."

A look of pride flashed across Prya's features. "Indeed."

"My mother was behind my father's imprisonment?"

Smiling, Prya bowed her head. "Brava, Princess. You guessed correctly."

Aria sank to the floor until her tail hit the sand. It might have been better if she'd never come here. How could she live with this information, knowing her mother had kept her father captive? "No wonder he hates humans now," she murmured.

Prya waffled her hand through the water. "Well, I don't see it the way he does."

Confused, Aria watched the older mermaid. "How is that?"

"Living in exile helps me gain a different perspective, Princess," Prya said in a condescending tone. "Your father has also taken blackness into his soul. It may not be dark magic, but his state of mind curses him well enough."

Aria considered her words. "You're saying that my father's bitterness and anger against the humans is his darkness."

"Yes. And I also say that humans are just like merfolk. Some are good and some bad. No one is born that way. All determine it through life based on their choices, their actions."

Brows raised, Aria found she was beginning to like the supposedly evil mermaid. "That's a very profound assessment, especially considering you're banished to live alone in this dark hole."

"You want to know why I'm alive while I live with dark magic?" Prya asked.

Aria drifted up from the floor. "Yes."

Pausing, Prya sat up. "I already gave you the answer. It's not my fault if you can't see it."

Aria frowned, wondering if she'd been crazy to have had sympathy for this mermaid.

"I'm finished with this conversation. I've answered enough for your payment. Time for you to go now, Princess."

"Oh." Aria tried to think of something else to ask, but her mind was too overwhelmed with everything she'd just learned.

"Leave," Prya hissed.

Aria bolted out of the cave, not wanting Prya to turn her into eel food. The mermaid had a strange flux of moods.

Once outside, Aria couldn't bring herself to swim home. She stayed a few feet from Prya's home, thinking of everything they'd discussed. Prya's question percolated in her mind. *What are you going to do?*

What should she do? It would be wise of her to confront her father about all of this. And yet, she didn't trust him to answer her questions. He'd probably tell her that it was all gossip and not to pay any attention to it. Once again, she thought about what a hypocrite King Caspian was.

Then an idea struck. *Why not follow his example, become human myself?* She could go to the surface and search for her mother. Aria didn't think she'd want to actually meet her, but perhaps watch her from afar, study the woman who seemed to be more evil than Prya was said to be—and be certain that Aria didn't share any of those wicked traits with her mother.

Her mind made up, she went back into Prya's cave.

"Back already?" Prya called from her pot. The mermaid was stirring something that glowed a dark blue.

"I have another request." Aria held out her arm. "How much of my blood in exchange for making me human?"

"Twenty ounces should suffice."

"That's it?" Aria was certain it would take more.

"That, and the knowledge that it will drive your father into a rage, is payment enough for me."

Aria paused at that. She was mad at her father right now but she wasn't the vindictive type. Perhaps she could get Kessida to cover for her so he would think she was staying with her sister for a while, as she often did. But she wouldn't tell Prya that. Let the mermaid think that Caspian would go ballistic if it entertained her so much.

Prya quickly went through the process of collecting Aria's blue blood and then returned to her pot. Aria supposed magic was used to prevent the contents of the pot from floating up into the water. Her head felt light from the blood loss, and she was shaking and weak.

"You knew I would come back, didn't you?" Aria asked. She had noted the lack of surprise of Prya's face when she'd returned.

Shrugging, Prya didn't bother to glance up. "I had a suspicion that you'd want to become human and seek out your mother. You can't very well take my word about her, now can you?"

Aria didn't like to think she was so predictable and didn't comment.

"Can you tell me anything more, Prya? To help me find my mother?"

Pursing her lips, Prya glanced at Aria. "Most of the information I could give you I cannot speak of. One thing I can tell you, she resides in the Kwardian kingdom. It's not too large, and I'm betting you'll recognize your own features in her face when you see her."

It was the same area Aria used to visit as a rebellious teenager. She could even go to that same lagoon she was familiar with to make the transition. Focusing back on Prya, she asked, "Does she have the same color hair as me?"

Prya shook her head. "It's similar but not exactly the same." She paused. "There is one more thing to discuss before we can proceed. I can see your heart is pure, Aria. You haven't brushed with dark magic. You realize this decision will make it harder to resist touching dark magic yourself? It's a very seductive power that can engulf you and very likely kill you."

Swallowing, Aria reflected on this information. She'd thought that if someone else performed dark magic for her, then she'd still be clean from it. Technically, she would, but it sounded like she'd have to work harder to resist it. So far, it hadn't been difficult to only tune in to the white magic. She'd never been even a little tempted by dark magic. Eternal happiness was more important to her than anything else in her mortal life. Surely she'd still hold the same convictions. "I'm willing to risk it."

Grabbing a vial, Prya threw the entire thing into the pot. Sparkles of dark blue magic exploded, dissolving quickly.

Prya picked up a bottle and swirled her fingers through the water in a strange pattern. The blue liquid floated out of the pot and flew into the bottle. Putting a stopper into the bottle, Prya handed it to Aria. "It might be small, but it's powerful. This will prevent you from using your gills, so take it when you're on the surface. And only touch the sea water when you're ready to return because it'll instantly transform you back into a mermaid."

Aria accepted it with shaking fingers. Was she really going to do this? "Thank you for your help, Prya."

The older mermaid nodded and turned away. Her fingers danced through the water once again and the pot slowly sunk beneath the ground.

Pausing just before she reached the exit, Aria stopped and turned around. "You're not as bad as people say. I don't know everything about the past, but I do believe you were wronged. I'm sorry for that."

Prya kept her back to Aria as she responded softly. "You're wiser than your father. Perhaps you'll do better among the humans than he did."

CHAPTER 3

The sun colored the sky a warm pink when Aria reached the surface. She'd sent a shell message to Kessida, and her sister had reluctantly agreed to cover for her while she was away. She'd also gone home to keep up pretenses, only her maid knowing that she'd been gone all night.

King Caspian had encouraged Aria's decision to stay with Kessida for a while. "Your sister needs more rest with the baby so close to coming. I'm glad you're going to help her with those boys. They have more energy than a hundred baby clams."

Aria had almost changed her mind at her father's words. Kessida really could use the help, and Aria suddenly felt selfish for leaving everything behind while she searched out her real mother. But then her father had gone on a rant about the feckless humans when an advisor reported that another shipwreck had littered a kelp farm with all kinds of debris.

She'd left in the middle of his tirade, once again bitter about how he'd lied to her all these years. *How can he even love me if I'm half human?*

Aria's world had shattered. She couldn't stay in the sea when the answers were on land.

Now in the lagoon she'd played in years ago, she glanced around the beach and saw two men walking along the shore. She dove back under, hoping they hadn't seen her.

Swimming over to a large boulder, she peered out of the water again, the rock hiding her. The men had stopped and were talking. Clinging to the boulder, the waves gently rocked her up and down as she waited. Air nipped at her face. The gills behind her ears twitched as the lungs in her chest took over and she breathed deeply, a strange pressure entering her throat. *When will they leave?*

Losing patience, Aria decided to tap into her white magic and listen so she'd have a better idea of whether their conversation would end. She reached past the dark magic within and clung to the pure white, allowing it to fill her mind. She focused on her sigh and her hearing, letting the soft tingles accentuate her senses.

Suddenly, the early morning light was overwhelming. The men on the beach were seen in perfect clarity. The noise of birds shifting in their nests scraped against her nerves, but she did her best to ignore the other sounds of lapping water and worms wriggling through the dirt to focus on what the man was saying.

"Looks like you really can influence the prince, after all, Rollo," the shorter man with thinning hair was saying.

"I told you I've been manipulating him all my life. It may have taken longer than we expected, but he finally signed the treaty last night." This man was taller and younger looking. She assumed he was Rollo.

The shorter man pulled out a cloth and dabbed at his forehead. "Excellent. We'll proceed with the plan, then. I'll send my assassins to kill him tonight."

Rollo tensed, his shoulders rising. "You said you'd make it look like they're rebels from my kingdom, Hanthorne. If a professional kills him, your country will be the prime suspect, treaty or not."

Puffing out his chest, Hanthorne stepped forward. "Yes, that's still the plan. They're ready to carry it out as soon as I send word to them."

"Make sure they only kill the prince. I need to be close to him when it happens for my alibi. I'd be quite upset if your men made me collateral damage during the process."

"And that's why I'm having the professionals carry this out. They know what they're doing." Hanthorne shrugged. "I can sweeten the deal and make sure you're injured in the attack. It will help your alibi."

Rollo narrowed his eyes. "Wouldn't it look suspicious if only the prince dies and I'm merely wounded?"

"He'll be in an open setting. There will be plenty of bystanders who can die or get injured during the attack."

Acid rose up her throat, and Aria gripped the boulder tightly.

"That makes sense," Rollo said.

Aria saw another man approaching, his footsteps muted in the sand. Rollo and Hanthorne didn't appear to notice yet. They were finishing up their conversation in low tones.

The newcomer was dressed in a jacket similar to the other men, except his shoulders were much broader. He moved as smoothly as a graceful eel and held his head as regally as her father. He also looked very familiar.

Aria's mouth dropped open. She'd played with him as a boy. When Aria came to the surface four years ago, there was a boy who sometimes swam in the lagoon. They'd played together a few times, splashing and chasing. She'd never spoken to him and had tried to keep her tail from view, but they'd had a fun time together. He must have been twelve or thirteen at the time, and she'd fondly thought of him as the little brother she'd never had.

Of course, she grew up and stopped visiting the surface. And now here he was, all grown up.

Rollo and Hanthorne stopped speaking when they noticed him. As one, they bowed from the waist.

The man glanced between the two for a second, his left eye twitching. "I have something for you, Ambassador Hanthorne." His voice carried so well that Aria winced from her sensitive hearing. He held out a rolled-up parchment. "Signed by myself and witnessed by one of my advisors."

A genuine smile slid over Hanthorne's lips. "Highness, I'm thrilled that you decided to sign." He took the treaty with one hand and held out the other. "May this be marked in history as the turning point for peace between our kingdoms."

The prince took Hanthorne's hand and shook it. "It is my sincere wish that your prediction comes true."

Hanthorne made a hasty yet polite retreat. The prince watched him go, and while Aria couldn't see the monarch's face, his stance made him look pensive as the ambassador walked away.

She wished she could swim up to them and tell the prince everything she'd heard. She'd never been good at sitting idly by while unfair politics brewed under her nose. It had gotten her into trouble with some of the visiting dignitaries, but her father had always respected Aria's sense of fairness and rarely reprimanded her for it.

"I'm doing the right thing, aren't I, Rollo?" The prince turned and looked over the water. He stared in her direction, and she darted behind the boulder.

"It's like I told you yesterday, Elex." Aria peaked around the rock again to see Rollo place a hand on the prince's shoulder. "I think this is the best approach to achieving your goals. You'll be the first in your line to attempt peace instead of war with Olandia. Everyone knows you're more noble than you father or grandfather ever were."

Prince Elex gave a halfhearted smile and patted his cousin's hand before crouching down and running his fingers through the sand. "You know that's what I want. No more wars."

"Your father must be turning in his grave," Rollo said wryly.

Prince Elex nodded. "Along with my grandfather and all my other ancestors." He flexed his jaw. "But it's time our blood feud with Olandia ended. Too many of my people have died, and for what? A petty rivalry?"

Behind the prince's back, Rollo glared at him. "And you've finally convinced the queen that signing the treaty is best?"

Lips twisting, Prince Elex shook his head. "It doesn't matter. When I turn twenty-one next week, she'll no longer have a say in how I rule."

"It was very wise of you, Elex, to sign the treaty now. It may not go into effect until next week, but your mother won't have a chance to stop you from signing."

Aria scowled at Rollo, who was playing his role perfectly. The poor prince had no idea how devious his cousin was. And now that the prince had signed the treaty, his death was imminent. She chewed on her thumbnail, wondering if there was anything she could do to stop it.

She waited several more minutes as the two discussed his birthday and how much responsibility he was taking on. Finally, they began walking toward the castle that stood further back on land.

Aria let go of the rock and continued to watch their retreating forms. Prince Elex was about to be betrayed in a much worse way than Caspian had betrayed her. He seemed like a decent man, and it rankled Aria to know he'd meet his end this very night.

Not if I can help it. She was just about to become human. She could protect go to the prince and warn him about the assassination that would take place that evening. It would only be a small detour from finding her mother.

Swimming cautiously, Aria moved farther down the beach, away from the castle. She would have to get used to her legs first and then somehow warn the prince about the assassins. *How will I find my mother?* She pushed the thought aside. One thing at a time and Prince Elex's life had a fast approaching expiration date if she didn't hurry to help. She'd figure out how to find her mother after that.

The waves gently lapped over her back as she dragged herself to the dry sand, her lungs again taking over once more. She felt heavy out of the water, and it took effort to pull herself over the sand. The little granules dug into her forearms and the dry air made her skin itch, but she kept going. Sand clung to her scales, and Aria had the impulse to turn back to the comfort of her home. *No, I'm committed now. I won't go back yet.*

The rising sun bathed her in its heat as she turned onto her back and reached for Prya's bottle. Even the straps on her belt felt strange outside of the water and it took longer to untie the bottle. Once she did, she sat up and took out the stopper. The potion smelled earthy and rotten.

Wrinkling her nose, Aria held her breath and drank. The liquid was thick, coating her throat and threatening her gag reflex. Dark magic filled her chest and then rushed to her tail with a strange icy burning sensation. Pain rippled through her shortly after and she gasped, her head tossing back and her body convulsing. Her muscles seized uncontrollably, and she accidentally bit her tongue, her mouth filling with salty blood. Darkness crept around her vision, and then there was nothing.

CHAPTER 4

A voice stirred Aria from unconsciousness. It was a man's voice that had a rich baritone quality that Aria found quite pleasant. "You poor thing. Looks like you were shipwrecked."

Long fingers gently stroked her cheek. "Miss? Can you hear me?"

The physical touch helped Aria open her eyes. She squinted against the glare of the sun and found the man kneeling next to her. His kind, brown eyes drew down in concern, dark hair falling over his forehead as he leaned over her.

They stared at each other for a long moment, the man looking as transfixed as she felt. He was leaner than any merman but exhibited a graceful air.

The man blinked and cleared his throat. "Are you alright, milady?" Once again, his voice carried over her in a soothing way that made her want to lie back and savor its richness.

His question finally penetrated, and Aria nodded. "Yes, of course." But nothing came out. Frowning, Aria touched her throat. "I think—" Again, no sound at all. The vibrations at the back of her throat worked, but she couldn't make the sound carry on the air the way humans did. Speaking in the water was different than on land.

"Something wrong with your voice?" He asked. "May I inspect it? I'm a doctor. I can help."

Aria nodded, though she doubted he could help her. He may be a doctor but didn't know mer anatomy. The thought reminded her that she was currently human.

She moved the doctor's hands away from her neck and sat up, staring down at a pair of very human legs connected to her torso, her vest brushing over her thighs. Biting her lip in concentration, she wiggled her toes. A triumphant smile broke out when she saw them moving.

"I don't understand," the doctor said. His gaze lingered over her legs. He cleared his throat, his face tinging pink, the looked into her eyes. "Did you think you were paralyzed?"

"It's not that," she tried once again to speak, but the vibrations disappeared on the air. Giving up, she smiled and shook her head.

"Do you have any injuries?" he asked.

She shook her head, staring at her legs.

"Here, please accept my coat." He shrugged off his outer layer of clothing, giving Aria a better view of his shoulders and chest. He was as broad as Prince Elex, but she could see his lean muscles through the white sleeve of his shirt. And he certainly appeared taller than the prince. He wrapped the coat around her shoulders, and she eased her arms through the sleeves.

The material was slightly rough against her skin, but she enjoyed how it smelled. Like earth and saltwater and the doctor's own musk. She pulled her chin back as she realized what she was thinking. This was a human, not some handsome merman for her to feel an attraction to.

The coat was like a blanket and fell to her calves, completely covering her vest.

Shifting at an angle, she once again studied her new limbs. They looked so strange on her, and yet the thrill of being human was overwhelming. She couldn't wait to walk and run.

Pulling her legs under her, she started to rise.

"Let me help." The doctor held out his hands. Her father had always taught her that humans were volatile and easily violent, but the doctor had only showed her kindness.

Grateful that this handsome and friendly man was with her, she placed her hands in his. His palms enveloped hers completely, but she liked the feeling. His skin was warm against hers and his touch helped her to feel more relaxed than she had since learning her father's secrets.

With his gentle pull, she stood, the coat sliding up past her knees. She noted that the doctor was studiously keeping his gaze on her face.

She lifted a leg to begin walking, but her feet felt like sharp blades were placed underneath the soles. She wobbled in the first two steps, like a newborn lobster, then at the third step, she pitched forward and would have fallen if not for the doctor's arms around her shoulders.

"Easy there," he soothed. "Let's take it nice and slow." His arm eased under both of hers, his body warming her back. He gave a smile of encouragement that made her stomach flutter. Or maybe it was his close proximity. Either way, she was enjoying every minute on land so far.

With his assistance, she walked several meters without falling. Aria learned that she had to concentrate on her balance to walk, using her stomach muscles. Each step was a little less painful on the soles of her feet, though her skin was still abraded by the sand.

She looked at the leather shoes that covered the doctor's feet. *I'll have to get some of those. They must certainly protect him from this pain.*

"You're doing well," he said. "Do you think you can walk on your own now?" He eased his hands away but kept them up as if prepared to catch her.

Aria focused on staying balanced and walked. It took a lot of concentration just to do that. How did humans accomplish anything else throughout the day?

"Very good." The young doctor kept pace with her.

Grinning, Aria stopped and looked up at him. She wished she could shout her joy at this. It was such a unique experience.

The doctor matched her smile as he looked deeply into her eyes. "How can one be so joyful by simply walking?" he murmured. She wasn't sure if he was asking her or just talking to himself.

I bet running is even better.

"What are you thinking?" he asked, amusement teasing his expression. "You look like you're excited about something."

It shouldn't have been possible, but her grin widened even more. She took off, keeping her strides long as she ran. The feel of muscles working in her legs was incredible. She didn't even mind the sting of the sand on her feet. The wind blew against her face and spread her undone braid behind her.

A burst of joyful laughter erupted, lost in the air.

Her foot landed at an awkward angle midstride, and the next thing she knew, she stumbled against her own feet. Her arms windmilled for balance, but she continued down until she landed in a soft thud.

"Are you alright?"

Turning onto her back, she laid there, catching her breath.

The doctor knelt over her, his brows drawn together.

Smiling, she reached up and traced the lines in his forehead, wanting to smooth them away.

It worked. His face softened, and he held her wrist still, keeping her hand against his face.

Heart stuttering, Aria felt transfixed by this man. There was an intensity stirring in his brown eyes that she found alluring. These feelings were unlike anything she'd experienced before. Sure, she'd flirted and kissed a few mermen, but she'd never felt anything so strong as she did with this man, and she didn't even know his name.

Is this because I'm half human? Am I more attracted to men than mermen? Or is this how Father felt with my real mother?

The thought of King Caspian brought a flush of guilt. She'd been raised to stay away from humans, and yet she continued to lay, staring up at a human man who made her feel like she'd never felt before. Yet the guilt didn't stop her. She laid, unmoving, absorbing every second.

Aria didn't know how long they stayed like that. It was finally interrupted when he cleared his throat and stood. "What must I be thinking? There may be others who need rescuing." He reached out and helped her stand. "My name is Dr. Moore. Please allow me to escort you. It's a short walk to the castle," the doctor said, holding out his arm. "I'll report your shipwreck to the chief guard and he'll send out a search party."

His mention of the castle reminded Aria why she was here. She started to move forward, but Dr. Moore still stood with his arm lifted. She blinked down at it, uncertain what she was supposed to do.

A smirk lifted the corners of his mouth and his eyes crinkled with amusement as he picked up her hand and placed it over his arm. "They don't have this custom where you're from?" he asked.

Relief flooded through her at his understanding, and she shook her head, feeling once again at ease.

"Well, allow me to enlighten you." He started walking and she went with him, her hand resting over his arm. It almost felt like dancing. She enjoyed the feel of his muscles shifting under her fingers and wondered what it would be like if they didn't have any fabric between them.

"This is considered a gentlemanly gesture. It shows respect that a man has for a woman." His voice was so rich and smooth, it piqued her senses and made her wish to listen to him all day.

She noticed that he didn't walk at the full pace he could have with his long legs. Aria realized he was walking slower on her behalf. The kind thought made her soften toward him even more.

Glancing up at the sun, she saw that it was well in its descent. *How long was I out?* It was obviously for most of the day.

A sense of urgency washed over her. If she wanted to save Prince Elex, she couldn't allow herself anymore distractions.

The ambassador and Rollo had said that the assassins would be disguised as rebels from the prince's own kingdom. Where would they have opportunity to kill Prince Elex?

"You look like you're pondering very serious things," Dr. Moore commented as he escorted her into a building just off from the gates.

Aria nodded, wishing she could speak and tell the doctor everything that would happen soon.

"Are you worried about the other passengers from your ship?"

She shook her head.

"No?" His eyes widened in surprise. "Why ever not?"

Sighing, she pointed to herself and then held up one finger.

"You were the only one on the ship?" When she nodded, he frowned. It looked like he wanted to say more, but she stopped walking and put a hand to his chest, then pointed at the castle.

"You wish to visit?" He pursed his lips. "I'd be happy to take you, once I've reported your shipwreck and received word from the queen or the prince on whether you'd be welcomed."

Gesturing with her hands at the mention of the prince, Aria again pointed at the castle. When she saw the doctor's dubious expression, she looked around, hoping to find some way to communicate. She picked up a piece of driftwood and held it as if it were a sword.

"A spear? Weapon?" he guessed.

She nodded. Then she raised her hand and mimicked stabbing him.

"Someone wants to kill me?"

She teetered her hand.

"I'm close, but not quite guessed it?"

She nodded. Then pantomimed killing the doctor again but pointed to the castle.

"Someone wants to kill the queen?"

She shook her head.

"The prince?"

Aria nodded vigorously, relieved that he understood.

Dr. Moore stared at her, his head tilted to the side and his eyes narrowed. "How can I trust this information?"

Shrugging, she gazed up at him helplessly. Glancing at the sun, she twirled her hand, hoping to indicate that they should hurry.

"It's going to happen tonight?"

She nodded, tugging on his arm.

"You think it may be happening right now?"

Again, she nodded.

"I consider Prince Elex to be a good friend. I'd do anything to keep him safe." His eyes roamed her face. "I honestly don't know if I should believe you, but I'd never forgive myself if something really did happen to him. So I'm choosing to trust you, milady." He stepped close enough that she had to crane her neck to keep looking into his eyes. "And if you're lying, I'll personally ask the prince to throw you into the dungeon to rot."

His serious tone struck deep. She understood he was gambling on her information. Though they'd just met, she liked him. And the threat he'd made only reflected his loyalty.

She bowed her head, then tugged on his arm again.

Dr. Moore hesitated, then seemed to come to a decision. "Do you think you're up for running, milady?" He held out his hand.

She grabbed it, and together, they ran toward the castle.

"The prince is scheduled to distribute goods to the poor in a few minutes. It'll be just outside the church, which is on that hill." He pointed to a grassy hill that overlooked the ocean and was just to the side of the castle. The church sat at the top, its back facing them.

They continued to run. The new muscles in Aria's legs were hot with fatigue and she could hardly draw breath, but she forced herself to keep up with the doctor.

They were halfway up the hill. The ground shifted from sand to grass, tickling Aria's feet with every step. It was difficult to run because the incline was steep, so it was more of a fast climb than anything else.

There was a strange wetness at the back of her neck. It was like water, but it leaked from her body. Was there something wrong with the spell that had turned her human? *Can't worry about it now.*

While they ascended, the doctor gave her a side glance. "Are you certain the prince is in danger?"

Stopping and holding his gaze, she nodded firmly.

Sighing, the doctor once again took her hand, and they finished their ascent.

There was a large group of people before them. Many murmured or spoke to one another. Prince Elex was walking through the throng while handing out bits of food that a trailing servant handed to him. Aria spotted Rollo behind the servants, leading two white horses.

Glaring, Aria watched the traitor, hoping he'd give some indication of where the assassins might be. Rollo studied the people around him, a small smile coming and going from his lips. He gave no indication of who would make the attempt on the prince's life.

There was a shout from the center of the crowd. Aria didn't hear what they said but rushed to the sound instead of waiting to see what happened.

The prince glanced up, his eyes widening in surprise when he spotted her running toward him. His guard stepped in front of the prince with his hand out, as if to say halt.

Aria slowed and scanned the people as she trotted and finally saw a shorter man moving with purpose. He went forward swiftly as more shouts cried out around them. He pulled out a crossbow from his cloak and aimed for the prince's head.

She pointed frantically at the man, staring at the guard with wide eyes. The guard looked in the direction she indicated and sped forward. The guard landed on the man just as he pulled the trigger, making the arrow go wide. It landed in Rollo's arm.

He cried out and cursed, cradling his arm against his stomach.

"Sire!" she heard the doctor cry. "Watch out!"

Looking up, Aria spotted another assassin with his sword already drawn and only two meters from the prince. The doctor ran to the assassin while Aria rushed to the prince. She wasn't a warrior like some of her sisters, but she could act as a shield, if nothing else.

The guards were in the middle of sprawling with two more would-be assassins. *How many murderers are in this crowd?*

"Protect the prince!" the doctor shouted. He'd knocked the sword out of the assassin's hand and was wrestling with the man.

The prince frowned at Aria once she stood before him and looked as if he were going to demand that she step away, but another man popped out of the crowd and threw a dagger toward the prince's heart.

On pure instinct, Aria overlapped her hands as she raised them to stop the lethal blade. The knife sliced into the center of both her hands, trapping them together in a painful snare. Screaming from the pain, a gurgle of sound emitted.

Guards who had been further behind the entourage finally broke through the throng and surged forward with spears and swords out.

They surrounded Prince Elex and took him into the church. The other guards had their suspects bound and escorted them away.

No one else jumped out to attack. Prince Elex was safe. Aria sighed and looked at her bleeding hands. Large, blue drops flowed to the ground. White magic would help the internal damage, but the rest would have to heal on its own.

A force knocked her onto her back. Aria coughed and gasped for air while two guards bound her wrists in scratchy rope that dug deep into her skin and pulled against the blade still embedded in her hands. She tried to protest as they escorted her with the other assassins into a wagon, but her words were lost on the air.

"Wait!" She recognized Dr. Moore's voice but couldn't see him. "She was trying to save him."

He said something else, but she couldn't hear it from inside the closed wagon that was rumbling down the hill.

CHAPTER 5

*I*t was cold. Aria had heard the guard call this place a dungeon. Wasn't that where the doctor had threatened to place her if she lied? Now that she was sitting in a tiny cell with moldy straw and rats for company, she realized his threat was far scarier than she'd thought. The only light came from the stars that shined through a small slit in her cell.

Aria was grateful for the coat that the doctor had given her. Not only did it help ward off the cold, but she kept her face inside of it to smell the doctor and ignore the scents of rotting decay around her. If not for that, then she wasn't sure if she'd survive the night. As it was, she was frightened of what the future held for her.

The guards had removed the knife from her hands. Aria wished she could have screamed when they'd done that. They'd stared at her bleeding hands in shock before finally wrapping dirty cloths over each hand. It was enough to staunch the flow of precious blood but did little else.

The other assassins had glared at her as they'd been moved to the dungeons. Aria was relieved to see that she wouldn't have to share her cell with those men.

She opened her mind to white magic, but it felt distant, as if she were reaching through slimy seaweed to get to it. The dark magic was there, available and waiting. The dark magic would heal her and help her escape from the dungeon. It felt as if it would be much easier to reach out to the dark, but Aria pressed her lips together and concentrated on mentally touching the pure, innocent magic. She'd not trade her soul or her life to save herself from this moment.

When she finally found her white magic, she drew it to her hands. It didn't feel right, and she was positive it was because she wasn't in the ocean. But it slowly entered her deep wounds, mending the delicate bones. It didn't quite finish the healing, but it soothed the pain until her palms went numb. It would have to be enough.

Sleep came in fitful moments. The raw hay poking her and the rats crawling over her legs kept her up most of the night. Was this what it was like for her father when he was held captive? Tears fell down her cheeks, thinking of her strong and noble father reduced to sitting in the cold, dry dungeon. No wonder he hated humans so much.

Sunlight trickled through the small windows. In the dim light, Aria saw a guard open one of the other cells and pull out the smaller man who'd tried to kill the prince with a crossbow.

Another guard joined them, and they dragged the man away. A few moments later, screams echoed from a different corridor. The screams died down for a few moments, then started back up again, even higher pitched than before.

Aria hugged her knees to her chest and blew out slowly. Were they going to torture her too? Was this degradation something else her father had endured? *I should have listened to you, Father!*

After a long while, the guards brought back the man to his cell. He was unconscious and bloody. The guards then preceded to take the next assassin, who kicked and struggled the entire way, down the hall.

More screams of agony rent the air. Aria huddled into the stinky straw, her core shaking.

The morning progressed in this fashion until the guards reached her cell.

Use the black magic. It can save you! But she ignored the thought. She wouldn't let these barbarians force her into giving into the darkness. She would only use white magic, which couldn't help her now.

Instead of fighting, Aria forced herself to stand tall and walk as gracefully as she could between them. She has a princess through and through. Even pain should not deter her from acting as such.

The guards eyed her suspiciously but only held her upper arms as they led her down the long corridor of endless cells and to a windowless room that was only slightly bigger than her cell.

It smelled metallic and of fear. There was a man standing by a chair that had metal clamps over the arms.

"So you're the witch that tried to help kill the prince," he said with a glare.

Aria shook her head, reaching out to the white magic. It came slowly, but she was able to read the man's aura by the time the guards had her strapped into the chair. What she saw in his aura chilled her bones. There was blue to show loyalty, but a lot of angry red and dark purple, which meant he wasn't a stranger to killing. At least there was no black, which meant he wasn't completely coldhearted.

"My name is Rimsley, and I have been appointed by the queen herself to find out every person involved with the attempted assassination." He went to an open fire and pulled out a long metal stick, its end glowing bright red. "The other men claim that they don't know who you are, but you must have known something about the assassination, yes?"

Staring at the rod, she nodded.

Rimsley brought it close to her cheek, and she could feel the searing heat it held. Water sprang from her forehead and her hands shook. Could she withstand this torture? She couldn't even speak to clear her name.

"So you admit to having knowledge about the attempt on Prince Elex's life?"

She nodded slightly, worried that the hot metal would burn her skin if she moved any more than that.

"Did you hire the men to kill the prince?"

Again, Aria was very careful as she shook her head no.

"What exactly were you doing at that gathering yesterday?"

Lips trembling, Aria tried in vain to respond. She did her best to push the vibrations from her throat as far as she could, but her words still didn't carry over the air.

"Speak up, witch." He brought the red end closer to her head, and Aria could smell her hair burning.

She panted. Fire had never scared her before. She had seen plenty of it, but she'd always been in the water, where the flames couldn't touch her. It could make the water hot enough to sear her, but she always healed. It appeared that fire thrived in the air, and she panicked at the thought that she'd never see the ocean again.

"Tell me," Rimsley insisted. He watched her closely as he slowly brought the rod to her neck. Eyes narrowed, he pushed the hot tip to the side of her neck.

The pain was so intense, she felt it all the way to the back of her throat and her fingertips. Her neck pulsed with angry pain. Her mouth opened in a wide, soundless scream.

Rimsley finally took the rod away, frowning. Aria panted, tears leaking from her eyes. The pain didn't leave with the hot metal. It continued to burn fiercely, pulsing with her heartbeat. The smell of her burned flesh had her stomach twisting.

"What's the matter with you?" Rimsley grumbled. He placed the metal stick back into the fire. Turning, he grabbed a handful of her hair and pulled.

Aria winced, her scalp stinging. Was he going to pull out all of her hair? Her neck protested any movements, and more helpless tears escaped and trekked down her cheek. It set of waves off sobs that couldn't be heard.

Rimsley let go of her and leaned back, frowning.

The door open with a loud, grating sound. Prince Elex stepped through, followed by Dr. Moore.

Rimsley bowed deeply. "Your Highness," his voice was breathless. "What brings you down here?"

Aria held her breath, hoping that the doctor was aiding her once again.

"Dr. Moore insists that this woman was trying to save my life, not terminate it." Prince Elex said. He scanned Aria from head to toe as he spoke and grimaced as if she were a pile of expired oysters. "He's convinced me to come down here and question her myself."

Rimsley stayed in his bow. "Begging your pardon, Highness, but I think there may be something wrong with the chit. She won't speak, no matter how scared or how much pain she endures."

"I told you, Prince Elex," the doctor said. His voice was lower than usual, with a roughness to it. "She can't speak. How can this man interrogate her? He'll kill her before he figures it out."

Rising, Rimsley fixed Dr. Moore with a glare. "Like you, doctor, I do my job quite well. I've barely hurt the woman yet. And it was easy to figure something was off about her."

"Do you believe her to be dangerous?" the prince asked. He held a white linen to his nose as if he couldn't stand the smell in the room another moment.

The interrogator shrugged. "I don't trust her, that much I can tell you." He rubbed his chin as he studied her. "But I don't think she's dangerous. She didn't even fight the guards when they brought her to me."

Everyone waited, looking to the prince.

Aria breathed slow, trying to look insignificant, hope warming her chest.

"My mother won't be pleased," Prince Elex murmured. "But I trust your judgement, Rupert." He nodded to the guards. "Release her." He turned to Rimsley. "Assign some of your men to follow her at all times while she is in my kingdom. They have permission to subdue her with force if she acts suspiciously."

As Rimsley bowed again, the guards unlocked the manacles.

Aria stood on shaking legs and held onto the chair for support. She couldn't believe how much her burn still hurt.

Dr. Moore swept past the prince and Rimsley to hold her up. Aria gave him a small smile as his arm slid under hers.

"Rupert here tells me I should owe you a debt of thanks, milady," Prince Elex said as he took two more steps into the room. He pulled the handkerchief away from his nose. "If that is true, I'll be sure to send you my regards. In the meantime, I'm allowing you to be released from the dungeons, but not from my palace. You will be under guard until I have the answers I want."

Aria nodded her understanding, keeping the prince's gaze. She wanted to convey that she was royalty too and understood the caution of giving one's trust. But he didn't seem to understand as he stared at her with continuing wariness.

He blinked after a moment and tilted his head to the side. "Have we met before?"

Lips pursing, Aria debated on how to answer. Yes, they'd met as children, but how could she explain that to him? It was years ago. She shook her head, hoping that was the right answer to give.

The prince shook his head and muttered something she couldn't understand. He turned and left, everyone but Aria bowing to his retreating back.

Dr. Moore gently grabbed her elbow. "I'll be taking this woman to my office to treat her wounds," he said to Rimsley as they walked out of the room. "You may send your guard there."

Rimsley didn't say anything, but nodded to one of the guards, who quickly caught up to them as they left the room.

Aria leaned into the doctor heavily as he escorted her up two flights of stairs and then outside where the sun shined and the breeze played with her hair. The scent of something cooking drifted over the air along with fresh grass and dirt.

Not only was she grateful that he'd come to her rescue, but now that she was out of danger, her energy plummeted. Her legs threatened to give out, and she sagged against him even more.

"Don't worry," Dr. Moore murmured in her ear. "You're safe now, I promise."

It was a promise he couldn't keep, since he wasn't a king or a prince, and yet Aria still took comfort in his words as well as his presence.

CHAPTER 6

*D*r. Moore's office was large, encompassing a polished piano, desk, and bookshelves brimming with leather-bound books. There was also a cot, which he led her to. He closed the door in the face of the scowling guard and grabbed cloths, which he then dipped in a bowl of water.

He brought them to her and placed them on her hands.

Aria froze, wondering if the water would turn her back into a mermaid. Hadn't Prya said that she just had to touch the water to change back? But nothing happened. The water Dr. Moore used must not have been seawater. She exhaled slowly in relief.

"What in the blazes?" he muttered as he cleaned her wounds.

There was little pain as he ministered to her, and she was glad that the white magic had helped with that.

"Your blood is *blue*!" he exclaimed.

Frowning, Aria shrugged. Of course it was blue. Then she paused, remembering the assassins who had been dragged back to their cells. They'd been bleeding red blood. It hadn't registered at the time because she'd been so scared. *I guess Prya's spell doesn't make me a full human, after all.*

He stared into her eyes, his lips turned down and his face twisted with befuddlement. "You're certainly not from around here, are you?"

She shook her head, watching to see what he'd do next. King Caspian had always told her that humans were too delicate to know about the existence of merfolk. Merpeople were able to acknowledge the idea of humans and had even studied them from afar, but humans couldn't accept that knowledge in turn. The idea of trying to convince humans of their existence would force them to react violently because they couldn't handle the concept.

Yet Dr. Moore, while appearing confused, didn't look like he was about to turn on her.

As if noting her wary expression, he smiled and patted her shoulder reassuringly. "I would love to learn all about where you come from. I've never heard of anyone with blue blood before. It would be fascinating to know what makes your people so different from mine."

Relaxing on the cot, she smiled.

"It's good to see you smiling so easily after what you've endured." He continued to clean her hands and then applied a strange-smelling ointment to them before wrapping the wounds with clean linens. His touch was gentle while assertive. He moved on to the burn on her neck, putting a different salve on it, which cooled and soothed the injury.

Aria could tell that this man was confident in his abilities and had a soothing nature. She wondered if he was a born healer. Reading his aura would probably tell her, but she didn't want to do that. She didn't need to open her mind to white magic to know that Dr. Moore was kind and honorable. Besides, it was difficult to reach her magic while on land. A sudden longing for home struck her, and she bit her lip, wanting the soothing water around her and her father to hold her. Dr. Moore was the only comfort she had on land.

Sitting back on his heels, he peered into her face. "Did you sleep much?"

Aria grimaced as she shook her head. She didn't want to think about her night in that frightening cell.

Dr. Moore frowned and looked down at his hands on his knees. "I'm so sorry I couldn't get you out sooner. It was madness after you'd been taken away, and no one would allow me to see the prince until this morning." He raised his head, regret shining through his brown eyes. "I even tried to meet with the queen, but she was too busy trying to investigate who had hired those thugs."

Straightening, Aria pointed to herself.

His face contorted. "Please don't say that you hired them."

Huffing, she shook her head and waved her arms, trying to give him an emphatic no.

"Okay," he drawled. "I'm not certain why you pointed to yourself then."

Chewing her bottom lip, Aria thought about how she could tell him. She held a hand to her ear and watched, hoping he'd understand.

"You overheard something? Is that how you knew the prince was in danger?"

Pleased at how astute the doctor was, she nodded.

His lips pursed to the side. "Are you telling me that you know who was behind all of this?"

She nodded vigorously, hurting her burn in the process and getting lightheaded. She put a hand to her head.

"Milady, this is a serious situation you're embroiled in." Dr. Moore helped her to lay on the cot. He must have thought she needed to since she'd been touching her head. "You're still under suspicion right now. While you're not in the dungeons, you're still a prisoner, just more like one of nobility." He rubbed the back of his neck. "We need to figure out a way to communicate better so I can get all the details from you. Depending on who hired those assassins, they may be working diligently to frame you for it, since you're such a convenient target."

Aria's eyes widened in shock. She hadn't thought of that. Her situation was certainly precarious. If it hadn't been for Dr. Moore intervening, she'd have been thoroughly tortured and, if Dr. Moore's assessment was true, then also condemned for the crime.

Reaching out, she gabbed his arm and tried to squeeze it. Her injury prevented her hand from working properly, but the doctor seemed to understand.

He stroked her cheek. "I saw it myself; you were trying to save him. I'll keep vouching for you, milady." His gaze lingered on hers. There was something behind it that made Aria feel special and cherished in a way she'd never experienced before. "Get some sleep. I'll send for some food and make sure you're well rested before I release you from my care."

Aria stiffened. She didn't want to leave him. Dr. Moore was the only human who'd showed her any kindness.

"Not to worry," he soothed as he lightly caressed her hair. "I won't be far and will check in with you twice a day. But unfortunately, I don't have the power to keep you in my care, and I'm afraid I must see to other patients or I will lose my place as royal physician."

She didn't want him to lose his position. She settled back down, hoping that staying captive as a noble would be less dangerous than in the dungeon. There had to be some way to prove her innocence. She still needed to find out who her mother was and certainly couldn't accomplish it as a prisoner.

The doctor urged her to get some sleep again. Aria was surprised that she felt safe enough to follow his advice.

She wasn't sure how long she'd been asleep when hollow metal clattered and woke her. Opening her eyes, she saw the doctor at his desk with platters of food before him. He was dishing different things onto his plate and paused when he saw her.

"You're up already?"

She sat up and shrugged. Her hands ached but seemed more functional as she flexed and bent her fingers. Even her neck didn't burn as much, though it felt itchy. Her injuries would heal quickly, though it would have been faster if she was in the water and more in touch with the white magic.

"There's plenty of food here. Would you care to join me?"

Aria nodded, realizing she hadn't eaten since breakfast yesterday. She couldn't identify the smells wafting from the desk, but whatever it was made her salivate.

Standing took more effort than it should have, and she teetered but didn't fall.

"I'm betting your muscles are pretty stiff, huh?" Dr. Moore walked over and took her wrist in one hand while placing his other at the small of her back. The heat of his skin through the material was pleasant, and Aria sadly felt the withdrawal when he seated her and let go.

He dished something that almost looked like kelp mixed with a white sauce onto her plate, then added some meats she didn't recognize along with a fluffy yellow substance and a light-brown lump that smelled delicious.

She tried to pick up the fork, but she'd never used the instrument before, and with her hands still healing, it was impossible to hold it the way she saw the doctor did.

Opening his mouth to speak, Dr. Moore hesitated, then cleared his throat. "I realize this may be crossing the boundaries of propriety, but would you allow me to feed you? Everything will be cold if we wait for a servant to come and do it."

Nodding, Aria wondered why they had such strange rules here. How was it considered bad if he helped her to eat? She clearly couldn't do it herself. Though at home, they didn't need to use their hands to eat. The food floated in the water and they simply swam to it with their mouths open to catch the fare.

Dr. Moore scooped the green stuff with white sauce and brought it to her mouth. Perhaps she could understand why this was frowned upon, after all. Being so close to the doctor and him feeding her made it feel incredibly intimate. Was it wicked of her to enjoy it? She was certain only the doctor could make her feel this comfortable about such intimacy.

He seemed affected as well since color rose up his neck and his pupils dilated.

The green stuff definitely wasn't kelp, but the flavors danced on her tongue and she groaned with pleasure. Part of her groan wasn't lost in the air and her eyes widened at the sound.

Dr. Moore paused and glanced at her mouth. "When we're finished eating, I'd like to examine your throat. Perhaps your vocal chords aren't as damaged as I thought."

Hope shifted through her chest at the idea.

Dr. Moore's attentiveness as he fed her and himself was something Aria had never experienced before, even though she was a princess. While servants had been taking care of her all her life, no one had ever shown such concentrated attention. Being the youngest of five girls, it had sometimes been easy to feel invisible in her childhood.

"I see you favor the rolls." He smiled. "If you like bread, I should give you a pastry or croissant. They're my favorite."

They finished breakfast, Aria's stomach feeling weighed down by the food. It was a strange feeling, like she needed to rest from eating, and yet it also felt pleasant to be so satisfied.

Next, the doctor led her to a chair and helped her sit. He instructed her to open her mouth and examined her throat. While the position certainly wasn't as enjoyable as when he'd fed her, she was able to see little flecks of gold in his brown eyes and smell an alluring musky scent from him as he inspected the back of her mouth.

"Very interesting," he murmured. "Can you try to say 'ah'?"

She attempted it as he instructed and was surprised when a tiny sound escaped. It was still lost in the air, but there was sound for just a moment.

Dr. Moore pursed his lips as he stood back, looking pensive. "I'll need to think about this. Your throat and neck are in good working order, and I can feel movement in your vocal cords as you tried to speak. That's a good sign." He smiled down at her. "I'm going to mix a tonic and see if it helps you recover your voice."

A knock sounded before a maid entered the office and curtsied, her black hair pulled back in a bun to show her round face. "Begging your pardon, Dr. Moore, but I'm to take the mistress to her room. The queen says you've had plenty of time to repair her wounds."

Dr. Moore's eyes tightened and Aria had the impression that he was frustrated. But he smiled and helped Aria to stand. "Of course. I will be stopping by her room later after I've mixed a tonic to see if it will help her speak."

The maid curtsied again and looked at Aria for the first time. Her hazel eyes widened as she took in Aria's hair and face. "If you'll follow me, milady." She turned and left.

Aria hesitated, glancing at the doctor. He was her only friend here, and leaving him made her feel unsafe again.

"You'll be alright. I promise to visit you as soon as I can."

You'd better, she wanted to say. He smirked and she wondered if he'd been able to interpret her look accurately.

A different guard followed them. This one didn't glare as much as the other.

Aria took in the surroundings as she followed the maid. She had to walk fast to keep up and concentrated on her balance to make sure she didn't fall. They walked into the castle through a side entrance and climbed several sets of stairs.

Panting as the muscles in her legs shook with fatigue, Aria wondered if they were going to lock her into the highest tower. The guard's presence behind her was a reminder of how much worse it had been this morning.

When the maid opened a door into a well-lit hallway, Aria sighed in relief. She'd be happy to never take stairs again. Curtains hung from floor to ceiling and paintings hung on the walls, some of them depicting pictures of horses with men in armor riding them.

The maid opened a door to their left and ushered Aria in. The layout was similar to something she'd see at home, with an antechamber that held a desk, chairs, and a settee in front of a place in the wall that had a space where logs burned. There was another door that must lead to the bedroom. There was a wooden tub filled with water in front of the unlit fireplace. Two other maids were standing next to the tub with cloths and bottles in their hands.

"Come now," the maid said. "We must get you washed and dressed as quickly as possible." The maid paused and sent a pointed look to the guard, who muttered under his breath and stepped out of the room, closing the door behind him.

The youngest maid helped Aria disrobe and ease into the lukewarm water. It was nothing like floating in the ocean, but a sense of home hit her as she laid back. She wondered what King Caspian was doing at the moment. He wouldn't miss her, thinking she was with Kessida.

Aria kept an eye on the doctor's coat and her vest that connected to her belt. They took the coat out of the room but left her vest in the connecting room that sported a large bed.

The maids set about their tasks immediately, scrubbing and washing her hair. Flowery scents she couldn't distinguish filled the room and covered her skin. The smells were pleasant and helped her relax into the water.

"Your hair is beautiful, miss," commented the youngest maid. "And your skin is . . ." She stared closely at the arm she was scrubbing. "Your skin is different, so pale it's almost translucent. Where do you come from?"

Aria smiled at the compliments but didn't even try to respond.

The maids exchanged glances before continuing their work.

The maid with black hair scowled as she inspected Aria's neck and hands. "Poor miss," she sighed. "To think of how you were treated after saving the prince." She stopped and met Aria's gaze. The empathy shining from those hazel eyes were a balm on Aria's soul. "I don't care what they're saying. I can see in your eyes that you're a good woman. Don't know how anyone can think otherwise."

Torn between grinning or crying, Aria offered a faltering smile.

The maid patted her shoulder gently. "You're safe now, milady. The name is Sandry. I've been assigned as your personal maid while you stay with us. Don't worry—I'll watch over you."

Aria patted Sandry's hand to express her gratitude. *There are good humans in the mix of bad. It's like what Prya said.*

They helped her climb out of the water and dry off before having her step into several different layers of clothing. One of the undergarments laced snugly around her ribcage, sucking in tightly and pushing her breasts far higher than was natural. Aria took shallow breaths until her lungs adjusted to the restriction.

Why in the world do humans wear such binding attire? It was no wonder that humans moved slowly and women were known to have fainting spells.

The young maid tried to have her step into a shoe with a high heel. Aria stubbornly shook her head. She'd barely figured out walking, and those heels would make her trip and fall all over again. Sandry stepped in at that point, her lips twisting to hide a smile, but Aria could still see it. She produced another pair of shoes with a flat, leather bottom.

They pinched Aria's toes, but she kept them on, grateful for Sandry's compromise.

She thought they were finished, but when the oldest maid steered her toward a chair and they started working on her hair,

Aria decided this was a different kind of torture from what she'd endured that morning.

They didn't put her hair in a simple plait but pulled it in different directions, twisting it this way and that. Then they put over thirty pins in her hair to hold it up. Her head hurt and some of the pins scratched her scalp.

When her hair was finally to their satisfaction, they curtsied and left.

"I'll be back later, to see to your needs," Sandry said as she exited.

Aria watched the door they exited through, wondering why there was such urgency to clean and dress her, only to leave her in the rooms alone.

She went to the bedroom. A bed with poles at each corner took up much of the space. Aria knew that humans liked to sleep in soft beds, but she decided they made a room feel cramped. She liked her own room much better, where seaweed wraps kept her secure to the wall as she slept and didn't take up all her swimming room.

She picked up her discarded vest and pulled the purse off. It still contained her money and she didn't want it laying where anyone could find it. Lifting her skirts, she tied it to what the young maid had called her pantaloons.

Then she went to the window and admired the view. If she were to be a prisoner, at least she could enjoy the scenery, which was lush with green hills cascading a forest of trees. There was so much life on land that it was humbling to behold so much in one sight. Her mother was out there somewhere. Aria wanted to find her, to discover for herself if the woman was as bad as Prya had indicated. Surely, she couldn't be all bad, right? Her father had loved her at one point.

The door opened, and Aria turned to see a servant announce Prince Elex, who then walked into the room.

Aria bowed her head to show respect to his station.

Prince Elex frowned at her.

She wondered if she was supposed to curtsy like the maids had done, but her natural inclination was to bow like she did for her father at home.

The prince's entourage came in behind him, making the large room feel cramped. Two of the men with the prince were dressed in fine clothes unlike the servants. Aria immediately recognized Rollo, her spine stiffening.

The prince's cousin studied her with a critical eye and sniffed. "She certainly looks like she's capable of nefarious actions, your Highness."

Holding his hand up to silence Rollo, Prince Elex also studied Aria. While she was accustomed to attention as a princess, the current scrutiny made her uncomfortable and it was all she could do not to fidget.

Aria forced herself to meet the prince's gaze, hoping to convey that she wasn't afraid, and that she wasn't his enemy.

"My good friend Dr. Moore is convinced that you're innocent, that you saved my life instead of trying to end it." Prince Elex came further into the room toward her. "I understand that you cannot speak, but I'd like to ask you some questions all the same. I need to judge for myself if you appear as he states."

Aria tried to clasp her fingers together, but her injured hands prevented that, so she rolled her shoulders back and nodded for him to continue.

"Did you try to save my life?" he asked.

All the men watched her closely as she nodded. Aria chose to ignore them and focus on Prince Elex, though she kept Rollo in her peripheral vision.

The prince looked down at her hands. "I do remember you stepping in front of that blade that had been thrown at me." His expression softened for a moment before his lips pressed together in a determined line. "But how did you know about the assassination? Dr. Moore said you ran to the commotion before any attack had happened. You knew it was going to take place."

Rollo took one step forward and narrowed his eyes as he watched Aria closely. She swallowed, hoping that he wouldn't convince the prince she was behind it like Dr. Moore had predicted. Either way, she had to be wary of the man. He had the prince's trust and she certainly did not.

Opening her mouth, Aria tried to speak, but it was to no avail. She looked up helplessly and held her hands out to the side in a gesture of futility. There was obviously no way to explain.

The prince sighed and glanced back at Rollo and the other man. Rollo folded his arms and shook his head. The other man had a more pensive expression with his lips pursed to the side.

Turning back to her, the prince asked more questions. "Were you shipwrecked?"

She nodded, knowing it was the easiest explanation for humans to accept.

"Do you know who is behind the assassination attempt?"

Aria nodded, keeping her gaze on the prince instead of allowing it to stray to Rollo. She was tempted to point at him but didn't think it was the right time. He was the prince's most trusted advisor. They'd assume she was lying and wouldn't believe her. She needed to find a way to prove that Rollo was behind it. And in the meantime, how could she tell the prince that another attempt would likely happen? She couldn't try to stop it, being a prisoner in his castle.

"Are you working with this person?" the prince asked.

She shook her head.

Rollo stepped forward. "Highness, may I ask some questions?"

"Of course." The prince stepped aside and gestured for his cousin to come closer.

Aria's heart picked up a fast rhythm and she forced her breathing to stay even. What was Rollo up to?

"Can you really not speak?" Rollo asked. He was close enough for her to smell fish on his breath and see a lighter version of the prince's blue eyes.

She nodded, her chest tight with anxiety.

Rollo turned to Prince Elex. "She could be faking. I suggest we send her back to the dungeons. Your mother's interrogator can deduce whether or not she can't speak."

Shoulders tense, she watched the prince with wide eyes. The burn on her neck tingled with the memory of Rimsley.

Prince Elex shook his head and held Aria's gaze. "He's already determined she can't speak. He said she would have cried out at least once when she was with him this morning."

"Even if she's not faking, it doesn't point to her innocence, your Highness. I feel in my bones that she's heavily involved in this treasonous plot." Rollo spoke it with conviction, and Aria wished she could talk. If she could have a private audience with Prince Elex and explain everything, she was certain she could convince him of what really happened. As it was, her only option was to hope that the prince could weed out the truth for himself. And perhaps Dr. Moore really could help her gain her voice.

The prince turned to the other man. "What say you, Nedil?"

The other advisor continued to hold his thoughtful expression, still studying Aria. "I can't say yet, Highness. I don't get the impression that she's capable of such treason, but it's difficult to determine."

Lips thinning, Prince Elex turned back to her. "Why bother to save my life? You may look familiar, but I don't recall meeting you. And you're clearly not from my kingdom. That shade of red hair is rare in this part of the country. So why go to the trouble of saving me?"

Again, she met his gaze directly. "Because I could," she mouthed.

The three men exchanged glances, looking blank.

Finally, the prince responded. "I trust Dr. Moore's judgment, and my instincts tell me that you're more friend than foe." He bowed from the waist. "Thank you, milady, for saving my life."

Rollo scowled but said nothing.

Swallowing, Aria bowed her head to him.

"You'll continue to stay here until a thorough investigation has been completed. A guard will escort you wherever you go, but you're welcome to leave this room." Prince Elex stepped close and leaned in until their noses almost touched. "If you betray me or the trust I've decided to give you in any way, I will cut off your arms and throw you into a pit of criminals for them to do with you as they please. Are we understood?"

Aria nodded, doing her best to hide the shudder in her torso.

They left the room, Rollo scowling at her until he left. When the door closed, Aria's knees gave out and she crumpled to the floor. How was she going to convince Prince Elex that Rollo was his true enemy and not her?

CHAPTER 7

Though the prince said she could leave her room—and Aria really wanted to explore the human world as well as seek out her mother—she didn't venture out. Part of it was because she was occupied with wracking her brain about what she could do to reveal Rollo as the villain. But also because Dr. Moore said he'd come and check on her. And she had to admit that she wanted to be in his company more than anyone else, whether merfolk or human.

The thought gave her pause, guilt swimming through her chest. Her father had taught her to stay away from humans. Not only had she gone behind his back and come to the surface to find her mother, but now she was entertaining thoughts of a human man. Dr. Moore was more than just kind; he awoke things in her that she'd never experienced before. *Am I more human than mermaid?* She mentally ran away from that idea. She loved her father and she knew he loved her. He'd have discarded her if he saw that she was more human than mermaid.

Sighing, she hung her head. This was getting her nowhere and only made her more confused. She laid on the bed, the pressure on her lower back easing. Gravity certainly felt different to her body on land. She wondered if she'd ever get used to the heaviness that humans seemed not to notice. The corset was uncomfortable, but she didn't know how to take it off; the maids had laced her into it from behind, and she knew she'd need Sandry's help to have it removed.

Sleep didn't come, but being able to relax alone helped her think more clearly and come up with a plan. She needed to take Dr. Moore to the beach where she could write in the sand—it would be easier there than etching into stone. Then she could explain that Rollo was behind the attempted assassination.

But she still wasn't certain how to convince the prince of Rollo's treachery. Her account alone might not be enough. Perhaps Dr. Moore could help her think of something.

It was at least another hour before a knock sounded at her door. Sandry entered and announced Dr. Moore, who walked in right after. He was tall enough that he leaned his head down to fit through the doorframe. No wonder his coat had covered so much of her when she wore it yesterday.

He walked forward and picked up her hand, lightly kissing the tops of her fingers. The heat of his mouth sent a pleasant shiver up her arm. When he looked at her, he must have seen her puzzled expression. "Another custom you don't have among your people?"

She shook her head.

"It's what gentlemen do to greet ladies." He leaned close and whispered. "Some ladies we look forward to greeting more than others." His wink made her giggle silently.

Dr. Moore led her to a chair in front of a desk and helped her sit before reaching into a pouch at his waist. "I put this tonic together in hopes that it will help you find your voice again." He pulled out the stopper and handed her the bottle. "A few sips should be enough."

When the potent, foreign smell hit her nose, she twisted her lips.

"I know it doesn't smell great, but it tastes a lot like brandy. So hopefully it won't be too bad."

She'd never tasted the drink he mentioned, nor had she heard of it when she was taught about humans, but decided it was worth a shot. She took two sips in quick succession. The flavor was unlike anything she'd ever tried. It was sweet and fiery and burned the back of her throat.

She handed the bottle back, her hands flying to her neck. She could feel blood rushing to her face as she tried to remember how to breathe. Finally, a choking cough emerged. She coughed several times, her eyes watering, until she could breathe normally again.

Dr. Moore squeezed her shoulder. "I'm sorry. I didn't realize you weren't used to liquor."

She glared up at him. Was anyone supposed to get used to something so vile? Were humans actually masochists?

The smile he tried to hide was an odd mix of contrition and amusement. "Well, it's done now. How does your throat feel?"

She swallowed. It was raw from the drink but otherwise fine. "Try to speak."

Coughing one last time, she opened her mouth and spoke. Nothing came out.

Dr. Moore's wide lips turned down in disappointment. "Hm. Maybe if I tried some different herbs and mixed another toni—"

He broke off when she glared and shook her head. No way was she going to drink anything else he came up with. She wasn't fully human, after all, and it wasn't worth it to choke down his tonics to humor him into thinking he could cure her. She was pretty sure she couldn't speak simply because she was on land instead of in the sea.

Chuckling, the doctor put the stopper back in the bottle and put it in his pouch. "Alright, I see you're unwilling to take doctor's orders in this case."

She folded her arms and looked up at him with the most mutinous expression she could muster.

His chuckle turned into a belly-deep laugh. It was warm and Aria found herself smiling. She noted that Sandry looked down to hide her grin. This man's emotions were downright contagious.

"Well then," the doctor said as his laughter died down. "I heard that you're not confined to your room." His expression softened. "Would you like for me to show you around the village? There's quite a market just outside of the castle." He watched her with a vulnerable, hopeful expression.

Grinning, Aria nodded. Not only was she looking forward to seeing more of the human with Dr. Moore by her side, but she could keep an eye out for an older woman that Prya had said she'd recognize as soon as she saw her. Aria hoped that was truly accurate and not some exaggeration. She'd also be able to lead him to the beach so she could write words in the sand and try to communicate better with him.

Dr. Moore returned her smile and held his hand out. He helped her stand and kept her hand resting on his arm, just like the previous day.

They walked down the corridor, Sandry trailing behind along with the royal guard. Dr. Moore led her down the same way she'd come, and the stairs made her legs shake with fatigue. She was grateful when they finally were on a level floor.

Then the doctor led her through a new corridor out to a stable. Aria wrinkled her nose at the animal and earthy smells. It wasn't unpleasant, really, just scents that she wasn't sure if she'd become accustomed to.

A groomsman saddled horses for them to ride. When the groomsman offered his hand to help Aria mount, Dr. Moore waved him away. Then he grabbed Aria around the waist, his long fingers almost touching at her back. She missed his touch when he let go after making sure she was settled on her mare.

"Have you ever ridden before?" he asked.

She shook her head.

"Then I shall lead the horse while you relax." He nodded to the groomsman, who led the other horse away.

Even though the doctor led the horse, Aria still had to use her core to stay balanced atop the creature. She enjoyed the scenery as they walked in silence for a few minutes. Once they were outside the castle gates, Aria silently gasped at the rolling hills and animals grazing along them. People were out tilling their farms, laughing with each other and sharing pieces of fruit. She didn't see anyone who looked like they resembled her mother.

When they reached the market, Dr. Moore helped her to dismount, his hands lingering on her waist. She wanted to savor his touch every time she felt it, even knowing it was wrong to feel this way about a human. They left the horse with a boy, whom the doctor had given a coin to, then they entered the bustling market.

She'd never seen so many people in such a small space. She was glad to cling to Dr. Moore's arm and let him lead her through the throng. There were hundreds of vendors selling everything from fish to jewelry. The noises of people calling out and conversing was almost as overwhelming as the smells of hundreds of different body odors combined. Aria realized that the sea kept merpeople from smelling at all—something that she was now grateful for.

They stopped at one of the tents selling jewelry and Dr. Moore picked up a necklace with a blue-green stone at the bottom. "What do you think?"

Studying it, she thought it was pretty. The stone was something she'd never seen in the ocean. Smiling, she nodded to tell him it was nice.

"It's yours, then." He stepped forward and clasped it behind her head. He was close enough that she could smell his familiar scent and feel the heat from his chest.

When he stepped back, she looked down at the necklace. It was even prettier upon closer inspection. Warmth suffused her chest and she smiled her gratitude.

Dr. Moore payed dropped a few coins into the seller's hand and returned Aria's smile.

They walked the entire length of the large market. Aria studied any older woman that she noticed. Disappointment weighed on her when she didn't find a single person who looked like she could be remotely related to. The futility of her search made her want to give up, but she straightened her back, determined to find the woman whom King Caspian had been with all those years ago.

The sun was well in its descent when she signaled to Dr. Moore that she was ready to go. She'd have to continue her search again tomorrow. He nodded and informed their escorts. Her maid sighed, as if relieved to be going back. Aria wondered if Sandry felt similar discomforts that she had. Aria's nose and cheeks had a strange burning sensation, her back ached, and her stomach felt like it was twisting with hunger. And her throat was parched. How did humans live like this?

Aria looked for the beach on their way back as the doctor led her horse. She couldn't see it, but she could hear the lapping waves to her left.

When they reached the stables and returned the horse, she grabbed Dr. Moore's hand and tugged in the direction of the ocean.

"You want me to follow you somewhere?"

She nodded.

Though he seemed hesitant, he still took her hand and held it, making sure not to hurt her wound. "Then lead the way, milady."

They walked to the beach, holding hands the entire way. The crashing waves and smell of saltwater eased Aria's nerves, even with the scowling guard behind them. Home. She already missed it, and yet the idea of going home soon saddened her. *If only I could move back and forth—live in both worlds.*

Once they were on the soft sand, Aria searched for a twig or a stick, but couldn't even find a piece of driftwood.

"What are you looking for? Were you hoping to show me something?"

Sighing, she crouched down and used her finger instead, starting with her name.

"Aria?" Dr. Moore read aloud.

Smiling, she nodded and pointed to herself.

"That's your name, Aria?" A spark entered his eyes. "It suits you." He brushed a strand of hair off her cheek. "You must call me Rupert, then, if I call you Aria."

Laughing silently, she nodded. He wouldn't be able to hear her say his name, but she would definitely think of him as Rupert from now on instead of the doctor.

"I'm pleased you can write. How did I not think to ask you before? Now we can communicate." He pointed to the castle gates. "I have a blackboard in my office. Shall we continue the conversation in there?"

She didn't know what a blackboard was but hoped that he would help her figure out how to write on it. Nodding, she placed her hand in his again and they walked to his office.

Sandry trailed behind with the guard, her gaze on their connecting hands. When she caught Aria looking at her, the maid grinned and winked.

When they arrived, Sandry and the guard waited outside the office. Rupert walked to a bin and pulled out a rectangular board that was the length of his forearm. Then he grabbed a little white stick and handed both over to her. When she stared at him blankly, he took them back and patiently showed her how to use the chalk to draw on the blackboard. Then he grabbed a cloth and erased the letters he'd drawn on it.

Admiring the neat little contraption, Aria wondered if it was made by magic. Something that you could draw on and then erase certainly seemed like something Prya could come up with.

She flexed her fingers, then took the stick. While the wound in her hand made writing difficult, she was able to put some legible letters onto the blackboard.

Prince in danger, she wrote. The chalk felt strange in her hand, like it was powdery even though it was solid.

"Yes, but you saved him—" Rupert began. She held up her hand to stop him and erased her words to write more.

Still in danger. Rollo trying to kill him.

"Rollo? The prince's cousin." Rupert paced the room while he rubbed the back of his neck. "I can't believe that, Aria. They grew up together. They're more like brothers than cousins. They've always been close."

Rollo made deal with Olandia. Agreed to kill prince after signed treaty. Even though she was skipping little words to shorten her sentences, her hand was getting tired from the writing, and her healing cut ached fiercely. Talking would be so much easier.

"The prince mentioned something to me about a treaty recently. It was only in passing, but he made it sound like he had some doubts about the integrity of Olandia and that Rollo had put his mind to rest on the matter." Rupert stopped pacing and looked at her. "How do you know all this?"

Glancing down, Aria felt her face turning blue. It was so embarrassing to admit, but she had to tell the truth. **Overheard.**

"Overheard or spied? How did they not notice you as they spoke of such grave matters?"

Aria glanced away, knowing she couldn't give him the full truth. While he'd accepted her differences well so far, she wasn't ready to tell him she was a mermaid.

His sigh sounded like it was full of frustration and she wondered if he would turn her over to the authorities.

"I may not know much about you, Aria, but I can see that you care for the prince. So I have to believe that you were not being nefarious." He picked up her hand and she glanced at him.

The affection shining from him warmed her to her core. She smiled, and his gaze dropped to her lips.

He leaned toward her.

"The effect you have on me, Aria," he whispered. "I cannot think of anything except you, even when I'm not with you."

Biting her bottom lip while she grinned. He watched the action with rapt attention.

Aria silently laughed and felt her cheeks turn blue again.

"How in the world does your skin turn such a color?" He mumbled. But he didn't seem put off by it. He stared at her so intently, it made her feel like she wanted to either get up and run or lean into him. Instead, she stepped back and pointed to the piano and then to him. She'd studied about humans and how they played music. It had always intrigued Aria to know how their music sounded compared to merfolk's. Not to mention she needed a distraction from the heat pooling in her stomach.

"You want to hear me play?"

She nodded.

Smirking, Rupert sat at the piano and patted the empty spot on the bench.

She sat where he indicated, their shoulders and legs brushing against each other.

When he pressed the keys into a slow melody, she stared, transfixed by the soft music and his graceful fingers flowing up and down the row of keys. It sounded incredible.

When Rupert opened his mouth and sang, Aria couldn't stop staring at him in fascination. How did he make his voice belt out in such a smooth and vibrant way? She thought she knew what singing was—it was something merpeople did, but all the music she'd ever heard was nothing like what Rupert sang and played.

When the song ended, she clapped.

Smiling, he seemed pleased that she enjoyed his song. "That was one that I wrote. It's about a sailor who saw a mermaid and fell in love with her. He spent the rest of his days sailing the ocean to try to spot her again, but he never did. He died at sea, ever in pursuit of the mermaid he loved."

Aria tilted her head. Do humans know about merpeople, after all? This was the first time she'd heard any human refer to a mermaid. She had thought the song sounded romantic, but his description was more depressing than anything.

"I see you don't love that concept." He chuckled, and Aria wished she could wrap the sound around her like a blanket. "I'll play another that is a lullaby my mother used to sing to me."

He played new notes and sang. Aria brightened at the tune. This was one she knew from childhood as well. She closed her eyes and let Rupert's deep, soulful voice pour over her. Feelings of being sung to by her father as a child brought a new warmth to her chest. Her eyes still closed, she opened her mouth and sang along.

She didn't think any sound would come out but was shocked when a powerful voice emerged from her throat, singing in key with Rupert.

He paused and stared at her, his fingers frozen. She stopped and looked at him, equally surprised. Blinking, Rupert hastily resumed the song. He sang and she joined in again, her voice carrying over the air perfectly. They finished in perfect sync.

Rupert stared at her with wide eyes. It was as if he saw her in a whole new light. "I've never heard anyone sing so beautifully," he whispered.

Aria smiled, pleased that she could sing as a human. And Rupert was right; her human singing voice sounded much better than when she sang in the sea. But singing felt exactly the same to her vocal chords in both places.

His brown eyes were warm and inviting. Rupert looked at her as if she were some precious and rare pearl. It made Aria want to stay on land forever, just to bask in his adoration. This man did things to her she didn't know she could feel.

His face inched toward hers.

It was as if a strong current was pushing her forward, closing the distance between them.

When his lips touched hers, she melted. His arms came around her, warm and secure. His mouth moved over hers in a sensual rhythm, making her heart pound and she felt like the moment could last forever.

They finally parted, their heavy breaths mingling into the air between them.

Rupert stroked her hair. "Aria, I—" He broke off and shook his head. It was quiet for a moment, then he cleared his throat. "You were able to sing perfectly. Does that mean that you can speak after all?"

She opened her mouth to answer, but no sound came.

"Interesting." He rubbed his chin as he thought. "Your vocal chords are obviously intact. You're able to use them when you're doing something that uses more of the back of your throat." He went quiet.

Aria lifted her brows, hoping he'd go on. Could he help her to speak like humans? Or would she only be able to talk under water? Singing whenever she wanted to say something seemed too ridiculous.

"Sing these notes." He proceeded to play a key and then paused for her to mimic the note. She was able to do it perfectly. It was interesting to hear her voice carry on air instead of water. It made her voice sound higher in melody than she remembered in the sea.

Rupert played every key on the piano and she was able to sing each one in succession. "Your pitch is absolutely perfect." Again, his eyes were round with wonder.

Aria lifted a shoulder. Of course she could match all the notes. She suspected any merperson could.

"You don't understand how impossible that is, do you? I've never heard of anyone who could hit every single key." He stroked her cheek. "You are so very rare."

Warmth pooled into her stomach. *You don't know how rare you are, Rupert.*

They leaned toward each other again. His breath tickled her lips and Aria craved the taste of him.

Rupert kissed her harder the second time, his mouth coaxing hers to open, and nibbled on her lower lip.

Aria groaned at the sensations he evoked, then pulled back and gasped, pointing to her throat. A sound had come out.

Rupert grinned. "Yes, I heard it too. Perhaps the perfect remedy to cure your muteness is more of my kisses."

Laughing silently, she shook her head.

"In all seriousness, though, I'd like to work with you later today. I'm pretty sure if you keep singing, it will train you to use your vocal chords for normal speech."

Excitement trickled through her. It would be such a relief to be able to talk.

Rupert blinked and looked around as if he woke from a dream. "What am I thinking? We need to focus on the thing you said about Rollo." He grew serious. "Are you quite certain that he's a traitor to the prince?"

Aria straightened and met his gaze. She nodded, understanding the position she was putting Rupert in. He barely knew her and could be risking the wrath of his liege if she was wrong. Then a thought occurred to her. She grabbed the blackboard.

The treaty is important, she wrote. Needs to be studied. Something in there points to the advantage of the prince's death.

"Yes, of course." He looked at her with open admiration. "I can't wait to learn more and more about you Aria. You save princes, understand politics, sing like an angel, and have the most beautiful eyes that make me feel like I could get lost in them. I look forward to the other talents you'll show off as I spend more time with you."

If only you could see me swim. She giggled at the thought, and a squeak sounded.

Rupert laughed. "I've never heard anyone sound like that when they laugh."

She playfully hit his shoulder.

He chuckled some more before sobering. "Now, we must focus on the prince." He searched her face, leaning closer. "Just one more kiss first," he murmured. His mouth moved over hers so smoothly, it was like their lips were designed to fit together.

When they pulled apart, Aria wasn't sure how she'd be able to leave Rupert when it was time to go home.

CHAPTER 8

$\mathcal{A}$ria went with Rupert into the throne room. The style of it was very similar to her Father's, except King Caspian's throne hung from the ceiling, where he could sit and look down on all the merpeople floating before him. The queen sat on her throne, which was on a platform that kept her a few meters above those standing before her. Aria couldn't see the woman's face, as it was covered with a black, lacey veil. Her hair was pulled up with a large crown resting atop it. There were streaks of silver, black and red in her tresses. Aria wondered what the queen's hair color was like before she started going grey.

She tapped Rupert and gestured over her face then pointed at the queen.

"You want to know why the queen wears a veil?" he asked.

She nodded, glad he was so perceptive.

"Her year of mourning isn't over yet. Until that time, she'll wear a veil over her face and that black mourning band on her arm."

Aria glanced at the queen again and noticed that there was a black band over the sleeve of her lavender dress. How strange. Were humans supposed to take a break from living to mourn their loved ones? Merfolk were taught that death was a reminder to celebrate every day one was alive.

The prince was sitting in another throne, candles lit all around them on the platform. It was fascinating to watch the flames flicker and dance, smell the wax as it slowly melted.

Both Prince Elex and his mother were listening to a courtier who presented his three daughters with wily glances at the prince.

Aria thought the young ladies were quite pretty, with hair the color of the sun and tall, lithe figures. When she glanced at the prince, she could read the speculation there. He was sizing them up the way she'd seen mermen do when they were inspecting squids for purchase. It was very different than how Rupert looked at her. She felt respected and adored whenever his eyes met hers.

When the prince glanced up to see the two of them approach, his eyes narrowed with suspicion. It was not going to be easy to convince the man about Rollo.

The doctor held a commanding presence as he whispered to a servant who stood just before the platform. The servant nodded, then walked up the steps to say something into the prince's ear.

The prince nodded in Rupert's direction, then continued the conversation with the courtier.

When the courtier was excused, a merchant approached. Aria and Rupert waited while they spoke with him. Her feet ached from standing for so long, and there was a pressure at the small of her back. She had to admit that it was much more comfortable being a mermaid. She could wait for hours with no discomfort if she were floating in the water.

When the queen excused the courtier, Prince Elex whispered in her ear and then stood and walked out a side door.

Rupert grabbed Aria's elbow and led her to a different side door that a servant was holding open for them.

They entered a room where the prince sat at a table laden with food.

Rupert bowed and Aria followed suit. "Your Highness," Rupert greeted. "Thank you for seeing us in a private audience."

"Of course, Rupert," the prince said. "I know you'd only request it if it was important."

"And it is." Rupert patted Aria's shoulder. "I've been communicating with Aria through writing."

Prince Elex's eyes sharpened as he studied her. He swallowed his bite of food before speaking. "She can write? I suppose she must be of high class if she knows writing."

Aria frowned. Common folk didn't receive the privilege to write, possibly read? Merfolk all benefited from the same education.

"While we were communicating," Rupert continued, "she told me that she'd overheard men plotting against you, majesty.

And that's how she knew to rescue you at the time of the attempt on your life." He glanced down at her before continuing. "She also said that something about the treaty between you and the other kingdom was mentioned. It sounds to me that there may be something in there that will be to their advantage in the case of your death."

The prince leaned forward, his elbows resting on the table, his face tight. "Rollo and I reviewed the treaty extensively. Yes, I had some reservations about signing it, but Rollo explained every line to me. It sounded reasonable."

Aria's stomach clenched as she waited for Rupert to tell them how Rollo was involved, but he stayed silent. She tried to give him a look to spur him into action, but he only put his hand at the small of her back and remained silent.

The prince pushed his plate away, curling the fabric underneath it. "I'll have *all* of my mother's and my advisors go through it again. If they know what to look for this time, they may find something that will shine light on all this. And, possibly, a loophole to get us out of the treaty if need be." The prince waved to a servant standing by the door. "Get all of the advisors at once and send someone to bring me a copy of that treaty."

The servant bowed low and left to do Prince Elex's bidding.

The prince turned back to Rupert, a satisfied smile teasing the corners of his mouth. "Good work. This goes beyond your duties as the royal physician, and I appreciate all that you do for us."

Rupert bowed. "Happy I could be of use, your Highness."

"This woman's name is Aria, then?" Prince Elex asked. After Rupert nodded, he bowed his head toward her. "You may be assured of my sincerity this time when I say thank you. It appears I owe you a debt of gratitude for my life. And if I find useful information in the treaty, as you've indicated, that will be a second boon to grant unto you." His eyes narrowed in thought as he gazed upon her. "I *do* know you, don't I? We swam in the lagoon as kids."

Softening at his words, Aria smiled at the prince and nodded. It pleased her that he remembered. Before yesterday, that had been her only interaction with humans, and she was fond of the memories.

Tilting his head, Prince Elex's blue eyes lit up. "I know we only played a few times, but those were happy times for me. Now I know why you never spoke. Just swam all around and played tag. I see you're still just as much of a mystery to me now as you were then."

They shared a smile that lightened the mood in the room.

Aria was glad she'd gone to the trouble to rescue the prince. From the little interaction she'd had with him, he was a decent ruler and she was glad he'd survived the attack.

Prince Elex excused them and sat to eat more of his food.

Rupert led Aria from the room and toward her own chamber. "I see there are still more surprises from you," he said. "You swam around with Prince Elex when you were children?" he asked lightly, but there was an undercurrent in his tone, like he was jealous.

Shrugging, she waved a hand.

"Mm." Was his only response.

They continued to walk, and a thought niggled at the front of her mind. Why didn't he bring up Rollo? How could he omit such an important detail? She frowned at him with confusion.

"I know what you're thinking," Rupert said as they walked. He glanced around to make sure no one was in the corridor. "Trust me in this, Aria. I pointed them in the right direction. But if I had told them about Rollo," he said softly, "the prince wouldn't have believed me. He needs to discover it for himself. Rollo is just too close for the prince to believe what I might try to tell him."

She'd had the exact same thought when she first met the prince and Rollo in her room, but Aria still didn't love the idea. The prince wouldn't know how much danger he was in.

As if reading her thoughts, he said, "And now the prince knows that the attempt on his life is likely to happen again. He'll be on guard. And I know the commanding military officer. He'll do anything to keep the prince safe when he learns of this threat."

Sighing, Arai decided that he was right.

They arrived at her chambers, her legs burning from all the stairs. Once in the doorway, Rupert stroked his hand down her shoulder in a sensual way that made her shiver. "I need to check up on some patients. I visit the queen's mother every evening to be sure she's comfortable. But after I've done that and you've eaten your dinner, would you like me to bring you back to my office? I'd like to continue our voice lessons."

Grinning, Aria nodded, hoping that the lessons would include more of his kisses.

He raised her hand to his mouth, kissing her knuckles. His dark eyes bored into hers, making Aria feel as if he could see deep down into her soul. "I look forward to seeing you again."

She watched him leave before entering her room, hoping that their time apart would pass quickly.

Sandry brought in a tray of food that Aria consumed quickly, even with the awkwardness of her injured hands. All the excitement of the day, from going to the marketplace to kissing Rupert, had left her famished.

She'd just finished and stood when a shadow passed over her. Gasping, Aria spun to the window.

The man moved quickly, rushing forward and pushing her to the floor, his heavy body pinning her in place.

He smelled like he hadn't bathed in months, and when he opened his mouth to speak, she was repulsed at the sight of his rotten teeth. His sour breath poured over her as he spoke. "Rollo sends his regards." The man laughed cruelly and shook her. "You frozen with fear, or can you really not speak like they say?"

Recovering from her shock, Aria struggled underneath him, trying to yell, but only a small gurgle came out.

He laughed again. "Scream, girly." He slapped her.

The impact snapped her head to the side, making her vision blur. The pain stung and panic set in. Aria continued to flail, trying to scratch his arms.

Black magic would save her. The temptation was overwhelming to reach out to the darkness and let it fill her so she could throw this man to the sea to drown.

"I could do anything I wanted to you. And no one would ever hear." He said it as if the thought were a fun new concept. He laughed, low and cruel. "I'm going to take my time with you." His hands grabbed at the top of her dress and ripped it down her front.

Aria pulled out a big clump of his stringy hair as she struggled to get out from under him.

He punched her, his fist colliding with her jaw in brutal force.

Blood pooled from her gums to the back of her throat. Aria opened her mouth and spit it into his face.

The man growled and pushed himself off of her.

The relief from his weight was temporary. She was unable to flee before he grabbed a fistful of her red hair and pulled her up. Her scalp burned, and she jumped up, hoping to take the pressure off. He punched her in the gut and then spit on her face, his hot saliva sliding down her cheek. She reached out with her mind, past the white magic that wouldn't help her and to the darkness. It beckoned her, promising salvation, but she paused. It would save her in this moment, but her soul would be damned to hell if she accepted the black magic. *I'd rather die here than suffer for eternity in the next life.*

Aria gasped for breath, her stomach screaming and her lungs freezing up, but she mentally shut herself off from the magic.

He tore the other side of her dress, cold air hitting her shoulders and the tops of her breasts. He slapped her again and chuckled.

Disoriented, the assault made her feel helpless and out of control. Anger and indignation rose up through the panic. No one had ever touched her with violence before. This man didn't know who her father was. King Caspian would leave the sea and hunt this man down, torturing him for weeks before gutting him.

More material ripped loudly as he pulled at her skirts. She didn't have time to wait for her father to eke out revenge. Rollo had sent this man to kill her, and he was going to assault her first.

Screaming out all of her rage and fear, she lashed out, scraping her nails down the side of his face. She pulled off a good amount of flesh, leaving deep gouges in his face.

The man cried out and held both hands to his cheek.

Aria turned toward her door. She had to get away.

Before she reached it, the man plowed into her from behind. She landed with a hard thud, his meaty hands wrapping around her neck as he sat on her back.

Air was cut off from her lungs and she turned blue. Her arms flailed, trying to pull his hands off her throat. The gills behind her ears shuddered, trying to breathe through water. There was no oxygen to be found.

Her vision became spotted with black and she knew it was the end. *Rupert!*

As if her silent plea was heard, Rupert and Sandry rushed into the room. They froze when they saw the two on the floor. The man loosened his grip and Aria gulped in air, hacking and coughing painfully.

Rupert yelled incoherently and ran to them. He pulled the man off her. Aria rolled onto her side and continued to gasp between her uncontrollable coughs, her neck throbbing. She was aware of Sandry bending over her and the harsh sounds of flesh pounding on flesh. She wanted to get up, to make sure Rupert was alright, but pain and the coughing prevented her from moving.

Suddenly, it was disturbingly quiet. Aria forced herself to lift her head, but she needn't have worried. The man was in a heap near her bed, unconscious. Blood pooled under his head and he had several cuts on his face.

Rupert came to lean over her, his eye swelling. His knuckles were bleeding as well. But his attention was focused on her.

She saw the concern and the wildness in his eyes, but his jaw was set hard, as if he was trying to keep a doctorly composure as he examined her. He gently prodded her neck and she winced.

"Bring several cold compresses after you've alerted the guards," he instructed Sandry.

She nodded and left. Rupert looked down at Aria again. He gently pushed strands of hair from her forehead. "You'll be okay, Aria. I promise. I won't leave your side tonight."

His voice and words were a balm to her shaking core. Her limbs quivered and her chest heaved. A sob escaped, and she grabbed his hand, clinging to it, even though it hurt her hand to do so. Tears welled up in her eyes.

Rupert picked her up and held her against his chest, holding her tight.

Aria clung to him as she continued to cry.

When footsteps sounded, she pulled away, using the sleeve of her ruined dress to wipe her face.

When the guards entered, Rupert didn't let go of her.

"This man is a hired goon, sent to assassinate Aria. Report this to the prince immediately. I'm sure he'll want this man taken to the dungeon for questioning."

The guards nodded. Two of them picked up her would-be killer and dragged him away while the other one left to report to the prince.

CHAPTER 9

Rupert sent someone to fetch a blackboard and chalk so Aria could tell him what had happened. She wasn't sure if he'd be able to read her handwriting. She shook so hard that her words were barely legible. She had to use both of her hands to hold the chalk, and kept taking breaks to regain her strength. But he patiently held the board for her and read through everything, even though it took almost an hour for her to relate everything.

"Rollo sent him." Rupert's lips were set in a grim line. "I should have seen this coming. Once I reported to the prince that you'd overheard the plotting, Rollo would have heard of it and known that you were a threat to him."

He sat next to her on the bed and pulled her into his arms. "Thank God you were able to make some sounds. The maid told me when I arrived that she'd heard a strange sort of cry so we came right in instead of bothering with proper etiquette." He squeezed tight. "I thought we were too late when I saw you on the floor. Your face was so blue." His voice cracked and he went silent, hugging her close.

The prince came in at that moment and paused, taking in the sight of the two of them together. Clearing his throat, he strode to the bed. "I can see with all those bruises that it's true. Someone attacked her."

"Yes." Rupert didn't say anything else.

"While I appreciate you taking care of her, Rupert, I don't believe you need to embrace her to help her heal." The prince gave a pointed look.

"Perhaps not her physical wounds," Rupert countered. "But it does soothe the emotional ones."

Aria noted the tightness around the prince's mouth and how his fingers twitched. She'd bet anything that Rupert usually never spoke to the prince in this way.

Clearing his throat, the prince straightened to his full height, looking more regal than ever. "I personally oversaw the assassin's inquisition. He broke and told us everything. He was hired by one of my trusted advisors, but he didn't know his employer's name."

The prince looked at Aria. "Did you ever hear any names mentioned when you overheard the plot for my assassination?"

Swallowing painfully, she nodded, hoping that the prince was ready to accept the full, painful truth.

"Well, then, give me the name." The prince's tone was coiled, like he could hardly contain his anger.

Aria tried not to take it personally. After all, he was about to discover that his most trusted advisor was the traitor.

She wrote Rollo's name on the blackboard, moving slowly to keep her trembling under control.

"No," the prince whispered before she finished writing. He stepped back, as if she suddenly smelled like rotten tuna. "It can't be true."

"If that's what she says, your Highness, I'm inclined to believe her," Rupert said as he stood. He reached out an arm, as if he wanted to somehow help the prince, but let it drop.

Prince Elex's normally handsome face was pale, almost green. He shook his head but said nothing. He walked quickly out the door, not acknowledging any of the servants as he passed them.

Rupert sighed heavily. "He took it better than I thought."

Aria twisted her mouth, thinking the prince hadn't reached deep waters yet. But at least he knew.

Glancing up at Rupert, a flush of gratitude filled her. She was glad that she'd become human. She couldn't imagine being in a world without Rupert now. It was easy to understand how her father determined that humans weren't good. The soreness in her body and face could attest to that. And yet . . . not everyone was cruel. The prince seemed to have good intentions toward his kingdom and she understood that his desire for peace was genuine. Her maid, Sandry, had been kind to her from the beginning. And if it weren't for her overhearing her gurgled screams and telling Rupert, Aria would be dead by now. Even with what had happened, she wasn't afraid to be among humans. Especially with Rupert at her side.

At that thought, she realized she couldn't leave him. She could stay with him on land and together they could figure out who her mother was. But that kind of choice came at a high price. It meant she'd never be able to enter the ocean again, never see her father or sisters. It would be a betrayal to her father, who wanted her to stay away from humans, but to go back home would be a betrayal to her heart.

If nothing else, she'd have to send a message, to say goodbye.

Wiping the blackboard clean, she wrote, **Take me to the beach?**

After reading it, Rupert studied her. "It's dark out and you've had quite the ordeal. I'll take you in the morning, after you've had some rest."

Shifting, soreness shot through her torso, neck and face. **Too much pain to sleep.**

He went to his leather pack and pulled out a vial. "This will help with that."

She cringed, remembering the awful taste of the tonic he'd given her before. She didn't want to hurt his feelings, so she tried to lighten the mood.

Magic potion?

His laugh sounded rusty, but genuine. "I don't practice magic, Aria. Just medicine."

She tried to smile but her face was too swollen. **Your lips are magic.**

His laugh was stronger this time. "When you're healed, I'll happily remind you of the magic that our lips share when they meet."

A shiver of anticipation flitted through her stomach.

He held the vial to her lips. "Just two sips should do it."

She took a sip, then made a face at the sickly sweet, fermented flavor. It wasn't as bad as the other tonic, but certainly not pleasant either.

"I know. But I promise it'll help."

Aria took another sip as he instructed, then wrote on the blackboard. **Trust you.**

"And I you."

He rubbed small circles over the back of her neck. Aria felt fuzzy, like a murky water come over her mind.

The pain lessened and her eyelids became heavy. She slowly blinked up at Rupert. He still looked handsome, even with the black eye. It was the last thought she had before darkness engulfed her.

CHAPTER 10

The next morning, Aria woke to find Rupert sleeping at an awkward angle next to her bed. The chair he slept in was made from hard wood and didn't look like it cushioned him at all. She lay still and watched him a moment. His breaths were long and slow, with a strange soft noise rumbling with each exhale. She wanted to run her fingers through his tangled hair, to lean into him and smell his natural scent, but didn't want to disturb him.

Aria moved gingerly, her body protesting as she got out of bed and rang for the maid to help her dress. When her maid arrived, Rupert woke up and left to give her privacy.

"I'll be back soon," he promised. "And then I will take you to the beach."

Sandry clicked her tongue when she saw the bruises on Aria's body and face. "That man deserved what he got," she said. "I'm glad we got to you in time, milady."

Aria tried to smile reassurance, but the swelling seemed even worse today.

Rupert was waiting as she left her room, looking as if he'd washed his face and changed his clothes. As promised, he escorted her straight to the beach.

She stood for a moment, staring at the water gently lapping at the sand. *Home.* She would miss it dearly. Would miss feeling buoyant and the comforts and conveniences that didn't exist on land. But it was so much more than that; she'd never see her nephews grow up. She'd never see Kessida or her others sisters again. It was ironic that she'd come to the surface out of anger toward her father. And now she was staying, even though she could forgive him now. He'd lied, yes—she still didn't like that. But he'd had a terrible experience up here. Had been kept in captivity and endured things she couldn't comprehend. She wished she could at least explain to him that she understood. That staying on land had nothing to do with bitterness and everything to do with love.

Tears trekked down her cheeks as she said goodbye to the sea, to her family.

Frowning, Rupert came forward and placed a hand at her back. He didn't say anything, but his quiet strength was exactly what she needed.

Smiling through her tears, she leaned up onto her toes and kissed his cheek, then turned to complete the task she came for.

It took a few minutes to find the right shell. Rupert asked her what she was looking for, but she hadn't brought the blackboard and couldn't explain it to him.

She almost gave up on her search when her toes touched something smooth in the sand. Crouching down, she dug a little and pulled out a small conch shell. Wasting no time, she held it to her throat and opened her mind to the white magic. Since the magic was still difficult to reach, she was glad to have practiced this spell since she was little. It was something all mermaids were taught at a young age to use in emergencies. Most used the spell to send messages to their friends. It had driven the teachers crazy since the shell only revealed the message to its intended recipient.

With the conch shell at her throat and her mind tapped into the white magic, she spoke, knowing that every word would go into the shell even if humans didn't hear it.

"Father, I've become human. I won't tell you who helped me, and if you find out, don't blame them. This was my decision and mine alone. I did it in order to find my real mother. Yes, I know that I'm half human. I was upset at first, but no more. I love you, Father.

"But while I've been up here, I've found someone special." She looked at Rupert, who watched with a curious expression, but there was no hint of judgment. "I love him. I've decided to stay on land and spend my life with him. I'll turn back into a mermaid as soon as I enter the sea, so this means I'll never see you again. I'll miss you, Father. More than you'll ever know. I promise to send messages to you as much as I can. Please know that I'm happy. I wish for your happiness also."

The shell vibrated with the message in her fingers. She closed her eyes and brought up an image of her father. The shell lifted off of her palm and shot into the air, then into the water. It wouldn't stop until it found her father and he heard her message.

She turned and saw Rupert staring at her with wide eyes. "Did you just make that shell float into the sea?" He rubbed the sides of his head. "Maybe that hit to my eye gave me hallucinations."

Smiling, Aria decided to sing to catch his attention, even if she felt a little silly doing it. "Rupert," she sang out. "There is magic. Your lips are magic." She made up the tune and felt like she could have come up with something prettier, but Rupert walked to her with a heated gaze.

"*You* are magic," he said. His hand traveled behind her head, and he pulled her in for a kiss. It was gentle, and she appreciated his mindfulness of her injuries, but she wanted more. Toes digging into the sand, she rose up and deepened the kiss like he'd done the previous day. They moaned in unison when her tongue grazed his upper lip.

Rupert's hands traveled down to the small of her back and pulled her close, making their fronts touch.

Aria could have been lost in his kisses all day, but a loud crack in the air broke through her lusty haze.

Rupert grunted and released her. She looked on with confusion. His face was a mask of pain and surprise.

Then red blossomed along the shoulder of his shirt. She touched it. It was warm and sticky. His chest was bleeding.

Rupert fell into the sand, gasping.

Another loud crack rent the air, and something stung the side of her neck, grazing her skin and making her hair flying out behind her.

Looking for the source of the wretched sound, she saw Rollo striding toward them. His face was blotched red with fury and his clothes disheveled. His lip bled a smooth trickle down his chin.

"Damn you!" he screamed at her. "I could have been king if it wasn't for you!" He raised something in his hand and pulled his finger into it, but nothing happened. Swearing, Rollo tossed his weapon and rushed to her.

Aria ran away on instinct but spun to find Rupert.

He watched her with wide eyes as he lay on the ground. Blood seeped into the sand under him and some trickled out the side of his mouth. She froze and stared with indecision. He needed help or he'd die.

"Run!" he shouted.

She couldn't save him herself, and she wasn't strong enough to fight Rollo. The guards at the castle would know what to do. Nodding, she turned back toward the castle, but it was too late.

Rollo reached her and grabbed her hair. She kicked out as hard as she could, her heel meeting his knee. He lost his grip. She ran as fast as she could. Hands grabbed her shoulders and pushed her into the sand.

"You'll pay!" He roughly turned her onto her back and straddled her. He gripped her shoulders again and shook her. "You ruined my life."

She wasn't going to reach the castle. She did the only thing she could think of. Aria took a deep breath and belted out a melody. It had no words, just a strong song; the lullaby that Rupert played for her and the one her father used to sing to her. She put all her fear and desperation into the melody as she sang out.

Rollo sat back, blinking at her strangely. "What are you doing?"

She didn't respond. Just kept singing as loudly as she could, hoping that someone would hear and come find her.

"Stop it." He hit her cheek, making the tune sound garbled, but she kept singing. His face contorted, and he punched her jaw.

She hadn't recovered from the blow before his fist landed hard in her gut.

Gasping for breath, Aria couldn't sing. She could barely even see. Black dots sprouted over her vision, and she realized that hands were crushing into her neck with brutal force.

She struggled to move, to hit and claw at anything her hands found, but Rollo dug his fingers painfully into her jaw.

Once again, she couldn't breathe. Panic was at the edge of her mind, and she fought to break free, small sounds escaping her mouth.

Suddenly, Rollo lifted off her, levitating into the air.

Aria sucked in deep, painful breaths and stared as Rollo floated on nothing. His eyes were wide, looking all around. When he glanced toward the ocean, color drained from his face.

Aria glanced in the direction he was staring at to find her father standing, waves lapping against his thickly muscled legs.

Prya was further back in the water, a dark cloud above her and her hands in front of her. She was clearly using black magic to lift Rollo.

Prya twisted her fingers and Rollo sailed toward Caspian. The king grabbed Rollo from the air and growled. "No one touches my daughter." He placed his fingers at the sides of Rollo's neck and squeezed until Aria heard bones snapping. Rollo's body went limp and Caspian tossed him aside, a splash erupting around the corpse.

Without a second glance, he walked to Aria on the sand.

She heaved out a sigh of relief, but her father's eyes stormed with anger. He lifted her up and carried her toward the water's edge. "Please tell me that your message was a mistake. Surely you can see now how dangerous humans are." He pointed to the bruises on her face. "And it looks like this isn't the first time someone hurt you." His body trembled, and Aria felt the barely coiled rage inside of him.

Caspian stopped walking and hugged her, cradling her to his chest. "I'm so glad you're alright." His voice cracked.

Aria tried to speak, but no sound carried on the air.

Caspian touched her throat and she felt his royal magic trickle into it, as well as to the other injuries in her body. "It's like speaking in the water, but you have to use your diaphragm to bring sound out. Just like when you're singing."

Following his instructions, Aria pulled her belly in and used her diaphragm. "You figured out how to speak when you were human before?" Her voice sounded strange—light and airy. "When you were with my human mother?"

"Yes," Caspian sounded tired. "I'm afraid to say that woman didn't have a nurturing bone in her body. As soon as she saw your tail and fins, she tried to kill you. Claimed that you were a demon." Regret and sorrow dimmed the light in his eyes. "I told her that I was really a merman, but she wouldn't hear any of it. She put both of us in the dungeon. The guards came and gawked at you in your water tank. They even snuck others in for a fee. If it wasn't for Prya coming up and rescuing us, we would have been fish meat twenty years ago."

"Her guards?" Aria questioned. "Who is my mother, father?"

Caspain closed his eyes and sighed, his face sagging with defeat. "The queen, Aria. Prya told me you rescued a prince up here. He is your younger half brother."

The news froze her with shock. "The prince is my brother?" she mumbled through stiff lips.

It wasn't until the water touched her feet that Aria broke from her shock and realized that her father had been guiding her back to the ocean. "No!" she called out. But it was too late. The saltwater seeped into her toes, crawling up her legs with dark blue magic. The fabric of her pantaloons tore and suddenly her tail shimmered in the sunlight.

"Father, no." Tears welled. "I want to stay with Rupert."

They were deeper in the water now, waves lapping at her chest and her sodden dress weighing her down.

"The man just tried to kill you. I killed him, Aria. You can't be with him anymore."

"That was Rollo," she insisted. "Rupert is over there. We must help him, father. He'll die!"

"It's for the best, Aria. He'll break your heart in the end. Trust me. Humans are too selfish not to hurt each other."

"No!" Desperate, she searched her inner magic. It wasn't very powerful. But *something* had to work. She couldn't leave Rupert like this. Twisting out of her father's grasp, she swam to Rupert. She reached the shore in mere seconds and pulled herself over the sand with her arms until she was by his side.

He was still alive, blinking up at her. But his skin was so pale, and the sand under him was an angry red from his blood.

"Rupert, please."

He smiled and looked up at her. "You're magic, Aria."

His arm reached weakly for her and she grabbed it, wishing she could save him.

"I love you," he whispered.

"Don't. You can't die," she choked. She reached out with her power and felt his aura. It was nearly gone.

Tears streamed down her face as sobs threatened to choke her. She couldn't lose him. She *wouldn't*. But that meant one thing. She had to turn to dark magic. It was the only thing that could save him. Could she sacrifice her soul, accept an eternity in Hell for this man? She might not even survive long after she gave in to it. *I'll do anything for you, Rupert.*

Keeping her grip on his hand, she closed her eyes and reached out, ignoring her white magic and searching for the darkness. It was there, waiting for her to give in and let it fill her. She just had to take it in.

Before she could accept it, a force brushed past her. Opening her eyes, she saw a dark blue magic fill Rupert's body, expanding his lungs and filling him with life.

Blinking, she looked behind her and saw Prya in the water, her hands reaching out, using all of her energy to send healing magic into Rupert.

Caspian was pulling on her arm, yelling for her to stop, but she ignored him.

The magic fizzled away and Rupert sat up, gasping.

"You're alright," she exclaimed.

He held his hands to his chest. It was completely healed. "How did you do that?"

Aria shook her head. "It wasn't me." She gestured behind her to Prya and Caspian, who appeared to have become a merman again.

"She was going to use black magic for that man, Caspian. A mermaid only does that when she's truly in love," Prya was saying.

"But you did it for me, to make me human all those years ago," her father countered.

Prya was quiet.

It took a few seconds for realization to dawn on Caspian's face.

Aria turned back to Rupert. "I would have given in to black magic for you, Rupert," she whispered. "I love you."

He traced her cheek with his finger. "I love you, too Aria." He glanced down toward her feet, and his eyes widened. "Aria, are you . . . I mean, it looks like . . ." He trailed off.

"Yes, I'm a mermaid," she whispered. "I had Prya," she pointed behind her, "change me into a human." She smiled. "And then I fell in love with you and decided I would stay here for you."

Shifting into a sitting position, she let Rupert get a better view of her tail, the scales shimmering in the sun. Sadness filled her. "My father pulled me into the water, though. Now I'm stuck as a mermaid."

"You can't be human again?" He asked. His face was open and pleading.

Chewing her bottom lip, she glanced at her father and Prya. Caspian was looking at Prya as if she were a whole new person that he'd never seen before.

"I don't know," she said honestly. "But I'll certainly try. Wait here." She kissed him before leaning onto her stomach to crawl into the water.

Rupert's arms came around her. "Let me help." He picked her up and carried her into the ocean, soaking his clothes as if it were of no consequence. But she knew all too well from the dress she had on how uncomfortable sodden clothes were.

When she was floating on her own, she kissed him again. Then she turned and swam to her father and Prya. It was obvious there was an undercurrent of tension between them, but she interrupted anyway. They could sort out their problems after Prya had turned her back into a human—hopefully. "Prya? Please. Can you make me human again? Just name your price. I'll pay anything."

Rubbing a hand over her forehead, Prya sighed wearily. Bags had formed under her eyes and her skin had taken on a green cast. "Not today, Aria. After turning your father human and the other two spells I just performed, I need to rest for at least a few days to recover."

"You will *not* come back to the surface, Aria," her father boomed. "I'll keep you under lock and key if I have to. But I will not lose you to those bastard humans."

Forcing herself to show patience she didn't feel, Aria kept her voice steady. "Father, you don't understand. This isn't like some affair you had with the queen. I love Rupert. We want to be together."

"He'll turn on you, Aria."

"He already knows what I am and he still wants to be with me." She fixed him with a hard glare. "Maybe if you'd been honest from the start, my mother wouldn't have thought I was a demon when I was born!"

Grinding his teeth, Caspian shook his head. "You don't know them like I do."

"Yes, I do!" she shouted, her composure shattering. "I've had two men try to kill me. I see the bad in them as you do. But I also see the good." She glanced at Prya, remembering the mermaid's words. "Humans are just like merfolk. Some are good and some bad. No one is born that way. All determine it through life based on their choices and their actions. Why can't you see that?"

Caspian opened his mouth to reply, but Rupert spoke from behind Aria. "Can you turn me into a merman?"

Everyone stopped and turned to Rupert, who was treading water.

Aria studied his face, which was earnest.

The only sounds for several seconds were the crashing of waves and seagulls calling out overhead.

Finally, Prya broke the silence. "Are you saying that you'd be willing to leave your life behind, leave any family or friends, and turn into a merman to be with Aria?" she asked softly.

Her father studied Rupert with suspicion, but he waited for the doctor's reply.

"Of course." He swam closer to Aria and smiled at her with affection. "She was willing to do the same for me. How can I say I love her just as much without doing so in return?"

Smiling, Aria wanted to say something, but no words came. He'd said it all.

"If you're willing to leave your life behind, it means everyone will think you've died, drowned in the ocean," her father stated. "Can you do that? Allow everyone to think you've passed on? How do you know you'll enjoy the life of a merman? You may regret your choice and resent Aria for it."

Rupert shook his head. "If I'm with Aria, I'll be happy, whether we're on land or sea."

"Yes, Rupert," Aria felt warmth suffuse her entire body. "That's exactly how I feel about you."

He stroked her hair, then turned to Prya and Caspian. "Can it be done?"

Caspian's mouth pressed into a thin line. Before he responded, Prya placed a hand on his shoulder.

"I'll do it," she said weakly. She looked like she'd lost weight in the last few minutes, but her face was determined. "I see the love for each other in your auras. Such devotion toward each other should be rewarded."

Studying Prya, Caspian's face softened. He grabbed her hand and held it. "I'll do it myself," he said. He looked at Rupert. "Just know that if you do anything to hurt her, I'll keep you alive for the next twenty years and torture you for every one of those minutes."

Rupert swallowed audibly but his grip tightened on Aria. "I'll do everything in my power to make her happy."

Glaring, the king placed his hand over Rupert's shoulder and white light shined between them.

When he lifted his hand away, Rupert looked down. A long, green tail was in place of his legs. He smiled at Aria. "We can be together now."

Smiling broadly, she leaned into him and kissed his mouth. With his tail, Rupert stayed steady and kissed her back, their arms encircling each other.

CHAPTER 11

Two months later, Aria laughed as she swam. Rupert kept asking to race, but she always won.

"How do you do that?" he asked, warmth shining from his eyes. It had taken practice for Rupert to learn to speak underwater, but he'd caught on quickly. He still sang for her, and everyone in the kingdom agreed that he had an incredible talent for music. He'd written a song and played it at their wedding, winning the hearts of most of the merfolk then and there. Even King Caspian had been impressed.

Her father was slowly warming up to Rupert and was even asking Aria when he could expect to have more grandchildren to play with.

"Magic," she joked with a wink.

Rupert hugged her close and kissed her. When they pulled apart, she looked up at the sun. It was on its descent. "We better hurry," she said.

Together, they swam upward until they broke the surface. The prince was already there, sitting in a rowboat and looking over the water.

"Elex," Aria called.

When the prince saw them, he smiled. "I'm glad you could make it."

Aria stomach sank when she noted he was alone. "Your mother couldn't come?"

Elex's mouth tightened. "*Our* mother isn't ready to meet you yet. But give her some time. I believe she'll come around."

Forcing a smile, Aria did her best to push back the disappointment. Her father had warned her to leave the queen alone, but she still had hope to meet her real mother. Prince Elex helped to keep that hope flowing.

"How are you, Elex?" Rupert asked.

The prince groaned. "I still have trouble seeing you as a merman. It's beyond strange, Rupert." He straightened. "If you ever want to become human again, there's always a job waiting here for you. Our new physician isn't half as talented as you."

"Thanks, Highness, but I could never leave Aria." His arm wrapped around her waist.

Aria smiled and rested her head on his shoulder. Not only was she with the man she loved, but her half brother was open to the idea of them getting to know each other better.

Elex even mentioned making a treaty with her father for the two races to exchange goods. Aria just had to convince King Caspian to swim up and meet with the prince. She hadn't succeeded in changing her father's mind yet, but Prya was making progress. The king rescinded her banishment and welcomed her back into the kingdom as one of his advisors.

"I brought you two a treat." The prince held up a box, and Aria groaned in anticipation.

The two merfolk pulled themselves into the boat and rested their tails over the side.

Prince Elex handed over the box of croissants and pastries.

"This is what I miss the most," Rupert said. "Fish and kelp don't hold a candle to pastries."

Aria nodded, her mouth too full to respond.

Sitting there with her love and her brother, she truly felt she had the best of both worlds.

THE END

About the Author:

Adrienne Monson is an award-winning hybrid author who has been hailed by MSN as a "vampire expert". She has always had a voracious appetite for reading and enjoys all kinds of fiction. While she is primarily known for her vampire novels in the Blood Inheritance Trilogy, she also writes historical romance, dystopian, and other genre mash-ups.

Join her readers club at
https://www.adriennemonson.com/news-letter/.

Follow her on Amazon (https://www.amazon.com/Adrienne-Monson/e/B00BEJLHA8) to get info on her newest releases.

You can also follow her on Instagram
 (https://www.instagram.com/adriennemonson/) or Facebook
(https://www.facebook.com/adriennemonson/).

Under the Moonlit Sea

Moonlight Fantasy

By

Teri Harman

Under the Moonlit Sea
Copyright © 2018 by Teri Harman
Original cover design by Ampersand Book Covers Copyright © 2018
All rights reserved.

Published in the United States by Tork Media

CHAPTER 1

Far off the coast of Maine, in the deep Atlantic
August 1989

The Anchor hummed its eternal rhythm, pulling on the moon's gravity to engineer the ocean tides. Quila listened closely, the intricacies of the Anchor's song as familiar as her own breathing. She knew when it was storming in England or when it was full moon just from the changes in the ancient device's hum. She curved her tail—the same soft hue as blue lace agate and iridescent in the murky depth—to swim her way around the massive stone Anchor. Her long charcoal-gray hair trailed behind her in waves.

The Anchor sat at a depth of three hundred feet, the same width across as the rock pillar formation it sat atop. All around it was vast open sea, the waters plunging to depths of ten thousand feet. It was as wide as three submarines side by side, twelve feet tall, and shaped in a perfect circle, echoing its parent, the moon. Around the outside edges were intricate etchings of the lunar phases, said to have been carved by a prehistoric octopus. Housed within the large circular edifice was a spiral of glowing white moonstones.

Quila's swim brought her full circle to where her father floated, waiting for her report. "The tide is on schedule," she said, stopping at his side. "But I'm worried about the moonstone at the center of the circle. Its energy wanes."

Mayar, steward of the Atlantic Anchor, nodded his understanding. His skin was the same moonlight gray as his daughter's and his eyes the same brilliant sea green. The moon mermaids all shared these qualities, varying only in hair and tail color. His pearl-white hair, reaching as long as his shoulders, floated around his square-jawed face. His tail, inky black, moved gently to keep him in place.

"What would you like to do, my Queen?" Mayar asked Quila.

Quila frowned. That title would never sit comfortably. Though she'd been ruling for twelve years, the mantle of queen still felt awkward, unwanted. Each time someone called her queen, it brought a slap of grief. *I'm queen because Mom died. Dad should be in charge, not me.* But kings didn't hold the ancient magic; that passed from mother to daughter. Quila had the moon magic, the deep connection to the Anchor, not him. She took a steadying breath. "As soon as high tide passes, we'll start the regeneration. They should be here by then." Her frown deepened. "Late, as usual."

Quila looked over her shoulder in the direction of their palace. Her seven sisters—one daughter for each phase of the moon— were often late to tide check. She gritted her teeth against the familiar annoyance. A moment later, she felt a tremor in the water. "Here they come." *Finally!*

The girls arrived in a flurry of tails, hair, and laughter. Deva, second in line, waning gibbous sister, called out in a singsong voice, "We're here! Did we miss anything?" Her cerulean hair and cream-colored tail were perfectly groomed.

"Of course we didn't," Lyria, fourth and new moon sister, answered. She was the only sister who kept her hair short. The silver locks bobbed just under her ears, and her dove-gray tail brought her close to Quila. "Something would actually have to happen for us to miss it." She rolled her eyes, bored.

Quila sighed impatiently. "I know your schedules are *so full*," —a sarcastic smile—"but just once it'd be nice *not* to have to wait for you."

"Why should *we* be on time?" Deva shot back. "We're not the one the Anchor needs. No one cares if *we* are here." A saccharine smile in return.

I didn't ask for this responsibility.

I wish Mother were here to tell us what to do instead of me having to make all the decisions.

"Stop being dramatic, Deva. We are all important to the Anchor."

Deva scoffed, "Hardly. If we disappeared tomorrow—"

"That's enough, girls," Mayar cut off the banter. "Deva, please show some respect for your and your sister's positions. The

Anchor is not to be taken lightly. You know that. And today we have a problem." He looked to his oldest.

"Some of the moonstone needs regenerating," Quila told her sisters.

Lyria groaned. "Didn't we just do this?"

"No," Quila answered firmly. "That was five cycles ago."

"I like singing to the moonstone." This was Hala, the youngest and eighth daughter, waxing gibbous. Small and sweet, she was usually the only sister to offer Quila support.

Quila put a hand on Hala's moonlight-gold hair and gave her a thankful smile. "It won't take long."

With a few sighs and rolls of eyes, the sisters gathered around the Anchor, equally spaced to line up with the etched carving of their moon phase. Mayar floated above the Anchor, astutely monitoring the moonstone. He signaled for the song to begin.

Quila's voice came first, a lilting alto, rich and resonant, she sang in the language known only to her people and the moon. The hum of the Anchor changed pitch to match hers. Soon her sisters joined in, one at a time, the swell of their voices warming the cold Atlantic water. Quila felt that same heat in her chest, the sensation of her energy passing to the moonstone.

They sang for several minutes before a new awareness ran down her spine, a twinge so strange her voice cut off mid-word. She had time to look up at her father and meet his concerned eyes before the moonstone cracked open with a violent wrench that sent a shock wave of energy rushing out of the Anchor.

The wave hit Quila and her sisters, sending them tumbling backward. Quila watched her tail flip over her head twice before the world went black.

***

Anson Lacey checked his air gauges and his watch. His air was good, his time was not. He had only about five minutes left to explore the shipwreck before he'd have to start his hour-long decompression ascent. He lifted his head slowly to avoid stirring up more silt. The visibility through his mask was horrible, the water murky with silt, rust, and oil. His thick dry suit protected him from the frigid temperatures, but he was far from warm. His joints grew stiff from the cold and the effort of moving so slowly.

He spider crawled his fingers along what was previously the ceiling of the luxury yacht. The boat had belonged to a Spanish prince in the 1920s. Prince Miguel had been notorious for his extravagant, salacious parties at sea. But in the deep-sea diver's world, Prince Miguel was famous for getting so drunk he had failed to notice when his boat caught fire and sank—valuable artifacts and all—into the freezing waters off Maine.

Anson had dived this ship several times with his father, the most successful and famous pioneer of the exclusive sport. Robert Lacey was god past two hundred feet. Those new to the sport prayed for half his physical stamina, mental control, and pirate-like roughness. Anson wished only to step out of his father's hefty shadow. Where his father was all grit and grind, Anson was careful intelligence, exhaustive research, and an incredible ability to see a shipwreck as it had once been even as it lay an eviscerated, upside-down disaster.

And though Robert Lacey had pulled several valuable and enviable artifacts from Prince Miguel's *Princessa,* he'd never found the coveted brass clock from the bridge. Anson was determined to claim that find.

But he had only moments left on this dive, and there was no sign of the grand timepiece with its twelve o'clock three-carat emerald.

The inhale hiss and exhale boom of his regulator seemed to fill the whole ocean around him. *HissBOOM. HissBOOM.* Anson brought himself to a stop, carefully scanning the sea anemone–encrusted metal and spider's web of wires in front of him. He knew he was in the remains of the wheelhouse where the clock had originally been mounted. He could see the original shape and form of the space in his head and match it to the chaos before him. That was his gift, something he did better than other divers. So much better.

Oil fogged his mask, but he didn't reach to wipe it away. He couldn't waste the movement and risk worsening the silt. His headlamp was useless in the grime. Frustration thumped loud in his nitrogen narcosis-impaired brain. Narcosis killed more divers than all the other dangers of diving combined. At two hundred feet down, every breath was seven times the volume required on land. Nitrogen was quickly leeching into his blood and wreaking havoc on his brain and muscles.

Anson paused to take a slow breath, fighting back the insanity trying to creep in. His father's words echoed in his mind. *Problems don't kill divers. Panic does. Keep your cool, ALWAYS.* He checked his watch again and mentally swore. Ignoring the desire to spend just a few more minutes hunting—his father also said, *Stick to your schedule or die; simple as that*—Anson laboriously turned to rewind his swim back out of the wreck. The narcosis screamed and whined at him. *You're a failure. Can't even find a clock. You'll never be as good as your father.*

Anson took slow, controlled breaths.

And focused on the map in his mind.

He pushed through a mess of wires, carefully keeping his double air tanks clear, and turned to the right. The exit, a jagged jack-o'-lantern-sneer opening near the massive propeller, was only a few feet ahead. Anson resisted the urge to speed up his swim, his fins remaining immobile behind him as his fingers moved him along.

An odd feeling prickled up his spine. He stopped, rocking in his own subtle wake. Had there been a noise, movement? What had caused him to stop? Anson swiveled his gaze back and forth. Panic burned the back of his throat. The water around him moved in a way he'd never experienced. His teeth clamped down on his regulator, and he kicked his fins hard. *Screw the silt; I gotta to get out now.*

A booming rock of waves hit the wreck. Metal groaned and screamed.

Anson slammed hard into the wall to his left, pain exploding through his shoulder. The ship tilted under the power of the wave. His mask got dragged into his eyes, his regulator nearly came out of his mouth, but he bit down hard and took a big breath. Pushing away from the wall, he swam hard for the blackness of his exit. The wreck continued to rock and shift all around him.

His heart pounded a jungle rhythm in his ears.

The narcosis taunted, *You're going to die here. No escape.*

The exit was a foot away. Muscling his way through the swaying water, Anson reached it. Just in time for the metal to collapse and bite down on him like a giant mouth.

CHAPTER 2

Quila blinked back to consciousness, the ocean black all around her. She groaned at the ache in her body, slow to realize her head hung below her tail, upside-down. With a painful flex of her tail, she managed to right herself. She pushed her dark-gray hair from her face, leaving her hands on her temples to push at the throbbing in her head.

What happened? Holy moon, what went wrong?

The only explanation was a failure in the moonstone. Her father had once mentioned that it was possible, that it'd been centuries since any section of the moonstone had collapsed. She closed her eyes and listened for the Anchor's hum. It was there, but wrong, limping along and out of sync. She turned to swim back, but something stopped her.

Quila swiveled back, peering out through the dark water in the direction of land. She held out her hand to feel the water, to listen with more than her ears. *What is that?* The Anchor was pulling on her, demanding she return, but this other feeling could not be ignored. She swam forward and then stopped.

Go back to the Anchor. Whatever this is, it doesn't matter.

But some deep instinct told her it *did* matter.

She took a thoughtful breath, the gills under her ears flexing. *I have to know what it is.* She swam fast toward the sensation, slicing through the water. She ignored the pulse of fear that came when she realized she had crossed over into human territory, into waters her people *always* avoided. Into waters her father had *forbidden* them to swim into after her mother's death.

Quila skidded to a stop.

I can't be here. This is where my mother died.

She looked around, the Anchor's tugging sensation filling her body now. But that other feeling was still there, equally as strong. She recognized it as fear, as panic, hard as coral and sharp as urchins. But the fear didn't belong to her. *So whose is it?* What if this was connected to the Anchor? What if the wave had affected something and she needed to know?

Cautiously, she swam forward.

Her sharp mermaid eyes could see through the darkness several hundred feet. Her hands undulated and turned as she swam, listening to the water for clues. After several minutes, she saw the outlines of a sunken ship, its jagged unnatural edges reaching up from the ocean floor.

As a child she'd been fascinated by the human world, curious about these creatures who lived on land but chose to sail on and swim in her ocean, sometimes to their own peril. Often she had slipped away from the palace to swim through these wrecks, puzzling over the objects she found. But all her fascination came to a jerking, painful halt when her mother was killed. Quila had been only ten years old.

Mayar's angry, grief-stricken voice filled her head. *Obey the rules established by our ancestors: Stay away from human waters at all costs and at all times. I'll not lose another to their ignorant, selfish curiosity.* If her father knew why her mother had broken these rules, he would not say. Elara's disappearance and death remained a mystery that no one was allowed to talk about. The only fact Quila knew was that human divers—the kind that strapped their air on their backs to explore the depths—were responsible.

What do I do, Mom?

Staring at the mangled ship now, Quila grimaced at the familiar pain of missing her mother, of wanting to know what had happened, and of needing her expert guidance. Quila was supposed to have had twenty-one years to learn under her mother's expert watch before Elara turned over the full moon responsibilities to her oldest daughter. Instead, at the tender age of ten, the weight of the Anchor had been handed to her. *You must take over for your mother,* her father had solemnly told her. *Our people look to you now, Queen Quila.*

And I'm going the wrong direction when the Anchor needs me.

A fleshy sense of dread pressed on her chest.

I can't be here.

Quila turned to leave, but movement caught her eye. Near the rear of the ship a human diver was caught in the jaws of a great tear in the metal. Her heart stuttered as she realized the fear and panic she felt belonged to this human. Had the shock wave from the Anchor caused this? *Is that why I feel his fear? Because the Anchor is responsible for this?*

Quila floated, unable to move forward or back. Unable to decide if she should save a human life or leave him to his fate.

***

The shock of the impact had Anson reeling for several terrible moments. The top of the exit had collapsed directly onto his tanks, pinning him to a bent but luckily flat section of ship below. *Pinned, like a butterfly in a case. No—squashed like a cockroach under the heel of a shoe.* The weight of the ship made it almost impossible to breathe. Though he'd managed to keep his regulator in his mouth, his torso was severely compressed. The small sips of air brought on the panic and the narcosis. The narcosis was yelling at him now, taking control of every thought, every emotion.

You're dead.

No way out of this.

Dead in the ship your dad is famous for. Won't Robert hate that?

Anson's heart rate was way too high.

One thing at a time. His rational mind finally broke through.

Anson looked at his watch. It had been only three minutes. There was still time to escape and ascend. But he'd have to work quickly. There was no rescue for deep-sea divers. No one was expecting him for over an hour. No one had dived with him because in this dangerous world partners got you killed. He was completely alone.

One thing at a time. One small thing first.

Anson put his gloved hands on the metal below him. He tried to look at his surroundings, but the waves had turned the ocean into a sandstorm. And there was a shallow pool of water in his mask; each time he shifted his head the salt water sloshed into and stung his eyes. So he had to rely on the map in his mind. *I'm facing out to the open sea. The anchor line to the boat is above and behind me near the center of the wreck. I'm pinned to the engine room floor, propeller to my left, bow to my right. The sun above me.*

A tiny breath, in and out.

Anson put pressure into his hands and tried to pull himself forward. Nothing happened. He tried again. And again. His breathing rate shot up, and his brain twisted back to panic. *Trapped. Trapped. Gonna die. Dead.*

Anson forced himself to calm down. He torqued his right arm back to try to feel the metal. He found a deep dent in his air tank. He tried to reach for his knife, thinking that maybe if he cut the straps off his tanks he could slither out. But to lose the weight of his tanks—even for a moment—could send him rocketing to the surface to meet a horrible death from the excruciating pain of the bends. He wasn't positive he could keep control of his tanks without the secure straps.

The knife was pinned under his right hip anyway.

Options. What are the options?

There are no options. Dead, dead, dead. Your father will laugh when he comes for your body. If he comes.

Anson couldn't slow his breathing anymore. It huffed and raged against his regulator. His heart beat an incessant, horrible pounding in his ears. He let his face rest on the metal beneath him, the mask pressing into his forehead. He gave in to the urge to pound his fists like a two-year-old in tantrum.

The water churned around him. Something had changed. He jerked his head up, coming face-to-face with a beautiful gray-skinned woman. He blinked and blinked again. He held his breath.

This is a hallucination. A common side effect of narcosis.

She is not real. This is my burned-up brain.

Or is it?

Oh, she's real all right.

The woman narrowed her eyes at him. Eyes that were an odd, brilliant sea green. *Those look like . . .* His mind slipped from her eyes to her hair. Dark gray like the metal of his tanks but shiny and silky. Her light-gray skin, like some kind of marble, and her chest covered only by that long hair. And her blue tail.

A blue tail.

Her tail moved gently in the messy water. Anson watched it, trying hard to dig through the narcosis to find his logic. Instead he thought of a necklace his grandmother had always worn, a pale blue stone laced with white.

It's the same color.

I'm seeing things. Crazy things.

She's incredible.

The woman, the *mermaid*, put her hands on his shoulders and looked side to side. She frowned, her brow lowering in concern. She felt along his regulator and touched his tanks. Anson shook his head quickly, panicked to lose his air. She ignored him and reached again. This time he started to thrash, the dam on his fear burst wide open. He heard his heart and his breath and felt himself thrashing like a hooked fish but couldn't stop it. She brought her hands to his cheeks, and though his head was encased in his dry suit hood, he felt the heat of her hands as if on his skin. The gentle pressure was enough to calm his body. The deep reassurance in her eyes enough for him to hand over his life to her.

She held his gaze for another breath and then released his face. She tucked her head and dove away from him. His eyes went wide trying to follow her. *Come back! Don't leave me.*

She came back with a long iron pipe. Carefully, she wedged it under the top section of metal, creating a lever. Then with unbelievable strength, she pressed down and lifted the section off his back. Too shocked, he couldn't move. She scowled down at him and used the end of her tail to whack him into action.

Anson swam free.

He turned to watch as she released the pipe and the metal came crashing down, closing the entrance permanently. Ignoring the destruction, she swam hurriedly to him, searching his face. He felt a peculiar rush in his legs and arms, his blood racing out into his limbs much too fast. Spots appeared in his vision, bright, flashing sparks. Anson reached out for her, feeling her hand grip his a half moment before he lost consciousness.

CHAPTER 3

Quila scooped one arm under the diver's right arm, and with her other hand she shoved the breathing piece back in his mouth. Was he dead or just injured? Could he still breathe if he wasn't awake?

What do I do?!

Closing her eyes for a moment, Quila tried to recall everything she knew about humans under the water. It wasn't much, but there was something about the deep water hurting their blood, their minds. *Ugh, what was it?* A shadow of a conversation she'd overheard flickered to life. Her father had been criticizing the divers. "They poison themselves. If they only knew to find some forma."

Quila's eyes flashed open. *The forma, of course.* They thrived on nitrogen instead of oxygen. Rebalancing the man's weight, Quila held out her hand and called to the creatures, her energy reaching out to them. *Please help.* Soon a swarm of the tiny shelled amoeba-like creatures came drifting up from below. *Find his skin, find his blood.* She pulled off his gloves and yanked up the sleeves of his strange black clothing. She knew the cold could hurt him as well, but the layer of forma would help insulate his fragile body. Soon the man was covered in a crowded layer of the brown and black shells.

Quila lifted her head toward the surface. *I've never been above the waves.* She swallowed her anxiety and swam upward, slowly, so the forma had time to work on the diver's blood. But the pace made her anxious. She had to get back to the Anchor—the hum had changed again, weaker. If the tides got off schedule . . . *disaster.* Her mother had taught her that fact early on: *If the tides fail, the earth fails. The fish, the plants, the weather, the humans, us—we all rely on the ocean's rhythm. Which is why we protect it so fiercely. Quila,* always *protect the Anchor first, no matter what.*

Quila glanced down at the diver's face. *So why am I risking the Anchor for you?* With his skin covered in forma all she could see was the section of face under his mask. His closed eyes, dark lashes resting on his cheeks. *What is your life like?* As she looked at him, a peculiar rumble of instinct moved through her chest. This moment, this man, were important to her. She didn't know why or how, but she felt it as deeply as she felt the rhythm of the Anchor.

Who are you?

Morning sunlight sliced down through the water, pulling Quila's attention from the man. The glassine surface was close. *Off you go, forma. Thank you.* The creatures detached from the man's skin, gathered together in a clump, and descended out of sight. Quila slowed, her apprehension roaring back as she looked at the barrier between her world and his. Her head broke the surface, the bright sun blinding. She blinked several times, her deep-sea eyes unaccustomed to so much light. She squinted up at the sky. Gorgeous white mounds of clouds, soft as jellyfish, piled high above the ocean, thick and delicious. That sky—so wide and endless. So like the ocean itself.

Quila sighed, amazed.

The diver stirred in her arms. She hurried to take the breathing tube and mask off his face. Then she looked for land. He needed his solid sand. She swam fast toward an empty beach of black rocks, a tall white lighthouse standing on a nearby outcropping. Quila kept close watch for other humans; exposure to one man was already too much.

Careful with his limp body, Quila eased the man onto the black shore, dragging him with her out of the waves, awkward with all his heavy equipment and her tail. She instantly missed the water, her body rejecting the thin air. But she found she could still breathe, though it was taxing. She pushed the hood off the man's head, surprised at the short crop of light-brown hair underneath. Unable to resist, she ran her hand over it, smiling at the tickle on her palm. His eyes fluttered open, immediately coming to her face. She gasped, surprised at the color of his eyes, which she hadn't been able to see clearly in the dark, murky water below. It was the same as hers, the same as all her people. *How is that possible?* The expression in his eyes told her that he, too, was startled at the sameness. She touched his face. He brought his hand to hers, pressing her palm harder to his cheek. His eyes closed briefly.

"Who are you?" he whispered, his voice strained and rough.

She offered him a small smile. "You are safe. Back on your land."

"How? What—what happened?" He moved to sit up, but her hand on his shoulder kept him lying back on his air tanks.

"Not yet. Rest." Quila pulled in a labored breath.

His eyes widened. "What's wrong? Are you hurt?"

She shook her head. "I must go."

He gripped her hand. "Wait, not yet." His eyes searched her face. "Are you real?"

Quila pressed her teeth together, a tug of emotion in her gut. "No, only a dream. Forget me."

The words made him grimace. She carefully pulled her hand free of his grasp. Instead of going straight back to the ocean, Quila surprised them both by pressing her lips to his, soft and barely there. A jolt moved down her spine. She pressed her lips down harder, her chest aching. His hands came to her back. The warmth of it was too much. She pushed away from him and in a swift, graceful arc dove back into the sea.

***

Anson lay motionless on the beach, his eyes unable to leave the spot in the water where the mysterious mermaid had retreated and left him alone. He ached for her in a confusing, exhilarating way. If his equipment and painful exhaustion hadn't weighed down his body, he knew he would have dived after her.

Mermaid. Mermaid? No.

He flinched, pushing his palms to the rock next to him to force his body upright. His head jerked side to side as his brain replayed the memories in the shipwreck. "How am I here?" he mumbled to the waves. Slowly, he slipped his tanks off and yanked away his fins. His whole torso felt compressed and sore from the weight of the ship. It hurt to breathe. He palpated his ribs, waiting to feel a broken one. "Only bruised," he reassured himself. *A miracle, really.*

He thought of the mermaid lifting the broken metal off him, her superhuman strength. *That's because she's not real, idiot.* "This is narcosis. She was a hallucination. Has to be." Anson brought his fingers to his lips. *But her kiss . . .* He shook his head hard. Pulling his hand from his lips, he saw tiny, perfectly round red welts on his skin, dozens of them. *Where are my gloves?* He turned his hand over to find the same small marks everywhere. He inspected his other hand and touched his face to feel the raised marks. Every inch of exposed skin.

When he was ten, Anson's father had taken him to a cabin on a lake in Utah during summer vacation. It was the first time they'd gone to a body of water that wasn't the ocean. Excited and ignorant of mountain water, Anson ran into the lake. Three leeches immediately latched on to his bare legs. He'd been terrified but forced himself not to cry in front of his father. *Just leeches, boy. Man up!* Robert had yanked off the slimy beasts, leaving behind small round welts, just like these.

Anson looked all around him for leeches but found nothing.

He touched the marks on his neck and shivered. *I was trapped in the ship and then . . . mermaid. No, not mermaid.* "But then how did I get free, get here? How am I not dying of the bends right now?" He looked down at his legs, waiting for a spasm, a cramp. "What just happened?" He lifted his eyes back to the ocean and thought of the impossible mermaid with her smooth-as-marble skin, long hair tangled around her torso, and vibrant green eyes the same hue as his. Her supple, salty lips.

He swore under his breath. "How will I explain all this to my dad?"

***

Quila swam as fast as she could back to the Anchor, dreading the moment of facing everyone there and trying to keep her emotions out of her expression. She pressed a hand to her chest, trying to push away the hurt that had taken root there since leaving the man on the beach.

Stop it!

Why did I kiss him? Holy moon, what is wrong with me?

She thought of her mother. She forced herself to imagine her struggling and terrified as the human divers pulled her from the ocean. The horror and pain of it. She tried to call up anger and hatred for the man she'd just saved. "You cannot feel this way about a human," she told herself. "You should have let him die."

What did I do?!

No one can ever know.

Quila's stomach turned, and she felt cold all over. In the black ocean ahead of her she saw a figure swimming her way. A bolt of worry moved through her before she realized it was her best friend, Daria. "Quila! That you?" she called out over the distance between them.

"It's me." Quila slowed as Daria came close. Her friend reached out, and Quila let her take her into a hug. Daria had pearly white hair and big friendly eyes, and her tail matched her hair exactly, a rare and gorgeous combination.

"I came to the Anchor just after it happened," Daria said in a concerned rush. "No one could find you. I've been looking all over. Are you all right?"

Quila pulled back, relieved at the sight of a friend. Daria's mother, Sedna, had worked in the palace archives. Sedna and Elara had been close friends until around the time of Daria's birth, only a few weeks before Quila's. When Quila asked why the friendship had ended and why Sedna left the archives, Mayar had grown quiet and said only, "They had a serious disagreement." Sedna lived a solitary life on the outskirts of the village. Quila had only vague memories of her friend's mom; she hadn't seen Sedna in years. Strange rumors circulated about her and the way she lived withdrawn from everyone. But Daria had always been there; Quila felt closer to her than to her own sisters.

"Do you know what happened?" Quila asked.

Daria shook her head. "Not sure. Your dad said something about the moonstone."

Quila bit her bottom lip. "I need to get back."

"Wait!" Daria held her arm as Quila tried to swim away. Daria searched her face. "Something else is wrong. What happened?"

Quila shook her head. "Nothing."

Daria lifted one eyebrow in her signature *I know when you're lying* look. She fisted her hands to her hips. "Tell me. It'll take two seconds. Then we can go."

Quila pressed a hand to her knotted stomach. She badly wanted to tell Daria, to ask for some advice. *This is dangerous information. I shouldn't tell anyone. But I tell her everything.* Quila met Daria's expectant gaze. "I rescued a human," she blurted out before she could stop herself.

Daria's large eyes opened to their widest. For a tense moment, she said nothing. "Okay. So maybe we need a little more than two seconds."

"Not now, though. I *have* to get back. I have to fix the Anchor before the tides get too far off schedule."

Daria nodded. "Yes, right. But after that . . ."

"I'll tell you everything."

The girls raced back. As the Anchor came into view, Quila tried to shake off her feelings and bury them deep.

"Quila! Where have you been?" Mayar yelled out as soon as he saw her. He was huddled with her sisters, close to the edge of the Anchor. Her sisters' eyes were wide with worry.

"I got pushed so far," she answered, hoping her voice didn't sound as shaky as it felt. "And I blacked out. I came as fast as I could. Did the moonstone collapse?"

Get to work. Solve this problem. Forget the human man.

"Yes, unfortunately." Her father frowned. "A huge section in the center. I sent Hala back to alert the miners. Titan and new stone will be here soon." Titan was the Anchor's engineer. He managed and cared for the structure and moonstone.

Quila nodded as she moved forward to put her hand on the Anchor. She closed her eyes to listen to its song. "The tides are slowing. We need to hurry or the rhythm will have a hard time catching up. I'll sing until the stone comes."

"Very good. That will help." Mayar looked at the ancient device. He shook his head. "I've only heard stories about this happening. It's so rare."

"I did not feel that the stone was so weak. Did I make a mistake?"

He shook his head. "No, I'm certain you didn't."

"Then . . . what happened?" Quila caught her father's eyes, her worry transmitting through her expression.

Mayar sighed. "I wish I knew. But it will be all right. Fixed in no time." His expression didn't hold the same conviction as his words. "Tell me what you felt right before the collapse."

Quila frowned. "It happened so fast. There was just this . . . pulse of energy. Like a twinge in a muscle. I knew something was wrong, but beyond that . . . And then the explosion." She shrugged.

Mayar put a hand on her shoulder. "You couldn't have prevented this. Sometimes things just go wrong."

Quila nodded, trying to convince herself of the same. "We will fix it," Quila reassured them all. "It'll be fine." *Will it?* She had no idea if it would, but this was her job as full moon sister, as queen: to reassure, to be strong, no matter how she felt. She turned to her sisters, who watched her with expectant eyes. "Come sing with me, please. We need to help the Anchor until it's restored."

"Why is Daria here?" Deva asked, petulant. "She's not supposed to be here. No civilians during Anchor rituals. Especially not ones with crazy mothers who were banished from the palace." She eyed the other mermaid.

Daria's expression flickered with hurt, but she answered coolly. "Quila asked me to be here," Daria answered, voice low but authoritative.

Deva scoffed. "Oh please. What can *you* do?"

"Stop it, Deva!" Quila cut in, holding back an annoyed sigh. "Daria is always welcome, and you know it. Now, get to your place, *please.*" *Sedna was banished?* Quila had never heard that particular rumor. But she didn't have time to wonder about that now. She headed to her place at the head of the Anchor.

Deva huffed, her eyes dark with angry jealousy, but she went as commanded. The sisters sang to the Anchor. Quila felt the moon reach back in response, bolstering the ancient device to continue its eternal job of pulling the ocean in and out. As she sang, Quila tried to calm the pull of her own emotions.

Everything is fine. Everything is fine.

I'll make sure it is.

***

Anson lugged his gear up to the Portland Head Light ignoring the wide-eyed looks of camera-happy tourists. The late-summer sun beat down on him, his dry suit too thick for the heat. He stomped into the foyer of the attached house area, sweating and huffing, and faced the white-haired woman behind the desk. "Need your radio," was all he could manage through his bruised-rib, too-hot breathing. The old woman blinked at him, taking in his gear, his welts, and his ragged breathing. After a moment, she sprang up from her seat. "Come over here, you poor thing. Sit, sit. Radio is right there. Are you okay?"

Anson dropped his tanks and fins to the wood floor with a loud clank. He shuffled to the chair she indicated. "Water, please," he huffed. She scrambled to fetch him a water bottle from a small fridge under her desk. He mumbled his thanks, took the bottle, and drained it in a few hard swallows. Her eyes went wider and full of questions. Anson turned away from her to the radio. He picked up the microphone and adjusted the frequency. "Zephyr come in, Zephyr come in. This is Anson ... from Portland Head Light" He released the talk button and listened to the static.

"This is Zephyr. Anson, what the *hell*?" Robert Lacey's deep pirate voice answered.

"Had some trouble."

Static hissed. Anson could almost hear his father ranting to the crew, wondering why his son had screwed up a perfectly normal dive. "What's your status?" came the curt reply.

"Gear intact. No bends." The mermaid's face filled his mind. He imagined telling his father about how he'd been rescued by a gorgeous mermaid. A small, desperate laugh came out of him; it sent bolts of pain through his battered torso. He glanced back at the lighthouse tour guide who stood behind him, hands clasped anxiously and brow furrowed. He rubbed at his forehead, taking a slow breath to quell the little pulse of hysteria. He pushed the talk button. "Just need a ride home," he added evenly.

"Ten-four. We're headed back now. Stay put. Anson . . . ?"

"Yes, sir?"

"Did you find it?"

Anson let out a long sigh before answering. "No, sir."

No reply came. Anson turned off the radio and leaned his elbow into the desk, fighting the urge to lay his head down and fall asleep. He heard the old woman moving behind him before a napkin holding two large chocolate chip cookies was thrust under his nose. He looked up, offered a weak smile of thanks, and took the food. "Okay if I wait here?" he asked.

"Of course, yes. You sure you don't need an ambulance? Your poor skin and—"

"No, ma'am," he cut her off. Anson dropped from the chair to the floor to lean against the wall and spread out his legs.

"I, uh . . . did you say the *Zephyr*?" she asked.

Anson looked up, all too familiar with that tone of awe. He resisted the urge to growl with annoyance. "Yes."

"That's Robert Lacey's boat, right?" The woman grinned. "My husband is a *big* fan. He's followed Robert's career from the beginning. Who are you? You said Anson, right? Isn't that . . . ?"

Anson took a big bite of cookie to delay answering. He swallowed hard. "Anson Lacey."

"Oh wow! Yes, the son!" The woman crossed to her chair. She was dressed in khaki capris and a white blouse. Her gray hair was stylishly short, her makeup simple. "Were you with him when he found the *Princessa*? I've read all about Prince Miguel— what a life! I'd love to have a piece of his dinner china. That pattern is gorgeous, isn't it? Your dad has several pieces, if I remember."

Anson groaned inwardly. He did *not* have the energy for this. "Yes, I was there."

She shook her head. "Amazing. Just amazing. I can't believe you men do *that*. So deep, so dangerous. Is the narcosis as bad as they say?"

"Worse," he mumbled through a full mouth. *It makes you see mermaids and not know how you escaped certain death.* He closed his eyes, hoping the woman would allow him some peace.

She didn't.

"So you must have been diving just now. How did you end up *here*?"

"Just got off course on my return. Lost the anchor line."

She hummed sympathetically. Anson kept his eyes closed, feeling sleep creeping into his body. He let his arms drop to his sides. As he drifted, Anson felt the mermaid's lips on his. He saw the look of concern and anxiety in her eyes. He missed her, an unexpected longing filling his heart.

Are you real? I want you to be real. How do I find you?

Stop it! She's not real. And even if she were . . .

Just stop it.

Anson pushed his mind to more practical matters. Like the story he would tell his father when he arrived. The anchor line thing was good. *Yeah, that will work. A weird change in the currents, no viz, and no anchor line. Maybe it shifted and I couldn't find it.*

Yeah, that's good.

Anson's body felt heavier now. Sleep overtook him.

Anson woke with a start. Had it been one second or one hour? Two faces were pushed close to his. One with glasses, one without. The one without said, "Sir, wake up? Sir, can you open your eyes? Ah, there you are!"

Anson took in the faces, the blue uniforms, and rubber gloves. And swore like a pirate. The glasses-wearing paramedic laughed. "Seems okay to me."

Anson pushed away their hands. "I'm fine. I'm fine."

"Mrs. Lucas here thought you'd died on her," No Glasses said.

Anson looked over the paramedic's shoulder to the old woman. He wanted to scowl at her but offered a weak smile instead. "Really, I'm fine. Just fell asleep."

"You have welts all over your skin. Can you tell me where you got those?"

"I was diving. That's what I do. I deep-sea dive."

"He got lost," Mrs. Lucas chimed in.

Anson frowned deeply. "Could you just"—he took a breath, not wanting to give in to the urge to punch both men and shove his way out of the lighthouse—"back off. I'm fine. Seriously. Just a rough ascent."

"Any pain in your legs? Cramping? Headaches?"

"No, no bends. I'm *fine!*"

"What's going on?" At the booming sound of his father's voice, Anson closed his eyes. *And here we go.* Robert arrived behind the medics, who turned to look up at the six-foot-five muscle-thick form of Robert Lacey. Anson opened his eyes and saw the automatic admiration in theirs.

Glasses decided to answer. "This man has an elevated heart rate, low pulse ox, and unknown injuries on his skin. Possible bends from diving. Who are you?"

Robert Lacey smiled, charming and rugged, with his neatly trimmed black beard and shiny bald head. "Boys, this is my son, Anson Lacey, and I'm Robert. We are deep-sea divers. It's a rough sport, but I *promise* you, he's fine. All that is normal after a dive."

The recognition came. "Oh wow. You the guys that go into ships like five hundred feet down?" No Glasses—obviously the dumber one.

Robert smiled, indulgent. "Only about two fifty, actually. Hard on the body but we are professionals. I'm gonna take Anson home. You boys can head out."

The paramedics stood, Anson now mostly forgotten. "You're sure?" Glasses asked.

"Yep, yep. Sure thing. Thanks for coming. Appreciate it." Robert shook both their hands and urged them out the door. Anson knew he hadn't inherited that aura of authority. No one listened to him like that. Not rookie divers they took out for first dives, not his only serious girlfriend, who'd told him he was too in love with the ocean to love her, and not even servers at restaurants who constantly brought him the wrong dish. He wondered—as he did often—if he were more like his mother. Was she shy and introverted, quiet and reserved? Robert refused to talk about Anson's mother. Anson didn't know if she was alive or dead, didn't know what she looked like, where she was from. He didn't even know her name.

When the medics were gone, Robert squatted next to Anson. "What happened?" he voice was low, so Mrs. Lucas couldn't eavesdrop.

"A strange current came though. I lost the anchor line. Came up offshore here." Anson held his breath, hoping his dad bought his story.

Robert nodded thoughtfully. "What's all over your skin?" He grimaced as he bent closer to inspect the marks.

"Not really sure," Anson answered honestly.

"Maybe broken blood vessels from the narcosis? Kind of weird looking, though." Robert shrugged. "Too bad about the clock." He met his son's eyes, the disappointment there behind his gray irises.

Anson swallowed his anger. "Yeah, too bad."

CHAPTER 4

The moonstone miners worked late into the night to restore the broken stone. All the dead stone had to be removed and the new placed together perfectly. Titan supervised with an astute eye. Quila was there every moment, watching the delicate work and listening to the Anchor. Her sisters had long since retreated to the palace. Even her father had covered a yawn and then slipped away to bed. At least Daria had refused to leave.

Quila looked back toward her home, to the palace and her cozy bedroom. She was tired but knew it was better to stay at the Anchor. *I couldn't sleep tonight anyway.*

She thanked the miners, eager to be alone with Daria. The workers gathered their tools and began to leave. Titan lingered, inspecting a small piece of the dead stone. Quila went to him. "What's wrong, Titan?" He'd been the engineer for nearly one hundred years. His body was lean from hard work, and his eyes were deeply lined from his jovial smile. But he wasn't smiling now.

"See this mark here?" He held out the section of stone, no bigger than a pebble. He ran his finger over a barely noticeable white line. "That looks wrong to me."

"Wrong how?"

"When the stone ruptures, the lines are jagged, erratic. There are no straight lines after a moonstone failure. But that . . ." He traced the line again. "Almost looks cut."

Quila suppressed a shiver. "What does it mean?"

Titan shook his head, brow furrowed. "I don't know."

"Would a mark like that *cause* the stone to fail?"

"Unlikely. There are imperfections in all the stones." He sighed. "Maybe I'm overreacting. It's just . . ."

"What?" Quila moved a little closer, her stomach tense.

"That stone should *not* have failed."

Quila pressed her teeth together. *I knew it.* She took a steadying breath. "Could someone do this to the stone? Could they sabotage it by cutting it?"

He thought for a moment, turned the pebble over in his palm. "I don't see how. The Anchor is designed to be impervious to harm. Someone with your abilities, *maybe*. Magic might be able to harm the stone. But still . . ." His sea-green eyes met hers. "Not that I'm saying you would—"

She lifted a hand. "I know. Thank you, Titan." She held out her hand. "I'll take that."

He shifted the suspect rock to her keeping and cleared his throat. "I'm sorry to ask this now, but . . . have you found my replacement yet?"

Titan had asked to retire months ago, ready to pass on the hefty responsibilities and take his wife off to tropical waters. Quila sighed, "No one is as good as you. Many of the miners are capable and knowledgeable, but I'm not sure they have your instincts, your creativity, and your sharp eye."

Titan smiled warmly. "I appreciate that but . . ."

"Don't worry, Titan. I promise to find someone soon."

"Thank you. Goodnight, my Queen." Titan left, leaving Quila and Daria alone.

Quila looked down at the pebble in her hand, worry twisting in her gut. *What do I do now, Mom?*

"Okay," Daria said as she approached. "Tell all, please."

Quila sighed, rolled her neck against the tension built up in her muscles. "I really shouldn't tell you."

"Of course not. I'll just leave, then."

Quila looked up at her friend's playful smile and laughed, and a tiny sliver of tension left her. "You know, I was totally joking before. Why would I do something that crazy?"

"Ha ha, funny joke. And here I was hoping you'd actually rescued a human and could entertain me with the whole juicy story."

Quila laughed again, but the sound cut off short. "What did I do, Daria?"

"I don't know. You still haven't told me."

Quila quickly told her friend the story. She finished with "Maybe that shock wave damaged my head."

"Totally possible. And likely," Daria agreed. "Unless it didn't. Then . . ."

"Yeah."

They were quiet for a moment. Then Daria said, her voice gentle, "My mom told me a story once of a mermaid who fell in love with a human. The story doesn't end well."

Quila scoffed lightly. "Of course it doesn't. And I'm not falling in love with him. I just . . ." She looked at the Anchor, its hum loud and steady now. There were a few hours until high tide. She should rest but knew sleep would be impossible. She lifted her chin. The surface was so far away, and yet its call to her felt intolerably loud.

It's not just the surface.

It's him.

Daria went on, "Remember when we used to pretend we were humans? And how romantic it would be to fall in love with a human man, live on the surface? You felt compelled to rescue him. That's not insignificant. There must be a reason."

"Yes, but it doesn't make sense. And this isn't some make-believe game. I'm the queen. I can't . . ." She wanted to know if the diver was all right. She wanted to ask him about why he'd been searching a deadly ship. She wanted to make sure he remembered her and didn't think her some illusion. She wanted to kiss him again.

Gripping the stone tightly in her hand, Quila fought the urge to swim upward.

"You should go," Daria whispered.

Quila jerked her head down to look at her friend. "What? No!"

Daria coolly shrugged her shoulders. "How are you supposed to know what to do unless you find out more? I know it's forbidden, but how can you ignore this? And you're the queen, Quila. If anyone can bend the rules it's you, right?"

Quila looked back up to the far-off surface.

He won't be there.

Stay where you belong.

But what if he was there? What if he wanted to see her as much as she wanted to see him?

"I'll go with you. I've been dying to see the surface for as long as I can remember."

No one will know. Quila shook her head. "I can't."

"You could."

I'll just go up and back, fast. Quickly. No big deal.

"You'll help me?" Quila met her friend's gaze.

"That's what I'm here for." She smiled. "That and to make Deva as jealous as possible. My goal is to make her so mad at me that her head explodes and messes up that perfect hair."

Quila laughed. Daria could always make her laugh. "Super fast?"

"As fast as we can, my Queen." Daria grinned, knowing Quila hated when she called her by her official title.

Quila took a big breath and nodded. "Let's go."

She flicked her tail and sent herself rocketing up to the surface. She didn't stop until her head thrust up into the nighttime air. Floating on the surface, she looked toward the black-stone beach and the white tower. The lighthouse beamed a bright light over the water, swinging around and around. There were smaller lights dotting the surrounding land, like glowing plankton.

And above her, the moon.

Quila gasped. She'd only ever seen the moon in carvings and drawings. This thing that controlled her whole life, that commanded her destiny, and she'd never seen it with her own eyes until now. *It's beautiful.* It was waning crescent, a thin curve of white, nearly the same shade as Daria's hair and tail. Daria bobbed next to her, her eyes locked on the sky too.

"It's bright and soft all at once, like the inside of a clam," Quila said, awestruck. Daria nodded silently. Hanging in the sky, enchanting and astounding, the moon was like nothing Quila had seen in the sea. She lifted her hand as if to touch it, outlining its shape.

A pulse of energy throbbed in her chest. A response from the moon.

Then another pulse of energy, much different.

She lowered her head to follow the feeling to the beach. Her capable eyes found him easily, sitting on the terraced black stone. Sitting there alone, in the dark, and staring out at her ocean.

He's here.

Oh no, he's here.

"He's here." Daria whispered. "You have to go over there. Romance demands it."

"This isn't about romance."

"Well, whatever it's about, you better go find out."

Quila hesitated, unable to send herself forward. "I can't. I can't do it, Daria."

***

Anson could not think of one logical reason to be sitting here on Portland Head. Not one. And he liked logical reasons, such as torque and currents and buoyancy and rate of decay. These were logical things that occurred in diving and broken ships. One thing happened to cause another thing, and if you knew about those things, you could figure stuff out, solve problems. Logic and reason and knowledge. But *this* . . . waiting for the impossible chance of an imaginary mermaid appearing in the middle of the night . . .

I've gone insane.

The narcosis ruined my brain—permanently.

He had tried to go to sleep; he needed it badly. After he'd escaped the lighthouse and his father, he'd hurried home to shower and crash. He'd been lying in his bed wanting nothing more than the relief of sleep, when the moonlight had slipped through a crack in his blinds. The light cut across his bed near his face, and suddenly the idea was there in his mind: *Go wait for her. She'll come to you.* Before he realized it, he was carving through the sleepy streets on the 1939 Harley-Davidson Knucklehead Bobber he'd painstakingly restored.

"Yep, full-on nuts. That's me," he said aloud now, shaking his head.

Movement in the waves cut off his self-depreciating thoughts. He leaned forward over his crossed legs, sucking in an anxious breath.

No, nope. Not a mermaid. Just waves.

Please be just waves . . .

The mermaid's graphite-dark head emerged from the water. Her eyes found his instantly, and then he wasn't breathing at all. She held his gaze for a long moment, water dripping down her face. Smoothly, she eased herself out of the water to sit on the stones only a few feet in front of him. The waves lapped over her blue tail. She tugged at her hair as if anxious, rearranging it over her small breasts. A flash of heat moved though him and he purposefully lifted his eyes to her face. Anson felt he should say something—they'd been silently staring at each other for far too long—but what could he say?

Finally, she was the first to speak, voice quiet, sensually low, "Are you all right?"

Her genuine concern made his chest ache. His own father hadn't asked that question. Anson swallowed hard. "Yes, I'm okay."

Her eyes roamed over his face, curious. "Good. I was worried."

"You were?" he asked. She dropped her eyes and looked away, sweetly shy. Anson wanted to move closer, to hook her chin with his finger and bring her eyes back to him. She shifted on the rocks, and he worried she would leave. "Thank you," he said to keep her attention. "I don't know how you did it but . . .

thank you." She turned back, nodded. He noticed that her chest was heaving. He moved closer. "Are *you* okay?"

"It's much harder to breathe up here." She touched the area under her ear, a small flap of skin. *Gills. She has gills like a fish.* Anson blinked, then hurried to look away, not wanting to stare.

"How long can you stay?" he asked. Easing even closer. She smelled of the sea: salt and seaweed and the unknown.

"Not long. I just . . ." She shook her head. "I didn't think you'd be here."

"I didn't think I would either." He offered a smile.

She returned it, her teeth like a row of pearls. "Why did you do it?" she asked.

His brow furrowed. "Do what?"

"Come into the ocean, go in that ship, risk death."

Anson sighed. He shook his head. "For a lot of reasons, I guess. My father basically invented deep-sea diving, so I've done it all my life. And I'm good at it. It's an interesting challenge. Because . . ." She looked at him so intently that he found he couldn't give her the surface answers he gave everyone else. *Why do I dive, for real?* He thought of being under the water. "Because there's a quiet and solitude under the water that you can't get anywhere else. Because every time I get in the water I have only my body and my brain. Nothing else. It's simple, clean."

"But the danger?"

"The danger helps focus my mind. Every thought is on purpose, every movement deliberate. Diving strips away the unnecessary. Unlike real life, which is messy, overcrowded, and junky." He laughed. "Sounds dumb, I guess."

She shook her head. "No it doesn't. I think I understand. I feel that way when I sing."

"You sing?"

A blush flushed her gray cheeks. "It's a family thing."

She moved her tail lazily in the water. He wanted to touch her icy-blue scales, make them real with his hands. He thought of her kiss, and his eyes came to her lips. "Your name?" he whispered. "What's your name?"

"Quila." Her low, quiet voice sent a shiver through him. "And you?" she asked.

"Anson."

She repeated his name slowly, the expression on her face changing.

"What is it?" he asked.

"I should go." She turned away from him to look at the sea.

This time he didn't resist touching her. His hand came to her upper arm, a gentle grip. "Not yet. Please. Just a few more minutes." The cool texture of her skin under his palm made his whole body flush with heat. He looked at his tan hand on her gray flesh. *So different. So . . . unreal.*

She looked down at his hand, half smiled. "A few more."

He nodded, relieved. "This is also gonna sound dumb, but . . . you are *real*, right? I'm not imagining all this?" He let his hand trail down her arm to rest on the back of her hand.

She shook her head. "My people are careful to avoid contact with yours. It's better if we remain a story to you."

"But then . . . why did you help me?"

"I . . . I'm not really sure. I shouldn't have. It's forbidden."

Anson blinked in shock, his gratitude increasing, but with it a sense of apprehension. "I'm sorry. But you're safe with me. I'm good with secrets." He smiled. "Mainly 'cause I don't have any friends. So who am I gonna tell?"

She gave a little laugh that sent a tremor through him. "It's just . . . I have certain responsibilities," she added. "To my family, my people. If anyone found out . . . ," she sighed, her eyes moving to the moon.

There was weight in her words that he understood without knowing the details. He felt the same kind of obligation to the Lacey diving legacy. "I get that. My dad is a piece of work. He'd lock me away if I even mentioned the word *mermaid*." He shook his head, pushing thoughts of Robert Lacey out of his mind. "I'm sorry you risked so much for me."

"I think the ship collapsed on you because of what happened with the Anchor. The shock wave—" Her eyes widened, the words clamped off. She pulled her hand away from his.

"The Anchor?" he prompted. She shook her head. Her breathing was worse now. When she wouldn't answer him, Anson shifted to the edge of the rocks, pushing off to drop into the cold water. He grimaced at the slap of icy water, his jeans sucking close to his skin and his boots filling with water. The area was just deep enough to stand in. He smiled at her confused look. "You need to breathe. Come on." He waved her into the water. She eased in with a grace he never hoped to match. Her head went under for a moment. *Don't leave. Please. Not yet.* She bobbed back to the surface, a tentative smile. "Better?" he asked.

"Yes, but your clothes. And it's so cold."

"I'll be okay for a few minutes." His gaze met hers, their faces only about a foot apart now. "I gotta ask about the eye color thing." Anson moved a little closer, the waves helping to push his body to Quila. "Why do we have the same color eyes? That's weird, right?"

"Very weird." Her hand lifted from the water. She traced a finger along his brow line, leaving a cold trail of water as she intently looked at his eyes. "Do other humans have it?"

"Not that I've met." He shook his head. "People have made a big deal of my eyes my whole life—because it's so different."

"All my people have this color. I never thought of a human having it too. So strange."

Anson shivered, unsure if it was the cold water or her answer. "So I have mermaid eyes?" He tried to make it a joke.

She understood his humor. "*Moon* mermaid eyes. That's different than regular mermaid. More rare." She smiled as she pulled her hand away.

"Moon mermaids? Sounds mysterious. What's the difference?"

She bit her lower lip briefly. "We help the tides."

Anson nodded at her clipped, vague answer, knowing he wouldn't get more than that. "And what do regular mermaids do?"

"Swim with dolphins and polish their tails."

Anson had to laugh at the condescension and superiority in her tone. "Wow. Tell me how you really feel."

Quila offered a sly smile. "We aren't really friends."

"Yeah, I got that." Anson laughed again. A shiver moved though him; his legs felt a little numb from the water.

"You're cold."

Anson wished he weren't, wished he could hold off the shivering, but without a dry suit his body couldn't handle the icy Maine waters. "Yeah, but I'm fine."

She laughed. "Then why are your teeth chattering?"

"This is t-t-totally n-n-normal."

Quila laughed louder, and for a moment Anson wasn't cold. But soon the smile left her face. "I should go anyway. I've stayed too long. It'll be high tide soon."

"I want you to stay," Anson said quietly.

Quila brought her cool, wet palm to his cheek, like she had when he woke up on the beach earlier that day. He pressed it there with his own hand again, savoring her touch. "I'm glad you're okay," she said.

"Meet me again?"

"No, I can't."

"Yes you can."

"I shouldn't."

"But you want to?"

She sighed, her breath shaky. "It doesn't matter what I want," she whispered.

"So I'll never see you again."

"It's for the best. We are . . . too different."

She was right. Anson felt reality slap him across the face. What was the point of meeting her again? What future could they have? This wasn't a first date with a great girl. This was . . . *What is this?* The cold in his body sunk deeper. "I understand, Quila. Thank you again. I owe you."

"Please be careful when you dive, Anson."

He nodded, feeling a rush of anger or sadness or . . . *something* he couldn't quite identify. Quila moved to swim away, but he gripped her upper arm. "If I'm never gonna see you again . . ." He pulled her body back to his and found her lips. A small gasp escaped her mouth, her breath teasing his. Then she met his urgent passion. Her slick body melded against his. He'd never felt such a fiery connection come from a kiss. Her lips hot against his, a little taste of tongue. A whirlwind in his head. The waves pulsed against their bodies, urging the kiss to go deeper. Quila's hand moved over his buzzed hair and then gripped his neck with solid strength. His own arms locked around her slender waist.

Abruptly, Quila broke the kiss. Her hands came to his chest and shoved hard. Anson hit the shore with a painful grunt, dazed and reeling. She dove away from him, gone in half a second.

CHAPTER 5

Quila sliced though the water, her speed pulling the tears off her cheeks as fast as they fell. Every part of her felt scorched and wasted. She felt the pull of the Anchor and the pull of Anson equally strong, in opposite directions. She was certain she'd tear in half before she reached home.

The strength of his arms around her, muscles flexed with the effort of keeping her so close. The hunger in his kiss, lips so warm. The pleasant scratch of his unshaved chin. His smell—so many scents she didn't know.

What did I do? Holy moon, what did I do?

"Quila, stop!" Daria called from behind, her swimming speed no match for Quila's. "Stop! Please."

Quila didn't want to stop. If she stopped she'd have to tell Daria what had happened. She felt as if describing those blissful moments with Anson might change her forever. And not in a good way.

What do I do now? I don't know how to feel, what to think.

That kiss may have broken me.

Though she didn't want to, Quila slowed. Huffing for breath, Daria stopped beside her. "I really . . . hate that you can . . . swim faster . . . than me." Daria took a deep breath to steady her talking. "*What* happened?"

Quila hugged her arms tightly around her. "I told you I shouldn't have gone."

"Why not? Come on, details!"

"We . . . talked. It was so easy to talk to him. He's funny. And then . . ."

"And then . . . ?"

Quila grunted. "He kissed me, Daria."

Her best friend's eyes went wide. "Holy moon!" she whispered, drawing out the words slowly. "Well, that is . . . unexpected." She blinked a few times before her signature humor came back to her face. "Did you want him to kiss you? Is he kissable?"

Quila winced. "Yes."

"Wow. A human kiss—was it as good as a mermaid kiss? Better? It had to be better than Orca when we were thirteen. He was *awful*." She made a face.

Quila allowed herself a little smile at the memory of her first kiss. Both their first kisses, actually. Orca, a boy their same age, scrawny and too confident for his own good, had offered to kiss them both. Just so they could all know what the big deal was with kissing. Laughing, the girls had accepted, as curious as he was.

Quila gave a small laugh at the memory. "That was like kissing the side of a whale."

"Right. Exactly! *So* gross." Daria smiled, her eyes soft. "But this time . . . ?"

"Not the side of a whale."

"Encouraging."

"No, bad. So bad. It was like"—Quila shivered at the memory—"seeing the moon for the first time tonight. Only ten times *better*."

Daria sighed. "You're right. No good. Can't have that."

The girls sat in silence for a moment. Daria spoke next, "What did his neck feel like? They don't have gills—that's so weird."

"I was too busy touching his short hair. It's like algae on the coral but . . . rougher."

Daria hummed her fascinated acknowledgment. "Maybe we should go talk to my mom. She might know what to do."

Quila looked over in surprise. "Really? I mean, will she see me? And how could she help?"

"She studied humans while she worked in the archives," Daria explained. "She's only told me a few things here and there, but I can tell she knows more." Daria lowered her eyes. "I know the rumors. I know what people say, and I'll be the first to admit that she's . . . eccentric, but if you want some advice, she's the best person I can think of. Unless, of course, you want to go to Mayar."

Quila winced. "No way. Since Mom he's become so bitter. He'd never understand."

Daria shrugged. "I think my mom would. She's been through a lot."

"Did she tell you what happened between her and my mom?"

"No, not really. She said they were like sisters, so close before the fight. She said Elara did something she could never forgive but refuses to say what exactly. And even though they hadn't been friends for so long, she told me it was horrible to be the one to find Elara's body that night."

Quila flinched at her own memories of that dark night. She saw clearly in her mind Sedna approaching the palace, Elara's body in her arms. The queen had a black belt around her waist, a human diver's weight belt, and there was a fatal injury to her head. Quila remembered the blood floating around her mother's head, a morbid crown. Sedna had quietly laid Elara at Mayar's feet. "I found her not far from my home. She was already dead."

Mayar, his face pale with shock and anger, asked, "You *found* her?"

"Yes, Mayar. I had no hand in this."

And then Sedna swam away. Quila had wanted to go after her, ask for more. Demand an explanation. But the shock had her frozen at her father's side, looking down at her dead mother.

Quila nodded now, a strange desire to see Sedna growing in her chest. "Okay. If you think she can help . . ."

"I *hope* she can."

"Then let's go."

***

Anson swam back and forth along the shore for half an hour. Hoping Quila would come back, hoping he could figure out where she'd gone. But all he discovered was just how cold he could get before he wanted to throw up.

Shivering badly, he climbed out of the water and collapsed on the rock. Huffing for breath and gritting his teeth against the cold in his bones, Anson thought only of her body pressed to his. He thought of the handful of girls he'd dated since high school and couldn't even find enough to compare to Quila. His body had reacted to her in a way he hadn't even known existed. So completely, with a wild sense of freedom. So powerful.

Like the pull of the moon on the tides.

He shook his head at the comparison, thinking of how she'd said her people help the tides. He didn't know what that meant, but he knew she had worked some magic on him. He lifted his head to look back at the waves.

Maybe it's like those sirens. She did mention singing. Maybe she put me under some twisted spell . . . ?

He let his head drop. No, he didn't want to think there was anything suspicious in her actions or false in his feelings. Because it felt like the most real thing he'd ever experienced. As real as the first time he dove below the two-hundred-feet mark and the world had changed forever.

Anson knew he needed to get warm or risk hypothermia but couldn't bring himself to move yet. Plus his bike felt a million miles away. Real life felt a million miles away.

Maybe I'm not really here.

Maybe I'm dreaming, asleep in my bed.

But the nonstop shivering told him he was very much awake. And Quila's kiss had been agonizingly real.

What do I do now?

"Nothing. I should do nothing," he whispered, teeth knocking against each other. *She's a freakin' mermaid. There's nothing I can do but forget this ever happened.*

Anson sat up. His chest ached at the thought of never seeing her again. Despite logic, he had to find her. If there was one thing he was good at it was solving a problem in order to find something. He had a good boat and a lifetime of experience diving the ocean. And he could find things no one else could.

But first I gotta not die from this cold.

Anson lunged for his leather biker jacket, which he'd left higher on the beach earlier in the night. Shaking, he managed to get it on. Then he forced himself to walk back to his bike, rubbing at his chest to get some heat back. The movement helped, and the August night air grew hotter the farther he got from the ocean breeze. The five-minute ride home helped dry out his clothes, but he was still shivering as he stumbled up the stairs to his apartment.

Straight into the hot shower, he sat on the tile floor, the water beating down on his head. When he finally felt warm, he started forming his plan to get a boat and find Quila.

Tomorrow, I will find her.

And I won't let her swim away from me.

***

A quaky sense of anticipation grew in Quila as they neared the outer edge of the village boundaries. The village wasn't large; there were only a few thousand mermaids at the North Atlantic

Anchor. Built on an old expanse of coral, the village of tiny cottages, each carved into the coral like caves, encircled the modest palace. The outside of the cottages and the palace were decorated with sea life of all kinds, a living reef inside and out.

Sedna had always felt like a phantom—this sometimes real, sometimes not real person who floated outside normal existence. Quila knew Sedna had once been very important to Elara and to the archives. Quila had wanted to see Sedna many times over the years to beg her for stories about her mom. But her father had told her to stay away. He had, almost harshly, made her promise not to ask Sedna anything about Elara. *"She's dangerous, Quila. Please listen to me about this. I need you to stay away from her."*

"But Daria . . ."

"I'm not talking about Daria. We've always welcomed your friendship. She shouldn't be punished for what Sedna did."

Quila had sensed the weight of responsibility and shame in her father. *"What did she do?"*

"Never ask me that. I cannot tell you."

Quila had kept that promise. But now, she wondered if she could resist asking Sedna a question or two.

There were whispered rumors that Sedna had gone insane. That she spent all her time pulling at her hair and mumbling words no one understood. Some said she stayed in her cottage because she'd gone bald. Some said finding Elara's body had made her paranoid to swim in open water. Some said they saw her swimming away from the village in the darkest hours of night.

Quila glanced over at her friend. For Daria's sake she hoped that it was all just gossip. A punch of guilt hit Quila in the chest. *I never ask Daria about it. I pretend like her mother doesn't exist while I constantly wallow in grief for my own. Does she hate me a little for that? Do I hate her a little because her mom got so much time with mine?*

Daria slowed outside a tiny coral cottage set apart from all the others, isolated on the rocky edge of the reef. She looked at the entrance, not Quila. "There's nothing wrong with Mom. She avoids everyone because they ask her about Elara; they look at her like it was her fault. But she's not . . . It wasn't . . . ." Daria's expression closed down, her face pinched.

"I know, Daria. It's okay." Quila hoped her friend heard the apology and empathy in her tone.

Daria nodded. "Follow me."

They swam forward and ducked through the round opening. The space beyond was dim, cramped. Quila's eyes quickly adjusted, but her mind was slow to make sense of what she saw. Hung from the ceiling were hundreds of stark white bones. Strung from thick bands of seaweed, eerily swaying with the soft current. Bones everywhere. Not mermaid bones. Mermaid bones were thin and light. These dense, thick bones could only be human.

Quila only barely managed to hold back a grunt of disgust. *Daria lives* here?!

Daria finally turned to her. "I told you she knows about humans." She gave a sad, embarrassed quirk of a smile.

Quila swallowed. "Where did it all come from?" she whispered.

"Shipwrecks. I have a thing for broken ships."

Quila felt a chill move through her as she turned to see Sedna hovering behind her. There was *nothing* decrepit or twisted about her, as rumor suggested. Instead, she was surprisingly gorgeous, catch-your-breath vibrant, and deeply intimidating. Sedna's sleek black hair flowed in waves nearly as long as her body. Her tail was the same white as her daughter's, long and lean. She wore a thumb-size stone around her neck, half-white and half-black, hung from a thin metal chain. Her bright, intelligent eyes took in Quila in one quick look that left Quila uneasy and self-conscious.

Sedna swam closer. "Hello, Quila. You look very much like your mother did at this age. Though she had more . . . confidence, I think. Much more *arrogance*. Tell me, do you enjoy being queen?"

Something in the way she said this made Quila's stomach twist. She chose to ignore the poignant question. "Hello, Sedna," she answered, hoping her voice sounded more confident than she felt. Sedna's sly smile told Quila that Sedna saw past her poised façade. "I hope it's okay that Daria brought me here. I . . . uh . . . have a problem."

Sedna hummed, intrigued. She lifted her hand and ran it across a line of bones. They knocked together: *thunk thunk thunk* in the heavy water. "And you think I can help? Why?"

Quila hesitated, wary. Daria gave her an encouraging nod. "It involves humans," Quila said. Her gaze flicked to the bones.

Sedna hummed again, moving slowly closer to Quila. "Did you know a human body has two hundred and six bones in it? We have only one hundred fifty. They have so much ... *stuff* inside them. And when they drown in a ship, *every*thing washes away or is eaten away except those bones." Sedna caressed a lower jawbone, teeth still intact.

Quila shivered. *I shouldn't have come here.* She looked back at the door, wondering how she could gracefully escape. Sedna ran a finger down Quila's arm, jerking her attention back. "You're in love with one of them, aren't you?"

Quila pulled her arm away. "What? No ... I ..."

Sedna laughed, a throaty sound. "That's the only reason you'd come here. So tell me the story. Because I do have the answers." Sedna leveled her gaze on Quila, one arched black eyebrow lifted in anticipation.

Quila looked to Daria, who again nodded her encouragement. Her friend didn't look at all nervous or uneasy. So maybe Quila didn't need to be either. *But the way Sedna's looking at me ... And these bones! Maybe the rumors aren't far off.*

"She rescued a diver from a shipwreck," Daria cut in. "A man. He kissed her tonight on the beach." Quila gasped quietly, unsure whether she should thank Daria or reproach her.

Sedna blinked slowly. "A diver. Good choice. They know the ocean better than most humans."

"I shouldn't have done it. It was a mistake."

"Too late now," Sedna called out in a singsong tone. "But you don't need to be so regretful, so scared. Did you know our people used to go to the surface? That we used to talk with, laugh with, *fall in love* with the humans?"

Quila shook her head. "That's only a story. Contact has always been forbidden."

"That's what Mayar wants you to believe."

"Why would he lie about it?"

"Because his father lied to him, and his lied to him, and so forth. Back for many generations. When humans became more numerous, more prosperous, the relationship between our peoples broke down. The Mer didn't like how the humans were treating the ocean, and the humans thought themselves superior, refusing to listen. So the line was drawn. We retreated, and our historians tried to erase the past. But I found the truth many years ago, buried deep in the archives." She sneered. "Your mother knew as well."

"What?" the word barely left Quila's mouth.

"In fact, *she* was the one who granted me access to the most protected vaults. There I found the stone books, carved in the old moon language that told of Mer and human living together. In those pages we also found the magic of the New Moon Change." Sedna said these last words slowly, tantalizingly.

Quila moved involuntarily closer to the woman. "What is that?"

Sedna smiled, her eyes growing brighter. "A long, long time ago *we* were human. When the moon asked for aid with the tides, some humans volunteered and were transformed into the Mer. The moon promised our first ancestors that on the night of each new moon we could return to land."

Quila shuddered, unable to stop the excited increase of her pulse. Anson's face filled her mind. The feel of his kiss flushed her face. "Return how?"

"It's simple, really: Go onto land on the night of the new moon and your tail will transform into legs. That's the magic of the promise. You'll be fully human for that one night, sunset to sunrise." Sedna slipped closer, lowering her face near to Quila's. She trailed a cool finger down Quila's cheek. Lowering her voice, she repeated, "One night as a human, each month."

"It's new moon tomorrow," Quila whispered back. *I could go to him. I could be with him. Stand on land. With Anson. I could . . .* Sedna laughed quietly. Quila jerked away from her, logic snapping back. "No, you're lying."

She let out a short burst of a laugh. "How does it make you feel, Quila? That the man you love is a diver just like your mother's killer?"

Quila winced. *Why does Anson have to be a diver?* "He didn't kill my mother."

"True." Her face darkened for a silent moment. She looked away from Quila for the first time in a long time, moving her hands back to her bones. Touching them, twirling them.

Quila's mind spun, an eddy of conflicting emotions. Her desire to be with Anson filled her, heavy in her gut. But she was queen; she couldn't leave the Anchor for a whole night. It needed her there in order to work correctly. If she left it . . .

"Your mother did it," Sedna said, looking back at Quila through the curtain of bones.

Quila's breath froze in her gills. "What?"

"I know what you're thinking. You can't possibly leave the poor Anchor. But it's not true. Elara did it *all* the time. She *loved* going on land. We both did." Another wicked smile. "The Anchor doesn't need you every second, Quila. That's another lie you've been fed."

"My mother would not—"

"Of course she would. You don't *know* her. You don't know what she would do or not. What she *did*."

Quila recoiled from the idea. *Yes I do. But . . . no, I really don't. I don't know anything about my mother. I never got the chance.*

"I was *there*, Quila, standing on my own two *feet*, on solid land, next to Elara. Month after month." Sedna pushed through her bones, sending them swinging as she quickly came back to Quila. "So, the only question is this: *Will you try?*"

CHAPTER 6

"*Y*ou're not taking the boat."

"Yes I am."

"Nope. We got that what's-his-name executive with too much money coming this afternoon to dive the *Pontiac*. Boat needs a good scrubbing down. We didn't do the full cleanup after your . . . incident yesterday."

Anson frowned at his father. The *Pontiac* wreck was far south, not at all the direction he needed to go. "What about Louie? Is his boat available?"

Robert looked up from his morning newspaper and lifted his coffee mug to take a sip while he surveyed his son. Anson tried not to fidget under his father's astute gaze. "Why do you need a boat so bad? We're diving this afternoon."

"I want to look for that clock. I think I was close."

"You can't do that by yourself."

"I'll be fine."

"You mean like yesterday?"

Anson looked away. His father's house was a small beachfront property, furnished to be practical, not cozy. His kitchen was all no-nonsense stainless steel and open shelving. The worn round wooden table—Robert on one side, Anson on the other—had been there since Anson's birth. The only real warmth came from a small oil painting of Portland Head lighthouse behind the table. It had always been there as well, but Anson had never really looked at it until now. Quila filled his mind. *I have to find her.* He felt a jittery sense of panic about this need to find her. *Like an addict needing a fix.* He frowned at that thought. "Is Louie around or not?" he asked.

Robert shook his head. "Took a group out at dawn. Gone all day. So is Billy and Horace and Guy. It's the busy season, if you recall. We all need our boats for making money."

Anson swore under his breath.

"What's your deal, Anson?" Robert leaned his thick forearms on the table. "You don't normally get all worked up like this? You rattled?"

"I've never been rattled."

"It happens. Even to the best—"

"Stop insulting me."

Robert raised an eyebrow. "What *really* happened down there?"

"I already told you." Anson kept his eyes on the painting. The part of the beach where he'd sat with Quila was there, just on the left edge by the thin driftwood frame.

"You shouldn't dive today."

"I said, I'm *fine*."

"Yeah, I heard you. But I don't believe you. I looked at your gear last night. Never seen such a deep dent in the doubles. Strange you didn't mention the cause of *that*." Robert waited while Anson turned slowly to face him. "If I had to guess," he went on, "I'd say you were pinned. Bad. Like half a ship on top of you bad. The kind you don't swim away from."

Anson swallowed, his throat tight. He'd been too out of it last night to think of hiding his gear. "Just knocked them hard. When that current tossed me around."

"Try again."

Anson clenched his jaw. The clock above the stove ticked, filling the silence between them. He thought briefly of spilling out the truth. *Why not?* But there were at least a dozen reasons why not, least of all was his chance of getting a boat. Robert leaned back in his chair, sipped his coffee. Waiting.

Anson said nothing. His eyes slid back to the painting. His mind felt fuzzy, overloaded with the memories, emotions, and sensations of Quila in his arms. He couldn't seem to see through it to a solid lie.

Robert set down his mug. "If you dive long enough—if you're lucky to *live* long enough to dive a long time—you see things in the ocean no one else sees. You experience things no one knows about or talks about. You don't want to tell me what really happened, *fine*. But you don't dive for me until you do. And you won't dive for anyone else either. I can't put a man in the water if I don't know where his mind is at." He stood. "Think about *that* while you sit around your apartment today. Ronny will help with the rich guy."

Anson kept staring at the painting, teeth clenched, while he listened to his father leave out the back door. The clock ticked. After several long moments, Anson propped his elbows on the table and dropped his face into his hands. "What am I *doing*?" he mumbled into his palms. Diving was his whole life. He couldn't risk it over some strange (possibly imaginary) girl. *No, not girl, mermaid.* A laugh burst out of him. The idea of being kept from the ocean, from the deep waters and the mazes of wrecks, gave him a hollow sense of panic. He rubbed his face and then pulled in a big breath.

"That's enough," he said as he stood. "No more. Forget her." He went to the back door, already formulating the lie he'd tell his father to get back in his gear and back in the water. He'd help this rich guy dive the *Pontiac* and let the ocean clear his mind of Quila, the mermaid.

***

Quila kept thinking of her comfortable hammock in her room in the palace. Lovely, deep sleep. A place to escape. A place to forget. A place where she didn't have to think of walking onto land under the new moon. A prickling sense of dread, or perhaps twisted excitement, had lingered with her all day. Sedna's powerful presence and tempting revelations tugged at Quila's desires. Her lips tingled, refusing to forget Anson's kiss.

To walk with Anson on the shore, sand under my feet. Feet! To breathe freely sitting beside him on the rocks.

Quila's tail suddenly felt heavy and awkward. *To be human . . .* She looked over at the humming Anchor. "Stop it!" she hissed to herself.

"You okay?" Daria was there, hovering behind her, refusing to leave her side.

Quila looked around, checking to make sure they were alone, and then leaned in close. "What am I supposed to do? What am I supposed to believe?"

"Why would my mom lie to you?" Daria looked wounded.

Quila sighed. "No, it's not that. It's just . . . she believes one thing, and I was taught another. They can't both be true."

"You could ask your father."

"No. No I could *not*." She shook her head as she looked at her father hovering above the Anchor with Titan as they checked the function of the new moonstone.

Daria frowned. "You are queen, Quila. Mayar answers to you. If you ask him as queen—not as his daughter—he might tell you. It seems like this is stuff you need to know."

Quila bit down on the inside of her cheek. "You're right, but I just . . ."

Daria watched her intently. "You don't want him to know so he won't try to stop you."

Quila pressed the heels of her hands to her forehead. "Ugh. I don't know!"

Daria moved a little closer to put a hand on Quila's back. "Okay. So let's try it first? See if it really works. Then we can ask the big questions. I'll go with you. You know *I* want to try it. We sneak up to the surface—just like we did last night—sit on the

beach and wait. If it works"—her face lit up with a big grin—
"Quila, *if it works*! How many hours did we spend pretending to
be humans when we were little? And now we might actually be
able to do it. How can you pass that up? I mean, if it works it'll
be *amazing*. And if it doesn't"—a casual shrug—"we come back
and return to our normal mermaid lives."

Quila slowly shook her head. "But what about—"

"Questions *after* we try it, remember? I mean, really, how can
we *not* try this?" Her smile turned conspiratorial. The same smile
Quila had seen too many times during their childhood exploits.
She had to smile back.

"Okay, okay. *Fine*. But, Daria . . ."

"Yes, my Queen?"

"Not a word to *anyone*. Not even your mother. Okay?
Promise?"

Daria pressed her hands together at her heart. "I promise, my
most glorious, illustrious, beautiful Queen."

Quila slugged her in the shoulder. "I can have you sent to the
Black Sea Dungeon."

Daria's grin stayed. "Then who would get you to add a little
fun to your serious life?"

Quila's smile faded. There was too much truth in Daria's
words. Quila's life had been nothing but serious responsibility
since her mother's death. The only time she forgot about the
Anchor or enjoyed herself was when Daria came to the rescue. So
even with her trepidations banging on the door of her mind, she'd
go to the surface tonight. She'd see if Sedna's ancient magic was
real. And she'd see if Anson was waiting on the beach.

What could it hurt?

***

Robert didn't believe Anson's lie about being trapped in the entrance of the *Princessa* until a freak shifting current freed him. So Anson was slouched on his couch, a third beer in his hand. Some game show was on the TV, but his head was turned to the large picture window that faced the sea. The last splashes of pink and orange sunset faded from the sky. He was seriously thinking of drinking until he passed out so he couldn't go to Portland Head.

Alcohol is portable.

No, nope. Staying right here.

The canned applause of the game show filled the room. Anson sipped his beer. What had his father meant by all that talk about the unknown and seeing things in the ocean? Had his father seen a mermaid? Anson laughed out loud, choking on a swallow of beer. He spit it out all over his jeans. Looking down at the dark drops, he laughed again. "I am officially pathetic."

He set his beer on the hardwood floor and went to the bedroom to change. He stripped off his jeans, threw them in the hamper, and went into the bathroom. He might as well shower before drinking himself into oblivion. But on his way, he caught his reflection in the mirror. He stopped. *My eyes, her eyes.* "Why? That has to mean *something*." He leaned over the counter to look closer at his sea-green irises. These eyes had gotten him plenty of attention from women over the years. High school, college, any bar he went into now. But none of those women had made him feel like Quila did. "And she has the same eyes." He narrowed his gaze, looking closer. "Screw this. I have to know why."

Anson pulled his jeans out of the hamper and grabbed the keys to his bike.

***

Quila and Daria waited until the palace and village were deep into sleep before slipping away. Quila wanted to back out; she couldn't dispel a slithering feeling of anxiety. *If you do this, something will go wrong. You'll regret it.* But Daria's encouragement and the possibility of seeing Anson again were enough to make her ignore her loud anxiety.

Silently, the girls broke the surface. Quila's attention went immediately to the spot on the shore where Anson had kissed her. He wasn't there now.

Where are you? I'm here because of you. You have to be here!

"So . . . how should we do this?" Daria finally whispered. "Just pop up on the beach and wait for legs? Do you think it'll hurt?"

"We should go back." Quila's pulse stuttered, her stomach sour.

Daria sighed. "No way. I'm not letting you back out of this. I'm sure it won't hurt. Come on, let's go to the beach."

"It's not that. I just . . . have this *feeling*."

"Well, I'm sure that feeling will go away the second you stand on your *feet*, face-to-face with Anson." Daria gave Quila her token wicked grin. "You worry too much. Come on." She started off toward the shore. Quila bit her bottom lip briefly and then followed. Daria waited for Quila to join her at the rocks. She dramatically smacked her hands on the rocks and then hoisted herself out of the ocean. She spun around. "Your turn!" She patted the rock beside her.

Quila rolled her eyes but lifted out to sit beside her. "Now what?"

"I have *no* idea." Their gazes lifted to the sky, thick with stars but no visible moon.

"I wish I could see the moon every night, see this sky," Quila whispered. "It's . . . incredible."

Daria lifted her face. "It really is." She sighed, amazed. "I feel so *light*. I never realized how heavy the ocean feels."

Quila recognized with a start that she felt it too. Sitting on the rocks with Anson last night had been a struggle, but tonight she breathed freely. Effortless and . . . different. "I think your mom was right, Daria." Quila pressed her hands to her tail. A slight tingling sensation started under her palms and spread along her blue scales, quickly intensifying. "Daria?"

"Yeah, yeah. Me too."

Quila gritted her teeth against the powerful sensation, not exactly pain, but still eye-watering intense. It felt as if she'd swam a thousand miles; as if the muscles in her tail were stretching to their limits; as if massive hands kneaded her into liquid. The base of her tail, where her fins forked, suddenly wrenched apart into two burning blue limbs. She cried out, reaching for Daria, who reached back to clutch her hand as her own tail split in two. Quila watched, blinking quickly, as the sections of their tails sprouted toes, formed ankles, and grew knees. Her skin faded from gray to peachy white.

By the time the sensations began to fade, Quila and Daria breathlessly collapsed to the rocks, still holding on to each other. Daria managed a weak, "Holy moon!" And then she started laughing, loud hiccups of amazement. Quila had a hand on her own chest, trying to slow her heartbeat, but felt a smile spread her lips. Soon the two were giggling and kicking their fresh legs in the salty night air.

***

Anson had been walking a mile-long section of the shore, back and forth, for hours. His feet hurt, his head ached from the beer and lack of sleep. He turned around and decided to head back to his motorcycle. *Enough, you idiot. Go home.* He shoved his hands into his pockets and hung his head heavy on his chest to watch his feet as he walked over the black stone. The incessant pulse of the ocean—a sound he usually relished—grated on his ears.

And then there was another sound on the air.

Light, bubbling laughter.

Girls' laughter.

Anson stopped, lifted his head. Technically, this area was closed at night, so who else would be down here? He worried he was about to intrude on a lovers' late-night escape. He peered along the beach, waiting for the light to swing this way to help him see. When it did, the light swept over the form of two women lying on the beach, rolling with laughter. They were naked. And their hair was the wrong color.

Anson's heart twisted. He recognized that dark-gray hair.

"Quila?" Her name slipped out before he could stop it.

The laughter cut off immediately as the two women jerked to seated and turned to look his way. "Anson?" Quila's voice answered back.

His whole body flushed with heat. He hurried closer, puzzled by the tangle of legs. *What the hell?!* He stopped, frozen by his confusion. He looked from Quila's face to her legs. No tail. Legs. His partly drunk brain lagged annoyingly behind. He felt nearly the same way he'd felt when he saw her face for the first time beyond his mask as he'd been trapped in the mouth of the *Princessa.*

Dumbly, he repeated, "Quila?"

"It's me, Anson. I . . ." She pressed her teeth together. The other woman (*another mermaid?*) whispered something to her. Quila nodded. To Anson, she said, "I know this looks strange. I'm sorry. This is Daria, my best friend. We . . . we uh . . . have legs."

The other girl, Daria, snort laughed and pressed a hand to her mouth to stop it. Quila shot her a warning look and turned back to Anson. She smiled softly. Slowly, Quila rose to her feet, unstable and unsure. She lifted her hands out to steady herself. She took a sluggish step forward and lost her balance. Anson rushed to catch her, her warm body falling against his. She straightened her knees and met his gaze. He kept his hands around her waist. "Thanks," she whispered.

"Quila, you . . . I don't . . ." He scanned down her body, covered mostly by her long dark hair (but not completely), and stopped at her legs. He ached to kiss her, to touch her wet skin. He cleared his throat. "What happened?"

"It's hard to explain, but we discovered that on the night of the new moon, mermaids can come onto the land. And walk, like you do." She shrugged, her eyes wary, nervous.

"But I . . ." Anson looked over her shoulder at the other mermaid who sat on the rocks watching them intently. He shook his head. "So just for tonight? Tonight you're . . . *sort of* human?"

"Right."

He shook his head again. He hadn't even resolved the idea that she was a mermaid and now this. "But you're still a mermaid?"

Quila smiled. "Yes. Are you all right?"

He laughed. "Just a little confused. And drunk. Or maybe too sober." He laughed again, his undisciplined eyes moving down her bare body.

She lowered her voice. "I wanted to see you again. And this way I can breathe and you don't have to freeze in the water. And we can spend time together. Like humans do." She narrowed her eyes, studying his face.

A burst of excitement cleared his mind. *She's here, standing in my arms. For one night.* He smiled. "So we can leave the beach?"

She looked past him, inland. "Yeah, actually." She trapped her lower lip in her teeth for a moment. "We can."

Another pulse of excitement. "Want to go for a ride?"

Quila's eyebrows lowered. "What do you mean?"

He looked down at her body again, gorgeous and unclothed. His cheeks flushed hot, his stomach tightening. "Well, you can't do it naked," he said with a laugh. "Here." He tugged off his leather jacket and then his plain gray T-shirt. "Put this on." He helped slip the shirt over her head and tug it into place, the shirt only barely long enough to cover her.

Quila smiled, glancing at his bare chest. Which made his own smile grow. "If you only have a few hours, I want you with me," he said.

"That's why I came."

"Good." He thought of kissing her again, but she turned her head to look at her friend.

"Go!" Daria said, waving at them. "Don't worry about me. But, Quila . . ." Her eyes flicked from Quila to Anson and back. "Back before first light. Remember: sunset to sunrise." Her tone was more serious with this. Anson wondered why. Was there some severe consequence if they stayed too long in the sunlight?

Quila nodded. "I will. You sure you'll be okay?"

"Of course! I'll just sit here and enjoy the sky and my legs. Go!"

Anson offered Daria his jacket. "Will you be cold?"

"No, I feel great. Really, just go. Like Quila said, you're why we came."

Anson nodded, the reality of that sinking in. He took Quila's hand. "Follow me."

***

Quila couldn't get enough of the speed. The motorcycle—as Anson had called it—raced forward, growling its way along the road. The air moved over her face, through her hair, and down

Anson's borrowed shirt over her skin. She pressed her chin to his shoulder, the leather of his jacket smooth, and tightened her arms around his waist. She forced her eyes to stay open against the wind so she wouldn't miss a single detail.

Anson's body moved with the machine, tensing and releasing with the curves as if he were a part of it. Quila relished her open legs, spread along his. Legs had so much range of motion and so much surface area. So much sensitive skin that loved to be touched. Anson's left hand kept wandering away from the handlebars to reach down and grip her calf, his hot palm on her wind-cool skin.

Anson turned his head to speak to her, to point out this landmark or that place. Quila knew a lot about the human world from her childhood curiosity. She knew the vocabulary, the basics, but seeing it all in person made her feel more alive than ever before. The new lines and textures. The odd smells and bizarre plants. The words Anson used and how his voice formed around them with hints of memory and thought.

Quila was most captivated by the sound of his voice and the curve of his profile. The feel of his back against her chest. She leaned closer. "Can I see where you live?" She wanted to see how this human man spent his days when he wasn't diving in her ocean. Where he slept, where he ate, the things he kept around him. Anson smiled and leaned the bike to the left to turn down a side road.

He slowed to a stop in front of a tall building divided into sections by large windows and balconies. It reminded her of the coral cottages but stacked on top of one another. Anson settled the motorcycle, its growl cutting off. "That's mine, there." He pointed to the top floor, right corner.

"It faces the ocean," she said, smiling.

"Yeah, of course." He turned and held out a hand to help her as she swung her new legs off to stand beside the motorcycle. Her body hummed from the ride, her legs deliciously shaky. Anson got off and took her hand. "This way," he whispered as he led her inside. They went through a couple of doors and then climbed several flights of stairs, her legs tiring quickly.

"This is me," he said, opening another door. She followed him into a small dark hall. Photos lined the walls on both sides. Quila smiled, leaning forward to look at each one. "These are all from your diving?" she asked.

"Divers are big on documenting." He smiled, proud.

She touched the glass frames, admiring the gear and treasures. "You rescued all these things."

Anson gave a small laugh. "I never thought of it that way, but yeah, I guess. We always think of it as *finding*."

"Which thing do you like the most?"

Anson's eyes brightened in the dim light. "I'll show you." He walked down the hall and into an open room. There was one long gray couch, a black box on a small table—*I don't know that. What is it?*—and floor-to-ceiling shelves loaded with books and salvaged items. The only light came from the big window, curtains left open to let the streetlights in. He went to the shelves on the right and lifted a small brown book, severely warped with water damaged. He opened it carefully, the spine cracking. "It's a journal, a book for someone to record their lives in. It was wrapped in a white silk scarf and locked in a suitcase. Someone cared for it, wanted to protect it. But when the pleasure cruiser went down, the water washed away *every* word." He tilted the book closer to her. "See the pages, the ink all blurred, nearly gone. Not even the name in the front survived."

Quila touched the page, relishing the rippled texture. "A whole life erased. The water took everything." She felt a pulse of sadness. "Like a small death."

Anson's eyes widened slightly. "Yes, yes. Exactly. That's why I kept this. It reminds me how important but how fleeting our lives are. And just how devastating the ocean's power can be. I thought of these blank pages when I was trapped."

Quila nodded slowly. She understood exactly why Anson loved this book. "My mother kept records for our people. And she studied the ancient texts. She knew things no one else did, and when she died . . ."

"It was lost," he finished.

"Yes. Or at least, some of it was. Mostly her experiences."

"This new moon transformation—was that part of her lost knowledge?"

"It seems so." Quila sighed, suddenly feeling the pull of her home. She narrowed her eyes, realizing that she didn't feel the Anchor. She felt a wave of relief followed by twisted concern. If she couldn't feel it, how would she know if something went wrong? Her body suddenly felt hollow and achy.

I didn't expect to lose that connection. I've had it with me for so long . . .

Anson pressed his fingers to her arm. "You okay?

She shook her head. She didn't want to waste time worrying. "Yeah. Just thinking about my mother."

"I'm so sorry she died. I never knew my mom. Don't even know her name. Dad won't tell me anything."

"I'm sorry too. That must be frustrating."

"How did she die—your mom?" he asked tenderly.

Quila pressed her teeth together and turned away. She thought of lying, but then answered with the truth. "She was killed by a diver."

Anson went quiet behind her. She heard the journal close and settle back on the shelf. "You mean a diver . . . *like me*, like a deep-sea diver?"

"Yes. She was found with a heavy black belt around her waist and a fatal wound in her skull." Quila half turned in order to read his face. His expression was genuinely pained. "Sedna—Daria's mom—found her."

Anson shook his head, eyes pinched in thought. "But why would a diver kill a mermaid? And . . ." He sucked in a hard breath and then swore quietly. "When did this happen? I know all the divers in this area."

"About twelve years ago."

"How old were you?"

"Only ten."

"So we're the same age." He reached for her hand. "I'm so sorry." He offered an empathetic smile. "Twelve years ago, huh? That's about when my dad was really getting serious about diving. There were only a handful of divers then." His eyes widened. "I probably know the person who did it." He leveled his gaze on her. "Quila, I . . . how can you even stand the sight of me? And you rescued me. How do you not hate me?"

A shiver moved through Quila. Her anger toward the diver who killed her mother was raw, a constant sting in her heart, but it didn't attach itself to Anson. She tightened her grip on his hand. "It wasn't you. You're not responsible for what happened."

"But you must be so angry?"

"Yes, at the man who actually did it. Not you." Anson's expression changed. He moved his eyes to the window, his jaw flexing. "What's wrong?" she asked.

He didn't look back. "Something my dad said today." He shook his head, turned back. "Did this . . . Sedna ever tell you what the man looked like?"

"No. She didn't see him. We really don't know anything. Only that my mother broke the rules about going to the surface and she died because of it." Quila's stomach went sour. *Just like I'm doing.*

"So you're breaking the rules too?" Anson asked, his voice weighted with understanding. There was a pause of tense silence as they both absorbed this. Finally, Anson said, "Well, I can check into old ships logs. See who was diving around that time. What was the date, exactly?"

"On your calendar . . . October 4, 1967. It was new moon." A chill rushed down her spine. "Holy moon, it was a new moon."

"What does that mean?" Anson asked, but then his eyes widened. "Do you think she was up here, on land?"

Quila closed her eyes and let out a long exhale. "Maybe. Sedna said my mother did this. That she came onto land." A stab of frustration made her flinch. "I hate that I don't know."

"I'll see what I can find. Okay?" Anson leaned to the side to draw her attention back to him.

She nodded. "Thank you." She took a step closer. "Sorry—I shouldn't have talked about my mom. I don't want to ruin our few hours with that mess."

Anson shrugged. "I'm glad you told me. I want to know you. I'd stand here talking to you about *anything*." His eyes moved over her face, and his expression changed, softened. "You're really amazing." His fingers touched her face. "This gray hair—it's beautiful. And, of course, your eyes. I like those best. Something so familiar about them," he teased.

Quila smiled. "I like *your* hair." She lifted a hand to run her palm over the spiky texture. "I can't stop touching it."

"Touch away." Anson closed his eyes as she ran her hand over his head again. He sighed, his hand slipping to her neck. "Do you have to go back to the ocean?"

Quila's throat tightened; her eyes stung with sudden tears. "I wish I didn't. But I really shouldn't have left at all."

"I know, but I'm so glad you did." He opened his eyes to meet her gaze. Emotions moved through his sea-green eyes, sensations Quila recognized and understood. "Can you come back every new moon?" he asked, his arms circling her.

"Every one," she whispered, her desire stealing her voice. Her hands lowered to his bare chest, slipping into the space between the halves of his jacket. Anson shifted, bringing her closer. This time when he kissed her it was a leisurely, sweet exploration, instead of the fevered desperation of last time. He took his time moving over her lips, down her neck, and back. He took his time letting his hands move from cupping her jaw to gripping her hips to arms locked around her waist.

Quila's new knees went lax, a simmering heat building in her belly and chest. She pushed his jacket off his shoulders so her hands could discover the terrain of his chest, arms, and back. She hardly noticed Anson moving them back toward the couch, and then smoothly, her body was beneath his. She smiled against his mouth. He laughed quietly as his lips moved down to tease the hollow between her collarbones. Her trembling legs wrapped around his. His palms found her thighs, hips, and sides. His fingers tangled in her hair.

Anson's lips wandered but always came back to her lips, his breath swirling with hers, her name barely a whisper against her own mouth. The rhythm between them felt like the Anchor's constant song to the moon: a natural and necessary connection. Quila wondered how she'd gone so long without Anson, without this energy alive inside her. Her hands moved over his hair as his mouth pressed to hers again. Quila lost herself in the sensations, in pleasure so stunning she knew she'd never regret this night.

No matter what might come next.

CHAPTER 7

*A*nson silently begged the sun to stay in bed tonight. *Just this once, sleep in, and leave the world in darkness for a little while longer.* Because Anson had no idea how he'd ever let go of Quila and stand up from this couch. He didn't want to lift his hand from her hip; her skin was the smoothest, lushest thing he'd ever touched. Her kiss woke up parts of his body and mind he didn't know had gone into hibernation. His simple cloth-covered couch had never been this comfortable.

Quila was spooned back against him, their bodies breathing in sync. Her hair had finally dried, and like her skin, was silky against his chest. He ran a hand over it. *It looks like molten silver.* "Has your hair ever been dry before?" he asked.

She laughed, her body moving against his with the sound. "No, actually." She reached up to pull some of it into her hands. He adjusted onto his elbow to watch her face. Her eyes brightened with fascination. He loved that everything was so new to her, so fresh. Seeing things through Quila's eyes brought his world back to life. "It's so . . . light," she said with another laugh. "Everything here has so much air in it. Everything in my world is full of water." She turned a little. "You know that, though. You feel the difference all the time."

"Yeah, but not like you do. To you it's home, to me it's always trying to kill me." He grinned and she laughed. "But I've dreamed of living in the water," he went on. "I've dreamed of swimming on and on, deeper and deeper. It must be amazing."

Quila nodded, her expression somber. "It is." She sighed. "It's almost dawn."

"Just ignore it. Maybe it will stop."

She smiled, leaning back against him. "I have to go back."

"What would happen if you stayed?" Anson asked before he could stop himself. "I mean . . . I just . . . would it ever be possible?"

Quila stilled. "I have no idea. But I can't, Anson. I'm queen. I'm in charge of the Anchor and the tides. It was incredibly irresponsible of me to leave for one night. I could never . . ."

"I know." He pressed his lips to her temple. "I had to ask. Wait—you're a queen?"

She laughed at his surprise. "That's what happens when your mom is queen and dies very young."

"You've been queen since you were ten?" She nodded, and Anson didn't miss her discomfort. "You don't like it?"

"I don't like that being queen means my mother is dead. I don't like that so much relies on me. And I really don't like that look on your face. I'm just me here, with you. I'm not your queen."

He smiled, totally understanding how she felt. He knew that look; people looked at him in a similar way when they found out about his father. He got it, but he couldn't resist the chance to tease her a little. He pulled his smile away, giving her a serious expression. "Yes, Your Majesty," he said dramatically.

She punched his upper arm, a good hard punch too. Anson broke out laughing, and soon she was laughing too.

When their laughter slowed, Quila said, "But I do wonder what would happen if a mermaid stayed on land. Would she stay human? Or could it . . . *hurt* her?"

"I don't want you to risk it," Anson said, wrapping his arm around her. "I mean, of course I want you to stay, but I don't want that to cause you pain or problems."

She rubbed at the soft hairs on his arm. After a quiet moment, she said, "We *really* have to go."

"I know." Anson didn't move. Quila didn't move.

Several minutes ticked by in silence. Anson wondered what Quila was thinking, feeling. Had this night been as transformative for her as it had been for him? He didn't feel like the same person anymore. He'd kissed her and changed completely.

"Thank you," she whispered, voice trembling.

Anson adjusted onto his elbow and gently pulled back on her shoulder so she'd lie flat, her face looking up at him. "For what?" he asked.

"For tonight. For . . . *this*." She pressed her palm to his chest. "I've never felt more . . . free."

Anson watched Quila's eyes go wet with unshed tears. A powerful tug of emotion pulled at his heart. "Me either. Quila, I . . . I'm the one who should say thank you. You saved my life, like actually saved it, and now . . ." He touched her face. "I know it makes no sense, and I know it may be impossible because of who we are, but this is important to me. I want this. I want you."

A few tears slipped down her temples. "Maybe we can find a way." She closed her eyes and laughed. "I have *no* idea how, but I want this too. I think I may *need* this."

Anson inhaled deeply, studying her green eyes. "Okay. Good. Then I guess I can take you back to the beach, *if* I know I'll see you again. Even if it's a month from now."

"I'll find my way back. I promise."

"I'll take that promise."

Anson lowered his head to kiss Quila one more time in the haven of his living room.

***

Quila hated the motorcycle's speed this time. She wanted Anson to go slower. She wanted the bike to break down, refuse to go any farther. She wanted to stay with Anson and pretend she never had a life before tonight. But soon they were walking on a path through some trees, hand in hand, the coming separation too heavy to allow words to pass between them. She kept her head down, watching her miraculous, magical feet walk over the dirt. She didn't want to give them back.

The trees opened up to the beach. Quila froze the moment they stepped onto the black rocks. Her jaw dropped, her hand went cold in Anson's. Anson stood rigid beside her. "What the . . . ," he started, the rest of his words lost in the shock.

Quila swallowed hard, her throat pinched closed by a vice of panic. "The tides," she whispered. She and Anson gawked at the ocean sitting as quiet and solid as a mirror. No waves, no eternal ebb and flow. A full stop. "But . . . how?" Quila searched for her connection to the Anchor but found only that hollowed-out center in her chest. "What did I do?"

She ran fast over the stone. Anson called after her, only a few steps behind.

I broke the ocean.

I was selfish and I ruined everything.

Holy moon!

Quila prepared to dive into the water, but shapes in the corner of her vision brought her to a skidding halt. Anson stopped next to her, his hand clamping down on her arm. "Wait—" His words stopped as he noticed the shapes on the shore. The people. "Who's that?"

Quila squinted through the dark, though she could see clearly. She shivered, her stomach tightening. "It's Sedna. And . . ." Quila's breath caught in her throat. Daria was there, too, seated at her mother's feet, her hands bound behind her back, head hung low over her knees. And lying on the rocks in front of Daria was Quila's father, bound with thick rope from chest to knees.

Knees. My father has legs.

Anson's grip on Quila's arm tightened. Quila's gut twisted hard. She forced herself to walk forward. Daria lifted her head, eyes wide and scared. She shook her head in some kind of warning, but Quila kept walking. She moved her gaze to meet her father's; she'd never seen him afraid. Looking away from his terror-wide eyes, Quila turned her attention to Sedna. She wore a long lithe white dress, the neckline low to expose her black-and-white stone necklace. Sedna's intense gaze bore down on Quila, a disquieting grin on her lips. Quila lifted her chin.

I'm queen of the moon mermaids.

Whatever is happening, I'll fix it.

I'll pay the price for wanting Anson.

She pulled her arm from Anson's grip. He gave her an apprehensive look, but Quila ignored him. "What's going on?" She moved closer to Sedna, Anson behind her.

"Did you have a nice night?" Sedna asked, voice too silky.

"The tides have stopped. Why? I demand an explanation, Sedna."

Sedna laughed, the twisted sound floating on the eerily quiet air. "Well, I stopped them, my Queen."

"How?"

"It took me years to figure out the magic. *Years!* The spells were scattered throughout the ancient records; a piece here, a piece there. It was quite the puzzle. But I got it. Tonight it finally worked. *Finally!* I've waited a long time for this. And the timing could not have worked out more perfectly." Her eyes flicked to Anson.

"You stopped the Anchor with magic? But why?" Quila thought of the small pebble Titan had shown her.

Sedna reached behind her. A long, dangerously thin knife flashed in the darkness. Quila held her breath. Sedna said, "To put it simply, my Queen: this is my revenge. Your mother and father ruined my life. So, I've ruined Elara's precious Anchor. Mayar is looking at his daughter walking on land with a human man—his worst nightmare, by the way. And now you can suffer the same fate as your mother while he watches."

Quila looked back down at her father and saw confirmation in his broken expression. He looked between her and Anson, pain filling his face. Quila lost her breath, a stab of guilt and shame plunging into her chest. She sucked in a breath, trying to keep the fear out of her expression. "I don't understand. What did they do to you?"

Sedna's face turned to stone. "They took away my son; I have to idea what happened to him. And they kept me from the man I love."

"*What?*" Quila's chest constricted even more.

"Your mother and I used the magic of the new moon *many* times to come to the surface. We loved it here. Elara loved escaping the incessant, needy Anchor. She loved walking on her legs. She loved leaving Mayar behind. And then she fell in love with a human man." Sedna paused, her twisted smile growing as Quila took in the revelations. "Oh yes, she loved him, but *he* loved *me*. Not her. And that was too much for our poor spoiled Elara. Isn't that right, Mayar?" She lightly touched the point of her dagger to his exposed shoulder.

The pathetic way he slid his gaze to the rock told Quila that Sedna spoke the truth. Quila put the back of her hand to her mouth, the contents of her stomach churning.

No, this can't be right. My mother loved the Anchor. She loved my father. She was good.

"I know what you're thinking," Sedna said. "*All* lies," she hissed. "When I found out I was pregnant, Elara lost her mind. She banished me from the archives and had me placed under guard. When my children were born . . . she *took* him."

The panic in Quila's throat constricted harder. She put her hand there to try and release it. "Children?"

"I gave birth to twins: one mermaid girl and one human boy." She looked down at her daughter.

Quila looked at her friend too. Fresh tears rolled down Daria's cheeks. To Sedna, Quila asked, "Why did my mother take him away?"

"Elara declared him an abomination and claimed she had to protect the Mer from corruption. But really she was madly jealous and worried about keeping the secret of her new moon adventures. So she had the guards hold me back and she left with my son." Sedna pressed her teeth together, jaw flexing. "I don't know what happened to my baby, and Robert never met him or Daria."

"Robert?" Anson's voice cut in. Everyone turned to him. "Sorry—did you say Robert? Do you mean Robert Lacey? Because . . ." His head jerked to look at Quila. His green eyes suddenly looked much brighter in the predawn dark. Quila's whole body went numb.

"How do you know that name?" Sedna demanded, stepping around Mayar to stand face-to-face with Anson.

Quila watched his jaw tense and release several times. Silently, she begged him not to answer, not to speak the words aloud. *Don't say it. Don't let it be true.* Anson looked away from Sedna, holding Quila's gaze instead. "Robert Lacey is my father."

CHAPTER 8

*A*nson blinked at the bizarre woman in front of him. He wanted to laugh. He wanted to run back to the cozy protection of his apartment. He wanted to dive into the sea and swim far away. Because there was no way this terrifying woman was his mother.

"*What* did you say?" Sedna drew out the words slowly, her face suddenly pale.

Anson said nothing. He couldn't say it again. And he knew she'd heard him just fine. Anson lifted his hand to finger his temple. *I have mermaid eyes. Maybe this woman really is . . .*

Sedna continued to study him closely. Without looking away, she spoke to Daria. "You didn't tell me about his eyes."

"I didn't know," Daria blurted back. "I couldn't see in the dark. Is he . . . ?" She clamped her mouth shut.

Sedna burst into a laugh, a trilling sound that prickled Anson's skin. "Robert Lacey, the diver, is *your* father? And you're twenty-two years old?"

Anson said nothing.

Quila gasped. "No. No! Stop this," she yelled.

Sedna ignored her. She lifted a hand to Anson's face; his breath froze in his chest. She ran her cool fingers down his cheek. "Hello, my son. How are you *alive*?"

Anson jerked away, taking several frantic steps backward. Quila reached for his arm, helping to keep him from falling to the rocks. "If this is true," she said to Sedna. "If Anson is your son, then my mother didn't hurt him or kill him. You have no reason for revenge. Release my father; restore the tides."

"No reason?" Sedna scoffed and threw up her arm. "This is almost worse. Knowing she kept him from me. Knowing he has been *right here* all along. With Robert." Sedna shook her head. "All the years of grieving."

"That was the price, Sedna."

Everyone turned at the sound of a new voice from behind. Anson's whole body went cold. His father stood behind them, legs spread wide, face windblown with pain. A pain Anson had never seen before. "Dad?" he whispered, not really loud enough for Robert to hear. Robert didn't look at him; his gaze was bolted to Sedna. "What are you doing here?" he asked louder.

Robert's eyes didn't leave Sedna. "I come here every new moon," he mumbled. "But I didn't expect . . ."

"Robert?" Sedna breathed, some of her threatening power draining away. Her dagger-free hand came to her chest.

Robert stepped closer. "Elara brought me the baby the night he was born. She told me that the only way she'd let him live was my complete silence on the matter. I could never tell him about his mother. I could never tell anyone about you, about your people. And . . ." He winced, swallowed hard. "I could never see you again."

Sedna stepped toward him. "I waited for you, with Daria in my arms, *every* new moon for a year."

"I know." His words were an apology heavy with years of hurt. "I had to protect him, Sedna." Robert finally moved his gaze to Anson. Anson saw a stranger, a man he'd never seen through the ego and success. Through the wall Robert had built around his throbbing sacrifice.

Quila's grip on Anson's arm tightened. "Did you kill her, Robert?" she asked, voice rough like barnacled ship skin. "Did you kill my mother?" Anson's stomach twisted. *No. Please no.* He looked at her, but Quila wouldn't look back. She released his arm and stepped closer to Robert, leaving Anson behind. *Don't do this, Quila. Don't put this between us.*

Robert's eyes dropped to the shore. Everyone went quiet, knowing his answer before he spoke. *Don't say it, Dad. Don't.* Robert, voice low and broken in half, answered, "It . . . it was an accident. I came to the beach that night hoping to meet Sedna. I couldn't take it anymore—I needed to see her. Those first ten years felt like an eternity." His aching gaze went to Sedna. She stood as still as the tideless ocean. Robert went on, "So I broke my promise and came to this beach. Elara was here, waiting. She caught me breaking our agreement. She charged up the beach, going for Anson asleep in the truck. I ran after her. I grabbed her. She pushed me away. I grabbed her again and threw her to the ground. Her head . . ." He swallowed hard. "There was a rock."

Quila shook her head. Anson wanted to reach for her, but he couldn't get his body to move.

"I panicked," Robert said in a rush. "I grabbed a weight belt from the truck and put it on her. I threw her into the ocean. I . . ."

"Did you know this, Sedna?" Quila asked, shoulders slumped forward.

"No, I didn't know," Sedna answered quietly. "I found her with the belt on, so I knew it'd been divers, but I didn't . . ." She spun to Robert. "Why didn't you find me after that?"

"I tried! I waited. You didn't come. I dove all over, searching. I became king of the divers while I was looking for *you*." His expression turned bitter, rancid with anger. "It wasn't about the shipwrecks and finds; it was all for *you*, Sedna."

Sedna's eyes softened for a beat and then went startlingly cold, hard. Her hand flexed on the knife still in her hand. Anson tensed. Sedna moved faster than he imagined possible. She had Quila by the throat, the blade against the pulse in her neck. "Elara took *everything* from me," she hissed in her ear. "If she were here, I'd kill her all over again. But she's not. So I will take her family instead. Like she took mine."

Anson lunged forward.

But he was too late.

Sedna dove backward into the sea, Quila trapped in her arms.

***

Quila writhed against Sedna's surprising strength. She pushed at the woman's arm to move the knife away from her neck but managed to move it only an inch. The cold Atlantic water rushed around them, their human feet gone almost instantly. Sedna's powerful white tail drove them deeper and farther away from the beach. Quila's head filled with the look of panic on Anson's face the second before Sedna had launched them into the ocean.

What is happening? My mother. His father. How can it all be true?

Sedna tried to bring the knife down again, but Quila managed to keep it away. Barely. She twisted, pushing with her tail, but could not break the prison of Sedna's arms. "Sedna, don't do this. Please."

Sedna said nothing.

"I'm sorry my mother did all that. I'm sorry about Anson and Robert. You must be in so much pain. I understand."

Sedna brought them to a jerking halt. "You do *not* understand, Quila." Lowering the knife, she hooked her elbow tightly around Quila's neck. Quila pulled at the arm. "See this place?" Sedna hissed. "This is where I found her. This is where I found Elara's body."

Quila froze. They were near the ocean floor, only about a hundred feet deep. A small lone fishing boat sat crookedly on the sand, lost and forgotten. Schools of fish swam around its broken carcass, weaving in and out through large holes in the wood. There was something strange about their movements in the calm water. *They miss the tides; they are scared without the currents.*

"She lay in that boat," Sedna went on, "as if she'd been the captain who valiantly went down with the ship. Blood misted out of her skull, forming this odd pink cloud around her. At first, I didn't know what I was looking at, didn't understand. And then I realized Elara was *dead*. I'd swum up to the shore an hour earlier, missing Robert." She looked up. "Such horrible timing."

Quila pressed her eyes shut, tears burning behind her lids. "Stop this. Don't make it worse, please."

"It was an odd moment, seeing her lying there. We hadn't spoken a word to each other in years. She'd kept me under close watch, a Black Sea Dungeon guard outside my door as I raised my daughter. She brought Daria to the palace to be a companion to her own daughter." Sedna gave Quila a poignant look. Quila's heart broke. Sedna went on, "She let me go to the surface to wait for Robert knowing he wouldn't come. She hated me so much, and I hated her back. She'd once been closer to me than a sister. But after everything, I wished for her death many times. And there it was, right in front of me." She pointed the knife at the wrecked boat.

"But Anson is alive. You have your son, and Daria has her brother. You can get to know him, and you can be with Robert again. But not if you do this."

"She's right, Mother."

Sedna jerked around, Quila choking in her iron grip. Daria hovered a few feet behind, a freed Mayar at her side. Daria swam forward, pleading in her eyes. "Anson is alive. I want to know my brother. I want us to be a family. Don't you? Please stop this."

Sedna laughed. "Do you think they'll let us know him, Daria? It's too late. I'm already in too deep. I have to kill them if we want our freedom."

"No, no you don't," Quila said, fighting the pressure on her throat. "I'm queen now, not my mother. I decide what happens. And I want to fix this. Release me and we can figure it out. Kill me and you'll spend the rest of your life in the dungeon."

The pressure on Quila's neck increased. "There's no fixing this," Sedna hissed. She brought the knife back, the tip pressed into Quila's left gill.

"Sedna, please!" Mayar begged. "We thought we were doing what was right. I'm sorry. I'm sorry for everything Elara did. Everything I did to help her selfishness. Listen to Quila, please."

Quila felt the tender skin in her gill split open a little. A mist of red blood floated past her eyes. Panic brought spots to her vision. She tugged at Sedna's arm. "I'm not her, Sedna. Please."

Two black shapes appeared in the water. Quila blinked, wondering if the pain and pressure were playing with her eyes. But as the shapes got closer, she realized it wasn't an illusion. Anson and Robert, in their full divers' gear, swam fast toward Sedna. She flinched and drew back as they approached, keeping Quila locked in her arm. Quila met Anson's worried gaze through his mask. He grimaced and then turned his attention to his mother. Sedna kept trying to move away from him, swimming her and Quila back. But finally Anson was close enough to lay his hand on her arm. He shook his head, his face intent. His eyes begging. Sedna's grip softened slightly. Quila resisted the urge to push away. She waited. Robert approached on the other side and also put his hand on Sedna's arm, the one with the knife. She shifted her eyes to his masked face. And her arm loosened, then withdrew.

Anson pulled Quila behind him. Quila coughed and took a much-needed full breath, her left gill sore but all right. Robert drew Sedna against his chest. She shook with violent sobs.

Quila shuddered and looked away. She found Daria close behind her. She pulled away from Anson and reached for her friend, taking her into a firm hug. "I didn't know," Daria whispered through her tears. "I had no idea she planned to do this. All the things she manipulated. I tried to stop her when she showed up on the beach. I—"

"I know, Daria. It's okay. It's over." Quila pulled back. "I need to restore the tides. Come with me?"

Daria nodded.

Quila looked over at Anson. Anson pointed upward. She nodded. "I'll meet you on the beach as soon as we restore the tides," she told him. He nodded his understanding and briefly touched her face with his gloved hand.

***

Quila led the way to the Anchor. She heard the miners' frantic work as they drew close. Titan came swimming at her fast. "My Queen, where have you been? All the moonstone was destroyed. We don't—"

Quila lifted her hand to stop his explanation. "I know, Titan. I'll tell you everything later, but right now we must restore the tides. How much have you replaced?"

He looked from her to Daria and back. "We just finished."

"Good work. Thank you. Are my sisters here?"

"Waiting at their places."

Quila nodded to her sisters, ignoring the looks and questions they threw her way. "Anchor first," she told them. Quila took her place in front of the full moon symbol. Daria took her hand, solid by her side. Quila began to sing, quiet at first. Her sisters joined in the song, the swell of music rising. Quila felt the Anchor kick back into action, its rhythm filling her body. The water around her came back to life, its flow returned.

As the moon energy filled her, Quila realized just how much she'd missed it. And just how much she wanted it there inside her. For so long, she'd fought against her powers and her position. But now, she knew she wanted it and knew she could be the kind of queen her mother never was.

I can do this, and do it better, wiser. I will be the queen I should have been from the beginning.

The moon answered her declaration with a pulse of heat around her heart.

***

Anson sat next to his father on Portland Head beach, tanks, fins, and masks discarded behind them. The first rays of sun broke the horizon, slicing across the water. He squinted at the brightness. Sedna lay with her head on Robert's lap, collapsed from exhaustion. They'd made it out of the water with just enough new moon power left to change her tail into legs again. Robert stroked her black hair, a small, astonished smile on his lips. Anson's heart tugged at the sight of that smile.

"I wanted to tell you," Robert whispered.

"I know."

"Quila rescued you from the *Princessa*?"

"Yes."

Robert shook his head; his smile grew. "Like father like son."

Anson gave a quiet laugh. "Not the safest taste in women."

Robert laughed back and then sobered. "I didn't want to hurt Elara. I just wanted to protect you. I . . . didn't know what to do."

Anson nodded. "The whole thing is a mess. But it's not your fault she died. She started all this. And I think Quila will understand that." *At least, I hope she will. What if she can't see past my father's mistakes? What if she never wants to see me again?*

A rush of energy came over the water. Both men looked up. The tide had restarted. Newborn waves kissed the shore, the sound of the ocean's song rising on the sunrise air. Anson smiled. "She fixed it." His smile faded. "What do I do, Dad? See her for only one night every month? If she even wants me anymore."

Robert sighed. "That's all I had with Sedna. It was never enough. It was . . . hard. But it was better than nothing. Nothing almost killed me." He met Anson's gaze. "I only survived it because of you. Raising you got me through the hardest thing I ever had to do. And I wouldn't change that. I've been hard on you because your life is so important. It almost wasn't, so I wanted it to be great. Because you are great, Anson. Better than me." He smiled. "But don't tell anyone I said that."

Anson shook his head. "I'm sorry you suffered like that. I'm sorry I didn't know and couldn't help you."

"It wasn't your burden. But I guess you're about to find out what it feels like to love a mermaid." He nodded his head toward the water. Quila and Daria swam fast toward the shore. Anson's heart tugged at the sight of the woman he loved and the sister he hadn't known he had. He wanted to keep them both close to him, make them family.

I have a sister. I want to know her.

And I want to be with Quila. I can't live without her.

Does she feel the same?

The mermaids clung to the edge of the rocks, their eyes moving to Sedna. "Is she all right?" Daria asked.

"Just sleeping," Robert answered tenderly. At this Sedna stirred, her eyes slowly opening. "Daria?" she said. Then she jerked to seated, looking around frantically. Robert gripped her arm. "It's okay, Sedna. You're safe."

"But I . . ." Her eyes stopped at Quila. "Quila, I—"

"Don't," Quila stopped her gently. "It's time we all move on."

Sedna blinked. "You're not going to . . . punish me?"

"I think you've been punished enough. I want you to heal, not suffer more. You, Daria, Robert—all of us. But what you did, Sedna, *should* be punished. I can let you go free only with your most solemn promise that your desire for revenge is dead. My promise in return is that if you ever break into the archives or come near the Anchor or threaten my family again, I will swiftly send you to the Black Sea Dungeons. And you'll spend the rest of your life there. Understood?"

Sedna wiped at fresh tears. "You are definitely not your mother." She nodded. "Yes, I understand. And I promise that this is all over. I'll do whatever you want me to do as long as I can see Robert and Anson on new moons. As long as I can finally bring my family together."

Quila's eyes moved to Anson. He reached for her, but she withdrew. His whole body went cold. "So we can see them only on new moons? That's all we get?" Her voice broke, and the emotion gave Anson some hope that she cared for him as much as he did for her.

Sedna took Robert's hand in hers and took a long breath. "I've read everything there is to know about Mer and human connections. The new moon spell lasts only until sunrise. As soon as that sun hits my legs, I'll return to my Mer state. I can't stay unless . . ." She paused, shoulders sagging.

"Unless what?" Robert asked, leaning toward her.

"Unless a human is willing to take my place. Nature demands balance. The moon magic requires it. I didn't have someone to take my place and I couldn't leave Daria."

Anson's pulse quickened. "So a human has to agree to be a mermaid in order for you to become human permanently?"

Sedna met his gaze. "Yes."

"I'll do it!" Anson hadn't realized he'd made the decision until the words came out.

Robert turned to him. "What? No. You can't do that. You don't need to do that for us, Anson."

"I'm not doing it for you." He turned to Quila.

She blinked up at him, her expression concerned. "No. You can't leave your home, your life. Diving. Your father."

Anson shifted forward and took Quila's hand into his grip. "I have always felt more at home in the ocean. And I've never felt more at home than when I'm with you. This is an easy decision. I want to be with you, Quila. And Sedna and Dad can finally be together. I can get to know my sister." He smiled at Daria and held out his other hand. She took it into a firm grip. "And we can all hang out together, right here, once a month. We can be a family. If . . . you want me?" Anson held his breath, watching the emotions move through Quila's eyes. Her brow pulled together; her gaze shifted away. Anson let out a shaky, resigned breath.

She doesn't feel the same way.

"Quila?" He prompted, tugging slightly on her hand. In a swift, surprising movement, she sprung out of the water and threw her arms around his neck. They went crashing to the shore, kissing and laughing. After a moment, Quila pulled back, palms pressed to the stone on either side of his head so she could look at him properly. "You're *sure*?"

"Absolutely." Her turned to Sedna. "I'm sure."

Robert lifted a hand. "But what will you do? What about diving?"

"What better way to dive than as a merman I'll bring you the *Princessa* clock next month."

"And you can be our engineer." Quila's eyes lit up. "Yes, that's perfect!"

"Engineer?" Anson asked.

"The person who takes care of the Anchor's structure. Our current one is retiring. I've been looking for someone with the right instincts to take his place. You'd do an amazing job."

"I'll take it," Anson said, smile growing and heart racing with excitement. He turned to Sedna. "How do we do it?"

Sedna's hand went to the black-and-white stone slung around her neck. "With this. Something else I stole from the archives."

She unhooked the chain and placed it on her palm. "I never thought I'd use it. I wore it as a reminder of what Elara took from me. But now . . ."

Anson sat up, shifting Quila onto his lap. "Let's use it."

"This is a piece of obsidian and a piece of moonstone. Two worlds together but always separate. It's enchanted with special transformation magic. The same that occurs on the new moon but much more powerful. Anson,"—she looked up—"come over here, my son."

Anson kissed Quila's shoulder and then helped her slip back into the water. With his heart pounding in his ears, he knelt in front of his mother.

This is my mother.

And this moment changes everything.

Sedna took in a long inhale. "Place your hand on top of the stone, on top of my hand." Anson obeyed. His whole body trembled with anticipation. Robert's hand clamped down on his shoulder. Anson turned to look at his father. "You're sure?"

Anson nodded. "Yes. I am."

Robert shook his head slowly. He turned to Quila. "I would have done the same for Sedna. He loves you, Quila. And I want you to know how sorry I am about your mother. I hope you can forgive me."

Quila's eyes turned misty. "I will always miss my mother. I will always hate that she died. But I know now she wasn't the person I thought she was. She caused so much pain and hurt. If you can forgive her, I can most certainly forgive you. You were protecting Anson. And I'm so glad he's here now."

She reached for Anson's hand, and he held her fingers securely in his, his chest warming. Robert cleared his throat. "Thank you." He gestured to Sedna to continue.

Anson looked into his mother's intense, vibrant eyes. An astonished shudder moved through him. *This is really happening.* He took a deep breath.

"Repeat the ancient spell with me," Sedna said. Anson nodded. She spoke in a language he'd never heard. His tongue fumbled with the words, but he managed. A tingling sensation started in his chest, radiating outward as they repeated the spell again and again. The stone between their palms grew hot. Anson turned to look at Quila, who gazed back with wide, amazed eyes. He held her gaze as a powerful gripping sensation moved down his legs. Her clasp on his hand tightened, a sure anchor. He wanted to collapse to the stone but forced himself to remain kneeling as his legs morphed into a tail.

Sedna's voice cut off. Breathing hard, and different than before, he looked down at his tail. A deep blue-gray, like the thunderheads of a massive storm. He pulled away the ripped remains of his dry suit. His skin now matched the other mermaids, soft moon gray. He teetered on the bend in his tail, but Sedna reached out to steady him. She smiled. "It's finished," she whispered. He looked down at her legs, now bathed in sunlight. "Thank you, Anson," she added and kissed his cheek.

Anson felt a hand on his tail. Quila smiled up at him, tears in her eyes. "Looking good," she said.

Everyone laughed. Anson reached for her, flopping awkwardly into the water. A pulse of pleasant energy surged up his spine as the water surrounded him. He bent and flexed his tail. He pulled Quila against him and kissed her until they were both breathless.

Quila pulled away laughing, arms slung around his neck. "I can't believe you did this for me."

"This is where I belong. I feel it. Here, in the ocean, with you."

Quila kissed him again, one soft, slow moment. She ran her hands over his head. "But don't grow out your hair."

Anson laughed. "Wouldn't dream of it."

"Good." Quila laughed too.

Anson turned to his parents. "Thank you both. And we'll see you soon?"

"Right here," Robert answered. "And you better bring that clock."

Sedna leaned down to kiss first Daria on the forehead, then Anson, then Quila. "Thank you for giving me a second chance," she said quietly, tears in her eyes.

Anson squeezed her hand briefly and then pushed back from the shore. "Okay, girls, let's see if you can keep up."

END

About the Author

Teri Harman has believed in all things wondrous and haunting since her childhood days of sitting in the highest tree branches reading Roald Dahl and running in the rain imagining stories of danger and romance. She's the author of The Moonlight Trilogy: *Blood Moon, Black Moon,* and *Storm Moon* and the magical romance *A Thousand Sleepless Nights.* She also writes about books for ksl.com and contributed regular book segments to *Studio 5 with Brooke Walker,* Utah's number one lifestyle show. She lives in Utah with her husband and three children. Visit her at teriharman.com or follow on Instagram @teriharman.

Pua's Kiss

Magic Realism

A Fairy Tale Ink Story for
Fractured Sea

By

Lehua Parker

First edition eBook published by Tork Media in *Fractured Sea*, a Fairy Tale Ink boxed set.

Printed in the United States of America

This title is available as an eBook, paperback, and audiobook.

For mana wahine who never trade freedom for the illusion of a happy ending.

CHAPTER 1

PUA

*I*t's the sarong's fault.

Lying forgotten in the sand, it beckons to Pua-O-Ke-Kai like a bad wingman carrying too many piña coladas and not enough bail money. It's just a fringed strip of tropical flowers on a bright yellow background, a cheap souvenir destined to be worn for a week in Waikiki and later forgotten in the back of a drawer.

But even a sarong has dreams.

Big dreams.

As the great Niuhi shark Pua-O-Ke-Kai cruises along the reef, the sarong's siren call brings her to the beach like blood in the water.

She can't resist.

At least that's the lie Pua tells herself as she wades out of the ocean and wraps the sarong around her human form.

A glance up and down Keikikai Beach confirms what her Niuhi shark nose already told her: it's deserted. There's just one lone boogie boarder beyond the lava outcrop, out past Piko Point on the Nalupuki beach side.

Nili-boy, she thinks, wiggling her toes in the sand. *A born waterman, but his mother will be angry if she finds out he's surfing alone. Too bad he's much too young to be interesting.*

Raising her face to the sun, she smiles and stretches her arms wide, joints and sinews snapping and popping in ways foreign to a shark. She breathes deeply, giddy as the quick hit of oxygen buzzes her brain.

It's been a long, long time since I've stood on this beach in the daylight. I deserve to warm my bones in the sun. No harm in that.

Curled like a kitten on the sand, she tucks her arm beneath her head and closes her eyes.

Just for a minute.

Funny how easily destiny makes you her bitch.

CHAPTER 2

JUSTIN

iddling with the car's radio, I can't find anything but static and one station playing luau music. It's too much in this heat. I flick it off and face the grim reality.

I'm lost.

From Waikiki, it can't be this far to Lauele Town. The island's not that big. For the millionth time, I check the map the rental agent gave me and run my finger along the narrow two-lane road hugging the coast, looking for the tiny red x he drew.

Did the last road sign say Kaimuki? I think so. No, that can't be. According to the map, Kaimuki isn't near the ocean, and I'm definitely following the coast. It was K-something. Kapolei? Keawaula? Kahuku? Kaaawa? Crap. Nothing makes sense. Hawaiian place names are all Ks or Hs with too many vowels.

Give me a simple name I can find on a map. San Diego. Anaheim. La Jolla, even.

I peer through the windshield looking for the sun, but it's behind clouds. I can't tell if I'm heading west or south. Everything's palm trees, blue ocean, white sand, and towering green cliffs.

Probably circled the island at least twice by now.

I've been driving for days.

Or maybe just two or three hours. Nothing's normal anymore. It hasn't been for a very long time.

This is getting ridiculous.

When did I last see a sign that was more than a posted speed limit? The only car on the road in the last five miles passed me going the other way. No stores or gas stations in sight. Tank's half full, at least.

Keeping one eye on the road, I spread the map over the steering wheel. Oahu is littered with towns along the coast, but I'm surrounded by endless jungle on one side and ocean on the other. Beyond this two-lane highway and the occasional powerline in the distance, there are no signs of civilization.

In the heat, I shiver.

No wonder Mom's family left Lauele for California and never came back.

They couldn't find it again.

I take a deep breath. Relax, dumbass. It's an island. As long as I keep heading in one direction, the worst that can happen is I'm right back where I started.

Tossing the map, I wince as the car's vinyl seats tear at my skin like an aesthetician's wax strip. This sucks. I need to grab a beach towel from the trunk to sit on, maybe put a tee-shirt over the back of the bucket seat.

I've seen locals in beach cars.

I'd blend.

At the car rental counter at the airport, downgrading to a car with no AC didn't seem like a big deal, but driving with the windows down is like riding in hell's hairdryer. A glance in the rearview mirror tells me all I need to know. If I don't want to scare small children or get mistaken for a homeless dude, I'd better pick up a hat.

In a convertible, wind in your hair is sexy.

In this pregnant roller skate, it's just pathetic.

Sasha would never have been caught dead in a car like this.

Sasha.

Just thinking her name is enough to evoke her.

From my mind, Sasha pops into the empty passenger's seat. She turns to me and says, "That's the difference between you and me, Justin. I always go first-class. No regrets." She tips her head to the side and pouts, the red of her lipstick matching her manicured fingers and toes.

It's a look I know well, a look that says *my way*. With Sasha, there is no *else*, no *highway*, no possibility of any other way but her way existing in the entire universe.

I grind my teeth. I'm not taking the bait.

She sighs, and it's the sound of a martyr burdened with the terminally stupid. "But you couldn't even get that right."

I shake my head. I don't want to continue our imaginary conversation, but I do. Now that she's gone, I say all the things I should've said to her face.

It's your fault that I booked us a luxury, non-refundable honeymoon package, Sasha. You always go first-class? Right. Try picking up the check for once and see how long that lasts. This whole trip is use it or lose it, and it's all on me and my credit cards. Thanks for that. At least the guy at Aloha Car Rental did me a solid by allowing me to switch the Mercedes convertible you reserved for this POS. Maybe now I can eat more than ramen noodles next month. Hope you and that bastard Palo rot in hell.

She pulls down her Maui Jim sunglasses so I can see her roll her eyes. "Palo is a godsend. He taught me who I really am."

You're Sasha Maria Rodriguez. We were together for five years, five happy *years, until you got starry-eyed planning an extravagant fairy tale wedding, dumped me at the altar, and married our wedding planner instead.*

"Don't be mad. I just swapped the Pauper for the Prince."

Prince? You mean the guy pushing discounted floral arrangements and cheap cover bands? That's what you wanted?

"And what did you want, Justin? More art supplies?"

I wanted to get married, Sasha. I promised you I'd make you happy, and I always keep my promises. You're the one who broke faith.

She pushes her glasses back into place with a sigh. "It never would've worked, Justin. Like Palo says, I've evolved beyond you."

Palo's a pretentious prick who thinks people prefer lemon-thyme cake with tomato confit over chocolate. That's not evolved. That's Pinterest.

"Don't be angry. You would've tried and tried to make us work because that's who you are, Justin, but you could never satisfy my needs. Can't you be happy I've found someone who can?"

You sure about that, chica? No matter what you say, there's no way Fabulous Palo with the color-coded binders, bleached tips, and appetizers to die for doesn't play for both teams.

"Sticks and stones, Justin. True love—"

True love, my left—

The road curves sharper than I expect, and I take the corner too fast.

Oh, crap.

Tires squeal. The hotel's complimentary bottle of Dom Perignon tips and rolls against the passenger door. Heart thumping, I fight to keep four tires on the pavement and the car in my lane.

Without missing a beat, Sasha points to the bottle and says, "Where's the card?"

We almost died, Sasha.

She shrugs. "Not me. I'm only in your head. Where's the card that said Welcome Mr. & Mrs. Halpert?" She sniffs. "Did you keep it for your scrapbook?"

Pleeze. That's too catty even for you.

"But you kept the champagne." She puts her hand to her chest and pretends to look around. "No crystal flutes?"

No need for a glass when there's one set of lips, Sasha.

"A whole bottle of honeymoon champagne for yourself? Aw, that's so sad."

I'm not going to waste a drop. Not going to waste this trip either.

I wipe the sweat out of my eyes, refusing to look at her any longer.

Done.

I'm so done.

Done before I started.

I wiggle in my seat, eyes darting to the center console with the empty Super Big Gulp in the cup holder.

I even ate the ice.

Don't think about the pressure threatening to erupt.

It's hot. No AC. Can't drink champagne and drive. End of story.

I'm just going to swallow hard and ignore how the ocean crashes against the shore. I'm not thinking about how much this seat belt pushes against my guts.

Oh, man. Please, God. Don't make me be the guy who pulls off the side of the road to pee in the bushes like a three-year-old on a family trip. And if I really have to be that guy, please don't let me be the guy who also gets arrested for indecent exposure.

On his honeymoon.

Alone.

Sasha snickers. "Loser," she says.

Ugh! It's been a week. Get out of my head!

She blows me a kiss. "Don't worry, Justin. I'll still visit you in prison."

The vein in my temple bulges.

That's —

No, no, no. Bad idea. Bad. Don't get angry. Relax. Anger makes gut muscles clench.

Sensing weakness, Sasha goes for the kill. She rises from the passenger's seat to float in front of my face, banging a tin cup against prison bars.

"Look on the bright side. In addition to three hot meals a day, you'll finally get to use your fancy art degree to create prison tats."

Ka-BOOM.

I'm swearing so hard, I almost miss it: the big beach pavilion and public restrooms across the street from a store called Hari's.

Hallelujah! Saved.

I screech into the parking lot, peel my body from the vinyl seat, and sprint past the sign saying Keikikai Beach.

Another Hawaiian K place. What a surprise.

Standing at the urinal, the relief is immediate. I start to grin.

Sorry, Sasha. No prison cobweb or teardrop tattoos today.

But if I did them, they'd rock.

Washing my hands, I catch myself in the mirror: stubble streaked chin, red eyes, wild hair.

Crazy.

Or homeless.

I lean close and narrow my eyes.

Not crazy. Not homeless.

Dangerous.

I turn the water off and run my wet hands through my hair, sweeping it back and to the side.

Better. Less psycho, more Wall Street.

It hits me.

I can be different.

I don't have to be the guy who flies with an empty seat beside him in first-class. I can be the guy who finds a young couple flying coach and trades seats.

I don't have to be the guy who gets lost circling an island because staying alone in the honeymoon suite is just too hard.

And I definitely don't have to be the guy who allows the memory of his former fiancé to torment him with his own insecurities.

I can be New Me.

It's only afternoon, I have a bottle of warm bubbly all to myself, and I no longer give a damn.

Not going to prison.

Yet.

CHAPTER 3

JUSTIN

*C*oming out of the bathroom, I walk to the edge of the pavilion and survey the beach below. It's a wide bay split by an outcrop of lava littered with tidepools. The beach in front of me is calm and shallow, the water clear all the way to the sandy bottom. On the far side of the lava outcrop, the ocean is darker and wilder, hinting at deep water. I bet when conditions are right, the surfing's good over there.

Sunlight tickles the water as clouds reflect in tide pools. Patterns lie just beneath the surface. I feel a familiar twitch between my shoulder blades as my mind takes the shapes, the dark and the light, and twists them.

I flex my fingers, considering.

Behind me are picnic tables and benches. The pavilion sits on a rise above the beach. The breeze off the ocean is fresh and clean.

New Me says, "Seize the moment. Drive to Lauele another day."

He's right. It's time to create.

Back at the car, I get my sketch pad and a pencil. They're nothing fancy, but I keep them with me for times when memory alone isn't enough to capture what I'm seeing.

What I'm feeling.

As I lock the car, the bottle catches my eye. Picking it up, I know Sasha's right. Drinking honeymoon champagne alone is beyond sad.

New Me says, "Take it back and leave it for housekeeping."

I sigh.

There better be extra chocolates on my pillow if I do.

But before I can put the bottle back, a muse whispers in my ear. "Forget housekeeping. Sunset's only a couple of hours away. As the sun slips beyond the horizon, open the bottle on the beach, take a sip, and pour the rest into the ocean in honor of broken-hearted homies everywhere."

Beautiful! I'll do it.

"And then forget that wench, pick your lame ass off the ground, and never look back."

Whoa. Cranky muse.

But she's right.

Tomorrow's a new day.

A new Sasha-less day.

I'm gonna be New Me.

Now let's all hold hands and sing *Kumbaya*.

New Me shakes my head.

Maybe not.

Crossing the pavilion, I place the bottle on a picnic table and perch beside it. Flipping to a blank page, I lose myself in art.

Half-way through the sketch, I'm ambushed.

"Eh, excuse, yeah? You know what time the Waimanalo bus come?"

"Holy—!" Startled, my pencil jerks across the page and strikes the bottom of a walking boogie board.

"Eh, watch it! No ding my board!" The board shifts to reveal a boy's shock of surfer-white hair, fierce brown eyes, and a puka shell necklace. He checks the back of his board and scowls, licking his thumb to swipe at the pencil mark.

I look down at my sketch pad. There's a bold line that doesn't belong. No way that's going to erase as easily as the mark on the board.

Ruined.

I'll have to start over.

Perfect.

I sigh.

The boy says, "You lucky it only scratched!"

"Oh. Sorry. You startled me."

Mid-scrub, his eyes narrow. He raises an eyebrow and cocks his head to the side. "What you said?"

"I said I'm sorry about your board." I turn my sketch pad toward him. "If it makes you feel better, my drawing's trashed."

His shoulders sag. "You're not from around here."

I throw my hands up and laugh. "I don't even know where here is."

He spots the bottle and tips his chin. "You lolo or drunk?"

"I don't know what lolo is, but the cork's still in the bottle."

The boy cranes his neck and sees that the bottle is unopened. "Huh," he says, "not drunk, so you must be lolo, then. Only crazy people don't know where they are."

I smile. "Not crazy. Lost."

"Fo'real?" He looks around, waving an arm. "This is the pavilion above Keikikai Beach. There's a sign out front and everything."

"I was trying to find Lauele Town," I say.

"Lauele?" He wrinkles his nose.

I shrug. "It's complicated."

He shakes his head. "No, it's not, brah. This beach is in Lauele."

"Really?" I turn toward the road. "Where's the town?"

The boy throws his arm wide and spins in a half-circle. "This whole place is Lauele. Hari's store is across the street. Nalupuki beach is over there. Aunty Liz-dem's house is that way. Lauele Elementary is mauka—toward the mountains. The boat harbor is a couple miles, maybe, but still in Lauele. What you trying to find?"

I rub my eyes. No wonder it's not on the map. Lauele isn't a town, it's a wide spot in the road.

"Nothing," I say, pinching the bridge of my nose. "I just wanted to see it. My family came from here."

"Oh, so you're a Coconut," he says, shuffling his feet and rocking his board. "Shoulda known."

"What?"

He has the grace to blush just a little bit, but won't meet my eyes.

He mumbles, "When I first saw you, I thought for sure you were from around here. You were sitting on top the table like a local braddah. Your hair is dark. You're wearing surfer shorts. But when I get closer, I see you drawing, drawing, drawing, paying no attention to anything else. And then I see you're wearing shoes and socks AT THE BEACH! Ho, that's one classic Coconut move. Shoulda known you don't know nothing about buses."

"Coconuts don't ride buses?"

"Coconuts drive rentals."

"And wear shoes and socks to the beach? That's a Coconut?" I ask.

The boy flaps his hand. "Brah, Coconuts are brown on the outside, white on the inside. That's you. You look like a local, but you're not."

I eye the boy's golden tan and spiky blond hair. He's no pure-blooded Hawaiian, either.

"So, if I'm a Coconut, what are you?"

"Me?" The boy proudly squares his shoulders. "I'm a Cocoa Puff!"

I blink. "A what?"

"A Cocoa Puff! You know, a malasada with chocolate dobash filling." When I don't respond, he smacks his forehead. "It's like a chocolate-filled doughnut. Golden delicious on the outside, brown on the inside."

"I see," I say, and bite my lip.

"Eh, no laugh! All the wahines love Cocoa Puffs!"

"Wahines? Girls, you mean? How old are you?"

"Nine. Why, how old are you?"

"Old enough."

"For what?"

"To know what women really want," I say.

The boy tips his head to the side. "Uh huh. That's why you're sitting here all by yourself with a full bottle of wine?"

"Maybe I'm meeting someone."

The boy nods sagely. "Truth," he says, "but if you're going to share that bottle, you better get some glasses. Wahines don't like germs. Girls are funny kine li'dat."

"Thanks for the tip."

"No prob. So, Cuz, you don't know when the next bus coming?"

"Nope. Sorry."

"Shoots. My Mom's going be cockroach-killing, slippah mad when I'm not home before sunset." He shakes his head and looks at his feet. "An'den," he sighs.

"Anden? That's your name?"

"No, brah. Wow. You look local, but you're such a Coconut, like fo'reals."

I'm not entirely sure what he's saying. I flip my sketch pad closed, tuck my pencil behind my ear, and stand.

"So, you're good?" I say, grabbing the bottle. "You need bus money?"

"No. Thanks, but." The boy picks up his boogie board and shifted uneasily.

"What?" I ask.

He opens his mouth, then snaps it shut.

"What?"

He presses his lips tight and shrugs.

"You already called me a Coconut. It's all good," I say. "Just tell me. I can take it."

"Eh, you're not going swimming, right?" he blurts.

I look at him nonplussed. "It's a beach."

"Yeah, but…" He points to a sign near the showers.

Danger. Shark zone. Swim at your own risk. At the bottom is a picture of a swimmer one second from being a Jaws snack.

At first glance, it's hilarious. I've seen signs like this posted by locals in California to scare tourists away. Keikikai must be a locals only beach.

And then I get pissed.

I reach out and thump the back of his boogie board. His eyes go wide, and he flinches a little as I loom over him.

"Didn't you just come out of the water?" I say.

"Yeah," he says slowly, puzzled by my tone. "But it's different for me."

I stand tall, cross my arms, and look down my nose. "Sharks don't bite Cream Puffs?"

"Cocoa Puffs!"

"Right, Cocoa Puffs. Sharks don't bite you because you're a Cocoa Puff?"

He looks down, confused. After a beat he mutters, "Something li'dat."

I waver. There's more going on here; he's genuinely concerned for me. I relax my arms and shift my weight.

I say, "You aren't afraid of sharks."

His chin snaps up. "Only stupid heads not afraid of sharks," he spits.

I think for a second. "You aren't afraid of sharks *here.*"

"No, but—"

"Have you seen sharks here?" I press.

He swallows and looks away for a second, then decides. "Yeah," he says. "I seen sharks here." He points to the end of the lava outcrop. "That's Piko Point." He sweeps his arm to the right. "That beach is Nalupuki. Good surfing right off Piko Point. On your board, if you look down in the water there, you'll see choke reef sharks—black tip, grey reef, sandbar—"

I interrupt. "Not all sharks are dangerous."

He flashes me a relieved look. "Right! Those kinds of sharks you don't worry about. You just keep an eye on them. If they start acting funny, that's your warning to get out of the water."

"Got it. So why does the sign show a big shark about to eat someone?"

He points to the ocean beyond the lava outcrop. "Out there are other sharks—big sharks. Niuhi sharks. Unlike a reef shark, you can't just look down into the water to see if they're annoyed. You never see Niuhi sharks coming unless they want you to see them."

"Sharks are ambush predators. Why would a shark want me to see him?"

He blinks, surprised. "To make a point about something. To make sure you understand that they're the boss. You never want a Niuhi shark interested, you know, curious about you. If they mark you, you might as well say your good-byes because you're already dead and just don't know it." He meets my eyes. "Fo'real," he says. "No joke. If a Niuhi shark marks you, you're never safe. You're shark bait every time."

"The sign's not a joke? There really are big sharks out there?"

"Yeah."

"Can you show me?"

He shakes his head. "Not now."

"You were surfing five minutes ago. What's changed?"

He points to the sun two finger widths away from kissing the water.

"Sunset, brah. You don't want to believe me, fine. But never go into the ocean at night, especially around Lauele. Anybody'll tell you that."

"Okay. No swimming tonight. Just walking, promise."

The boy's shoulders ease.

"But honestly, I'm coming back tomorrow. I'd like to see some sharks."

"You sure? Maybe it's better if you stay in Waikiki. No sharks," he says.

"But more people."

"Truth. But that's why no sharks."

"I like sharks."

He dusts a bit of sand from his elbow and sighs. "You're one stupid head Coconut, for sure. Nobody likes sharks."

He leans his board against the table and walks to a spindly plant growing near the parking lot.

"If you're going to get in the water, you better know how to stay safe." He touches a leaf. "It's called a ti plant. Take some leaves and twist them into a lei to wear in the ocean." He holds out his leg so I can see the intricately braided ti leaf lei around his ankle. "Like this."

"Nice," I say.

"Here, you try." He breaks off a couple of leaves and hands them to me. In my palms, I roll them against each other. They're waxy and slender, like leaves on corn stalks. I lift them to my nose, but I don't smell anything special.

The boy clicks his tongue. "Never mind. I'll make it." Snatching the leaves back, he deftly shreds them into strips, weaves a simple braid, and presents the finished lei to me. "Of course, mine's more fancy, but that'll work."

"That's shark repellant? A braided leaf?"

"Underwater, all legs look the same. That lei marks you as a local and asks the Niuhi sharks not to bite. I mean, they'll still bite if they want to, but the lei just reminds everyone to be a good neighbors."

"Oh. Makes perfect sense."

He looks at me, unsure if I'm making fun.

At this point, I'm not sure either.

"My Mom says you don't need wear the lei in a specific place, but I put mine on my ankle 'cause I figure when you're sitting on a surfboard, sharks can't see a lei around your neck. Legs always dangle, yeah?"

"Smart."

He walks back to his board and gives me a little wave. "Okay, then. If you see a big shark out there—"

"—get out of the water."

His brown eyes turn serious. "You can't. By then it's too late. But you can always try to tell them you're friends with Nili-boy. It might help."

"Who's Nili-boy?"

"That's me."

"Of course it is."

Nili-boy lifts his board and balances it on his head. "Laters, Coconut." He flashes me a hand signal, thumb and pinkie extended, middle three fingers folded against his palm.

Shark sign language, I'm sure.

And he thought I was crazy.

"Bye, Nili-boy," I say. "Thanks for the lei. But what if I meet a tourist shark, and he doesn't know you?"

"Pray, brah. That's all you got left." He tips his chin toward the lei in my hand. "Better put it on now before you forget."

"I won't. I'm not going to forget any of this."

Shaking his head and muttering about coconuts, sunsets, and bus stops, I watch as Nili-boy carries his boogie board down the street and out of sight.

I read the sign again and snort.

Shark zone.

Right.

I put the ti leaf lei in my back pocket before slipping off my shoes and socks and leaving them on the rock wall near the sign.

As I head down to the water, the sand burns, so I step a little quicker.

Cooling my feet at the ocean's edge, I watch how the colors melt from clear turquoise at the shore to deep purple at the horizon, so different from the uniform gray of the California coast. The breeze off the water is refreshing, not freezing, and smells like salted flowers and sunshine.

Maybe if I lived here, I wouldn't want to share, either.

I tuck my sketch book under my arm and turn my attention to the bottle. Stripping the foil, I slip it into my pocket before popping the cork. Angry champagne froths down my arm. Warm and shaken too much, it's eager to merge with the seafoam at my feet and be done.

"To Sasha," I say, and tip the bottle to my lips. My mouth fills with sparkling air and the faint taste of sour grapes. The bubbles roll up the back of my nose, making my sinuses burn.

What a whole lot of nothing.

I turn the bottle over and pour the rest into the sea.

CHAPTER 4

JUSTIN

I walk.

Maybe it's to find shells. Maybe it's just to move a little before the long drive back to Waikiki. Maybe it's to finish becoming New Me.

Maybe it's fate.

All I know is one minute I'm walking along the beach at the sweet spot where the sand is firm and the ocean gently kisses your toes, and the next I'm noticing a bright spot of color against the white sand.

Someone's beach towel or mat?

Mildly curious, I look out to sea and along the beach, but there's no one around. Moving closer, a shape takes form—a dark head and curled legs.

Is that a body?

Heart pumping faster, I start to jog, watching for movement, for breathing, for anything to tell me to hurry or slow down. My hand reaches for my cell phone in my pocket.

911, right? Even in Hawaii it's got to be 911.

Closer now, I see it's a woman lying on the sand, wrapped in a bright yellow sarong.

Do people do that, just lie in the sand without a beach mat?

Is she hurt?

No blood.

Her hair is dark and her skin, copper. She looks local. Maybe islanders don't bother with beach mats.

When I get close enough to see her chest gently rise, I slow.

I pause a few feet from her.

Not dead.

Sleeping.

The setting sun is soft on her features. With her knees drawn up, ankles crossed, and her arm cradling her head, there's an air of innocence about her. Long lashes sweep high cheekbones; her nose is straight and narrow; her full lips rest in a Mona Lisa smile.

Like a sea nymph come ashore.

I squat, tipping my head this way and that, mesmerized by the way light moves over her, the way the breeze toys with bits of loose hair, the way small specks of sand cling to her cheeks. My fingers twitch with the need to paint, to capture this moment forever. I sink to the sand, pull my pencil from behind my ear, and start to sketch.

One sweep of a soft line to suggest her arm tucked behind her head. Another line forms the shape of her face—forehead, nose, eyes, lips, chin. A shadow creates the hollow in her throat. Stroke, smudge, slide—my pencil moves without thought as my eyes devour her.

The pink and gold of the sunset dances in her hair—Argh! I can't capture it with this black pencil! Her eyes are—

Her eyes are—

Her eyes are looking right at me.

Oh, crap. I'm THAT guy.

I'm sitting on the beach next to a beautiful woman, a stranger, practically drooling.

She blinks once, twice.

She opens her mouth.

I brace myself for the scream.

"Hi," she says with a sigh. She sits up and sweeps a stray bit of hair away from her face. "That was glorious."

What the what? Is she for real?

"What's wrong?" she says. "You look like you've seen a ghost."

"N...n...nothing's wrong. Sorry to disturb you." I snap my book closed, tuck my pencil behind my ear, and scramble to get up.

She tips her head to the side. "Are you sure? You look pale around the lips. You aren't going to faint on me, are you?"

Light-headed, I sit back down. "I don't think so. I was actually worried about you."

"Me?"

"I thought you might be dead."

She smiles. "How sweet. That's the nicest thing anyone's said to me in a long time."

I puff out my cheeks in disbelief. "I said I thought you were dead!"

"I heard you. You were worried. That means you care. I bet you're honest and trustworthy, too."

"You make me sound like a Boy Scout," I say.

"Is that a bad thing?"

"Well—"

"See? You can't even lie about that," she says, idly brushing sand off her shoulders.

"You don't mind the sand?" I blurt.

"What's to mind?"

I open my mouth and shut it again.

Did I just fall down a rabbit hole?

I shake my head and start again.

"So, you're okay?"

"I'm fine, but as I recall, we started this conversation wondering about your health." She raises an eyebrow.

"Well, I'm fine, too."

"Great."

"Great."

We look at each other.

"Okay, then." I stand. "Guess I'd better be going."

She raises her arms over her head and stretches with the grace of ballet dancer, her breasts straining against the sarong.

Is the knot going to hold?

I can't breathe.

"Going where?" she asks.

"Back to my hotel," I squeak.

"Waikiki?"

"Yeah."

She grins, and her face lights up like it's Christmas, the 4th of July, and her birthday all at once. "You're not from around here."

"No, I'm from the States."

The corner of her mouth twitches. "Yes, I've heard of it. Pretty big place."

Too late, I realize what I said. "I mean I know Hawaii's a state, I just…um…"

In my head, Sasha laughs. "Smooth as Ex-Lax," she says.

Shut up, Sasha!

"You sure you're all right? You've gone from pale to flushed."

I sit back down.

Up. Down. Up. Down. I'm worse than a bloody Jack-in-the-box.

"I'm sorry," I say. "I'm not very good at this."

"Hello, Not Very Good at This. My name is Pua-O-Ke-Kai."

My mouth stumbles. "Pua-O…"

"Call me Pua, for short. It means flower." She holds out her hand.

I take it. It's soft and warm and smooth as buttercream frosting.

I want to lick it.

I shake my head.

What is wrong with me?

"Hello, Pua For Short. I'm Justin. I have no idea what my name means. My parents chose it."

She laughs. "Mine, too. With this much in common, we're destined to be friends."

"Thank you for not screaming."

"Because we're friends?"

"Because you caught me staring at you like some weirdo while you were sleeping."

"Most women would have screamed?"

"Oh, yeah," I say.

Her eyes widen.

"I mean, it wasn't like that, I'm not a pervert..."

"Good to know," she says.

I stop and take a breath. "I told you I wasn't very good at this."

"You're doing fine. Can I have my hand back?"

"Oh! Sorry!"

"So, if you're not a pervert, what are you?"

"A painter."

"Of houses?"

"Of portraits." I wave my sketch book. "I was trying to visualize how I would paint you."

"Flattery. And you say you're not good at this."

I grin. "I also do some sculpting and ceramics."

"An artist."

"A jack of all trades and a master of none. At least my professors think so."

"Professors? You're a scholar?"

"More like permanent student. I'm on the five-year MFA plan at UCLA. ABD."

"ABD?" she asks.

"All But Dissertation. I haven't finished my portfolio for an art show."

"Is that why you're here?"

"It's complicated," I hedge.

"Maybe you'll feel inspired by the islands," she says, toying with her hair. "Many do."

"How about you?"

"Oh, I'm long done with school, but not with learning. The world's too interesting for that."

"I like that. Out of school, but still a student. So, what do you do with yourself?"

She smiles wider. "I travel."

"Trust fund baby."

"No, but you're right. I don't worry about money."

"Must be nice."

She looks out to sea. "No worries about money, but plenty about time. The sun's gone down. I've got to get going. Kalei's going to be furious if he finds out I've spent the afternoon on the beach."

I knew it. Girls like her are never free.

"Kalei's your boyfriend?"

She stands, brushing sand off her butt.

Butt.

Don't stare at her butt.

Absentmindedly, she shakes sand off the front of her sarong.

I wonder what she's wearing underneath.

Or not wearing.

I squeeze my eyes tight.

Maybe I am a pervert.

She reaches up and pulls her hair into a knot on the top of her head. "Kalei's my brother. I don't have a boyfriend," she says.

Want one? New Me growls.

Stop being a pig.

Bet I could make you forget time, too.

Just. Stop.

I swallow.

Keeping my eyes glued to her face, I say, "Your brother can't be that mad at you. Tell him it was an emergency. A beach emergency. You had to help a tourist out."

She says, "But now that you're okay, and I'm okay…"

"You have to go. I understand."

I stand and brush sand off my shorts, angling my butt toward her just a little bit.

Two can play this game.

Damn.

She's not looking.

Chillax. Just play it cool.

"It's time I headed back, too," I say.

I pause.

Go for it, New Me shouts.

"I'd like to see you again."

Surprised, she steps toward me. "You would?"

"If that's all right?"

"You're sure about this? You're choosing of your own free will to see me again?" Her lips curl inscrutably, like the cat that licked the cream.

I grab my cell phone out of my pocket. "What's your number?"

"I don't have one."

"You don't have one?"

"No."

"Oh. Do you want my phone number?" I ask.

"I don't have a phone."

I look at her. "Do you have a quarter? I can give you one."

"What?"

I sigh. "How are we going to meet again?"

"The usual way," she gestures, "along the beach."

"Along the beach?"

"Uh huh."

"You live around here?" I ask.

"Not far."

"Where?"

She steps close and leans toward me, gently placing her forehead on mine, nose to nose.

What the what? She wants to *kiss*? Here? Now?

New Me jumps to attention.

Don't wait for an engraved invitation, idiot! Kiss her!

I start to push forward to capture her lips, but she doesn't yield. She places her hands on my shoulders and holds me in place.

She exhales, her breath rising from her lungs to crawl up my nostrils and hover in the back of my throat. The scent of lemon, salt, sandalwood, and something I can't identify swirls around me. I feel lightheaded and dizzy like I've downed a shot or ten of tequila on an empty stomach.

I sway, but she holds me steady.

The air rushes out of my lungs, and it's her turn to breathe deeply.

She holds me just a beat longer, then steps back.

What the hell just happened?

I shake my head to clear it.

Crap! I run my tongue over my teeth. When did I last brush?

"I find you interesting, Justin. Don't worry," she says, "I'll find you. We carry a part of each other now."

"Pua…"

"Good bye, Justin. See you soon." She turns and lightly runs toward the lava outcrop that stretches out to sea.

I'm still too dizzy to do more than blink.

Seriously, what the hell was that all about?

Bemused, I watch her tiptoe barefoot over the rocks.

Oh, no. Her shoes.

I search the sand where she was lying, but she's left nothing behind.

When I look back toward the outcrop, she's gone.

What?

I scan the beach, but there's no sign of her.

Can't be. There's nowhere to go.

Did she fall?

I start to jog over, but with the sun down, it's hard to distinguish the water from the rocks.

A trick of the light. That's it.

I touch my nose, still feeling her forehead against mine.

What was that breathing thing?

Was she flirting with me? It didn't feel like flirting.

Did she want me to kiss her? I should have kissed her.

I'm such an idiot.

I don't see the wave that splashes against my knees.

Tide's coming in.

The usual way.

We'll met again *the usual way.*

I kick a rotten coconut husk as I turn toward the pavilion.

How many guys does it take for there to be a *usual* way?

How could she not have a phone?

Was she playing me?

She was playing me. No one that good looking and over 21 worries about what her brother thinks.

Of course she has a boyfriend.

He's probably the one with the trust fund.

I am an idiot.

I shake my head.

Get a grip.

You went from "she's the love of your life" to "she's a tramp" in one breath. Chill. You'll see her if you see her.

I'm such an idiot.

CHAPTER 5

PUA

Surrounded by ink-black ocean and cold lava rock, Pua waits for her brother Kalei. The moon isn't quite full, maybe in another night or two, but it still shines like a beacon over Piko Point. The ocean is calm, the sky clear, and the stars and moon sparkle like jewels in the large saltwater pool near her feet. She sits and toys with small hermit crabs, trying to decide how much she will tell Kalei about Justin, that strange young man who'd caught her napping in the sun.

All tourists are crazy. She should forget Justin and not meet him again, especially here on this beach.

She shouldn't, but she knows she will.

Pua hugs her knees, looking out to sea. She feels her brother Kalei walk up behind her, not because the echo of his slight limp reverberates through the lava—his missing right toe tends to throw-off his walking balance—but simply because she knows he's there.

Twins always know.

"Pua."

"Kalei." She doesn't turn around.

"You weren't at the harbor this afternoon."

"I'm sorry."

"I waited."

"I lost track of time."

"That's impossible."

She rolls her eyes. "It's the truth."

Kalei sits beside her. His fingers tug the edge of her sarong. "I've never seen this before."

"It's new," she says, eyes back on the sea.

Kalei follows her gaze and sighs. "You're distracted. What's wrong?"

"Nothing."

"I don't believe you."

"It's nothing."

"Your lips are pale. When did you last eat?"

She shrugs.

His eyes narrow. "You've met someone."

She shrugs again, not meeting his eyes.

"Pua? You did, didn't you? It's been decades since I've seen you like this, but I know I'm right. Tell me true." He licks his lips. "Is he delicious?"

She grins. "He is easy on the eyes."

"You naughty girl! You find him *interesting*?"

She nods. "We honi. I marked him. He's mine."

"Breath mingles in bodies? So soon! Details!"

"He's a tourist."

"Of course. Tell me something I don't know."

"Young. Mid-twenties. He's an artist from California. I really don't know much about him. He wants to see me again."

"He said that? Before or after the honi?"

"Before."

"How utterly delightful. He's baring his belly. How'd you meet? Waikiki? Is that where you got that ridiculous sarong?"

She fiddles for a moment with the fringe, smoothing it over her knees. "No, I found it on the beach this afternoon." She points to Keikikai in the distance. "Just over there."

Kalei stills, all joking pushed aside. "You walked on Keikikai beach in the daylight?"

"Napped, actually."

He puts his hand over his mouth for a beat, then shakes his head. "I don't have to tell you how dangerous that is."

"No."

"Why, Pua? You know Father's kapu."

"The kapu only says that no Niuhi-human sons may be born. It doesn't forbid napping on the beach in the sun."

"If you want to lie in the sun, go to the northern islands. Visit Aunty Ake at Respite Beach. Head to California or Tahiti for all I care. But you can't lie on the beach in Lauele. It's too dangerous."

"Father's rules."

"The Great Ocean God Kanaloa's kapu laws, Pua. You're playing with fire, and you know it. The only way for you to have a son is to mate with a human whose bloodlines come from Lauele—"

"—under a full moon and on the beach at Keikikai. I know, I know. And that's a world away from what happened this afternoon."

"Did anyone see you?"

"Nili-boy was surfing alone at Nalupuki. There wasn't anyone else when I came up the beach."

Kalei waves his hand. "I'm not worried about Nili-boy. But napping in the sun at Keikikai, that's risky behavior even for you."

"I couldn't help it. I was just so tired."

"Tired? Impossible."

"Not tired, exactly. Restless. I came to Keikikai because there was an itchy feeling right beneath my dorsal fin. No matter what I did, I couldn't scratch it. When I spotted the sarong on the shore, I had to have it. I was all the way up the beach before I realized what I had done. But the sun felt so good, Kalei, the air so fresh in my lungs—"

"You had to stay," he says, his tone flat as death.

"Yeah," Pua says.

Kalei leans over and inhales Pua's scent, confirming what he suspects. "You're kahe."

Pua bolts upright. "That's impossible! Father wouldn't allow it."

"He told you to stay away from Lauele. Did you listen?"

"I—"

"Let me see the back of your neck, Pua."

"No."

Kalei snatches her hair and twists.

"Hey!" Pua struggles, slapping at his arms, but he ignores her and lifts the braid off her neck. In the moonlight, the turtle tattoo is faint, but distinct along her nape.

"The turtle mark is there. You're kahe. Your body is ready to bear children."

"I don't believe you."

"It's there, Pua. I wouldn't lie to you about this."

"I'm Niuhi, not a bitch in heat."

Kalei drops her braid and slides his arm around her shoulders. "Think about it. Your maternal instincts are driving you here. Why else would you come to the one place that means death for us all?"

"And whose fault is that? I remember when you were kahe, Kalei, and running to Lauele like salmon up a river. I remember Nanaue, the son you had with a human mother, the son who turned into a monster and got us banished from our home."

In the darkness, Kalei flinches. "Nanaue became a monster because his human grandfather wouldn't deny him anything."

Pua's voice drops to a hiss. "Centuries ago, Father promised the villagers we'd never return to Lauele. Their sons and daughters would be safe. No more Niuhi-human children like Nanaue who lure friends into the water and eat them like poi. Banished from our ancestral lands! We have your son to thank for that!"

"Pua—"

"And because of you and your appetites, I can never be a mother. Did you ever think about that? No. All you worry about is your duty to Father and his laws."

Kalei explodes. "And why is that? Do you ever think about what it means to me if you break kapu? I have to kill you, Pua, you and your Niuhi-human son! If I don't—"

"Father kills us all. I know."

"Do you, Pua? Do you understand why I get so angry when you hang around Lauele—in human form, no less?"

"I am in control of my destiny, Kalei. I'm not a mindless rutting goat."

"Are you willing to do what it takes to not conceive, Pua? You're not so fond of red meat as I recall."

"Devour him, you mean? That's only necessary if the man is from Lauele, remember?"

"The man—that *interesting* man. Where did you find him?"

"He found me."

"Let me guess: on the beach at Keikikai when you were napping. This is exactly what I feared!"

"I told you, he's a tourist."

"You're sure?"

"He's staying in a hotel in Waikiki. It's fine."

"Fine?" Kalei closes his eyes. "You've already marked him."

"There's nothing to worry about."

"You're kahe. You've marked him. He'll find you irresistible."

"It's a dalliance, nothing more. We've both had them before."

"It's different when you're kahe. The risk—"

"—doesn't exist when your lover isn't the descendant of ancient villagers from Lauele." Pua leans her head on Kalei's shoulder. "Think of it this way. He'll scratch my itch and keep me entertained. If I am kahe—and I'm not saying I am—it'll pass. He'll get on a plane back to wherever he came from, and we'll go back to doing what we do best."

"I don't like this, Pua. Not one bit."

"He's a tourist. He'll be gone in a week."

"He could come back."

"I'll make sure he doesn't," she says.

"If they find any part of a body—"

"I don't need a lecture about how the shark hunts will start again. Rabid men slaughtering sharks by the dozens. Panic driving humans to kill indiscriminately. I'm not stupid. No one wants that. If I kill him, I'll leave no trace."

Kalei reaches down and scoops water from the big saltwater pool. It slides like liquid mercury through his fingers as he drizzles it over her feet. She wiggles her toes, flicking the drops away, each one tumbling in the moonlight before landing in the darkness.

Kalei speaks slowly. "Life is good now, Pua. We have a new home in Hohonukai. There's fish in the sea. We can travel wherever we want; humans don't bother us. Life wasn't always this easy."

"Me lying on the beach in the afternoon isn't going to change any of that. Like you said, we can go wherever we want. No one cares."

"What about Aunty Hanalei? She went to this beach and look what happened," Kalei says.

"Aunty Hanalei made the choice to live on land as a human. Her choice, not mine. Not ever," Pua says.

"She fell in love."

"Aunty Hanalei was crazy. Niuhi don't love what they eat."

Kalei's lips quirk in a crooked smile. "I used to think that, too, until I met Nanaue's mother."

"But still you left her and your child. We're Niuhi," Pua says. "We belong in the sea."

"Sometimes I wonder how things would be today if I'd chosen to stay back then."

Pua laughs. "Too many humans in the world have no room in their imagination for creatures like us, Kalei. They have no capacity to see the world as it is. Remember the newcomers' horror over Hawaiian wooden gods and sentient stones? A few high chiefs saw how foreigners lived and wanted what they had, so they ordered the villagers to tumble all the old gods to the ground, erasing traditions thousands of years old. Our father Kanaloa saw this coming, I'm convinced of that. Nanaue was only the excuse to hide us away."

"Maybe," he says, "but I miss the old days." He touches her ankle. "Your skin's too dry."

"Thank you for the compliments, brother dear. First my lips are too pale, now my skin looks dry. Do I need to brush my teeth, too?" She bares her teeth at him and pushes his dripping hand away with her foot. "Knock it off."

He shifts beside her on the cold, black lava. "Just trying to help."

"Don't. You're just irritating me."

"Pua?"

"What?"

"You do have to brush your teeth."

"Oh!" She pushes him with her shoulder, happy he's no longer so angry.

He nudges her back. "Well, someone had to tell you."

She thinks for a moment. "You're wrong about Hohonukai," she says. "It's a place we live; it's not our land."

"We have our land right here at Piko Point," Kalei says.

"Not all of it."

"What's done is done. They won't give us this valley back. Too many humans think they own parts of it now," Kalei says.

Pua says, "I know. It makes me sad."

"Makes me mad." He flicks a hermit crab into the water.

Pua touches his arm. "Kalei, I do know how dangerous it is for me to be here. If I could stop coming, I would."

"You're saying the valley is calling you? Is that it?"

She shrugs. "You ever heard of anyone having an itch like that?"

"Yeah." He grins. "Aunty Hanalei!"

She shoves him. "Shut-up and go if you're just going to make fun of me."

"You're the one talking chicken skin stories." In a high falsetto, he mocks, "Kalei, the land, the 'aina, is calling me; I have to go to the mysterious itching beach or die!"

"Technically, the beach is scratching. I'm itching."

"Whatever, Pua."

They watch the ocean spray dance above the lava as the waves crashed along the breakwater. The rhythm is soothing, like the heartbeat of their mother in the womb. They lean their heads together, lost in thought.

"I have to go away for a while," Kalei says. He lifts his chin to the ocean. "The ahi are running. Uncle Nalu says he needs my help."

"Do you want me to come?"

He shakes his head. "No. One look at you and Uncle Nalu would know you'd been at the beach."

She touched her face. "I burned?"

"You glow." He flashes his teeth. "But seriously, I want you stay away from this beach." He pauses. "I can't make you."

"No, you can't."

"But will you? Please? For me?"

It's the first time in their lives Kalei has ever asked her for anything. With all her heart, she wants to give it to him, but she can't make a promise she won't keep. She contemplates the stars, waiting for an answer to come.

Kalei sighs and follows her gaze to the sky. "Almost a full moon."

"Yes."

"Father left about an hour ago for the Big Island. When he asks, I'll tell him you went to Molokai for a while."

"To see Kamea. She's due soon. He won't think twice about that."

"At least that will help explain the tan. I hear all she wants to do is lie on the beach. I think she's trying to cook that keiki faster!"

He stands.

"Scratch that beach itch if you must, Pua, but be careful. You cannot afford to be seen, especially around here in the daytime."

He walks along the far edge of the saltwater pool to where it meets deeper, swifter currents through a passage to the open ocean. He stretches his arms over his head, looking back at her one last time.

"Sun bathing causes cancer, you know. Night is the best beach time."

Moonlight glints off his teeth, stark white against the shadow of his face.

Pua sticks out her tongue. "Since when have you ever worried about cancer? Enjoy your swim, Kalei. Tell Uncle Nalu aloha for me."

His face now grim, he says, "Remember Aunty Hanalei. She went fishing in landlocked waters and never came back."

He twists backward, throwing his body into the darkness. Splashless, he enters the water and dives through the tunnel into the open ocean.

"Show-off," Pua mutters.

She stands, wrapping the sarong tighter. Kalei's right. She needs to eat. She also needs to bathe; her skin feels chapped, rough from the sun, wind, and salt.

A change of clothes would be nice. Perhaps one of the Paris dresses. In five hours the sun will start to rise over the mountains.

She hopes Justin is an early riser. She can't afford to be in the sun too long.

CHAPTER 6

JUSTIN

*W*earing flip-flops and walking across the lava to Piko Point, I wonder if my footwear meets Nili-boy's approval. The dude at Snorkel Bob's just laughed when I asked him if locals ever wear shoes and socks at the beach.

It wasn't a nice laugh.

Whatever.

I rented snorkel gear and paid for a pair of flip-flops, climbed into my car, and headed back to Lauele.

As I carry my gear, I tell myself I'm here to find sharks, but Pua can't find me in *the usual way along the beach* if I'm not here.

I'm not as stupid as I look.

The sun's high in the sky. White pockets of salt and orange cast-off shells of crabs lie scattered across the lava. To my right, five surfers catch waves at Nalupuki. The waves aren't very big, but consistent, and I watch them pump fists and whoop as they ride all the way to shore.

Skirting around tide pools, I see schools of tiny grey fish and striped sergeant majors. The spines of sea urchins poke out from crevasses, and tiny charcoal black snails cling to the rocks.

On the wild ocean side, waves dash against the breakwater. I pause where the water splashes my knees and watch the currents. As long as I stick to the Keikikai side of the lava today, I should be okay. But I came to see sharks, and Nili-boy said they hang out on the Nalupuki side, the side where the surge can smash me into the rocks. To safely get there, I'll have to do a beach entry and swim out with the surfers.

I look toward the beach.

It's a long way back.

Looong way.

Maybe later this afternoon. I've come this far, might as well see it to the end.

I'm almost to Piko Point when I spot a medium-sized yellow dog snoozing on a ratty beach towel next to the biggest tide pool. Nearby is a pair of upside down flip-flops, the center post of the left one patched with a plastic bread tie.

"Hey, girl," I say.

She opens one eye, gives me the once over, and snuggles deeper into the towel.

I'm beneath her contempt.

Challenge accepted.

I set my bag down and walk to the tide pool's edge.

"Keeping an eye on your master's property while he dives, huh? You're a good doggie, aren't you, girl?"

I swear I see her roll her eyes and shake her head before turning her back to me.

"Aw, don't you want to be friends? I'm not going to hurt you."

Did she just chuckle?

Must be the wind.

Looking down into the water, I see different kinds of fish— yellow tangs, purple damsels, and Picasso triggers. A snowflake eel slips back into his home as an octopus hides near coral fans. The water's colder here and the surge is stronger than in the other tide pools—something's different. Stepping to the left, the light hits just right, and I see a large underwater archway leading to open blue water. At my feet are a couple of ledges worn smooth like steps.

Easy in, easy out. Looks like I won't have to do a beach entry after all.

"I bet this is where all the locals come to spearfish and gather lobster. Is your master out there, little girl?"

Not even an ear twitch.

"Hey, Pooch! I'm talking to you."

She squinches her eyes tighter.

I whistle.

Her body tenses, but she doesn't raise her head.

"Sweetie! I'm talking to you."

She tucks her nose to her chest and flattens her ears.

She's trying too hard to ignore me.

I'm going to make her love me.

"C'mon, let's be friends. I have something you'll like. Something my *friends* like."

I walk back to my snorkel bag and take out the snack I bought at Hari's store across the street.

"Beef jerky."

Her tail wraps tighter around her body. I slowly break the seal.

"Teriyaki. Ummmm, smells good."

Her whole body quivers.

I take a piece and wave it around.

"Looks tender."

I put it in my mouth.

"Wow. Delicious."

Her nose wrinkles. She raises her head, narrows her eyes, and chuffs one derisive chuff before flopping completely over to the other side.

I've been dismissed.

"Fine. Be that way. More for me." I tuck the jerky back in my bag, grab my snorkel gear, and sit at the edge of the tide pool. Mask rinsed, snorkel attached, fins on, I ease into the water.

I bob for a bit to get my bearings and then check out the arch. It's a clear shot through it and to the surface on the other side. In the tidepool, I hyperventilate a few times to prepare. One giant breath, and I bend at the waist and jackknife toward the arch.

Glancing back through the shimmery water I see the dog looking down at me, my bag of jerky in her mouth.

She got me.

She got me *good*.

It only takes four kicks before I'm through the arch.

The world's a little grayer twenty feet below the surface. I feel the surge tug against me, pulling me to deeper water. I relax and let it carry me away from the tunnel, then slowly kick to the surface.

It's ten minutes before the reef settles down enough for the first shark to appear.

I'm taking my time, cruising about fifteen feet above the reef, looking at all the sea life below, when a small white tip reef shark circles around a coral head. It's a juvenile, only about two feet long. I trail it as it glides along the bottom looking for starfish or octopus. I lose it when it turns and heads down through a crack in the reef.

Taking a moment to raise my head and get my bearings, I realize I'm about fifty yards from Piko Point, near where the surfers line up to catch waves.

I fill my lungs and jackknife, heading deep into dark water.

Twenty-five feet down, I wiggle my jaw again to make my ears pop.

Cruising along the bottom, I see them.

Nili-boy wasn't kidding.

Hammerheads, gray reef, blacktip, and even a galapagos shark all circle below me in an underwater ballet. Most are small, but a couple of the larger ones rest near the bottom where the current rushes over their gills.

I'm in love.

Too soon I have to kick to the surface for air. But I dive again and again, watching how they move and interact, wishing I could stay longer.

Scuba lessons, asap, I promise myself. Maybe Snorkel Bob can hook me up.

Another surface, another jackknife, a couple of powerful kicks, and—

Nothing.

This can't be.

Where'd all the fish go?

I surface and dive again, but the reef below is empty of sharks, butterfly fish, idols, parrot fish—gone, all gone. It's barren reef in all directions.

I'm on my way back up when I get hit from behind by a large brown blur that grabs me and forces me to the surface.

I spit my snorkel out and spin around, trying to figure out what's got my bicep in a vise. Suddenly, another mask surfaces next to me. He lets go of my arm, pulls his snorkel out of his mouth, and says, "We have to get out of the water. NOW!"

"What are you talking about?"

"Can't you feel it?"

"Feel what?" I look for the surfers, but they're headed back to shore.

"Didn't you see?" he says.

"See what? I didn't see anything."

"Exactly," he says. "Even the sharks are hiding. Follow me."

He puts his snorkel back in his mouth, holds his fishing spear parallel to the sea bottom, and kicks like an Olympic swimmer back to Piko Point.

When I come through the arch, he's already standing outside the tide pool, rubbing his legs with the ratty towel. He's an older man, part-Hawaiian at least, and he moves with a wiry grace that belies his age. Probably retired and able to spend his days spearfishing.

Lucky.

The yellow dog's nowhere in sight.

I surface and pull off my mask and snorkel.

"Here," he says, holding out his hand, "give 'em to me."

"Thanks."

"'A'ole pilikia," he says, placing my gear next to my bag.

"Ah-oh-lay…?"

He smiles. "'A'ole pilikia. It means no problem, no trouble. Sit on that ledge and take off your fins. Don't worry, no wana—sea urchins—live there."

I swim to the ledge, pull off my fins, and step out of the water.

"Towel?" he asks.

"I've got one, thanks." I dump my fins next to my mask and blot my face with one of the hotel's fluffy white finest, the ones they forbid you to take to the beach.

At their rates, they can afford to loan me a towel.

"You're not from around here," he says.

I slick my hair back and sigh. "Why does everyone keep bringing that up?"

He gestures to my ankle. "You're wearing a ti leaf lei. It threw me off when you didn't know 'a'ole pilikia."

I reach down, tug it off, and stuff it into the pocket of my swim trunks. "It's silly, I know. A kid told me it would protect me from sharks."

"You think it's superstition?"

I tip my head to the right, scrubbing harder with the towel. "Well, come on. If it worked someone would've figured out how to bottle it and make a buck, right?"

The old man opens his mouth, then screws his eyes tight, and snaps his lips closed. He swallows deliberately, then says, "But you wore it anyway."

It's the last thing I expect, a gentle chide that gets under my skin. "You're not wearing one," I say.

He blinks then throws his head back in a great belly laugh. "Oh, I wear one. Mine's just more permanent." He pivots to show me lines of triangles marching down his calves. He holds out his hand. "I'm Kahana."

"Justin." We shake, but then he twists his grip, and suddenly we're clasping thumbs.

"You need to learn how to do this like an island boy," Kahana says, giving my hand one last squeeze.

"I feel like there's a lot of things I need to learn." I point at his spearfishing pole. "That's a Hawaiian sling, right?"

"Yeah." He hands it to me. "Put your hand through the loop. Now twist. Pull back. Now grab the spear right there. See? If you let go, the surgical tubing shoots the spear forward."

"Cool."

"I catch a lot of dinners with this spear. I'm out here most days."

"Nice," I say.

"Beats a nine to five," he says, "even without weekends off."

"Retired?"

He smiles again. "Something like that."

"Hey, what happened out there?" I ask, handing back his spear.

Kahana takes it and throws his towel over his shoulder. "What do you think happened?"

"I'm not sure."

"You didn't feel the ocean telling us something?"

"Get out of the water?"

He nods. "Most of the time we never know why, but it's important that we listen. We'd outstayed our welcome."

"All the fish went into hiding," I say.

"That's the last sign." He holds out his arm. "The first is the hair on your arms stands up. You get a tingling in your spine. A hot spot forms on the back of your neck. You feel uneasy in the pit of your stomach. That's when you get out of the water. If you wait until you're the last thing swimming in the open, it's probably too late."

I nod. "I'll keep that in mind. Thanks."

Kahana slips his feet into his flip-flops and says, "This isn't a tourist kind of place. What brings you all the way out here?"

"I wanted to see sharks."

"Sharks? Are you crazy?"

"People surf with them daily. You swim with them daily. I wanted to see what they looked like up close."

Kahana rubs the towel across his face. "Pilikia," he says, "with a capital P. Sharks are trouble, brah, and up close they're even more trouble. Don't you have a TV? If you want to see sharks, do it from the safety of your living room. I hear there are entire cable channels devoted to that sort of thing."

"The documentaries only show teeth and fins. I can't see how light and shadows travel across their skin. I need to see how the whole shark moves if I'm going to get it right."

His eyes bug a little when I say this. A thousand words cross his mind, but he discards all except one: "Why?"

The truth? Since yesterday, I can't stop thinking about them. The curves of their spines. The edges of their fins. Their obsidian eyes with lids that snap from the bottom up.

Their rows and rows of teeth.

But I can't say any of that. Instead, I look at Kahana and tell him a secondary truth.

"I'm an art student in search of a project. I have an idea for an art show all about sharks. That's why—"

"—Waikiki Aquarium," he interrupts. "More better you go Waikiki Aquarium. Sit in front of the big and little tanks and sketch to your heart's delight. There you can get up close and personal with sharks without having to chase them over a reef. If you're feeling super adventurous, head to Sea Life Park. Costs more, though." He pauses to see if I'm hearing what he's trying to say. His teeth worry his lower lip. "You saw the sign at the pavilion, right?"

"Yeah."

"It's not a joke. There's no reason for you to recklessly endanger yourself here."

Mentally, I take a step back. Recklessly endanger? I'm a grown man, not a five-year-old.

"But it's okay for you to recklessly endanger yourself, right? It's what you do, every day you're out here hunting for dinner." I wince at my whiny tone. I don't mean it, but I can't help it.

His arm sweeps the ocean all the way to the beach. "This is my home. I don't have a choice. You do." He waits a beat, then adds, "You don't want to bite off more than you can chew, Justin. Things are not normal out there right now. I don't know why. I also don't want you—or anybody else—getting hurt."

I open my mouth to say something, anything, but before I do, there's a yip right behind me. I jump.

"Ah, Ilima," says Kahana, "there you are."

I spin around to see the jerky thief. "Finally came back for your master, huh?" I say.

"Master?" Kahana says. "Is that what you think?" He chuckles and wipes his eyes. "Oh, man. You hear that, Ilima? Master! That means I'm the boss!"

Ilima chuffs once and pants, tongue lolling past her chin.

Is that a smile?

"Ah, well. No fish today. Looks like we're having Spam and rice for dinner, Ilima." Kahana hefts his spear and gives me a tip of his chin. "Laters, brah. Like I said, better you go Waikiki Aquarium. It's dangerous here. But if you do come back, wear that ti leaf lei. It doesn't matter what you believe, Justin, only what the sharks do. Come, Ilima. We go."

He takes only a couple of steps toward shore before something on the lava catches his eye. Picking it up, he reaches back and hands me the empty jerky bag. "Yours, yeah? Make sure it gets in a rubbish can. Nobody likes swimming in a landfill."

"Right," I say, taking the wrapper.

Scolded like I'm five again.

I swear the dog is laughing at me.

I scowl at her, and she gives her whole body a shake that ends in an innocent *who, me?* look.

There's something up with that dog.

"I'll make sure the trash gets where it belongs. Thanks for everything."

"No problem," he says.

I tuck the wrapper into my pocket next to the soggy ti leaf lei and watch as Kahana makes his way to the pavilion, Ilima leading the way.

"Yeah," I mutter. "No problem. Ah-something-easy-for-you-to-say."

CHAPTER 7

JUSTIN

*a*t the showers, I rinse off my gear before stepping into the cold spray to scrub the salt out of my hair and the sand off my feet. My mind swims with images of sharks. How do I recreate the feeling—

Paint the floor.

It bursts into my brain like a symphony.

Put the audience in a bubble floating in the sea. A circular wall mural of ocean life from a center perspective that shatters as they walk. Paint the floor to look like bottom of the ocean as seen through glass, the ceiling like looking up through water to sunlight. Suspend sculptures throughout the exhibit space. Diffuse the light and layer shadows. Use fans to create currents against the skin and to move schools of fish strung on mobiles. Use humidifiers to waft salt scents through the air. Add an airlock to the room to increase the feeling of pressure in ears and sinuses. Play the sounds of fish nibbling, shellfish snapping, the roar of surf as it rolls against the shore, the distant calls of whales…

I'm so excited, hair raises along my arms.

Finally, a vision for my dissertation. I'll bring the ocean to the landlocked in the form of a bubble under the sea. An art show like this could do more than entertain, it could educate, engage, and inspire. School kids could—

"Aloha, Justin."

I wipe water out of my eyes and smile. "You found me."

Pua laughs. "Was there any doubt?"

I turn off the water and grab my towel. In a deceptively simple green and yellow sundress, she's stunning.

"That you could find me? No," I say. "That you'd want to, well, yeah."

She shifts her weight. "Why wouldn't I?"

"Are you kidding? Look at you in that Givenchy dress, oozing elegance. Look at me all covered in sand. You're so out of my league."

She walks over and places her hand on my arm. "I don't think so," she says.

It's like I've been hit by lightning. Every nerve in my body lights up. A blush warms from the back of my neck to my toes. I feel like a seventh grader at my first dance.

New Me hisses, "Get a grip. If she figures out how completely uncool you are, it's over."

I try for nonchalant. "You're too kind."

At least this time my voice doesn't break.

She squeezes my arm and says, "I find you interesting, Justin. I'd like to get to know you better."

I swallow and say, "What do you have in mind?"

She leans close and purrs, "Do you like games?"

Games?

I think of the way she inhaled me on the beach.

"Like—" I clear my throat, "like video games?"

The corner of her mouth pulls slyly. "No," she says. "What I have in mind is nothing like video games."

Oh, Lord. Am I going to need a safe word?

She turns and with a single come-hither glance over her shoulder, walks out of sight around the pavilion. I grab my stuff and scramble to follow. When I round the corner, she's not there.

I knew it.

Punked.

"Pua?"

"In here," she calls. "The other side of the oleander hedge."

It takes me a moment, but then I spot the opening. It's narrow, almost too narrow, and I push my way through, dragging my snorkel gear behind me.

It's a scene from another century.

The area is intimate, surrounded by ten-foot oleander bushes on three sides, but open to an ocean view overlooking the entire bay. Shading the space are two towering trees bursting with fragrant white and yellow flowers. The grass beneath them is stunted and scruffy, but it's mostly covered by a large woven mat. On the mat are a couple of lounging pillows, a bowl of fresh fruit, a tall gourd with coconut shell cups, and a small wooden board dotted with black and white pebbles.

"This is amazing."

Pua slips a flower behind her right ear, sinks onto the mat, and reclines against a pillow.

"Want to play?" she asks.

It's every male teenage fantasy come true.

I freeze.

In my head, Sasha laughs. "You are swimming soooo over your head!"

Shut up, Sasha!

"Um..."

"Sit," Pua says and pats the mat beside her.

"I'm wet," I blurt.

She raises an eyebrow.

"I mean, my swim trunks. From the shower."

"It's fine. This lauhala mat has seen worse," she says. "Unless you'd be more comfortable with them off?"

"No!" I squeak.

Her eyes light up.

I hastily clear my throat again. "I mean, no, thanks. I'm good. I'm sure they'll dry faster on. Unless, you know, you want me to. Do you want me to? No! Don't answer. I'm just going to—"

I walk over to the mat, slip off my flip-flops, and sit crisscross apple sauce, hands clasped in my lap.

In a corner of my mind, Sasha plops down in an easy chair with a monster bucket of popcorn. "This is going to be good."

I clench my jaw and try to ignore her.

"Comfy?" Pua asks.

"Uh-huh," mumble.

"You don't look comfortable."

Sasha crams a handful of popcorn in her mouth.

"I'm fine," I say.

From a side table, Sasha grabs a drink and starts sucking on the straw. When she sees me watching her, she gives me an enthusiastic thumbs up.

Bitch.

Pua gestures to the board. "Konane. Ever played?"

"No."

"It's not complicated. Black lava versus white coral pieces, alternating stones. This board is an eight by eight grid." She reaches out and removes a black lava rock and a white piece of coral from the center of the board. "Black goes first. You move by jumping over your opponent's stone into an empty space. The eaten stone is removed. You can only move in a straight line—no turns or diagonals. Jump as many of your opponent's stones as you choose as long as each jump lands in an open space and continues in a straight line. The winner is the one who can still make a move."

Is she joking? Is making a move some kind of island code? I look from the board to her face. She's smiling, but there's a definite air of challenge about her.

"Unless you don't think you can beat me," she says.

Game on!

I reach out and pick up a black stone, deftly jump over a white piece, and remove it from the board. Quick as a cat, she jumps and removes one of my pieces. The game progresses quickly, clearing out the center until I'm forced to start moving my edge pieces.

Finally, I have to stop and study the board. "This is harder than it looks," I say.

"It's not just a children's game. Everyone played konane. Chiefs and commoners competed in high stakes tournaments. Kamehameha the Great was said to be unbeatable."

"But you don't believe that."

"Everyone loses sometimes," she says.

"But he was the Great!" I say.

"Yes, he was very, very good."

"But you're better."

"Of course." A triple jump clears most of my remaining pieces. "I win," she says.

I blink.

"You ambushed me!"

She laughs. "Not bad for your first game."

"Again!"

"I warn you, I won't take it easy on you."

"It's not your nature," I say.

She smiles that inscrutable smile and starts to reset the board. "No," she says quietly, "it's not."

After the losing the second and then a third game, Pua pushes a pillow toward me. "Lie down. Get comfortable."

I prop myself on my side and help her reset the board.

"Something to drink?" she asks.

"Sure."

She pours a pink liquid into a coconut cup and hands it to me. "Guava juice with a little liliko'i mixed in."

"What's that?"

"Passion fruit. Shall I make the first move or do you want to?"

Once again, I freeze.

Sasha perks up. "Finally," she mutters. "This whole thing's dragging on longer than ketchup out of a bottle."

Nope. Buh-bye, Sasha! Hope all that butter goes right to your thighs.

I mentally slam the door in Sasha's outraged face.

Feels so good, I slam it twice.

"Justin?" says Pua.

I blink and snap back to the present. "I'll follow your lead, Pua, whatever you want to do."

She reaches out and removes two markers.

I have to admit, I'm a little disappointed.

We begin again.

"What were you thinking about back at the showers?" Pua asks. "You had such a look of wonder on your face." Her black jumps my white.

It's early in the game, so strategy doesn't matter much. All the big decisions happen in the end. I quickly jump the black piece closest to me and remove it from the board.

I say, "I was thinking about an art project to complete my master's degree. What if people could experience what it was like to be underwater without getting wet?"

"The word you're looking for is submarine," says Pua. "Or Jacque Cousteau."

"What?"

"The French—oh, never mind," she says with a double-jump.

My white coral eats another lava stone. "The world is more than seventy-percent ocean, and most people have never experienced what it's like to swim with fish," I counter.

Pua rolls her eyes. "They aren't missing much."

"I don't believe you. You're just jaded from living in paradise." I motion to Piko Point. "The sharks out there—"

In the act of removing a piece from the board, Pua stills. She waits until I meet her eyes. "What do you know about the sharks out there?"

Where's this white-hot anger coming from?

No. I'm reading this wrong. She's just concerned for me. That's all.

"Just what I observed snorkeling with them this morning. The sharks are why I came back to Lauele. Well, one of the reasons," I tease.

She pulls away from the game and starts rearranging the fruit in the bowl.

Oh, crap. I've somehow screwed the pooch.

"Who told you about the sharks off Piko Point?" she bites, every line in her body tighter than a drawn bow.

I open my mouth to say Nili-boy, but realize I can't tell her that. She's far too upset about something and Lauele's too small for them not to know each other. She'll eat him alive for spilling the beans about sharks. How—

Oh, yeah.

The stupid sign.

"I saw the sign."

"What sign?"

"The one warning people about sharks at the pavilion. People wouldn't post that without a reason, right?" I remove another stone. "Your turn."

She reaches out and moves stones without looking at the board.

This has gone way south.

In my head, Sasha's beating on the door, wanting to get out. I put a double-lock on it and take a deep breath.

"I'm sorry I scared you by ignoring the sign and snorkeling off Piko Point. I know how terrifying sharks can be to people—"

Was that a cough or a laugh?

I press on.

"—but not all sharks are dangerous. They aren't mindless eating machines hell-bent on eating people. *Jaws* gave them all a bad rap."

Pua won't look at me. She turns further away.

I say, "I think if more people knew that, they'd care more about sharks. They'd want to protect them."

Is she biting her lip?

Her shoulders are shaking.

Oh, no.

Is she *crying*?

"Pua, it's okay. I won't go back out there—not until you feel okay about it. In the meantime, we can do some observations and sketches together at the Waikiki Aquarium—"

She spins toward me, hissing like a wildcat. "The Aquarium? THE AQUARIUM? You want to take me to that soul-less morgue of death, disease, and confinement?"

"Uh—"

"How dare you? How dare you support the enslavement of free creatures? You're just like all the rest!"

Holy crap! How did we get here?

"Wait a minute! I never thought about aquariums like that. But doesn't that mean what I'm trying to do is a good thing? My art show will do all that an aquarium does to bring the ocean to people without harming a single sea creature. People go to aquariums because they can't dive or don't live by the beach. Aquariums show them an undersea world full of wonder. It's like dolphins—"

She throws her hands wide. "Dolphins? Dolphins? Of course people like dolphins. You know why they're smiling all the time? Because they're the stupidest suck-ups in the sea."

Wow.

She just doesn't get it.

"Pua, people just don't like dolphins; they adore dolphins. And what people love, they protect," I say.

She's breathing hard, but she's listening.

I think.

"Pua, when was the last time you played in the ocean? Splashed in the waves?"

She narrows her eyes and sets her jaw. "I don't *play* in the ocean."

"See, that's what I'm talking about. When did you last see a sunset from a boat deck?"

"I—"

"Never, I know. That's something tourists do, not locals. You're like someone who lives in the alps and never skis. I'm going to change that—"

"No."

"What?"

"You're not going to change me, Justin. I am exactly what I am. Nothing more, nothing less."

"Whoa, you're taking this all wrong." I look down at the board, frustrated. "You said konane was a high stakes game. Let's raise the stakes."

"Brave words from someone who's never won a game."

"I have two tickets for a catamaran snorkeling adventure tomorrow. If I win, you have to come with me and play tourist."

"And if I win?"

"Name it," I say.

"Later," she says.

Later? What does that mean?

"Bets need to be two ways, Pua. What would make you as happy as I will be if you go snorkeling with me tomorrow? Dinner at a fancy restaurant? New shoes? Tickets to a concert? Me to shave my head?"

Shave my head? What am I saying?

She looks down her nose at me. "I don't know what will make me happy, yet."

How bad could it be?

"Okay," I say. "You can decide later. But I have veto power over head-shaving or piercings or tattoos. Deal?"

"Deal," Pua says. "Your move."

We turn our attention back to the board.

In one glance I see exactly what I need to do to win. Her pieces are in perfect position for mine to double and triple jump. All I have to do is remove more of her pieces than she can of mine, and I'll win.

I make my first triple jump move and take three of her stones from the board.

She reaches out and eats one of my pieces. "That's game," she says.

"Impossible. I have way more pieces than you!"

"That's still game. You lose."

I sit up and study the board. She's right.

"You win. Guess you don't have to go snorkeling with me tomorrow."

"My father thinks like you," she says out of the blue. "He allows aquariums because he believes they help humans understand that they are only one piece in an interconnected world."

"Allows?" I tip my head back and finish my drink. "Is your father in government or something?"

"Or something."

She gathers the stones and puts them in a pouch.

Slowly, she nods. "The aquarium *is* the right place for you to sketch, Justin, better than off Piko Point. Your idea of an art show that brings the ocean to land is worth pursuing."

"Thanks."

I think?

She stands and smooths the front of her dress.

I jump to my feet, too.

She says, "I'll go on the catamaran tomorrow—"

"—That's—"

She holds up her hand. "Not because of the game, but because you asked me to."

I can't stop grinning.

"I'll pick you up. Where—"

"I'll meet you there," she says, and before I can say anything else, she slips through the oleander bushes.

"Wait! You don't know the time or the place or anything!" I call.

Her laughter carries through the hedge. "Don't worry. I'll find you."

"Kewalo Basin! 3:30 pm! The *Ariel*!" I shout.

But she's gone.

CHAPTER 8

PUA

*P*ua leaps into the ocean at Piko Point, changing from human to shark the moment the water touches her skin. Coolness washes over her gills as she flicks her tail once to propel herself through the arch and into the wild blue.

As the water churns, bubbles rise.

She turns and snap, snap, snaps at the silly, frivolous things, her jaws unhinged and gulp, gulp, gulping.

Humans are messy, she thinks. *So emotional. So sincere.*

So much easier to be a shark.

She doesn't have to scan the reef to know that it's empty. Sea creatures know their places. They don't lecture her—her!—about sharks or the benefits of aquariums. They don't try to tell her how wonderful dolphins are.

Dolphins taste like chicken, she smirks. *Warm-blooded and juicy.*

His arrogance is staggering.

He thinks he can persuade humans to love sharks with pretty pictures and toys. It's all about them, of course. He's given no thought to what sharks want or need.

They definitely don't need humans.

The world would be such a better place without them and their noisy, polluting ways.

She arches her back and rolls in the water.

Damn, that itch beneath my dorsal fin!

Father, I don't know why you're punishing me like this. As the Great Ocean God Kanaloa, on pain of death to me, my lover, and son, you forbade me from becoming a mother, something even the lowest invertebrate in your kingdom is allowed to do. But you've given me an itch that's driving me insane, and the only cure is to break your kapu. Why won't you take this urge away from me and let me return to creature I used to be?

It's not fair, Father.

You made me who I am. You know my nature.

The consequences are yours.

CHAPTER 9

JUSTIN

*S*he's late.

I'm standing at the end of the gangway, looking back to the entrance to the docks at Kewalo Basin Harbor. All the passengers but me are already aboard the *Ariel,* sipping drinks and shooting the breeze. The captain leans over the railing.

"We gotta go, man," he says.

"Just a few minutes more," I plead.

"We're already fifteen minutes past our departure time. People want to see the turtles."

"Give them another round of drinks on me."

"Can't dude. You coming or not?"

"I—"

He softens. "I get it. It happens a lot. People meet on vacation. There's an instant connection. You're certain you've met your soulmate. But then things look different in the morning. Chin up. There's always more fish in the sea."

"Not like this one," I say.

"Why don't you come aboard? You've already paid for the trip. Who knows, you might get lucky and see some dolphins. Everybody loves dolphins."

She's not coming.

I'm never going to see her again.

Sasha looks up from her newspaper and coffee. "Told you," she says and turns a page.

For the last time, you're not real. Get out of my head.

She blows me a kiss that turns into a raspberry. "I'm as real as you're going to get, Sugar. Get used to it."

"Hey!" says the captain. "Tick-tock."

I walk up the gangway as the deckhands cast off.

"Finally," I hear an overweight man say to his sunburned wife.

"Shhhh!" she says. "Don't be rude!" She thrusts out her hand as I squeeze past. "I'm Kari with an i from Oklahoma. This is Earl."

"Hi Kari. I'm Justin."

"Oh, my hell," says Earl. "I need another drink."

"Earl!" says Kari. "We just had lunch."

"It's five o'clock somewhere."

Earl gets up and heads to the bar.

"Don't mind him. He's just a little nervous to be snorkeling." She looks around and mouths *sharks*.

"Sharks aren't anything to be afraid of," I say.

"I read on the internet that they eat turtles. Aren't we going to be swimming with turtles?" says a bombshell in a blue bikini.

Her boyfriend flexes his bicep as he puts his arm around her. "Relax, Babe. I got you."

A teenage goth chick rolls her eyes and snaps her gum. "If a shark wants you, there's nothing you can do."

"Hey," interrupts a deckhand with a smile and a tray of drinks. "No shark talk. Captain's rules. Orange juice?"

"No, thanks," I say.

"Sunscreen?" Kari waves a Costco-size bottle at me. "Gotta protect your nose, you know." *Skin cancer*, she mouths.

I feel the urge to join Earl in something stronger.

"Excuse me," I say and head to the galley.

It takes us about half an hour to get to the snorkel site. Three other tour boats are already anchored. The dive master starts his safety spiel about staying near the boat and remembering we're on the *Ariel* and not the *Kahalakai*. As he demonstrates the proper way to inflate a snorkel vest, he says nothing about sharks or about what not to touch. Looking down into the water, I figure the reef's twenty feet below us. Wearing a snorkel vest, it's going to be tough to get that deep. Under protest, Goth Girl finally puts a vest on, but stubbornly refuses to inflate it.

"Sweetie, what if you drown?" her mother wails.

"Then it won't matter. I'll be dead."

I hoist my bottle of beer to her.

I like her.

Once all the fins are sorted and masks dotted with goo, the passengers start flopping into the water. Bombshell squeals when Biceps lifts her over the side and drops her in.

What a douche.

I bet they're perfect together.

"Getting in?" I say to Earl.

"Ppfft," he says.

I take that as a no.

Once it's just me and Earl and the deckhands, the captain swings by. "Not getting in?"

I shrug. "Seems rather pointless. You can't see anything that doesn't come up to you when you're wearing a vest. Too hard to kick down. Got any little boxes of cornflakes or cans of Cheez Whiz?"

He laughs. "The Great State of Hawaii frowns on that kind of behavior. Not good for the fish or reef."

"Great for the tourists, though."

"I tell you what. You wanna jump in without a vest, be my guest."

"Your dive master was pretty strict about that."

"That girl was under eighteen with nervous parents. You're an adult who knows about cornflakes and Cheez Whiz. I'll chance it."

I hand my empty bottle to the bartender. "Set my buddy Earl up with another," I say and slip him a twenty.

I put my mask and snorkel on and don't bother with the ladder.

The cold water shocks what little buzz I had going right out of my head.

What am I doing?

I should just cut my losses and head back to Cali.

I blow water out of my snorkel, put my head down, and kick away from the crowds and the boats.

The water's crystal clear, so I stop kicking and just float facedown for a while. The sunlight makes zebra stripes out of the shadows of the ripples. There're some barrel sponges and patches of something purplish on the reef, but most of the fish stay well away from me.

Is that an octopus?

Better check where the boat's at.

Don't want to get too far.

As I raise my head and turn, the shadow of something big, really big, passes below me. I whip around, but I don't see it. I tread water in a circle, my head on a swivel.

"Hey," somebody calls. "Where'd all the fish go?"

Something flashes past the corner of my eye. I spin, but I'm too slow.

The boat's 50 yards away.

My heart's pounding.

Don't be ridiculous.

You're psyching yourself out.

"Dah-dum," says Sasha. "Dah-dum."

Another shadow, this one circling to the left.

"Dah-dum. Dahdumdahdumdahdum—"

Knock it off, Sasha!

It's all in my head.

Flash.

No! I definitely saw something that time.

I fill my lungs and prepare to break the world record for a 50 yard snorkel dash. I lean forward, spread my legs for a scissor kick—

BAM!

Something reaches around my neck and squeezes.

"Miss me?" she says.

"Aiiiiiii," I scream and promptly swallow water.

Pua wraps her arms around my chest and hauls me to the surface. "It's okay," she says. "You're with me."

"Pua! Where? How?" I sputter.

"Told you I'd find you."

She's bobbing upright, barely treading water to stay at the surface. She's wearing a white bikini that shows off her golden tan.

And a whole lot more.

"Where's your snorkel gear?"

"Snorkel gear is for wimps," she says.

"Where's your boat?"

"Over there," she points.

Two of the other boats are underway, heading in different directions, while the third one's pulling anchor.

"Pua! Your boat left!"

She shrugs.

I look to my boat. The dive master's waving us all back to the catamaran. "Come back," he calls. "We're going to a better spot. All the turtles have left."

I shake my head. "Your boat must have miscounted its passengers! Let's get to my boat and tell the captain. C'mon."

We make our way to the *Ariel* and wait for the others to board. When it's just us left, Pua motions me ahead. I kick to the stairs, hand my mask, snorkel, and fins to the deck hand, and climb up. The deckhand leans past me to give Pua a hand.

I see his face go white.

I barely have time to break his fall before his head hits the deck when he faints.

There's commotion and confusion as people rush to us.

"Is he okay?"

"What happened?"

"Bring him here. Somebody get the first aid kit."

"Should we call the Coast Guard?"

"I've got a pulse. He's breathing. Let's just give him some space."

In the eye of the hurricane, I look up and see Pua standing on the deck, watching us. The captain spots her when he comes running from the galley with the first aid kit. He stops cold.

"She's with me," I say.

They regard each other for one long moment. The captain dips his head. Pua smiles and leans against the railing. Time speeds up. The captain kneels next to me.

"Keanu," he says to the deckhand.

"I think he fainted," I say.

"Keanu." The captain pats the deckhand's cheek. "C'mon, man. It's going to be all right."

Keanu jerks awake. "Knee-oooo-he," he moans.

The captain puts his hand over Keanu's mouth. "Shhhhhh," he whispers. "I know. Be cool."

Kari with an i holds out a baggie full of ice. "For his knee," she says.

"What?" says the captain.

"Didn't he just say he hurt it?"

"Oh. Yeah. Thanks," says the captain. Together we help Keanu sit up.

"For your sore knee," says the captain.

Still dazed, Keanu clasps the bag first to his left knee, then to his right.

Man, he hit his head harder than I thought.

The captain stands and addresses the crowd.

"He's fine, folks. But I just got word that conditions aren't good for snorkeling. There's a storm blowing in, so we're going to have to head back to the harbor now."

"What? No turtles, late start, early return, what a rip-off!"

The captain says, "I know it's a bummer, but safety is our number one priority. But our number two priority is a good time. Drinks are on the house until we get to the harbor."

The crowd cheers.

The captain continues. "After you get your whistle wet, see Becky—wave your hand, Becky—see Becky before you exit the boat. She'll either refund your money or give you a ticket for another day—your choice."

"That's more like it!"

"Becky, turn up the music. Maybe we can tempt some dolphins to put on a show for us."

"Yeah!"

The music starts to boom. People drift away, some to the bar, others to the sun decks.

"Let's go to the bow," Pua says, taking my hand and pulling. At our feet, Keanu closes his eyes and moans. She doesn't even spare him a glance. "Don't worry. He's fine."

"Just a second," I tell her.

I reach out and touch the captain's shoulder. "Hey, Captain, I need to report something."

He turns, wary. His eyes shoot past me to Pua. "I already know," he says.

"Somebody already radioed you about a missing passenger? I bet he was having kittens."

"Um—"

"My friend Pua is the one they left behind. It's unconscionable. Imagine if we hadn't been here to pick her up."

Pua puts her chin on my shoulder and leans over. "Yes, Captain. Just. Imagine."

The captain swallows. "We're, um, honored to be of service."

"C'mon, Justin," she says, "let's head to the front. I bet we'll see dolphins. Lots of dolphins. People like a show, don't they, Captain?"

He nods.

"Don't worry," Pua says as she breezes past, "I'm only here for Justin. He thinks I need to gain a deeper appreciation for the sea."

The Captain squeezes his eyes tight. "Tourists," he says. "Heaven helps us."

"Oooo!" Pua squeals. "Look!"

All around the boat, the water begins to roil. Suddenly, a dolphin leaps out of the water, his entire body as high as the safety railing. More appear, surfing the wake off the bow. Pacing us on either side are a dozen, then two dozen, then too many to count.

"It's a giant pod of dolphins," Kari says. "One huge family!"

"Whoa," says Biceps.

"Quick! Let's get a dolphin selfie," says Bombshell.

When the cell phones come out, the dolphins go nuts: spinning, leaping, clicking and squeaking. There's so much spray from their blowholes that it drifts over the water like smoke.

"Earl! Earl!" shouts Kari, "Come see the babies!"

Earl shakes his head and buries his nose in a beer.

"You're missing it!"

People line every vantage spot along the boat. Goth Girl puts her black lipstick in her pocket as she stands next to me, a frown on her face. "This is weird," she says.

"I think it's amazing," I say.

"But there are three kinds of dolphins out there." She points. "Those are spinners, those are spotted, and those bigger ones off the bow are bottlenose." Pua locks like a laser onto Goth Girl. "It's like a school assembly where the principal makes the jocks, nerds, and drama kids dance together."

Pua narrows her eyes. "You're saying it's a little too much?"

Becky interrupts with a tray of plastic champagne flutes. "Compliments of the captain."

I take two and hand one to Pua. When Goth Girl reaches for one, Becky tilts the tray away. "Sorry, adults only. I'll bring you a soda in a minute." Over Becky's shoulder a dolphin tail walks.

Biceps pushes between us. "Babe! You gotta see this."

A mama dolphin paces the ship as her baby circles and jumps.

Bombshell squeezes in. "It's so cute I want to die!" She grabs his shoulder. "I want one! They're so little, I bet they'd fit in the pond."

Goth Girl says, "A freshwater pond?"

Bombshell says, "Yes! Behind our apartment. Oh, it would be perfect!"

"Dolphins need saltwater—"

"No, they don't! They breathe air, not water like fish," says Bombshell. "They can live anywhere there's air. Ain't that right, Babe?"

"You know it, Babe. I bet Joey could catch us one the next time he's in the Gulf."

"You'd take a baby from its mother?" Pua asks.

"Oh, honey, it's not like that," Bombshell says. "They're fish. It don't mean the same to them."

Goth Girl says, "Dolphins are mammals, not fish."

Bombshell waves her hand. "Whatever. You know what I mean."

Pua stares for a moment at her champagne. Off the bow, dolphins are doing front flips.

"Are you okay?" I ask. "Do you want to get out of the sun?"

"I need some space." As Pua turns away from the rail, the dolphins suddenly submerge and disappear.

"Aww," Kari says. "Where'd they go?"

"Here," Pua says, handing Goth Girl her champagne.

"Thanks!"

"Don't you want it?" I ask.

Pua gives me her Mona Lisa smile. "I've had more than enough of bubbles lately."

"Want me to get you some water?"

"No. Let's head to the least crowded part of the boat," she says.

As we climb the ladder to the top deck, people spot three distinct groups of dolphins heading away from our boat.

"Looks like she was right," I say. "Three different kinds of dolphins, not one big family pod. Wonder why."

Pua brushes the hair out of her face. "Dolphins, whales, sharks—who can tell them apart?"

"See, that's why I think—"

The captain comes over the loudspeaker. "Folks, we'll be at the dock in five minutes. Time to finish your drinks, gather all your belongings, and get ready to disembark. If you haven't gotten your vouchers, be sure to see Becky. On behalf of the crew of the *Ariel*, we hope your island vacation continues to be everything you imagined. Aloha!"

We're the last ones off the boat.

At the gangway the captain hands Pua a sarong. "With your stuff lost on another catamaran, I thought you might like this," he says. "A tourist left it behind last week."

Pua smiles and wraps the orange and green tie-dye sarong into a dress. "Castoffs are my favorite kind," she says. "Smooth sailing, Captain."

"With your blessing, it's sure to be." He bows a little as she passes down the gangway. I move to follow, but he grabs my arm and pulls me close. "Be careful," he whispers. "She's—"

"Not your typical island girl? Told you," I say.

He takes a breath to say more, but then shakes his head and releases my arm.

"Good luck to you, Justin," he says. "I'll be praying it goes well for you."

I wink. "You and me both!"

CHAPTER 10

JUSTIN

"*J*'m parked over here. Where's your car?" I ask.

"I don't have one," Pua says.

I grin. "You were that sure you'd find me?"

"It's not hard. You're very predictable."

I unlock the doors and throw my snorkel gear in the back. "Okay, Smarty-pants, what do I want to do now?" I wiggle my eyebrows suggestively.

"Not that," she says. "Food now." She slides into the passenger seat. "That's later."

In my own private corner of hell, Sasha stands with her mouth open.

Suck it, Sasha.

I say, "I have a reservation for us at L'Couteux—"

"No."

I blink. "It's rated—"

"No."

"Where then? Pua, I want to take you somewhere nice. You mean a lot to me—"

"Start the car. Let's head to Lauele. I know just the place."

I hop in and turn the ignition. Lava-hot air explodes from the vents. "Sorry, sorry!" I say, frantically rolling the windows down. "There's no air conditioning!"

Pua gathers her hair, twists, and magically creates a bun on the top of her head. "What are you talking about? That's what windows are for." She reaches over and steals my sunglasses from the console. "That's better. The sun is always so bright." She leans back in her seat, sighs, and closes her eyes. "It's toasty warm in here, nothing like the deep ocean. To experience anything like this, you have to get close to a volcano."

"Watching a volcano erupt underwater would be incredible."

"Not really," she says. "Nobody wants to swim in sulfur. Itchy."

"I'd scratch your itch."

"Later," she says with another huge sigh.

All her bones melt.

Is she going to *sleep*?

Sasha rears her head. "Dude, she is totally going to sleep. It's a long drive in a sweltering car. She didn't want to go to dinner at the best restaurant in Honolulu. She wants you to take her back to Lauele so she can get away from your sorry ass. Read between the lines."

She had fun on the boat.

"Which part? The part where she didn't meet you at the dock, the part where she got left behind, or the part where her stuff got lost, so she's wearing a reject from the lost and found?"

The dolphins were cool. Everybody loved the dolphins.

"You sure about that?" Sasha gets comfy on pool lounger, sipping an umbrella drink.

"Pua?" I say.

"Hmmm?"

"What did you think of the dolphins?"

"The dolphins?"

"Yeah. I know we didn't get a chance to snorkel along the reef much, but did you see how excited people got seeing dolphins in the wild? It's why I want to create my art exhibit."

"You want to make people feel like they can steal a baby dolphin from the ocean and put it in their freshwater pond?"

"Those two don't count. They're idiots."

"People are."

"But that's why we need to educate them."

"It's a waste of time. Humans believe they are the most important creatures on the planet. Everything and everyone belongs to them. It's their nature to destroy. You can't go against nature. Might was well yell at the waves to stay away from the shore."

I turn onto the highway and head out of the city, thinking about what she's saying. "You sound angry."

She rolls her head on her shoulders. "Not angry. There's no sense in getting angry when a toddler does what toddlers do."

"That's harsh. What about Goth Girl—the one with the black lipstick. Do you think she's like the two who wanted a baby dolphin?"

Pua purses her lips. "No. She's aware. If more were like her, I'd have hope, but she's the exception that proves the rule."

"You don't believe in the power of one? One voice, one person, can change the world."

"Humans are herd animals."

I laugh. "But even herds have leaders."

"If you say so."

At highway speeds, the wind is whipping through the car. Tendrils of hair, loose from her bun, flail like octopus tentacles around her face.

"You didn't like the boat," I say.

"I liked it fine," she says. "Just don't fool yourself into thinking these kinds of encounters are more than superficial entertainment. It's a holiday, a break in routine, for everybody."

She shakes her hair loose, and the sweet smell of sandalwood and something I can't put my finger on—salt, maybe?—fills the car. Her hair brushes against my lips. She leans her head toward her lap and sweeps her hair up, twisting tighter and tighter until another knot forms on the top of her head.

"Hair," she grumbles. "I never know what to do with it."

"Please promise me you'll never cut it," I say.

"Cut it?"

"Yeah. No bobs or bangs or layers. It's beautiful just the way it is."

"Cut it?" She wrinkles her nose. "You can do that?"

The light through the windshield kisses her cheeks, her chin, and the long graceful line of her neck that ends in the hollow at the base of her throat.

I want to bury my nose in it and blaze a trail of kisses to her belly button.

I'm in love.

From her imaginary lounge, Sasha pulls out a fan.

"No, Justin. You're in heat."

CHAPTER 11

PUA

*I*t's hot.

Pua feels it all the way to the pit of her stomach. She doesn't have to glance at Justin to see that he's feeling it, too.

The air on her skin is almost too much. Soon she won't be able to stand the clothes she's wearing.

Her scent is changing. Even Justin's puny nose can tell. Behind the sunglasses, she watches as his nostril flare; his eyes dilate and darken with desire.

She runs her finger over the skin between her knee and the edge of the sarong, over and over, in little circles, and shudders.

Can I do this again?

She remembers other lovers, some tender, some fierce, and wonders what Justin will be like.

She inhales and uses her tongue to parse the scents flowing through the back of her throat.

Man sweat.

Soap.

Salt.

A mishmash of the people from the boat.

And something—just a hint—

The ghost of someone special, a woman, but not for a while.

There's a bitter afternote of heartbreak there.

Grateful. He'll be a grateful lover.

And I will finally put that itch to rest.

At least this time, I won't have to kill him.

It's the one thing tourists are good for.

CHAPTER 12

JUSTIN

When we round the last curve that leads to the Lauele, I turn to Pua. "Where's the restaurant?"

"Just pull into the parking lot at the pavilion," she says.

"You don't want to eat?"

"I need to eat. You do, too, to keep your strength up. You're no good to me weak."

Weak? Right now I can pound nails.

"Then where—"

"Just park."

I pull into a stall and shut off the engine. The sky is purple, rose, and gold as the sun sinks into the ocean.

Pua opens her door and steps out. When I start to follow, she leans back down. "Why don't you wait by the tables and watch the sunset? I'll bring us something from Hari's."

"I'll go with you."

"No. I need a minute to freshen up. I'll just pop into Hari's and be right back." She shuts the door and starts across the parking lot.

I scramble out of the car. "Wait! You don't have your purse!"

She waves without looking back.

"How are you going to pay without any money?"

She calls over her shoulder, "You worry about the strangest things."

I watch as she sashays across the street and disappears into the little convenience store.

Holy cow.

What have I got myself into?

I shake my head to clear the cobwebs. The whole drive back from the harbor is a blur. All I could think about was her sitting next to me in that little white bikini.

And without that little white bikini.

It's her perfume. It's driving me crazy. What's under—

I slap my cheek. Get it together, dude. You're a gentleman, remember?

New Me growls.

Maybe not.

I flee to the bathroom and splash water on my face. Hands clamped on either side of the sink, I regard my reflection.

My pupils are wide, too wide. My cheeks are flushed. Stubble on my jawline. I meant to shave again before dinner.

I meant to do a lot of things.

I sweep my hair back into my Wall Street look.

Pit check. Not bad, not good. Wish I had some deodorant for a quick swipe.

I look myself in the eye and start a little pep talk.

Here's what's NOT going to happen—

1. I'm not going to take advantage of her.
2. I'm not going to act like a pig.
3. I'm not going to assume anything.
4. And I'm definitely not going to tell her something crazy like I love you before she has a chance to know me enough to love me back.

Okay. Now for a DO list—

1. I'm going to listen to her and get to know her better.
2. I'm going to make sure she gets home safely.
3. I'm going to talk to University of Hawaii's art school to see about teaching opportunities.
4. I'm going to call my landlord tomorrow and see about putting my stuff in storage.
5. I'm going to meet her family.
6. I'm going to marry Pua.

I look at the guy in the mirror and smile.

I like New Me.

Chapter 13

Justin & Pua

Justin

I'm sitting on the table watching the last sliver of sun sink below the horizon when Pua returns carrying a plastic bag full of take out. I jump up and reach to take it from her, but she brushes past, steps off the pavilion, and onto the grass.

"Let's eat on the beach," she says.

"Sun's down," I say. "Sure you don't want to eat here?"

"I'm sure. The full moon is rising. Isn't it gorgeous?"

"You're gorgeous," I say.

"You didn't even look," she says.

I turn. Behind us, the moon is a pearl leaping from towering cliffs into the night sky. I watch as night closes in and the sky shines with the pinpricks of diamonds, feeling small and adrift in the vastness of the universe.

Yaddah, yaddah, yaddah. I know that's the vibe she's going for, but I don't care.

I swivel back to her. "You're the only thing I want to see," I say.

"Food first. Let's head to the beach," she says. "It's private. We'll be away from the lights at the pavilion and Hari's store."

She turns and wanders down the hill, her hips swaying with every step.

I haven't moved, but I'm out of breath. Blood pounds in my head.

Remember the dos and don'ts.

Sasha appears in a housecoat and curlers. "You are so screwed," she says.

From your lips to God's ears, Sasha.

I take a deep breath and head to the beach. When I pass the shark sign, I jump and slap it for luck.

Pua

*A*t the edge of the lava outcrop that leads to Piko Point, Pua slips off the sarong and spreads it out on the sand. Her body is thrumming; she's certain if she's not careful sparks will fly from her fingers. She sends her Niuhi senses out into the night.

The beach is empty from Nalupuki all the way to the pavilion. Not even that mettlesome dog is around.

Perfect.

She unpacks styrofoam containers and cans of juice, feeling Justin's approach through vibrations in the sand. She'll have to ask her questions quickly.

She knows the middle.

It's just the end that's uncertain.

It's also why her dinner is light.

She has no idea if she's eating dessert.

Justin

It's dark on the beach. I hesitate for a second, but then I catch a glimpse of a white bikini smiling like teeth in the darkness.

"Pua?"

"Over here."

"Ah, using your sarong as a picnic blanket. Nice."

"Some things are better without sand," she says, handing me a plate.

"What's this? Smells delicious."

"Teri beef, rice, macaroni salad. More guava-passion fruit juice, too. Typical man food."

"Man food? What are you eating?"

"Fresh ahi sashimi and a little tako poke."

"What?"

"Sliced raw tuna and a salad of octopus and seaweed. Want some?"

She holds out her chopsticks.

I hear the challenge in her voice.

In the moonlight, the thin sliver of tuna glows like a ruby.

"Sure," I say. "I'm not afraid of a little raw fish."

She brings it to my lips. I open my mouth, and she places it like a communion wafer on my tongue.

It's refrigerator cold. I hold it in my mouth for a second, warming it back to life. I expect salt, I expect slime, but what I taste is sweet. Tentatively, I chew. The meat is tender, almost melting in my mouth.

I groan.

"More?" she teases.

"Yes."

"Too bad. It's gone. All that's left is man food."

"What? How did you eat it so fast?"

"Practice," she says.

Pua

He's a little clumsy with the chopsticks, but not too bad. He manages to get rice and beef into his mouth, with the occasional morsel of macaroni and mayonnaise thrown in. She waits until his blood pressure stabilizes, when his heartbeat slows and his mind relaxes, before she circles with her opening move.

Justin

Pua says, "I know you're from California and an artist, but that's all I know."

I look up from my plate. "We really haven't talked about ourselves much, have we? I was born and bred in Garden Grove, California, and I'm finishing my MFA at UCLA. Only child, no siblings. You?"

"I have a twin brother, Kalei."

"A twin? Really? I'd love to meet him sometime."

She laughs. "I don't know about that."

"He doesn't like your *boyfriends*?"

I hold my breath.

"That's putting it mildly."

Boyfriend. She let that slide.

Score!

Sasha looks up from a magazine. "Desperate, much?"

For someone so in love with their soulmate Palo, you sure spend a lot of time in my head.

Sasha sniffs and turns a page.

" —in Hawaii?"

Crap. I missed that.

"It's complicated," I say.

Pua

"Do you know anyone in Hawaii?" Pua asks, stifling a burp. *A little too much chili in the poke,* she thinks

"It's complicated," Justin says.

Pua leans forward. It's the moment when a fish either turns and runs or gives up and presents its belly.

She likes offerings, but it's more fun to chase.

"I was engaged."

Horrified, Pua recoils. "To someone in Hawaii?"

Justin reaches for her hand. "No, no, nothing like that. Sasha and I were together for five years. We met at UCLA. She was a barista at the student union. We were planning our wedding. This trip was supposed to be our honeymoon, but she…changed plans, including the groom. Everything was non-refundable, so…"

Pua's eyes light up. "You came alone? What about your family or friends? Surely someone—"

Justin shakes his head. "There's no one. Over the years, Sasha kept me close. I didn't realize it until after she left that all my friends had gone, too. I haven't seen my best friend in years."

"What about family?"

"Gone, too."

"You're all alone in the world, aren't you, Justin?"

Pua stands in the moonlight as it bleeds into the ocean. The only sound is the lapping of waves along the shore. She hooks her thumbs into her bikini bottoms and shimmies.

"I can help with that," she says.

Justin

My mouth drops to my chest; my lungs fill with her scent of sandalwood and salt. She drops to her knees and tugs my shirt over my head. Her lips brush mine, and it's like connecting with a live wire. Every nerve in my body lights up.

"Pua—"

She pulls her lips away and replaces them with her fingers. "Shhhhh. You talk too much." She takes my hand and places it on her breast.

"Pua—"

"Shhhh," she breathes, and her breath is dark and deep as the ocean.

She slips her fingers under my waistband and tugs.

I break all my rules.

Pua

She was right.

Gratitude.

What she didn't expect was how thoroughly he scratched her itch.

Maybe she'll visit him in California.

She could use a pet like him.

Nestled against his chest, she counts his breaths, one for every two waves that roll onshore. The moon has passed its zenith. In a few hours it will follow the sun over the horizon. It's the time of night when humans sleep.

And others walk.

She should leave him here and walk into the ocean.

Easier that way.

She starts to stand when something crunches underfoot. She reaches down and pulls a ti leaf lei from his pants pocket.

Oh, no. Oh, son of a sea serpent, no!

"Justin," she urges. "Wake up."

"Wha—?" He blinks, reaching for her. "What's wrong?"

"Why do you have this," she says, waving the lei in his face.

He takes it from her, squinting. "Oh. A kid gave it to me." He laughs. "Said it would protect me from sharks."

She shakes his shoulder. "Why would a local kid give a ti leaf lei to a tourist?"

"He said it was because I was a Coconut."

"What does that mean?"

"Brown on the outside, white on the inside. I grew up in Orange County, but my mom's family's originally from Lauele."

Pua goes still as stone.

"Is there any more juice?" Justin asks. "I'm so thirsty."

Pua places her hand on her abdomen. Two faint points of light flicker, but aren't whole yet.

There's time.

"I can't believe I fell asleep," says Justin. "How can I make it up to you?"

Pua says, "A midnight swim makes everything better."

Justin

Pua grabs my hands and pulls me to my feet. I reach for her, but she dances away. In two seconds, she's knee-deep in the waves.

"C'mon," she calls. "The water flows like silk."

I walk to the edge where seafoam nibbles my toes.

"I thought islanders didn't swim at night?" I say.

"Scaredy-cat," she says. "What could possibly hurt you here?"

She wades deeper and dives under a wave, stroking out until she's treading water.

Still holding the lei, I walk out until I'm knee-deep.

"Are you sure about this?"

She comes back and takes my hand, water cascading down her body. "More sure now than ever, Justin. Come join me in the water." She sees the lei and twitches. "Get rid of that rotten thing. You're mine now."

CHAPTER 14

JUSTIN & PUA

Justin

*T*he ocean's different at night.

Pua guides me past the shore break and out to where the waves roll like a rocking chair. It's peaceful cradled in darkness. For the first time in a long time, I look at the sky and know my place in the universe.

"You were right," I say. "A swim is exactly what we need."

Pua side-strokes to my left.

I have to spin in the water to follow her.

I laugh. "This reminds me of a game we used to play. Marco Polo."

"I know it," she says and dives beneath the surface.

"Marco," I say.

I hear her come up behind me. "Polo," she says.

Water is tricky. Echoes bounce and distort distances. I know she can't be more than an arm's length behind me, but her voice comes as if she's twenty yards to sea.

Something splashes to my right. I spin toward it.

"Marco?"

Something cold brushes against my back.

"Polo," she whispers in my ear. Her arm snakes around from behind, and I feel her body spoon against mine. As she releases me, she trails a nail across my chest.

In the darkness, I shiver. I can't tell the sea from the sky. Every hair on my body stands at attention.

"You're good," I say.

She leans forward and kisses the nape of my neck, sending a pulse of energy down my spine.

She nudges me in the small of my back, and then she's gone again.

Is that her to the left?

"Marco?"

Treading water, something sweeps against my toes.

I feel her break the surface and circle to my right.

"It's so dark out here, I can't see you." I pause. "Maybe it's better this way."

Pua

They're out too far for Justin to scramble for shore, too far for anyone walking the beach to see or hear, even if anyone cared to look. The tide is heading out. If she's careful, not even blood will make it to shore.

In her womb, two sparks sputter. Twins. It's always twins.

He has no one. The most anyone will find is his rental car in the parking lot. Kahana and others may suspect, but no one will know for sure, and that way the shark hunts won't start up again.

Sharks eating humans create bounties. Bounties bring hooks and boats and leave blood dripping onto the docks from the mouths of innocent tiger, bull, and hammerhead sharks. Bounties and hunts bring photographs of shark bodies lining the docks in newspaper articles.

It brings fear and hysteria.

It's an endless cycle.

He's just a tourist, Pua thinks. *No one will even notice he's gone.*

Justin says, "Maybe it's better this way—in the darkness, I mean. You can't see my face. I don't want to scare you away, Pua."

As if.

"But I'm moving to Hawaii."

She pauses in the water, wary.

"I know you think this is sudden, but there's nothing for me in Cali. I've come alive here."

And now you're going to die.

Good-bye, Justin.

Good-bye, little sparks. You were dead before you were ever conceived.

But Pua flips on her back and floats, listening to his voice and hearing the truth behind his words.

"In Hawaii, I've discovered my purpose—I can create art here that changes the way people see the ocean. Thousands of people come to these islands. Just think of the impact my art will have on the world."

"You're deluding yourself," Pua says, gliding behind him.

Thigh or jugular?

Jugular.

That way he can't scream.

"No," he says. "Art moves people. If people care about the ocean, they'll stop polluting it. What we care about, we protect."

"You're one person out of billions," Pua says. "Why bother?"

"Because I love this place. I wish my family had never left. I wish we'd grown up together boogie boarding, going to prom, and watching the submarine races at Piko Point."

If we had, you would have known better when you saw me sleeping on the sand.

But I would've known you, too.

He sighs. "It's easier to talk this way in the dark when I can't see how ridiculous this sounds to you. I want you to know you've changed me, Pua. You're fearless."

"No one's fearless, Justin. We all have fathers."

"I don't believe you. You truly are fearless, Pua. You don't need me. You don't need anyone. You don't care about fancy cars or restaurants. A castoff sarong or a designer dress—it's all the same to you. You move through the world doing what you want, when you want. You publicly give champagne to a girl because you know it will make her happy even though she's too young. You don't have a phone or a car because things always work out for you in *the usual way*. The rules don't apply to you because you make your own rules."

462 L e h u a P a r k e r

I'm Niuhi.

I take what I want and make my own rules.

Pua cups a hand over her belly.

And what I want is you.

"And that's what I've come to love," Justin says.

She jerks, startled.

"Love?"

Justin sweeps a hand across his face. "I know, I know. It's too soon. You think it's the tropical night with the stars overhead, sex on the beach—it's out of some movie script, right?"

"I—" She fills her lungs and dives.

"Pua?"

Kalei will kill him.

Kalei will kill me.

Father will kill us both if Kalei tries to protect me.

Twins. One is bound to be a boy, the other a girl.

The boy I'll have to kill. But the girl—

The girl I will keep for my own.

I will be a mother.

She skims along the bottom, watching Justin's fluttering feet above.

He's a risk.

He needs to disappear.

One bump, then bite.

She spirals to the surface.

Justin

I'm tired. Treading water is exhausting.

Pua's head rises from the water sleek as a seal.

Pua's not winded at all.

"Pua? Say something. Anything."

"I don't have the words."

I lick my lips and taste salt.

I say, "I promised myself I wouldn't do this, Pua, that I would go slow and give you time to get to know me, to know us, before saying I love you."

"Do you always keep your promises?"

"Yes."

She splashes me. "That's a lie. You just told me you broke promises you made to yourself when you said you love me."

"You misunderstood. To tell you I love you is not a lie or a broken promise. It's the truth. My word is my bond, Pua. If I promise you something, I will die before breaking it."

"And your debts?"

"I pay them. All of them."

Pua

The konane board shifts and the stones realign to reveal another option.

Pua spots it immediately,

It's risky, so risky, she thinks. *It will only work if I can hide my son in plain sight. No one can know he is Niuhi. Kalei cannot suspect my son even exists. But then Father can't hold Kalei accountable for what he doesn't know.*

If this works, we'll be safe from the punishment of death for breaking kapu.

Kahana and that blasted dog Ilima will have to help.

And Justin will have to go and never come back or it all falls apart.

I can't have him recognizing himself in a son or chasing after me because he thinks he's in love.

But maybe, just maybe, if both twins are to live, he doesn't have to die.

Justin

Like a ship coming out of fogbank, Pua emerges from the darkness. She wraps her arms around my neck, her legs around my waist. With her body tangled in mine, it should be harder to stay at the surface, but she's buoyant.

For once I'm not struggling in the water.

She places her forehead against me and leans forward so our noses touch. I breathe in her breath, and it's like sunshine, lemons, and sandalwood.

"Konane," she says. "Do you remember it?"

"Of course," I say.

"The reason you lost at konane is because you think the game is all about devouring your opponent's pieces. It's not. It's about keeping your own options open and always having another move to make."

She swivels her head, rubbing her nose against mine once, twice.

"Eskimo kisses," I say.

"You owe me, Justin," she says. "There's a debt that's due."

I laugh. "The gambling debt? Do you know what you want?"

She nods and captures my mouth. Images of waves fill my mind; castles of coral rise from the deep; I hear chanting and drums as shadows dance in firelight.

She kisses and kisses until all the oxygen is gone from my body.

I begin to faint.

Darkness rolls like deep sea breakers on their way to shore.

I feel heavy and weak as a newborn pup.

I start to sink.

She pulls back and breathes life into my nostrils.

My eyes are open, but I see nothing, not even stars.

"Justin," she says. "I am not free. I can never be yours. You must swear on the debt you owe me that you will leave these islands and never, ever come back."

"What?" I'm so dizzy, my chin sinks below surface and water fills my mouth. "No!" I sputter.

"Swear it!"

"No."

She grabs my shoulders and pushes my head underwater.

She holds.

And holds.

I struggle.

She holds.

A light appears behind my eyelids. I feel my spirit rise and rush toward it like a bullet train through a tunnel.

Still she holds.

This is how I die.

I'm suddenly stone-cold sober and thinking clearly.

This girl is nucking-futz.

She's cray-cray Loonie Tunes.

She's going to kill me, and there's nothing I can do about it.

I'm no longer struggling when she pulls my head out of the water.

"Swear," she says.

"I swear," I say. "Just please let me go. I'll never come back."

Pua brushes her lips against mine. "Aloha, Justin," she says. "Remember your promise. Never come back. If you do, you've murdered us all."

She releases me and disappears into the night.

Epilogue

Justin

When I make it back to shore, the first thing I do is throw up. The second is gather my things and climb into the car. The concierge doesn't bat an eye when I stagger into the lobby, trailing sand and a broken heart.

He's a pro. It's just another day in paradise, right? It's like the captain said: it all looks different in the morning.

I'm just another tourist who fell victim to a local psycho.

Who doesn't have a phone or car?

Who won't tell me where she lives?

Who sleeps on the beach in the afternoon?

Mental patient escapees, that's who.

Why didn't I see it sooner?

Did she put something in my drink?

Did I get roofied?

From the honeymoon suite, I call the airline and change my ticket for the next flight back to California. I shower, throw my stuff in a bag, and get the hell out of Dodge.

Wheels up on the runway, I order a Coke, dump in some rum, and pull out my sketchbook.

Pua, asleep on the beach.

Why? Why do I always attract the crazy?

In the empty window seat, Pua tucks her hair behind her ear. "I said I wasn't free, not that I didn't love you."

You're telling me you're a prisoner? Of what, like the mob? Is your father part of the Yakuza? Is that what you meant when you said he allowed aquariums? Were you really trying to protect me by making me leave?

Pua smiles without showing her teeth. "Oh, Justin," she says, "We're going to have so much fun."

Pua

She swims to the arch at Piko Point where she rests in the big saltwater pool until daylight brightens the sky. For the first time in a week, the infernal itching is gone from under her dorsal fin.

Too bad she can never have Justin scratch that itch again.

Boy had talent.

The sparks in her womb are lively.

Hungry.

That little bit of sashimi and poke on the beach were never going to be enough.

She smacks her lips, considering.

Something warm and fatty. A dolphin or a seal? I'll head to the northern islands and hunt. Maybe visit Aunty Ake. She'll help me figure out how to hide a male child I cannot raise in plain sight.

Two shakes of her mighty tail send her out into the channel.

She doesn't look back to see the octopus slithering out of his hiding place.

The Great Ocean God Kanaloa smiles.

Things are going just as he planned.

The End

Justin and Pua's story continues in *One Boy, No Water*, Book 1 of *The Niuhi Shark Saga*.

ABOUT THE AUTHOR

LEHUA PARKER is an award-winning and best-selling author of Pacific literature stories that explore the intersections of Hawaii's past, present, and future. Her MG/YA magic realism series, *The Niuhi Shark Saga*, is used in public and private school curricula. Book One, *One Boy, No Water,* was a 2017 Hawaii Children's Choice Nene Award Nominee. Her publication credits range from short stories, poems, and novellas to essays, plays, and novels. A founding member of Fairy Tale Ink, her work also appears in *Fractured Beauty* and *Fractured Slipper*.

"Pua's Kiss" in *Fractured Sea* is a prequel to *The Niuhi Shark Saga* trilogy and part of the companion series *Lauele Town Stories*.

Originally from Hawaii and a graduate of The Kamehameha Schools, Lehua is an author, book doctor, public speaker, and business consultant. Trained in literary criticism and an advocate of indigenous cultural narratives, she is a frequent presenter at literary conferences and symposiums.

Now living in exile far from her tropical home, during snowy winters she dreams about the beach.

Catch up with her at

Website: www.LehuaParker.com

Facebook: https://www.facebook.com/LehuaParker/

Instagram: @LehuaParker

Twitter: @LehuaParker

FORBIDDEN WORDS

Historical Fantasy

By

Angela Brimhall

Forbidden Words
Copyright © 2018 by Angela Brimhall
All rights reserved.

Original cover design by Ampersand Book Covers

Published in the United States by Tork Media.

CHAPTER 1

Sometimes it's difficult to be completely silent, even though I have no voice. As I hurried down the carved coral hallway to my room, the curled tip of my fin swept several loose rocks on the ocean floor, slamming them into the wall. A reverberating wave undulated through the sea water behind me and I froze. I whipped my head over my shoulder to see if anyone had heard the sound and waited for a full minute before diving into my bedroom. I tried pulling the giant clam shell door shut but one of the hinges stuck. I tugged hard on it, but the door wouldn't budge. I peeked out into the hallway to check if anyone was coming and was relieved to find it empty still.

Father couldn't find out I snuck away today. He'd hang me on a fisherman's hook if he discovered my plan before Persephone fulfilled her promise.

I examined the hinges and saw a small pebble lodged just inside the pin. I dug it out and yanked on the door handle. It shut so hard I tumbled into my room, crashing into my vanity. An oyster shell holding a strand of pink pearls and my coral brush set launched into the water, but I caught them before they fell to the floor. The skittering pitter-patter of my heart pulsed at the base of my throat as salty water flooded in and out of my lungs.

Always the klutz.

I rolled my eyes and chided myself as I put my pearls and brushes back on my vanity. I never was very good at sneaking around.

After my heart slowed, I settled into my seaweed bed and took the newest slate journal from the stone bedside table. The many shelves lining my bedroom were full of these permanent journals, stacks of them in chronological order beginning with my first one at age five. I'm sure I could've counted a hundred of them at least.

I tapped my temple and tried to recall the details of my meeting. So much had happened, and I wanted to remember every detail. I opened to the first page, readied my fishbone stylus, and swiped it across the surface, scratching my only voice in this world across the pliable rock.

I've been mute since birth. Silent, except the words I write in my journals. But today, I met someone in secret who said she can fix me. I know it was risky. Wrong even. If Father found out, he'd be furious. But, it was worth it. Everything's going to change for me. Tomorrow I turn 18 and I've always known what that meant. At first—

A knock echoed on my door. My fingers stiffened, and I dropped the fishbone. I slammed the journal shut and slid it under my pillow just as the door swung open. Father peeked his head in.

"May I come in?"

The sound of his voice jumpstarted my heart, but I forced a wide smile and waved him in. He grinned beneath a flowing silver beard and swam toward me, seafoam eyes lit with anticipation and glee like they are every year on my birthday. His hands were tucked behind his back, as usual.

"I know Bastian has a huge celebration planned for tomorrow, but you know how I am. I tried to wait, my little Angelfish, I really did. But . . ."

I waggled my finger and furrowed my brow, trying to look stern but I couldn't help it—he looked like the cod that ate the canary rockfish. I smirked and signed my response using my hands. Only he and I understood the unique sign language we'd developed over the years.

Daddy, no. I want to be surprised. Let's wait.

Father's mouth spread so wide that his eyes nearly squeezed shut. "Aurianna, please. This is an extra special gift."

I looked at the ceiling to feign annoyance, then patted the space next to me on my bed. He sat, brought his large hand around front, and placed a golden, jeweled box in my hands. I turned it over and examined the opulent frame in awe, following the intricate carvings of seashells that seemed to float over the pink-coral and mother-of-pearl inlay. Small diamonds and pearls lined the perimeter of the box, framing it in a sparkling glow.

Father wasn't an extravagant merman. Even though he was Poseidon, a god, he preferred things simple over fancy. This kind of gift was very unusual.

"I know I should give you this tomorrow at your coronation, but I can't help myself. It's been fourteen years since we lost your mother and I couldn't bear to wait one more night. Go ahead— open it."

I leaned over and kissed father's nose, then bit my lip in anticipation as I lifted the lid. A soft violet glow shone bright for a moment before gentle chords vibrated into the water. The melodic notes blended with a woman's soft crooning voice.

When your heart found mine, true love came to be
Two souls so divine, joined under the sea
I'll always have you, you'll always have me
Together forever, my beloved you'll be

Two miniature merpeople appeared and twirled in the center of the pearlescent base, their fins intertwined. The two glowing faces gazed into each other's eyes with fondness only true love could etch. I recognized my father as a young man, his hair and beard much shorter, broad shoulders squaring off a rippling chest of muscle. His tail fin shone with a brilliant silver and gold sheen. The petite woman with him was unfamiliar for only moments. Then I realized, it must be my mother. A cascade of thick auburn curls fell against her narrow back brushing her the curve of her hips. As they turned I caught a glimpse of her heart-shaped face. Excitement and a shudder of sorrow gripped my insides. She looked just like me. A knot swelled in my throat settling just above my broken vocal cords.

The pirouetting figures rose from the center of the box and danced through the water around us as if they were alive, completely oblivious to their observers.

"I had this made for your mother the day you were born." Father let out a sad little laugh. "She told me she was going to teach you that song. She thought you could sing it to your true love someday."

I laid the jeweled box on my lap and placed my hand on Father's arm. His soft slick flesh warmed my cold fingers and his words set my heart on fire. He'd spoken of my mother only at the rarest of times. I knew it was very difficult for him to open up about her and what it did to him for days after.

"When we realized you couldn't speak, your mother cried one single tear, then never shed another. She straightened her fin and firmed up her gills. It was her mission to find a way for you to communicate." He put his arm around my shoulder. "It didn't take long, and to her utter delight, she realized you wouldn't need much help."

He raised his eyebrow and pointed to the stacks of slate journals lining the shelves.

"Not being able to speak from birth never stopped you from having a voice. Your lips couldn't speak the words of your heart, but you were determined to find a way to be noticed. The moment you could crawl, your little fingers searched the ocean floor for shells, rocks, anything you could get your hands on to make noise."

I shrugged my shoulders and signed.

And you haven't been able to shut me up since. Ha. Ha.

"Ah, Amphitrite adored that about you, you know. Loved that fire of yours. Said it went with your cascades of red hair. You're so much like her, my darling. She'd be so proud of the merwoman you've become." Father beamed, his eyes sparkling with pride. A rush of heat tingled my cheeks. I was never one to take compliments well.

He winked at me, then floated off my bed, pulled me up as fast as he could, and whirled me around the room. My miniature parents joined our cadence as Father hummed the tune emanating from the music box in perfect time with my mother's delicate serenade.

I knew he missed my mother. He'd never given his heart to anyone else, and the ache of her passing remained. When I was younger, I wanted to see him happy, so I hoped someday he'd find another love. But it never did happen.

My mother's voice slowed and came to a stop. Father dipped me down and flipped me back up, his chest pumping with loud laughter. I couldn't remember when he'd been in such high spirits and so free.

A pang of guilt jabbed at my stomach reminding me I had deceived him today but the reward that was to come was worth risking everything.

"Ah, ha ha. That was wonderful. But, I'd better be getting back before Bastian finishes with the choral dress rehearsal. I promised to put a stamp of approval on the performance for your birthday coronation tomorrow."

Thank you for the beautiful gift. I'll treasure it. I love you, Father.

He wrapped his arms around me so tight, it was almost uncomfortable.

"I love you too. I'll see you tomorrow. Good night, sweet Aurianna."

Father kissed me on the forehead. I hugged him once more. *See you tomorrow.*

"Yes, it will be a day to remember."

He winked, bowed, and disappeared through the doorway.

The ghost of Father's kiss still lingered above my eyebrow. I rubbed it in for good measure and realized in that moment just how much my father had done for me over the years. He was a single father with the burden of an entire kingdom upon his shoulders, but I'd always been his first priority. I never doubted that.

My young miniature parents caught my eye as they twirled near my closet, eyes locked in an eternal gaze. Mother's song had started over again and it was so tempting to keep my music box open just have her there with me—to memorize her beautiful song, but I decided there would be plenty of time for that tomorrow. I picked up the music box and as my fingers touched the clasp, the couple danced over to the center of the inlay where they started and faded. I breathed in deep as a blanket of satisfaction covered my heart. For the first time since I was four, both my parents had been with me. Baby guppies swam inside my stomach as I realized through Father's new gift, I could now see my mother anytime I wanted.

I placed the music box on the stone table beside my bed and reached under my pillow for my slate journal. I found the fishbone stylus that rolled to the bottom of my bed and opened to the first page. Another pang of guilt flashed as I reread the last sentence I'd started before Father came in, but I finished scratching my thoughts anyway.

I've been mute since birth. Silent, except the words I write in my journals. But today, I met someone in secret who said she can fix me. I know it was risky. Wrong even. If Father found out, he'd be furious. But, it was worth it. Everything's going to change for me. Tomorrow I turn 18 and I've always known what that meant. At first, I thought the goddess of the underworld a bit strange, even dangerous, but Persephone convinced me she has the magic I need. If I can gather the things she requested from Father's treasury and meet her at the edge of Seawood Forest before dawn, I can surprise Father at my coronation. Perhaps even try to sing him the beginning of Mother's song. I know he won't be happy about me taking some of the things she asked for at first, but I know he'll see it was worth the sacrifice. For the first time in my life, I'll have a voice!

CHAPTER 2

*J*finished my thought, shoved my journal and stylus under my pillow again, and sat for mere seconds. I couldn't keep my hands still. My fin tingled in anticipation as I watched the moon dial in the garden move from my only window. I'd never stolen anything or even attempted to deceive Father before. Tonight, some his most precious treasure would disappear at my hands.

What if I got caught? Would he be disappointed? Angry? Or worse—hurt?

I swam, tracing the curves of my room over and over. Minutes crawled by on a sluggish ebb for hours, making the wait that much more agonizing. With nothing to do but think, dark thoughts of my childhood swirled like poisonous squid ink inside my mind. Although Father and I communicated through our own sign language, he knew it would be too difficult and burdensome to teach the others I interacted with. We had to find another way for me to converse with others in the castle and the kingdom that made sense. When I was five, Father hired a tutor. She created several erasable sand tablets that I could trace letters into and she taught me how to write. Although I became quite proficient in my written communications, it did little to quell the whispers of the water nymphs and other merchildren in the coral village.

"Too bad she cannot speak. The king must be so disappointed."

"It's a shame Poseidon didn't have any other children."

"A tragic waste of royal blood."

"He'll never find a merprince to marry her. Who would want a mute?"

A pit, long buried, resurfaced at the memories breaking through the wall I hid them behind. A child so young should never have to endure the things I did, and it stuck with me for many years.

I remembered returning home in such a state, scribbling wildly on my sand tablet, listing everything I thought I was—helpless, hopeless, worthless, voiceless. Strings of iridescent tears would fall in silence as I showed my words to Father. He'd smile a sad smile, pull me on his lap, and declare, "My darling Arianna, when you understand the difference between what you think you are and what you can be, you'll find yourself and others will see you."

Eventually, I learned to ignore the incessant prattle of the merchildren and the kingdom gossipers and could swim by, head held high and shoulders erect.

The cruel whispers all bounced off me, except for one. No matter how they worded it, it caught me off guard every time:

Poseidon will never have a male heir to pass his throne to.

What kind of merprince could he get to marry her?

Not even the royal treasure will be dowry enough to convince a merprince from any of the four oceans to take her.

Flashes of the miniature version of my mother's face splashed inside my mind; sapphire eyes, high cheekbones, flowing deep auburn hair. Father always said he could see her in me. I saw the love he had for her and wanted to grow up to be as much like her as I could.

Earlier, when they danced around my room, Father gazed at the tiny version of her with such longing and love. For the first time in a long time, the ever-dodgy glimmer of hope flashed across my future.

I stopped circling and clenched my fists, willing the gnawing pit to rise into my pounding heart so I could crush it. The water nymphs of the coral village and the other merfolk had long since quieted their gossip at the passionate behest of my father, but I knew they would always secretly regard me as the poor mute daughter of Poseidon. In their eyes, mute equaled stupid, incompetent, unworthy of marriage or love.

Well, not after tomorrow.

With Persephone's magic spell, when my father presented me to our kingdom, I'd announce myself and prove to everyone that I deserved the throne, prove that I was worthy of the kingdom's trust. I'd quell those whispers on my own, and someday, someone would look at me like my father looked at my mother. Love me like he loved her.

All I needed was a voice.

***

When the moon dial passed the eleventh hour, I listened hard through the currents in the water for a good ten minutes. No one made a peep. A thrill of giddiness pricked my fingertips and the bottom of my fin. This was it. My chance to be heard.

I set my jaw and grabbed a sturdy net bag, a sand tablet, and the list of treasures Persephone wanted in trade. I peeked out the door, looking left and right, my heart crashing inside my chest like the tide on stormy day. No vibrations disturbed the water. My lips pressed together, I leaned forward, careful not to make any hard tail thrusts to create waves of my own.

I made it to the end of the hallway and peered around the corner, a tangled knot of fret holding steady at the base of my throat. The thought of getting caught terrified me, but I forged on. This was my only chance. Nothing was going to stop me. Once I got my voice, a lot of things were going to change.

I passed through the tunnels, cautiously exploring each one, and careful to look behind me before moving along. I thought of my mother again. I was so young when she took her place among the goddesses in heaven. Father never spoke of what happened, exactly, only that during the human war, a human king caused her death during an attack on the castle.

Father forbade me from interacting with them or even going to the surface.

I'd overheard some of the older merfolk talking in hushed circles about the times before the human war when Father wasn't around. They regaled the golden days when our kind rose from the depths of the sea to the surface where the light of the sun touched the waves. Their talk of skies full of glitter, stone castles on the hills of the coast, and the friendly humans who sailed our waters in their vast wooden ships mesmerized me. They spoke of trade with the surface and of solid friendships between the humans and merfolk that were almost like family. The land and ocean coexisted in harmony and supported each other for centuries before the war.

Deep down I knew I shouldn't, but I found myself fantasizing on sleepless nights of being a part of the human world. I had a strong feeling I couldn't explain that told me there must have been some misunderstanding. How could humans be so friendly for so long and then suddenly turn on us? There had to be a good reason.

Under the sea, people saw me as the mute. Helpless against the seduction of curiosity, I found myself wondering if I had a chance to meet a human and could find out what really happened, unlike the merpeople, a human would accept me.

As I turned the last corner and headed toward the treasury, I decided after my coronation, once my voice could be heard, I would travel to the surface and try to find a human. A tendril of electricity trickled up my fins, travelled past my seashells, and settled in my chest.

Maybe I'll find a human prince who'll see me like Father does and my first royal act could be reuniting the human kingdom and the all the underwater kingdoms in peace again.

Dizzy with the thoughts of the surface and the possibility of meeting a human prince, I arrived at the treasury unfocused and didn't think to check the corner. I swam right past it and collided with a tall muscular body swimming backward out of the door in a hurry. The impact tossed me back and I tumbled into the wall, slamming my shoulder into the jutting rock. I dropped my net bag as the armored figure turned around. He stared, his neon blue eyes open wide, and shoved his hands behind his back.

Bastian?

I hurried and snatched my bag from the ground, my shoulder twinging with the jerky movement. He blinked rapidly and opened his mouth like an idiotic codfish. Then he recognized me and snapped it shut. His left eyebrow rose into his dark wavy hairline and he pulled his tattooed shoulders back in a menacing stance.

"What do you think you're doing down here in the middle of the night, Princess?"

I shrugged my shoulders, cocked my head, and consciously widened my eyes.

"Don't be coy, young lady. Answer me."

Bursts of sour bile peppered my throat. I reached in the bag and tried hard to casually retrieve my sand tablet, careful not to rustle Persephone's list. Bastian wasn't part of the royal guard, but as Father's most trusted and decorated advisor, he had the power to ruin everything. I stiffened my shoulders and stood tall.

He furrowed his brow, swept a long strand of wavy black hair away from his forehead, and popped his square chin up to look me in the eye.

"Aurianna, it's after midnight. Shall I ask you again what you're doing out of bed, wandering the castle, or shall we go wake Poseidon and tell him of your insolence?"

Annoyed but trying to stay calm, I traced my words into the sand tablet.

I was just looking for something.

He sniffed and pulled down his lip. That sour-faced stooge. I would've fainted clear dead if he ever smiled or acted normal. I had no idea what Father saw in him. When I inherited the throne, he'd be the first to go.

"In here? What would you need in here?"

I wanted to see if I could find anything of my mother's in there to surprise Father tomorrow with a gift of his own.

Bastian's hard eyes softened. He released his set jaw and the thin lines of his mouth curved. I patted myself on the proverbial back for such a brilliant, off-the-cuff lie.

"I see. That's kind of you to think of that, especially because tomorrow is going to be very hard on the king."

Hard on him. Why would my birthday be hard on him?

What do you mean? I thought tomorrow would be a happy day for him. I'm 18 now, a merwoman. I'm not a mermaid anymore. I can help with the kingdom. I can marry and start my own life.

Bastian paled as if he realized he'd said something he shouldn't. It piqued my curiosity.

"I'm sure you're right, Aurianna. I just meant it will be a sad day for him to lose his daughter to adulthood."

I narrowed my gaze and stared him down.

Tell me what you mean.

Bastian pretended to yawn and patted my shoulder as if to coddle me like he did when I was young.

"It really is late, Princess. Come, come, it's too late for this. I'll escort you to your room and accompany you to the treasury in the morning. You first."

He gestured for me to lead. I hesitated but knew if I put up a fuss he'd be onto my mischief. I turned and swam up the winding tunnels of the castle and back to my bedroom with him in tow. The tension between us was palpable. He'd been down in the treasury for an unexplained reason and still hid something behind his back. I'd been sneaking down there for something I shouldn't have been. We were both dying to know what the other had been up to, but neither wanted the other one to find out.

When we reached my room, I pushed open the clam shell door and swam inside. Bastian spoke, his voice stern and authoritative. "Well, goodnight to you, Princess. I hope you sleep well. See you in the morning."

He waved his hand and bowed, hesitated as if he wanted to say more, then pulled my door shut and swam away. I could tell he wanted to question me further, or at least stay by my side until he knew I was asleep inside my room, but whatever he'd been doing down in the treasury was important enough for him to leave it be.

Frustrated at losing the chance, but not willing to give up, I circled my room and watched the moon dial for another hour. Every sliver of light that disappeared on that dial was less time I'd have to find the things on Persephone's list. The mounting pressure made my stomach curl.

What if I couldn't get to her in time? I'd lose my chance.

The moon dial passed the hour mark and I opened my bedroom door. I poked my head out and listened hard for any vibrations, but the only sounds I heard were two squeaky dolphins outside my window discussing the effects of a particularly bad batch of herring.

I headed down to the treasury again, this time hyper alert, looking over my shoulder just in case Bastian thought to be on the lookout. Incoherent thoughts raced around inside my head one after the other, not giving me the chance to focus on one worry before another crowded in. I swallowed and braced myself each time I turned a corner, clenching my jaw, anticipating Bastian's face to jump out at me, but the hallways remained empty. Once I reached the treasury, I breathed a heavy sigh and slipped inside.

Bioluminescent algae climbed the coral walls, casting a bluish hue onto the mounds of treasure lining the cavern. Fingers trembling, I placed Persephone's list next to a large patch of bright green fungi and counted out the five requested items: the golden belt of Heracles, the ring of Phorcys, the sword of Oceanus, the shield of Proteus, and the crown of Medusa.

Persephone sketched a drawing next to each item to make it easy to recognize the unique traits of the pieces.

Father truly wasn't a materialistic king now, but rumors of his frivolous and raucous youth had circulated throughout the kingdom during my entire childhood. He and my grandfather Kronos conquered many underwater nations in their time. There was no secret the royal treasure vault held vast and precious treasures from the most powerful oceanic gods all over the world and the mounds of gold and trinkets lining the floor were proof of his power.

I searched for hours through the mounds of gold, silver, and jeweled treasure, my heart leaping with each find: the golden belt, the ring, and the sword and shield. But the crown of Medusa was nowhere to be found. The tips of my fingers ached from overturning so many coins and heavy relics. No coin, cup, or statue was left unturned, I was sure of it. A cool lump settled at the back of my throat. Persephone insisted on all five pieces or she wouldn't make the deal.

Twings and twangs of worry yanked on parts inside me I didn't even know existed. Time had run out. I had to go. There was no other option. I closed my eyes, held the four precious treasures against my chest, and prayed silently to Zeus and Athena to have mercy on me. I hooked the ring onto one of the clasps of the belt, shoved the rest of the treasures into my net, and slung it over my shoulder.

Guilt slithered inside my stomach like a nest of anxious baby eels as I left the treasury. Whatever reaction Father had when he found out about the stolen hallows, I knew in my heart he would grant forgiveness when he saw what I used it for.

I peered around the tunnels to make sure once again that Bastian hadn't followed me, then swam as fast as I could toward Seawood Forest. The light in the water from the moon disappeared, leaving only minutes—perhaps even seconds— before the sun broke through the darkness.

CHAPTER 3

W hen I was a little mermaid, the merchildren of our servants in the castle used to tell me that Seawood Forest was haunted by sea creatures who would eat the scales off my fins and turn me into shark bait. There were rumors that the creatures used to be merpeople, cursed by Hades, the god of the underworld, to suffer an eternity of hell for the deals they broke.

I never believed them until now.

Quiet moans vibrated through the water, calling out to me as I approached the edge of the tall, thick seaweed.

"We see you there beyond the trees. Come to us and we'll set you free."

Fishbumps poked up through my scales and lined my bare skin. My tail weakened, barely keeping me upright. I squeezed the net closer to me and searched the water for any sign of Persephone, now painfully aware of my naivety at her request.

"Come to us. There's nothing to fear. Come closer, yes. You'll like it here."

The sounds of the ocean dampened. Dark vapor cascaded from above. Heavy water enveloped me, pulling me toward the thatch of dark green. I fought to move my fins, to escape, but every muscle inside me seized up. A thousand hands roamed over my body, down my tail, through my hair. I struggled and screamed voicelessly, trying to kick out but too weak to fight.

"Stop!"

A stern voice called out behind me and the vapor dissipated. Strange sensations jolted through my body, releasing the ebb and flow of the pull. I collapsed onto the ocean floor.

"My dear princess, I am sorry about that."

I gazed up and saw a bony hand outstretched, then followed the thin arm up into Persephone's golden smiling face. Sharp teeth rested on thick bronze lips threatening to pierce the skin at any moment, the curve not quite reaching her eyes, mocking my weakness. Knowing I shouldn't but desperate for her help, I nervously extended my one hand, and she pulled me upright. She stood on two legs, two heads taller than me, a tight, elegant weave of seaweed, rope, and what appeared to be the skin of a great white shark covering the top half of her gilded skin. A flowing sheet of canvas marked with strange runes cascading from her waist to her ankles.

"I told my beauties to leave you alone. But I guess you were too tempting to resist." She chewed on a long black fingernail as she eyed the shiny contents of my net. "I see you considered my offer," she said. Her turquoise eyes sparkled with a greedy glimmer.

I nodded, my head barely strong enough to make the gesture, and stooped back down to sift through the rocky floor for my sand tablet. Persephone tapped my shoulder. I looked up and saw her palm outstretched, balancing my tablet. Her mouth curved up into a seductive grin. Long strands of deep green hair swirled in the water around her as if dancing to an inaudible beat. I rose and took the tablet with a trembling hand. As I met her eyes, a cool chill traveled the length of my spine. I knew I was in trouble. My gut was telling me to grab the tablet and swim as fast as I could back home. But I took the tablet from her anyway and scribbled quickly.

Yes. I brought what you asked for.

Most of it.

The tips of my fingers tingled, knowing what'd they had just written was a lie.

The sparkle in her eyes turned to golden flame to match her skin, burning any trace of the turquoise there moments before.

"Yessss." The single syllable slithered out of her mouth. I fully expected to see a forked tongue flicker out of it but only a black tip slipped out to swipe her upper lip.

"Show me, child."

I rustled through the net my heart racking the sides of my ribcage. The metal of the objects sparked turning cold, grazing my fingers with an icy burn. It was as if the sacred hallows were making one last futile attempt to defend themselves—they could feel the evil seeping from Persephone.

Oh gods. I am truly sorry. May Zeus and the gods forgive me.

I gripped the hilt of the sword first and brandished it. Persephone watched the movement, her eyes ticking back and forth. Her grin widened, revealing her mouthful of frightening, thick barbs. When we'd met earlier today, she had called to me from the corner of the kingdom's community gardens where I was gathering sweet seagrass and red algae for a kelp cake for Father. A long hood had covered her face, only the swatches of green hair billowed out from the sides to rest just above her waistline. Her velvety voice, so mesmerizing and genuine when she offered her help, soothed me which I now realized came from her clever magic. Witnessing the full sight of her flaming eyes, sharp grin, and powerful presence terrified me to the gills.

I've made a terrible mistake, but I can't go back now. Stay calm.

I tensed my fin to keep it from quivering as Persephone reached out and gripped the blade, teasing it from my grip. As I let go, a surge of energy left my body I hadn't noticed was present until it was gone.

"The sword of Oceanus." She raised a thin green eyebrow and shivered as her skeletal fingers traced the intricate runes on the gilded hilt with her fingertip, similar to those on her skirt. She twisted it side to side, then leaned down to study the details of the embossed design. Two silver tiger sharks chased each other around the grip, blue sapphire jewels glimmering from their eyes. An elaborate carving scrawled down the blade in a strange language I couldn't read.

"What else did you find, Princess?" Her lips quivered as she pressed them together to suppress a laugh.

I reached inside the bag once more and retrieved the golden belt. A jolt of electricity convulsed through my forearm up into my shoulder. I wrenched back, nearly dropping it. She jerked it from my hand and examined the ring hooked on the belt clasp.

"Mmm."

She licked her lips and unhooked the clasp. The ring fell into her open palm. A breath of satisfaction bubbled from her lips, releasing a quiet giggle, and she tossed the belt aside.

"Ahh, Phorcys's ring."

Resonating light from the filtered sunlight just breaking above the ocean surface caught the scarlet jewel as Persephone slipped it onto her finger. Her eyelids fell shut and she clenched her fist. The facets of the gem pulsed, rippling the water around us. Streaks of violet lightning bolted up her veins in one swift jolt.

Persephone opened her eyes and peered eerily at me through glowing white pupils, the golden fire snuffed out.

"What else?" she asked, her hand outstretched, her fingers wiggling in anticipation.

Heat rose into my cheeks as I reached in to retrieve my last and final offering.

What is she going to do when she finds out this is the last treasure? Athena let these four items satisfy her greed. Protect me. Bless me with your wisdom. I need my voice. Please.

I drew out the shield but before I could get it out of the net, she yanked it from my hands and stripped the rest of the net from its edges.

"Proteus's shield."

Persephone thrust her ringed hand through the leather straps, and the body of the shield vibrated, causing the water around us to oscillate in soothing rhythmic circles. Schools of fish, eel, and jellyfish swam toward us, entranced. She moved her arm to the right and the mass of creatures followed suit. Persephone thrust her arm forward, then gracefully moved it left. The schools of sea life shifted and followed her lead, as if the shield controlled their every move.

"Ah ha ha. All I need is the crown and the set is complete. The crown, child. Where's Medusa's crown? Give it to me."

The crazed look in her white eyes unsettled me, and I swam backward to put distance between us. But no matter how scared I was about telling her, no matter how loud the voice inside my head was screaming to run, I couldn't. I wasn't leaving without my voice. I traced into the sand tablet.

That was all I could find. I searched Father's treasury for hours. He didn't have the crown. I brought you four of the five items. That should be more than enough to pay the price for my voice.

"Oh, you think so, do you?" Violet sparks blazed off her gold skin. The white of her eyes glowed so bright, the veins in my head throbbed. "That crown was the most important piece of the set. I need it. I must have it."

Persephone tossed the shield to the ocean floor. She rushed me and grabbed my arms. Searing pain surged up my shoulders into my neck and temples. Darkness bled into my vision, blinding me. I dropped my tablet and swung my arms, trying to fight back.

"Brazen and obstinate. I expected nothing less from Poseidon and Amphitrite's spoiled little brat. You're just like your mother." She spat.

I jerked my tail, thrashing to get away from her. The harder I fought, the more painful the bursts in my head became. I wasn't going to stop, not even if it killed me. Returning empty handed and living the rest of my life without my voice would be worse than death. I had nothing to lose.

"Stop fighting, Aurianna."

The moment the last syllable left her mouth, every muscle in my body froze. Her hands left me. The pain stopped. My stiff, heavy tail slid off the slick ocean sand beneath me, pulling the rest of my paralyzed body forward. My vision returned just as I crashed into a reef of coral—

rigid outstretched hands the only thing keeping jagged fragments of rock from impaling my face. Indigo blood blossomed in the undulating water, twisting and rising from the sliced flesh of my wrists in delicate tendrils.

I lay on the bottom of the ocean floor at her feet, frozen. Persephone mumbled a few strange words and sharp cuffs of coral coiled around me, caging me.

"Oh dear." Persephone clicked her tongue. "With those wounds, the sharks will scent your royal blood in mere minutes, and soon you'll be nothing but rotting flesh in their bellies."

My throat tightened and a voice inside my head chided me with ruthless truth.

How could you have thought this would work? That it could be so easy? You were a fool to believe something as valuable as your lifelong hope and dream could come true.

I caught sight of two large shadows circling above me. Long, thick bodies flicking their tails with slow deliberate movements.

Oh no. The sharks. Father. Zeus. I wish someone could save me!

The shark in the lead dipped his nose and slowly spiraled downward, closing the gap of space between us. A small bit of tingling had come back into my limbs but not enough for me to attempt to break free. The second shark followed, black soulless eyes fixed on the crimson blossoms still curling out of my wrists. The jaw of the larger shark fell open revealing razor-sharp triangles ready to slice into my exposed, helpless body, feet away from my face. I had just enough feeling in my face to shut my eyes.

Please, make it quick. Don't make me suffer.

A bright purple light flashed bright enough to penetrate my lids. The light dimmed seconds after it pulsed. I opened my eyes, expecting to see the gaping mouth of the shark preparing to devour me but, all I could see were large black flakes swirling like bits of fluttering sea grass in the water. Jolts of cold spikes rushed through my veins waking up every part of my body from the inside out in chilling pain. The lacerations in my wrists tingled, then sealed over.

A skeletal green hand appeared in front of my face. I gazed up to see Persephone beaming, her eyes ablaze with eerie white light. a mocking smile spread from pointy ear to ear. I hesitated, then took her hand. She pulled me up as if I weighed nothing and brought me in close, leaning into me so our noses nearly touched.

"Were you afraid, Aurianna?" she hissed, the pupil of her white eyes flashing with turquoise flame.

I nodded over and over again. My throat tightened. Every inch of me ached as I wriggled my fin, trying to stay upright.

"Good. I wanted to teach you a lesson about the power I hold now, even without the fifth hallow." Her clawed finger grazed over my vocal cords. "I had doubts you could find all five or if you'd even show at all. Four out of the five works." She slid her finger down, pressed it into my chest, and drug it across my collarbone, shoulder, and back as she walked around me. "I will find Medusa's crown on my own. With the combined magic of these four hallows, I can stand against anyone. Even Poseidon."

Fiery heat flooded my stomach. Anger and regret bubbled up and I longed to strike her face but feared it would be the last thing I ever did. I had to get away. Warn Father somehow.

"So, a deal is a deal. I never break my word." A terrifying, toothy smile spread across her face so large and triumphant, it swallowed her cheeks whole.

"I will give you your voice to satisfy that deal, if only for the few minutes you have left. It's only fair. But don't get the wrong idea. True, I saved you from the sharks, but I can't have you running off to tell your father about this new development. That would ruin the surprise."

Swim, Aurianna. As fast as you can. Get away. Go.

I steadied my fin, getting ready to bolt, but Persephone noticed the change and flicked her hand. Phorcys' ring flashed.

The muscles in my fin weakened. I swayed, sinking downward toward the ocean floor. She pressed her hands together then drew them into a square. A wall of water formed around me like a cage and held me upright.

"Before I let you have your last words, I need you to stay still and listen. I have a story to tell you, if only for my own satisfaction. I want you to know the truth before you die. You see, I'm not the villain you must think I am. There are no heroes in this story. Especially not your Father."

Persephone reached out and squeezed my jaw. I clenched my teeth as sharp pain lurched up the sides of my neck and pummeled my brain.

"I am the Goddess of the Underworld, the only remaining monarch of what's left of it. Your dearest father, Poseidon, killed my beloved Hades and stole our kingdom two centuries ago during the oceanic wars. For years I tried to defeat him, to get my kingdom back, but without the hallows, I continued to fail."

Her grip on my jaw squeezed tighter, increasing the blinding pain in my head.

"So, I did the unthinkable. I made a deal with the human king Alastair. He was fighting his own battle to save his kingdom, so I worked side by side with him. I even broke the laws of the gods by using my magic in exchange for his help."

Persephone's eyes blazed with blue fire again. Golden sparks of light appeared on the crown of her head and shot upward, igniting her dark flowing hair into sheaths of gilded straw billowing in the flowing current of the water.

"With our combined forces, he defeated his aggressor, but even with his armadas and my holy power, we could not defeat Poseidon's hallows." She let go of my jaw and placed her hands on my shoulders. The pain in my head dulled as I peered into her eternal eyes. "Now, my dear, I want you to listen very closely because this is the most important part. In our last attempt at overthrowing him, Alastair and I took your mother and held her, generously offering to trade her life in exchange for the hallows. But, even with your mother's life on the line, your wicked father craved power over love. So, I had the human king slaughter her on principle to show him what it felt like to lose."

A beam of light sliced through the darkness of my father's past searing my soul. The pinnacle of truth was finally revealed, and everything about Father's aversion and hatred for humans made sense to me. Father spoke of how much he hated humans, how they were to blame for my mother's death. He told me they killed my mother, but I could never get him to tell me how it happened. I'd tried to press him, especially as a young child, but he never yielded. I had guessed somehow, she'd been caught in one of their nets or swam too close to the surface. I never imagined they'd murdered her.

Persephone continued her tale. "You see, the man you know is not the man I know. His thirst for power and dominion over the seas cost your mother her life and his prideful insistence on keeping you uninformed about his past will be his downfall and yours."

She let go of my jaw and grinned. The skin where her fingertips had gripped flooded with tingling heat. Persephone gathered all four of Father's treasures and brandished them in front of me.

"You see, the beauty of this is, I never could overpower him as long as he held the mythic hallows, but it only took a little nudge to tempt his foolish, selfish child to bring them to me of her own free will. Four of the five hallows supplies me with more than enough power to find and retrieve the crown of Medusa. Once I do, I'll send your father to meet you and your mother in Elysium."

White hot rage churned inside me, and I ground my teeth. If I could've escaped the cage, I'd have clawed the grin right off her face. But I couldn't move. Her white eyes met mine and her gaze bore into my core, tunneling into the deepest part of my soul until it hit the bottom. After a moment, she closed her eyes, and a glimmer of joy briefly flickered on her face before her expression hardened again.

"You know, child. Now I see how helpless and pathetically inept you are, death seems just too boring of an end to Poseidon's legacy. Not nearly cruel enough for revenge's sake. Having to live with the knowledge you traded what you wanted most for what you loved the most—well it's just too delicious." Persephone laughed and mumbled, "I'm so cruelly clever, I impress myself."

Persephone stalked toward me, punched through the barrier of water, and forced the ruby of Phorcys's ring deep into my forehead.

"Vocalis humanus permanente."

A vortex of bubbling water picked up my limp body and spun me in twisting circles. Blistering pain cut across my throat, slashing it wide open from the inside. Salty sea water burned as it pooled in the valley of my gullet.

The spinning slowed, then stopped.

Hot stinging pricks erupted at the base of my tail fin. The intensity grew like a fever, lighting every scale with scalding fire. Patches of emerald iridescent flakes fell like dying embers, swirling in the water currents around me in droves.

A loud ripping sound echoed in my ears before the excruciating pain registered. I reared back. A strained keening wail exploded from my throat—for the first time in my life, I screamed.

I pitched forward and looked down to see two pink flesh-and-bone legs flailing in the water.

"The vile hideousness of humanity suits you, my dear. Your body now reflects the very thing that stole Poseidon's love. What irony."

I opened my mouth to breathe but a rush of sea water choked inside the back of my throat. Sparks of light swam in my vision.

Father!

I twisted my torso in frantic spurts, but it did nothing to move my legs. Persephone sniggered.

"Ah yes, one more thing. The ocean is no place for a human. I wouldn't want you to drown, my dear."

She flung her fist at me and a single flash of crimson light shot from the ring's center. The beam hit me just below my sternum and propelled me upward. Consciousness faded the higher I rose. Crisp air bathed my face for only a moment as I breeched the water's surface. Then, my vision turned black.

CHAPTER 4

Strong hands gripped my waist, digging into my hip bones. My eyes fluttered. Cognizance hid inside the limbo of mental fog weighing my consciousness down. I wanted to shove the fingers away, but the weakness in my arms forbade me. My entire body was drawn from the water and cradled in thick arms against a hard chest. A male voice called out.

"Get the boat, tie it to the rocks. Hurry, Colin, it looks like the storm is nearly upon us."

The thump thumping rhythm emitting from his chest nuzzled my cheek, but the loud piercing sounds of the crashing water and whistling wind beat inside my exposed ear. Frigid air raked across my raw naked skin. Each breath I drew in seared my enflamed throat.

Everything hurt.

"Sam, get her to the cave. Go!"

The man carrying me ran, bouncing my sore body against him in short bursts. An incoherent groan gurgled from my throat, surprising me.

"It'll be alright, milady. I've got you."

I opened my eyes and saw nothing but a dark, stinging blur so I slammed them shut. He slowed his pace. The sounds around me muffled. My stomach swooped, and his grip on me loosened. The warmth of his embrace separated from my skin, and I met with solid ground. Sharp hard granules brushed like sandpaper against my delicate new skin. The frigid air bit at me, causing the muscles in my arms and legs to shudder over and over. I squeezed my eyes and clenched my jaw to stop it from quivering.

Something ripped and a damp covering fell against my exposed torso, enveloping my breasts and new pelvis.

A soothing voice whispered in my ear as my hair was tucked behind my ear.

"Stay still. You're ice cold. I need to gather some wood. If I can't get you warm, you won't survive."

The covering over my body felt strange, like nothing I'd had against me before, but it was soft and pleasant. I peeked through my eyelids to test the reaction and found it less painful this time. I inspected my surroundings, but there wasn't much to see aside from the blanket of stars peering in from the cave opening.

Throbbing pain pulsed through my new legs and I cried out, bending them upward. It was almost as if I had two separate fins now, each working independently of themselves.

"I'm coming. It's going to be okay," the deep voice called.

I looked up and saw the silhouette of a tall figure rushing toward me. My heart slammed against my ribcage, beating hard as a rush of fear flooded through me.

A human.

He dropped a pile of wood a few feet away and proceeded to snap two small rocks together. Orange sparks emitted from their edges and a few fell atop the wood, sprouting into a rippling swatch of light.

The human man came toward me, bare chested, palms up as if to surrender to me. I hugged the covering and tucked my chin. He slowed his walk.

"My name is Sam. I know you're scared and hurt. I understand. I know I'm a stranger and you don't know me, but I can help you, if you'll let me. Will you trust me?"

I nodded hesitantly. He smiled as if relieved and ran a hand through his long chestnut hair.

"I'm sorry, I had nothing to cover you with but my shirt. It's not going to be enough to keep you warm. We need to get you closer to the fire. Can you move on your own, or do you need me to help you?"

Out of habit, I looked around for my sand tablet to answer him, then remembered it lay at the bottom of the ocean. A pang reverberated inside me, and the reality of the entire situation dawned on me. I lost my fin, almost lost my life, and soon my only family.

But for the first time since birth, I had a voice.

I looked up at Sam's waiting face and opened my mouth to speak but only strange sounds burbled out. Heat rushed up my neck into my cheeks. I clamped my jaw shut realizing I had no idea how to speak. I saw the words in my head and my mouth longed to speak them, but nothing was coming out the way I intended it to. With all my years of wishing and dreaming of the day I would be able to speak, I had never imagined that it would be so hard.

"Here, let me help you," Sam said and offered his hand again. I shook my head. I couldn't speak yet, but I wasn't going to show him I was completely helpless. I clutched the shirt against my chest and scooted my way closer to the swaying glow. He put his hands up and sat on the opposite side of the fire, putting some distance between us.

Warmth spread from the growing red-orange illumination. Everything in the ocean was cool and soothing. Here on the surface—the air in my lungs, the heat on my skin, the hard crystals of sand beneath me—it was all uncomfortable and foreign. Such strange sensations. All would be painful if not for the pleasure and relief they offered.

Sam stared at me, but I wasn't quite ready to meet his gaze. I looked everywhere but his face.

The fire cast eerie shadows on the face of the cave walls as if this peculiar light had power to infuse life like the Gods did. I wondered if the shadows were alive, if they could see me.

Rustling sounded behind me.

"I secured the boat, Sam. The storm seems to be moving south. Looks like we're in the clear."

I whipped my head over to see another human man leaning into the mouth of the cave, this one a head shorter than Sam, light sandy hair on both his head and his cheeks. Rushes of wind billowed through his clothes as the wind whipped him from behind. I hugged the shirt tighter against me, a jolt of panic lacing my veins. I was already overwhelmed with one human man. Now there were two.

"Good to see you up and alive, miss. You appear to be breathing, at least. Lucky we snuck out for an early-morning fishing trip or we wouldn't have been here to save your life. I guess you could call us heroes. Nothing new, though. Prince Samandrian and I, we've done lots of—"

"Ahem," Sam interrupted. "Thank you, Colin. Would you be so kind as to jog up to the castle and ask Johanna for some clothing? I believe she's around this young lady's size," he finished with a pointed look at the cave entrance.

"Yes, my prince. I'll be back as soon as I can." The man named Colin bowed, then winked at me and disappeared. I gulped in wild wonder and amazement. The air stung.

A prince? This man was royalty? What was he doing out in the middle of the ocean like this?

Sam chuckled and for the first time since we'd come to the cave, I rustled up the courage to really look at him. Dark ruffled hair waved against his neck like strands of seaweed tossed in a hundred different directions. Shadow hugged his clean jawline where merman's beards would be, as if shaved off on purpose. I'd never seen a man without one. It was bizarre and . . . beautiful.

He met my gaze through the flames. The amber light reflected in his deep brown eyes.

"Sorry about my friend there. He's a bit of a show-off." He laughed again then licked his lips. "So, uh, how are you feeling? Are you still chilled? I can stoke the fire until he gets here with some clothes."

I shook my head. The heat of the fire did soothe the chill on my front side, but the wind whispered up the bare parts of my back and buttocks. I hoped Colin hurried back.

Sam smiled, then scratched the top of his head. "It seems like you understand what I'm saying, but it doesn't appear you're in the mood to talk. I get it. You must have really been through something."

I observed his uneasy expression and longed to speak my mind. I eyed the flickering sand floor of the cave to find anything that would work as a writing tablet, like the one I'd lost, but I couldn't see anything.

I nodded and patted my lips, trying to communicate that I did want to speak.

"Oh." Sam's cheeks blossomed pink. "So, you want to talk but you can't?"

I frowned and clenched my jaw in frustration.

"Is it because you're hurt?" he asked. His brows raised, concern lining his face.

I watched his lips, how they moved in different directions when he formed the words. Determination swelled in my chest. My sacrifice was not going to be in vain. Persephone said she lifted the curse of my silence. I just had to do my part.

Goddess Athena, I invoke the name of my father, Poseidon, and his brother Zeus and call on you for this favor. Help my mouth speak the words of my mind.

I pursed my lips together, steeled myself, then opened my mouth to speak the word I saw Sam's lips forming in my head.

"Hu-r-rt." The sound that came out surprised me so much that I slapped my hand over my mouth. Joy resonated through me unlike anything I'd ever felt.

Athena had heard me. Persephone's spell worked.

I could speak. Actually speak.

Sam's eyes widened. He scrambled up and rushed to my side. "You're hurt? What can I do?"

What little Father would speak of the humans was negative and scary. He told me they were killers. Cruel and vicious warmongers that poached the sea. Taking everything and gave nothing back. I'd listened and tried to picture them that way but for some reason, the stories from the elder merfolk had felt more real and true. They'd painted a picture of the humans so fascinating and inviting I couldn't help but see them differently in my mind. Even after Persephone's confession about the human king, I knew there had to be more to the story. Deep down, I had a mysterious inexplicable connection to the humans. And this one—Sam—he was nothing like Father described at all. His determination to help me was genuine, even though he didn't know me. I could feel it.

I shook my head and smiled. "No. Not hu-r-rt."

"So, you're not hurt?" he said. "I'm sorry, I'm confused."

I waved my hands at him and gestured for him to sit down. He cocked an eyebrow.

"Alright." He sat back down next to me.

I sighed and closed my eyes. Speaking took more energy than I realized, so much more than just writing my words down. I tried to think of how to say what I was feeling.

"I have much to say." I opened my eyes to look at him and caught movement in the mouth of the cave. Colin came running toward us, his arms full something big and fluffy.

"Got it," he said.

"Wonderful. Thank you, Colin." Sam jumped up to meet him. "Wait, what's this?" he asked, looking down at the bundle in Colin's grasp.

"You said to get her something of Johanna's, so I grabbed the first thing I saw."

"Oh, Colin, an evening dress? That's really the first thing you saw?"

Colin chortled. "Hey, I did my best. It's clothing isn't it? Oh, and I grabbed a towel too. If she doesn't like the dress, you can wrap that around her." He laughed again.

"Why don't you take anything seriously?" Sam sighed. "Well, I suppose it'll do until we get her up to the castle. I'll let you explain to Johanna why she's in her favorite ball gown."

I stretched my neck to see what Colin handed to Sam. As the prince turned to me, the peach sunlight peeking up from the horizon caught something on the mound in his arms, and patches of sparkling pink lit up in every angle. He laid the heap next to me and stood.

"You'll have to forgive Colin. He likes to keep things interesting. We'll excuse ourselves and let you dress. Just let us know when you're ready, and I'll help you to the castle. I'm sure you're starving."

He turned and followed Colin out of the cave.

I touched the heap, not sure if the lights sparkling from it would be hot. The material was cool to the touch, just a little rough, like sand crystals or the ribs of a conch shell. I glanced over to the opening of the cave to be sure no one was looking, then let Sam's shirt drop. The seashells covering my breasts had disintegrated during my transformation and I cringed at the thought of either of them seeing my exposed chest.

He called this pile an evening gown. I wondered if human women only wore these at night and wondered why Colin brought me one since it was now daytime. Sam seemed annoyed. I wasn't quite sure why. I unfolded the heap and saw there was a hole at the top and bottom, and two long tubes on each side.

Having observed Sam and Colin, I could see the peculiar triangular shape was meant to cover my body. But, it looked very different than what was over their chest and legs, aside from the long tubes which seemed an obvious place for my arms.

Resolved not to make a complete fool of myself, I slid the largest hole over my head and pulled my arms through. The material fell over me, pooling in my lap, covering the whole of me. The soft feeling of the fabric on the inside against my skin soothed me, like I was enveloped by the ocean again.

I looked down and noticed the stars I saw before glimmering in the light of the fire. White dots appeared on the cave walls and followed any movement I made, just like the miniature dancing couple that came from my music box. My heart sank like lava rock into my stomach. Father would be wondering where I was by now, wondering why I hadn't shown up for my coronation. Somehow, I was going to have to figure out how get him a message to tell him to warn him about Persephone and tell him I was alright. But first, I'd have to get these humans to trust me enough to help me.

"Everything okay in there?" Sam called from outside.

"Yes," I said, trying to project my voice loud enough for him to hear.

Sam peeked his head in and saw I was dressed, then approached me. His brawny face lit up as a wide smile spread up his cheeks. I'd never before seen a merman as handsome as Sam was. It was fascinating to see his legs move and how graceful they led him one step at a time toward me. There was something about him that stirred feelings in me I'd never experienced.

I wonder if Mother felt the same way about Father the first time they met.

"Looks like I was right. You are Johanna's size."

"Jo-hanna?" I questioned, wondering who this person was that he kept mentioning, almost feeling jealous of the clear affection in his voice when her name rolled off his lips.

Please don't be his wife.

"Yes, she's my older sister. She'll be able to help us figure out something more appropriate for you to wear. You're going to love her."

Sister. Perfect.

"Do you need help to stand? I wasn't sure how you were feeling yet. We shouldn't rush after all you've been through this morning."

I nodded my head and reached for him. The soft flesh of his hands encircled mine and sent soothing warmth flooding into my body as he pulled me up. I tried to get my legs under me, but I didn't know how they worked. My knees wobbled, and I tumbled into him.

"Whoa," he yelped.

He tripped back a few steps then lost his balance. We both tumbled to the cave floor, and I landed right on top of him.

"Sorry," I said, trying to push myself back up.

"Little unsteady there," he chuckled. Then we both started laughing. My throat undulated in odd motions, much harsher than underwater. It was going to take time to get used to all the unusual body sensations my new voice introduced.

Sam stopped laughing and studied my face. We were so close his sweet breath tickled my lips, and I could see flecks of gold and green in his eyes. I stopped laughing too, and we stared at each other for what seemed an eternity. My heart rapped against my sternum, and I had a sudden urge to just let myself melt right into his chest and stay there forever.

"Whoa, hey. I don't mean to interrupt this little tit-a-tat, but I'm getting hungry." Colin's voice echoed inside the cave and broke the surreal reverie.

Sam blinked and gently slid out from under me. I rolled over on my back and he jumped up.

"I'm sorry about that. Uh, I should've known you'd be a little unsteady at first. If you'll allow me, I can carry you until we get you some breakfast. I'm sure you'll be feeling better after that."

"Yes," I said, not wanting to appear weak, but not yet knowing quite how to use my new human legs. I didn't want to make a fool of myself more than I already had. I was going to get this walking and talking thing down. Before long, I'd be show him the strong merwoman, um, human I really was inside.

Sam swept me up into his strong arms like he did when he plucked me from the ocean just an hour before, and we headed out of the cave into the sunrise.

CHAPTER 5

"Johanna, look what we caught fishing this morning!" Colin shouted as we walked under the threshold of the castle doors. The sun had risen higher as we'd walked up the shore and through the vast colorful gardens of the grounds. The foyer was a welcome relief from the hot rays and glaring light.

"Colin," Sam chided.

A petite girl with deep pink lips and hair the same sandy color as Colin's ran down the cascading staircase in front of us but stopped short when she saw me in Sam's arms.

"Sam, who's this? What happened?"

Sam pursed his lips and leaned into my ear. "I'm sorry, I was so worried about how you were feeling I forgot to ask your name."

I looked at the girl, again hoping my words wouldn't come out as a blubbering spurt of sound.

"Aurianna."

I breathed a sigh of relief. At least I could say my name.

"Aurianna, well, it's a pleasure to meet you. My name is Johanna. I'm Sam's sister." She curtsied.

Johanna's bright green eyes traced over the dress I was wearing, clearly recognizing it, but she didn't say anything. "Sam, why are you carrying her—is she hurt? What happened? I can go get—?"

"We haven't had a chance to really talk about what exactly happened or why she was out in the middle of the sea when a storm was coming in," interrupted Colin. "But I think she's probably okay by the way her and Sam were acting in the cave." Colin waggled his eyebrows.

"The cave?" Johanna put her hands on her hips. "Were you out fishing by Hades's Hole again? I told you not to go there, it's dangerous. You know how many men have been swallowed up in that vortex? We don't even know if there's a bottom."

Hades's Hole? Sam must know about the gods. I wonder what he would do if he found out who I was.

"Yeah, yeah, I know. But if you're going to be my wife, you've got to accept I'm going to have to be myself. And Sam and I like to—"

"Whoa, don't get me involved," Sam hurried to interject. "I'm her brother, she's stuck with me. You know the wedding isn't until next week, Colin. She can still change her mind," he teased.

Johanna pinched the bridge of her delicate nose, then turned to address me directly. "I'm sorry, we're being terribly rude. I'm sure you don't want to sit and listen to us banter. Sam didn't answer my question. Are you hurt? What can I do to make you more comfortable?"

My stomach flip-flopped and made an odd sound.

Hmm. I guess hungry has a voice up here on the surface.

"I'm okay. Just a little hungry," I said, trying to hide my amusement at the display. The three of them appeared to be very close, and Johanna seemed as kind as her brother.

"Of course you are. Sam, sit her at the dining table. I'll ask the maidservants to whip us up something."

Johanna disappeared, and Colin broke into a fit of laughter.

"Sure is good we found you. That's the first time she's ever let me out of an argument that easily. I'll go get you a shirt, Romeo. I'm not going to sit and stare at your naked chest all through breakfast. I'll lose my appetite."

Romeo? I thought his name was Sam.

Colin followed where Johanna disappeared, and Sam took me into a large room similar to the feast room in our castle. A rich wood table stretched nearly the entire length of the room. Tall-backed chairs lined each side, ornate carvings of seashells laid into the backs. Blooms of bright-colored blossoms that resembled some of the sea plants and coral reefs burst from a slender silver vase in the center.

Sam pulled out a chair and lowered me down, then sat to the side of me. He'd held me so long, it was like I wasn't a whole being now I wasn't in his arms.

"So, while we're waiting, can I ask you a few questions?"

I met his gaze and swallowed. Where would I start? I couldn't very well just come out with the truth. *Well, Sam, I'm not really human. I'm a mermaid. I unknowingly made a deal to with Persephone, the goddess of the underworld, for my voice, who is at this very moment plotting to kill my father, the sea god Poseidon, with some mythical weapons. Oh yes, and she also tried to kill me. That's how I ended up ruining my life, nearly drowning, and you having to rescue me. Yep, I think that about covers it.*

Instead, I managed to say, "I don't really remember how I got out there. I'm sorry."

Sam frowned slightly. "Okay. So, we can't answer that question. Where are you from? Do you remember that?"

I fidgeted with the sparkly beads on my dress. One of them popped off in my fingers. I inhaled and bit my lip. I let it fall from my hand to the floor, hoping Johanna wouldn't notice when she got it back.

"I'm not from here. I live in a different kingdom, uh, far away."

Sam folded his hands in front of him. "Oh really, how far?"

"Well, I suppose it's not really that far." The air in the room seemed to thicken. *Really, what was I going to say? I wish Johanna would come back with the food.*

My stomach made another loud gurgling noise, and I slapped my hands against it.

"Here we go. Bless them, they'd already made the omelets and started on the pastries when they heard you come through the door." Johanna and Colin walked in, three women followed behind them with piled trays. Most of what was on them looked very unfamiliar, but I was relieved she interrupted the questioning. Johanna put circular plates in front of us. The surface looked like the inside of a pearl and reflected the light in the room.

Colin helped put goblets full of an orange liquid at the head of the plates. The women put the trays in the middle of the table, then placed strange-looking silver objects next to our plates. The smell wafting from the trays was curious. Such strong yet inviting aromas. It surprised me when my mouth started to water.

"What would you like, Aurianna? We've got danishes, sweet bread, quiche, omelets, ham, bacon, cheese, and fruit. Anything look good?" Johanna beamed and waited for me to answer. I had no idea what she'd just said, and none of the food on the trays was recognizable. I looked it over and decided to try one of everything.

"I'll try it all," I said and handed her my plate.

Colin guffawed and looked at Sam. "Well, she's not shy, is she?"

He was making fun of me like I'd said something wrong. My heart started beating faster. "I mean, I'll have what you're having, Johanna. What's your favorite thing?"

Johanna shot a dirty look at Colin, then smiled at me. "Oh, Cook makes the best spinach-and-cheese omelet. And the cherry danish braid is divine. You can see what you think."

She piled some odd-looking shapes onto my place and handed it to me. I picked up the long green-and-yellow rectangle in my fingers and took a huge bite. An explosion of texture and flavor landed on my tongue. The tiny green squares tasted a bit like seaweed salad but sweeter. I wasn't sure what the soft yellow spongey substance was, or where it came from, but I liked it. I looked around and saw the three of them staring at me as if I'd done something wrong, then glancing at each other.

I eyed Sam. He held one of the pronged objects in his hand. It resembled Father's trident. A morsel of food was stabbed into the end of it. Hot prickles stung my cheeks. I put the food back down on my plate and poked it with the small silver trident next to my plate, breaking off a small chunk. I watched Sam put his food in his mouth, and I followed his action.

"Colin, you never said what happened this morning," Johanna said and took a sip of the orange liquid. Colin's face tightened as if he'd been caught doing something he shouldn't. He half-smiled, licked his lips, and adjusted the collar of his shirt.

"Well, Sam and I were out fishing this morning and the wind kicked up. A storm looked like it was coming, so we tried rowing to shore but got caught in the tide. It pulled us over by Hades's Hole. We'd just paddled away from there when this little fish popped up right out of the middle. Before I knew it, Sam had jumped ship."

Little fish? What had he seen? Even though I was chewing, my mouth felt dry.

Colin ran a hand through his long blonde hair and winked at Johanna. "I was going to go, you know, but he'd jumped in first. I kept the boat afloat while he grabbed her. He swam to shore and got her into the cave. The storm started blowing over, so I went up and grabbed your dress. The rest is history."

"Sam, you could've been killed," exclaimed Johanna.

"But I wasn't. And if I hadn't been there, she would've drowned," Sam defended himself.

"Well, thank heavens everything worked out. After we eat, I can take her upstairs and get her cleaned up. Get her some more *comfortable* clothes." She eyed Colin and he pointed his finger at her, clicked his tongue, and winked. She rolled her eyes and sighed. "Then we can figure out how we can get her home."

"Where'd you say you were from?" asked Colin as he chomped down on a thick piece of pink meat.

I fidgeted and shoved more of the yellow sponge into my mouth.

"She hasn't said yet," Sam answered. "Just said she's from far away, but not too far."

I sent a prayer to Athena that Colin wouldn't keep pressing, and Johanna thankfully answered it. She took my cue and steered him in a different direction, talking about the menu for their upcoming wedding celebration.

I sighed in relief and tried the crispy red-and-brown object on my plate. Johanna said it was a cherry braid. It was delightfully sweet and tangy. Sam watched me. I could see him glancing over out of the corner of my eye and had to work not to smile. I could see he was just as fascinated with me as I was with him. Part of me wondered what would happen if I did just tell him the truth.

We finished breakfast, and Johanna insisted on getting me "cleaned up." I wasn't sure what that entailed but was curious. Sam and Colin helped me up the staircase. With each step, my legs seemed to settle into the motion and grow stronger. By the time we were at the top stair, I felt like I could try it on my own.

"I think I've got this," I said.

"Great," said Colin and he let go. "We never got any real fish this morning, so I think I'll go down to the *safe* fishing hole and see if I can catch some for Cook."

He leaned over and kissed Johanna passionately on the mouth and made to pull away. She giggled, grabbed his shirt, and pulled him in for another longer kiss.

I smiled and teetered a bit. Sam's arm tightened around my waist.

"Break it up, kids. Go on. Make sure you catch a fish for me," Sam said.

The couple separated, and Colin bowed. "Milady." Then he jogged down the stairs and out the front door.

Sam looked at his sister. "You're marrying that scoundrel next week?"

"Hey, he's your friend. If you hadn't convinced Father to let him court me, this wouldn't have happened. It's all your fault."

They have a father? I wonder where he is and if I'll get to meet him too.

"Well, he was the only prince in the ten kingdoms that even came close to being worthy of you. You needed a challenge."

"Indeed," Johanna smirked. She reached out and wrapped her arm around me. "As do you," she said. Sam's cheeks flushed red. "I got her. Why don't you go ready the carriage? I'm sure she'd love to see the village."

Sam let go of my waist and smiled. "I'm sure she would."

He shot a look at his sister and she grinned. I couldn't quite tell what was going on, but it seemed like they were saying

something without speaking out loud. Something I wasn't meant
to understand. Sam turned and headed down the stairs.

"Are you ready?" Johanna asked. Her eyes sparkled with
such genuine kindness it made me feel safe and secure.

"I'm not sure what we're doing, but I think so."

"You're simply stunning, Aurianna. I'm just going to make
sure everyone else can see it too."

I put my arm around Johanna for a little extra support, and
she walked me down the hallway toward an open door.

Excitement and trepidation quivered in my stomach. I'd
always secretly wondered what it would be like to be human. The
stories of their big ships, colorful kingdoms, and large stone
buildings had me so curious about them as a child, wondering if
somehow Father was wrong or at the very least mistaken about
the whole of them being evil. The moment Sam plucked me from
the ocean, nothing but kindness and care had been shown to me.
I fought the thought and was even a little guilty to think it, but it
came.

I was happy to be human. At least for now. Perhaps this
would be a blessing instead of a curse. It may just be what I
needed to save my father and the kingdom.

Thoughts of what Persephone admitted she was planning still
haunted me and played at the front of my mind. But I found a
small bit of comfort knowing she didn't have everything she
needed to start her war. Persephone had tried to fight my father,
even recruited the human king and his massive armies, but they
had failed because she didn't have the entire sacred set of five.
She was missing one. I hadn't found Medusa's crown and thank

the gods I hadn't. As I entered Johanna's room, that fact gave me some relief. I knew I needed to figure out a way to get a message to my father soon. And maybe I could even get Sam, Colin, and Johanna to help me.

Persephone will still have to search to find the crown. It wasn't in the treasury, which means Father must have hidden it somewhere difficult to find to keep the five separated. He should be safe, for today at least.

CHAPTER 6

Johanna did all kinds of things to me, and not really knowing what else to do, I went with it. I found out what a bath was, what hot irons did to your hair, and about what human girls wear. She explained the difference between an evening ball gown and a regular dress. Once she compared them, I could see why Sam made such a fuss when Colin brought me the gown.

"See, these kinds of dresses are only worn for special occasions. Oh darn, it looks like one of the beads is missing. I'll have to have the tailor fix that."

I swallowed, knowing the missing bead was nestled in the rug in the dining room, but I was too embarrassed to admit I'd broken it.

The towel around me started to slip a little and I pulled it up. Now that I knew how it felt to be human naked, I much more preferred to have clothes on.

"With your sea-blue eyes, I'm thinking we should go with the either the turquoise or pink. What do you think?"

She held up two dresses. They were both very pretty, but I'd noticed an emerald green dress in her closet earlier and really hoped she'd let me borrow it.

It reminded me so much of my fin, and I ached to see it.

"Do you think green would look good with my eyes? I've always really loved that color."

Johanna nodded. "Yes, I think I have the perfect one."

She hung the other two dresses up on the rod in her closet and took out the green one. In the light, it had a slight shimmer that reflected a purplish hue, much like an abalone shell. She handed it to me then turned back to the closet.

"Shoes, shoes, shoes," she mumbled as she rustled around on the floor.

"Got it. Hat. Hmm. Yes, the white one'll do."

She came back with the dress and two oddly shaped objects dangling from her finger. I looked down at her feet and noticed she had on two of the same type of things. *Shoes.*

"I love it." I breathed. She offered the shoes to me and I took them as a knock sounded on the door.

"I'm not trying to rush you ladies, but I think the sun will be going down soon, and I wanted to show Aurianna the village."

Johanna rolled her eyes. "It's only noon, Brother."

I didn't know what she meant by that, but it sounded like we hadn't take as long as Sam thought we had.

"Go put the dress on. We'll put a little bit of pink on your lips, pinch your cheeks, and you'll be ready to go."

Pinch my cheeks? What does that have to do with anything?

I dressed in what she called the bathroom wondering if pinching my cheeks was going to hurt and returned to the room.

"Okay," Johanna walked up to me. She had a small bowl of pink-colored goo. She put a little on her fingertip and patted it onto my lips. "Rub your lips together. Yep, that's it."

She put the bowl down and pinched my cheeks. I winced, not sure what sore cheeks had to do with me cleaning up, but apparently it was important.

Johanna walked back a few steps and observed me. She quickly returned, adjusted the sides of my hair, then stood back and looked me over once more. An overwhelming feeling of affection for her swelled in my heart. I'd never really been taken care of like this. Growing up without a mother or sisters, I never knew how amazing it felt to just be cared for. My throat grew tight, and a flash of water pooled in the corners of my eyes.

"You know, I have to say . . . I'm good," Johanna said with a self-satisfied smirk. She put her hands on her slender hips and looked me up and down. "You're more beautiful than I expected. Are you ready?"

I nodded, suddenly feeling nervous and hoping that Sam thought I was beautiful now too. I fidgeted with the front folds of the dress and wriggled my toes inside the shoes. It was so odd to have feet, let alone have them confined in these contraptions.

"Ready!" Johanna hollered.

The door swung open and Sam stood there, dressed in a new white shirt, black pants, and tall shoes that came up to his knees. His gold-green eyes met mine and his square, clean shaven jaw dropped open. He stood there, mouth open wide like a trout. After a brief moment, he shut it, ran his hand through the top of his hair, and cleared his throat.

Johanna nudged me forward. "I told you I'm good," she said to Sam. "Now get going and have fun. Make sure you take her to the bridge. She'll love the view of the river. Oh, and stop by Maurice's. Get her one of his famous chocolate truffles. She'll love those." She turned away to gather some items from around the room. "I've got to get going. I'm late for my wedding dress fitting. The tailor's going to have a tantrum, and I'll have to pay him double if I don't get there soon."

Johanna disappeared into the bathroom. I walked toward Sam and he offered me his arm. After the bath and standing for so long, I felt pretty steady on my legs, but I took it anyway.

"You look very nice," he said, a half-smile spreading into his right cheek. "Green's actually my favorite color."

A school of butterfish sped around my chest and I could feel my heart beat in my fingertips. "Thank you. Mine too."

We walked down the staircase, but instead of going out the front door, Sam led me down a hallway in the opposite direction. I observed likenesses of different humans in large squares on the wall.

"Is this your family?" I asked, slowing our pace.

"Yes." He pointed to a man with a sharp angled face that had a white flowing beard like my father's, except a bit shorter. "This is my grandfather on my father's side." He pointed to another picture next to him. "This is my father."

I took a step closer to observe the tall, slender man with dark hair who resembled Sam, a gold-and-white sash across his chest, nestled behind a very attractive woman wearing a long red gown and sitting in a chair. I leaned in, admiring the crown of white glittering jewels sitting atop her head. Thick light brown waves cascaded down her shoulders, brushing against the head of a bald baby boy in her arms.

Sam pointed to the young girl with blonde curls, dressed in a dark purple dress standing beside the queen, a small smile forming her tiny lips.

"That's little Johanna standing next to my parents when she was five. The baby my mother is holding is me, right after I was born."

I looked at his mother's face. I could see Sam in the shape of her almond eyes and the plumpness of her lips, but the resemblance wasn't as obvious as the shape and demeanor of his father's face.

"My mother died when I was seven."

He lost his mother. Like me. My heart sank. I squeezed his arm.

"Oh, I'm so sorry. I understand. My mother died when I was four." It was remarkable we had this pain in common. Unusual and sad.

"I'm sorry for you as well. Perhaps you'll be open to telling me a little more about yourself while we're out."

My voice caught in my throat. We'd never finished our conversation at breakfast. I knew he had questions, and I was going to have to come up with satisfactory answers to appease him.

He led me past images of his father standing alone, and a few others of Sam and Johanna at different ages with animals, gifts, and elegant clothing. I loved seeing their age progression, and it was clear that their father loved them.

We reached a door that led into another garden. The sun was up, but it wasn't bothering my eyes like it had earlier. The hat was helping. Huge white fluffs spanned the azure sky. The ambient light seemed softer when the incandescent yellow bulb hid behind them. Puffs of cool air breathed all around me, cooling the heat of the rays.

"I've readied the carriage," Sam said. "There are a few places I'd love to show you. Our kingdom is quite picturesque."

We rounded the corner, and I stopped short at the sight of two large animals standing in front of a square box with four wheels. I stared at the beasts. Twitters pinged around my stomach.

"What's wrong?" Sam questioned.

"What are those things?" I said pointing to the enormous creatures. Sam furrowed his brow as if confused.

"They don't have horses where you're from?"

We have seahorses, but they surely aren't the same as these monstrosities. These things were as big small whales and covered in white fur. "No, we don't."

Sam pulled his mouth down. "Really? Hmm."

I could tell he wanted to start questioning me but resisted. I thanked him silently for his discretion.

"Well, I can assure you they are quite gentle." He took hold of my hand and led me toward them.

"Arod, Brego, meet Aurianna."

He guided my hand up to the furry muzzle of the one on my left and pressed my palm against it. The horse leaned into my hand, and I was in awe. Beneath the warmth, I could feel the majesty and power radiating from this animal's soul.

"That's Brego. He's mine. Arod is Johanna's horse."

I slid my hand under Brego's chin and scratched. The horse's ears flicked back and forth, and he closed his eyes.

"He likes you."

Arod snorted and huffed.

"Oh brother, do you need some attention too, Arod?" Sam rubbed his hand up and down the horse's neck and patted him. "Arod is just like Johanna. Stubborn and needy at the same time."

I laughed. This time the sound came out perfectly, like how the other human's laughs sounded. A rush of pleasure flushed in my insides. This action stimulated physical happiness and it was pleasant feeling. I laughed harder and my stomach shook.

Sam looked at me and grinned. "Glad to see you're enjoying yourself."

"These animals are enchanting."

"Yes, they are." Sam clicked his tongue. "Are you ready to take us to town boys?"

Brego neighed.

"Come on." Sam took my hand and led me to the side of the carriage. "Face me, I'll lift you up."

I turned around to face him, and he glided his hands around my waist. The heat of his hands filtered through the light, smooth material of the dress. Our faces came close. The gold and green flecks I'd seen earlier caught the light. Fragrant sweet smells wafted from the garden, and my mouth watered. I'd seen the water nymphs and other merpeople kiss, but I'd never experienced it before. I licked my lips. Sam lips parted slightly as he looked into my eyes. The energy between us flickered like the flames from the cave fire. He was going to kiss me.

"Ready?" Sam breathed.

Ready for what? Is this really happening? Yes. Yes. I'm ready to be kissed. "Uh huh."

Sam's hands squeezed my waist, and I rose off my feet into the air. He set me down in the carriage, and I tumbled onto the seat and scrambled to right myself. Instead of a kiss, he'd sat me down.

"Ha ha. Sorry about that, I thought you said you were ready."

I thought I was . . . "Yeah, oops." *That was lame, Aurianna. Seriously.*

Sam pressed his lips together, and I could tell he was trying not to smile. He jumped in next to me and took two long strips into his hands that appeared to be connected to the horse's mouth. He offered them to me.

"You want to drive?"

Drive? What does that mean? "You go ahead. I'll, um, drive later."

Sam smiled and clicked his tongue. "Let's take her for a ride, boys."

CHAPTER 7

The carriage jerked forward, and I grabbed onto Sam's arm to keep from tumbling from my seat. My eyes darted in every direction. Everything was in motion on either side, even underneath me, like I was swimming but without water. The air pushed my hat back, and I grabbed onto it just in time to keep it from flying off.

I knew I should probably let go of Sam's arm, but I kept mine intertwined with his. The weight of his body pressed against mine felt so natural and soothing.

"It's amazing how this gadget works," I declared. "This is incredible."

"Have you never been in a carriage before either?" Sam questioned.

"Oh, well, yes, I have. Just not like this one."

Sam's brow furrowed. "You said you'd never seen horses before so, how do your carriages work?"

Distract him. Distract him. We need to get off this subject.

"Kind of like this but without horses, of course." I quickly turned the conversation to safer waters. "So, what are you going to show me today?"

Sam flicked the long strips and the horses moved us forward even faster. "Everything I can."

Buildings similar to some of the larger ones in my kingdom dotted the rolling hills in front of us. Large plants surrounded us on either side, some tall that stood on sticks, others hugged closer to the ground. Everything here was so green but so much brighter than the sea gardens we had back home.

I wanted to talk to Sam so badly. I wanted to share all the details of my kingdom. Tell him about Father, and the water nymph villages, and all about what it was like to live under the sea. I was bursting to share my whole life with him—I wanted him to be part of my world and I wanted to be part of his.

After seeing the portraits of his family, I found myself wondering about them. If his father was stern but loving like mine and how it would be to grow up with a sister.

"Tell me about Johanna. How much older than you is she?"

"Four years. But she acts like she's my mother." He let out a quiet breath. "I guess she's had to. My father never remarried after Mother died."

A pang of sadness pulled on my heart strings. "Mine didn't either. I guess once you find the other half of you, no one else can fit into that missing piece to make you whole again."

I looked across the countryside and saw another odd-looking animal snacking on the grass not far from our road. This one was as big as the horses and had a similar build with four legs, but it had an odd sack hanging from its belly. As we passed, it uttered a loud mooing sound, and an unpleasant smell crept into my nostrils.

The creatures up here were so peculiar. I wondered what this one did and if it pulled carriages too. I would hate to have to sit behind an animal that smelled so bad.

We sat in silence for a little while. I soaked in every vision of the landscape in front of us, breathing in different pleasant smells floating in and out of the air. The white poofs in the sky glided along with us making different shapes. I found three seashells, one two-headed eel, and the better half of a clownfish. The surface truly was fascinating.

Sam broke the silence with a heavy sigh, then smiled.

"Anyway, back to sisters. Johanna is really great. She's always taken care of me. I was always getting myself into trouble. Then I met Colin, and she was always having to get one or both of us out of the pickles we'd get ourselves into." He laughed.

Pickles? I had no idea what was talking about but listened intently. The sound of his voice laced with excitement was enthralling.

"How old were you when you met Colin? Have you always been friends?" I asked.

"I met Colin five years ago, when I was sixteen. He came with his father to make some land deal with mine and even though there was a three-year age difference, we really hit it off. He's the brother I never had." Sam paused. "Well, I guess after next week, he'll *be* the brother I never had."

So that was how Johanna met Colin. They seem perfect for each other and really in love. I wonder how that will be.

"He never had any brothers or sisters. Just him. So when he'd visit, we started doing all the things I always wanted to do with a brother. He'd get me in the worst trouble. He still does." Sam chortled. Then his voice took on a more serious and thoughtful tone. "But . . . if it wasn't for him wanting to sneak out this morning and go fishing in Hades's Hole, I'd never have been there to—"

"Save me," I said. "And, I'm sorry, I haven't thanked you for doing that. So, thank you."

I curled my fingers under one of the folds in my dress and clicked the heels of my shoes together.

"You're very welcome."

Sam let go of one of the long strips and intertwined his hand with mine. Fire blazed up my arm and settled around my heart. He made me feel so alive every time we touched.

"It's okay if I hold your hand, isn't it?" he asked, his eyebrows raised.

"Um hm." I wanted to say something smart, clever, or even romantic, but my tongue refused to move. All I could do was just breathe.

We came up over a hill and rode through a large gate and into a wide area surrounded by tall buildings stacked up three times higher than those in my kingdom.

"Welcome to Galandria, our kingdom."

Groups of humans were milling around, walking, talking, and busying themselves with their own business. Sweet-smelling aromas like the scents from Johanna's breakfast infused the air. My mouth watered, and I wondered what new treats the humans could make that would be better than the red-and-brown cherry danish Johanna gave me this morning.

Smaller carriages, without horses, lined the streets, filled with large and small items—an array of bright and inviting colors. I saw one with blossoms like those in the vase on our table.

"What would you like to see first?" Sam asked and squeezed my hand.

"Surprise me."

CHAPTER 8

Sam and I spent the afternoon walking the streets of his kingdom. The people greeted us with kindness, and I could tell Sam's family was beloved in their eyes. After meeting Johanna and Sam, I knew why.

Sam bought me some of the blossoms with white petals from Carrina's Floral Shop. He called them roses. He said Johanna was using them to decorate for her wedding next week, and I couldn't blame her one bit. The perfume from the flowers was intoxicating. I kept shoving my nose inside them when Sam wasn't looking just to get another burst of the calm, enchanting feeling they offered.

We wandered into what he called a bakery next. That smell was almost as good as the roses. He used some metal coins, similar to some of the treasure Father had, and traded them for a plate of food like what Cook had on the breakfast trays. He also bought four round light-green spheres he called apples. He put them in the bag he was carrying and said they were a treat for the horses.

The man behind the counter called the layered things he'd stacked on the plate sand witches. I thought it a very unappetizing name and refused to taste them at first. I wasn't sure how sand witches were different than sea witches. We had sea witches at home, but they were real live evil beings. Father had imprisoned them all during the ocean wars. I wasn't sure how the humans had gotten hold of them and cut them into squares for us to eat.

We argued after we sat down at a table just outside the bakery and I told him I wasn't going to be forced to eat something that was made of evil sand beings.

Sam burst out laughing so hard, other people walking by stopped and stared.

"No, no, no, they're not made of sand witches—or any kind of witches. It's . . . well, how do I explain it? It's just a croissant with turkey and cheese and a little bit of lettuce and tomato. Just try it. It's okay. You'll love it."

"Does turkey come from a living being?"

"Well, uh, yes. I guess so. It's a bird."

I didn't know what a bird was, but for argument's sake I wasn't going to make him go into it. It didn't look anything like fish so just to be safe, I told him to take the turkey off it. He smirked, took it off mine, and added it to his.

We ate, and I did find the sand witch without turkey delicious, but I wasn't about to admit it. I especially liked the red tomato. It was sweet and juicy, like the red algae berries we had in our gardens I made Father's kelp cakes with.

He took his last bite before I took mine and I could tell he really wanted to ask me more about myself. I thought I better start talking and asking him questions before he could start asking his.

"Johanna said I should try the chocolate truffles from Maurice's. Are we going there next?"

Sam wiped his mouth with a small white square cloth.

"Not yet. I promise you'll get to try his famous truffles, but we'll go there a little later. I have a book waiting for me at the bookstore, that's why I was coming into the village today. Do you like to read?"

Books. Finally, something familiar. I had an entire library of books at home. Many of them my own life journals.

"Yes, as a matter of fact I do. I've done a lot of reading—and writing."

"You write?"

"You have no idea." I fidgeted with my fingers. He looked curious at my response and went on.

"That's wonderful. Johanna loves to write too. She writes poetry." He ruffled his hair, then tucked a piece of it behind his ear. "Perhaps she'll show you when we return home. I know she's working on one for the wedding," he rolled his eyes. "It'll be some sappy love poem she'll read to Colin who'll secretly love it."

He stood and offered his hand.

"Ready for the next adventure?" he said, his eyes twinkling with a playful glimmer.

"Yes," I said as I stood. I placed my hand in his and something tickled in my stomach. Every time our flesh touched, my body had a strong, yet pleasant reaction.

We walked quite a distance down the road, past many other stores full of clothes, tables and chairs, and even jewels. The villagers passing us looked down at our hands, then back up at Sam and smiled as they passed. Some of them even whispered after we strode by. I couldn't quite hear what they were saying but they seemed excited about something.

We stopped in front of a shop that read Rowling's Books, and Sam opened the door. A tinkering sound jingled in the air. "After you, milady."

I walked in and my jaw dropped. I covered my mouth and scanned the room. Every wall was stacked with rows of neatly stacked books, all different colors and sizes. A buzz of excitement filtered into my fingertips. I wanted to touch them, read them, see if they had pictures.

"Sam, it's amazing."

He squeezed my hand and I wondered if he too could feel the buzzing.

"Go ahead and look around. Let me know if you find a book you like."

I let go of his hand and strolled through the aisles, running my fingers across the spines. The texture wasn't unpleasant, just different from the slate and sand tablets I had. A deep-purple spine caught my attention, and I pulled it from the shelf. The cover read, "20,000 Leagues Under the Sea, by Jules Verne."

Curious, I opened it and found a black and white drawing of an enormous octopus-like creature wrapping its tentacles around what appeared to be some kind of underwater boat. I skimmed over the pages, catching words here and there about a mysterious monster that lived underneath the sea taunting sailors and wondered if Sam had ever read this book. The monster they spoke of sounded much like Hades' monster, the kraken. Father told me he had it killed after he defeated Hades.

I perused the bookstore and found Sam sitting at a table in the back corner. As I approached him, a wild temptation to run my fingers through the waves of his dark hair popped into my mind. The hair curled just past the nape of his neck, and I wondered what it would feel like. His shoulders moved up and down, a steady rhythm that matched his breathing. The way the shirt hugged his back made me wish we were in the cave again.

"Miss, have you found anything I can help you with?"

An old scratchy voice behind me interrupted my daydream. I jumped and dropped the book on Sam, which in turn made him jump and whip around. I turned to see a wrinkly human man with a curly gray mustache standing there, a smirk spread across his spotted lips. A metal contraption with two glass circles sat on his nose, enlarging his eyes to appear fish-like. He reached down and picked up the book that had tumbled to the floor.

"I'm so sorry, sir," I stammered out. I backed up, my hands in the air in front of me.

Sam stood up from the chair, chortling, a large gray book in his hand.

"It's quite alright young lady," the old man reassured me. He held his hand out, and Sam placed his book on top of the one I dropped. I noticed the title on the cover and the warmth in my face rushed into my stomach—*Eirene, Daughter of Poseidon*.

The man kept talking, not noticing my shock. "Prince Samandrian, shall I wrap this up for you as well? Looks like you're both into ancient sea myths."

"Yes, thank you, George."

I grabbed onto the chair to steady myself. The room started spinning and my palms felt damp. I swayed, the wet feeling now on my forehead and the back of my neck.

Poseidon's Daughter, Eirene? Eirene's my middle name. How can this be? Does he already know about us, about our kingdom?

Sam put his hand on my elbow in concern. "Aurianna, what's wrong? Are you feeling alright? You look white as a sheet."

"Why are you buying that book?" I asked, my throat so tight I could barely talk.

"Oh, that? It's for my father. He had it sent here for when he gets back tonight. Greek myths are a bit of an obsession with him. He's been reading them to me since I can remember. It's not a big deal—they're just bedtime stories."

Obsession? Sam's father was obsessed with Greek mythology? Gods and daughters of gods? Sam hadn't seemed to put any thought into it, like he didn't believe it was real. I prayed to Athena his father didn't believe it either. That he truly thought of them as bedtime stories. At least for now.

"Seriously, you look pale." Sam pulled a chair out and guided me toward it. "Here, sit down. I guess I've been running around with you too much today. I'm sorry, I forgot what a rough morning you had. I was just so excited to show you around. I'll go pay for these and we can go home."

My mind was reeling. How did the humans know about me and Father? Who had written a book just about me? I was going to have to get my hands on that book when we got back to the castle and see what was inside.

"No, I don't need to sit. I'm fine, Sam. Really. I think that old man just scared me. I'm good." I slipped my arm in his and walked with him to the front of the bookstore. "You promised me a chocolate truffle and I have no idea what it is, but Johanna made such a fuss about it, I'm going to insist we don't leave until I've tried one."

Sam laughed. "Well alright. Maurice's it is."

He paid the old man with more of his metal coins, and we headed further down the street until we arrived at Maurice's Confectionary Emporium. We walked in, and the sweetest smell enveloped me. My entire body tingled almost making me forget about the book incident. I sniffed the air again and again.

"What is that delightful smell?" I asked, the water in my mouth nearly spilling from the corners.

"You don't have chocolate where you're from either?" Sam questioned.

"Not yet," I said.

He chuckled and walked us up to the front of the store. Hundreds of small brown ovals with multicolored tops presented themselves in neat rows behind a curved wall of glass.

A young girl with red hair, almost the same color as mine, greeted us. Her face turned pink when she looked at our intertwined hands.

"We'll take two boxes, please." He leaned over to me and whispered, "Johanna will kill me if I don't bring her back a box."

He elbowed me, and I nodded trying to pretend to understand why Johanna would have such a strong reaction to not getting chocolate.

"Of course. Will that be all, your majesty?" The toothy stupid grin on her face made it obvious she was playing to him. I wondered if Sam noticed and if he did, if he thought it was as silly as I did.

"Yes, thank you." He nodded, then let go of my hand, patted his pockets and dug inside the left one. I supposed he was looking for more coins to pay with. He seemed uninterested in her display of obvious interest which made me want to laugh and feel sorry for her at the same time.

I wondered why everyone in the village was having such a strong reaction to us holding hands. It appeared to excite some and if I wasn't mistaken, this girl seemed jealous.

Sam put a handful of coins on the counter and the red-haired girl handed him two glittering boxes with large loops of gold tied in a bow on top. He tucked them under his arm, grabbed my hand and we walked out the door. I could feel the heat of her eyes on us as the door shut.

The clouds had now completely covered the sun and most of the blue of the sky. The breeze felt cooler, more pleasant. The village was bustling with people still, talking to each other and exchanging goods for coins. Some of them noticed us and others just went on with their business, seemingly too busy to care.

"Would you be willing to go one more place with me? It's just outside the village," Sam said as we made our way back to where we left the horses and carriage. He seemed more excited and anxious than he had before. I sensed this was an important place, so I decided to tease him a little just to see what his reaction would be.

"I don't know . . . I guess it depends on where it is," I said and put my hand on my hip. Sam's eyes widened. I hadn't let my attitude come through yet, but I was feeling so comfortable around him, I couldn't help myself.

He raised his eyebrow and rubbed his chin. "Well, I'm not going to tell you. Will you still come?"

I raised my eyebrow to mimic him and stared into his eyes. There was a challenge inside them and I was definitely up for that.

Feisty. I loved it.

"I suppose. But it better be good."

Sam guffawed. "I guess we'll see, won't we?"

CHAPTER 9

*W*hen we approached the carriage, Arod and Brego nodded their heads. Brego pawed the ground, expressing his annoyance.

"I know, Brego. We were gone for a long time. I'm sorry, boys. Here, I've got something for you." Sam pulled two green spheres from the bakery bag and shoved one into each of their mouths. "We've got two more apples, but you have to be good and earn them."

Arod snorted.

"I mean you, Arod." The horse moved his head up and down. I couldn't help but smile as I watched Sam's interaction with his horse, wondering what it would be like to have an animal of my own.

We galloped out of the village, and Sam took us down a road we'd only passed earlier. We entered into a huge mass of the green-topped sticks. I stared all around me, noticing the light wasn't shining as bright in here. Occasionally, a few white beams penetrated the thickness and connected with the ground. It reminded me of the reefs near the western shores of my kingdom. The water was so clear down there, the rays would impale the water and reach all the way to the ocean floor just like it did here. I played in the beams when I was a child, but when Father found out, he chided me for going so close to the surface and forbade me from ever returning.

Miles passed as we made our way through the thickness of the green. Sam spoke of his childhood and I spoke back, revealing as many details as I could of mine without raising too many unwanted questions.

The sun waned, breathing its multicolored air into the fading blue sky as we came upon a steep, rocky hill.

Sam stopped, tipped his head, and peered at me with a twinkle in his eye.

"I want to take you somewhere. Do you trust me?"

I pursed my lips, trying not to smile. "Should I?"

"Probably not." He rubbed his chin trying to look serious, but I could tell he was having difficulty holding his mouth still. I folded my arms and looked away as if I needed to consider his question just to tease. He brushed his leg against mine and a popping sensation bounced in all sorts of directions inside of me.

"Well, since you saved my life today, I guess I can."

Sam stuck out his elbow, and I hooked my arm inside his.

"You're going to want to hang on," Sam said with a mischievous grin. "Arod, Brego, giddyap."

Sam slapped the long strips against the horses' backsides, and the carriage leaped forward. My hat lifted off my head again. I reached up, barely caught it between my fingers, and held it on my bouncing lap to keep it from flying away.

The horses grunted as the carriage jerked and pulled toward the top of the steep hill with Sam encouraging them along the way.

I could barely stand it. I was dying to see what was on the other side.

We reached the summit, and a wide expanse of rolling green meadows unfolded before us. Pink and orange bursts from the sky reflected across a small crystal lake nestled on the far border. A narrow stone bridge stretched itself across the length of the water, leading to another steep patch of hillside.

"It's beautiful," I breathed.

"You haven't seen anything yet. Arod, Brego—you know the way. Hyah."

The carriage tipped forward, and the horses took off like a shot.

"Whoo-hoo!" Sam yelled as the carriage sped faster. My stomach lurched up into my throat and I had to swallow hard. I clasped onto his arm—both terrified and ecstatic.

"You're crazy!" I screamed. The strength of my voice gushing out of me was exhilarating. My heart flooded inside my ears, but I could barely hear it over the whipping wind.

"Wooooo!" I screamed again, and Sam burst out laughing. I should've been embarrassed at my improper, unladylike outburst, but I couldn't help it. I wanted to yell, scream, laugh, cry—make noise any way I could. Years of pent up feelings fought with such vigor to be freed, I had to clench my teeth to avoid scaring the poor man and letting it all out at once.

The carriage reached the base of the hill, and Sam slapped the long strips on the horses' backs. Arod and Brego ran down the pathway toward the bridge, then slowed their pace to a comfortable stride. The rich color of the sky faded, casting deep shadows from the green-topped sticks across the water. Light disappeared beneath the horizon and was nearly gone when we reached the bridge. Soft darkness fell, blanketing everything in a comfortable blue-gray, so familiar like an old friend. Like I was home.

"We need to hurry, it's almost here," said Sam and he jumped from the carriage onto the bridge.

"What's almost here?"

Sam reached for me. "Here, let me help you down and I'll show you."

I put my hands on his shoulders, and he lowered me to the ground. Cool air lifted the hair off my neck and we stood silent, eyes locked, his fingers trembling against my waist.

"You're so beautiful," he whispered. The sweet tang of his breath caught inside my throat, settling on my tongue.

Every function of my body halted for the smallest second. I forgot to blink, breathe, and could've sworn my heart skipped a beat.

No one had ever said that to me.

Sam drew his finger across my cheek, spreading wild fire inside my skin, and lifted a stray piece of hair. The corner of his mouth cocked up and he tucked it behind my ear.

"Come on, we have to get to the middle of the bridge."

He took my hand and led me across the stone arch. Miniscule silver lights started popping into the growing darkness of the sky. In awe, I stared up at them, not quite knowing what they were, mesmerized by the patterns. I wondered if they were the stars the elders had spoken of.

Sam pointed up at a tall mountain pressing against the far corner of the lake.

"Do you see the point of the mountain just over there? The tallest one? Keep looking at the sky behind the top of it."

"I don't see anything."

I continued to watch, seeing nothing. He rested his hand on the small of my back and pulled me into him. I took a shaky breath and blew it out of pursed lips.

"Just wait." Sam squeezed my hand.

Another minute rolled by. Just as I was about to admit I couldn't see a thing, a bright glowing light peeked out from behind the tip. I gasped as the sliver grew, enlarging into a silver sphere on the move, almost like an oyster's pearl floating across a black ocean.

"What is it?" I breathed.

"The moon? Don't tell me you don't have a moon where you're from," Sam joked.

I swallowed.

Think of something. Anything.

"Oh yes, ha ha. Of course, we have a moon. I meant, um, that." I pointed to a ripple that appeared on the edge of the lake.

"The ripple? Oh, that's probably just a pike. They see the stars reflecting in the water and jump for them sometimes."

I stared up at the inky black sky, her white orb, and the glittering lights. Sam pointed up at a pattern in the glittering lights above us.

"Cassiopeia. She's my favorite constellation of stars."

I snuggled in closer to him, and it was like we fit together perfectly.

"My father taught me to find the North Star when I was a boy, then trace it down and there she'd be. After my mother died, I secretly hoped the middle star was her, looking down on me from heaven."

I stared up at the sparkling sky and wondered if my mother could see me too. If humans and merpeople went to the same place.

"Its beauty is like nothing I've ever seen before," I gasped, overwhelmed at the sight.

Sam looked at me and took my hands in his. "Yes. Beauty like nothing I've ever seen before."

I met his gaze. My heart leapt, taking on a life of its own. Sam lowered his chin and gazed into my eyes.

"I know we just met, but everything about you feels so familiar. Like we've spent years together. I'm sorry, I know I'm being forward. I don't mean to be."

He brought his hand up to my face and brushed his fingertips up my cheekbone again, stoking the fire that hadn't yet faded from the last time.

"What are you thinking about?" he breathed.

How could I put into words what was racing through my mind? For years. I'd dreamt of having someone look at me like Sam was now. Someone who saw me, the real me. From the time I was young, I'd seen other couples swimming around our kingdom, hands intertwined— laughing, enjoying each other's company . . . talking.

Today was my miracle.

Every thought that came to me I'd spoken out loud and shared it with Sam. It was like I'd lived a lifetime with him over the last few hours we'd spent together. I was excited. Terrified. Overwhelmed. And, for the first time in my life, unabashedly happy.

"What am I thinking about? Oh, you know, lots of different things."

He opened his mouth to say something, then cocked his head, leaned forward, and pressed his mouth against mine. I closed my eyes. A collision of strange almost painful sensations crashed inside me, as if I'd been stung by a jellyfish or electrocuted by an eel. But then a pleasant sensation drowned the sting and I felt weightless, like I was back in the ocean in the warmest, gentlest undercurrent.

Soft, wet lips searched mine, and I chased them like we were playing a game. He ran his quivering fingers through my hair and something sweet tingled my nose. He let go of my other hand

and pressed it against my back. Like I somehow knew what to do, my arms rose, wrapping them around his neck. I pulled him close, flattening his body against mine.

Time stood still.

Then it started again.

"Brother!" A frantic voice behind me disturbed the gentle quiet. Horse hooves pounded the ground. Sam's lips left mine and he looked up.

"Johanna? What are you doing out here?"

She sidled up next to us on a large black horse.

"Sam, something's happening out in the water by the castle shore. Strange lights are coming from Hades's Hole. Water is jetting up from every direction. Huge tides are swamping the shore. Something's not right. It's like there's a war going on down there."

Oh no. Father.

I whipped around. "What kind of light? What color is it?"

Johanna furrowed her brow. "Well, there are many colors. Red, purple, green."

Persephone.

I turned back to Sam and spoke urgently. "Sam, I need you to take me back to the place you found me this morning."

He furrowed his brow as if confused. "What would you know about lights in the ocean, Aurianna?"

"I'm sorry, I can't really explain it. Just take me there. Please, hurry."

Sam nodded, and we ran to the carriage. He looked up and noticed her horse for the first time.

"How do you have Father's horse? Has he returned already?"

The horse stomped, lifting its head up and down and it panted through the bar in its mouth. She stroked its head. "He came back early. He'd just arrived when the lights began to stir."

Sam jumped up into the carriage and reached for my hands. "Meet us back at the castle, Johanna. We won't be far behind."

Johanna clicked her tongue and the horse took off.

"What's going on, Aurianna?" Sam finished helping me into the carriage. "Why won't you tell me what you know?" The sparkle in his eyes had gone. His brow furrowed and the color in his cheeks faded. He looked nervous, unsettled.

"I'm so sorry. There's just so much to explain. Please, just go. You'll just have to trust me."

I thought about the day—the time I'd spent with Sam exploring new and exciting things while Father was exposed, unaware of the danger. Guilt's ugly mouth opened, swallowing me whole.

I should've never gone to Persephone. Never stolen the things out of Father's treasury. She didn't have Medusa's crown, so I thought I had time. *What was I thinking? How could I have been so foolish up here on the surface gallivanting with Sam. He doesn't even know who I really am. Now Father's in trouble, and I don't know how I'm going to save him.*

"Arod, Brego, hyah. Take us back home, boys." Sam slapped the long strips on the horse's backs and the carriage jolted forward.

CHAPTER 10

Thoughts raced inside my head as we climbed. The hills blurred in multicolored motion. I closed my eyes to focus, and the dizzying sensation slowed. I remembered the joy on my father's face when I'd opened the music box and when he'd opened up about my mother.

Had that been only yesterday? It felt like a lifetime ago.

"Are we almost there?" I asked.

Sam ignored my question. "Are you going to talk to me and tell me what's happening? Does this have anything to do with where you're from?" He slapped the strips against the horse's backs and the carriage jerked forward, gaining more speed.

I chewed on the side of my mouth and looked at my lap. "You wouldn't believe me if I told you."

Sam growled. "Try me. Because I'm not going to stop asking you until you tell me. I can't help you unless I know."

You're going to think I'm crazy. "Sam, please."

We rode in silence until the spires of the castle were in sight. Hundreds of terrible scenarios had run through my head about Father, Persephone, Bastian—the entire kingdom. Many of them ended tragically for Father and our people. Heaviness filled my chest. Water gathered in the corners of my eyes, but I blinked it away.

We turned around a sharp corner and the wheel of the carriage lifted off the ground. Sam pulled on the straps and the horses slowed enough for the wheel to come crashing back down. Then he yanked back hard, and the horses stopped completely, a good distance from the entrance gate.

"I'm sorry, but I'm not just going to drop you off and have you go drowning yourself out there. We're not moving another inch until you tell me. I . . . I don't want to lose you."

A hundred different emotions flooded in all at the same time. The desperation in Sam's eyes melted my resolve, but despair, fear, and uncertainty tugged with relentless force on my heart.

If Persephone had somehow gotten past the royal guards and found Medusa's crown, she had started her war. There was no escaping it. I was going to lose Sam or lose my father today depending on what happened. How could I choose?

I buried my face in my hands. This was all because of me. I'd ruined everything by being selfish. Now that I'd found Sam, I had even more to lose. Somehow, I'd have to figure out a way to stop this.

"Okay. I'll tell you when we get to the castle. But you must promise to take me to Hades's Hole, no matter what I say or what you may think."

"Deal." Sam clicked his tongue and the horses started up their gallop.

We raced through the gates, wind whipping at my face. As we approached, I noticed Johanna standing next to a tall, silver-haired human man, who was waving for us to stop.

"Whoa, boys. Whoa." Sam pulled the straps and the horses slowed to a stop. He dropped the strips and jumped down. "Father." He ran to the man and embraced him. They pulled apart and I met the man's gaze. He tipped his head in my direction.

"Who's this?" he said, a half-smile spreading on his lips. Sam pulled his shoulders back and gestured toward me.

"Father, I'd like to introduce you to Aurianna."

The man's face blanched white. He put his hand over his mouth, then walked over to the carriage and put his hand out. "Hello, Aurianna. I'm King Alastair."

King Alistair? Thick air grew inside my lungs. Short breaths panted out of pursed lips as I tried to catch my breath. Arod and Brego snorted. Suddenly there were four horses standing in front of me instead of two.

Alastair? The human king who was working with Persephone against my father, the man who killed my mother?

A thrill of heat flared up my core like an eruption of volcanic lava. I shut my eyes to remove his face from my sight. My mother's smiling face flashed. My parents danced around the dark field of my eyelids. Father spoke her name and it echoed repeatedly inside my head.

Then everything went dark.

CHAPTER 11

cool, wet sensation spread across my forehead.

"Aurianna? Can you hear me?" Sam's voice sounded miles away. My eyes flipped open and he peered down at me, his handsome face lined with concern. He held a piece of damp cloth in his hand.

I tried to raise my hand to meet his, but my limbs were as heavy as clay. Soft flickering light danced from flaming candles surrounding the room casting shadows similar to those in Sam's cave. A black glittering sky stared at me from a glass-covered opening in the far wall.

"What happened?" I slurred.

"You fainted."

I tried to sit up, but he pressed his hand on my shoulder.

"Stay still."

I breathed a deep painful breath the air pressing against the tight space inside my chest. As my consciousness grew sharper, the recollection of what happened broke through.

"Your father. Your father is King Alastair," I said. A knotty lump welled in my throat. Sam pulled a chair to my bedside and sat next to me. He reached over and put his hand on mine.

"When you're ready, we can talk about that."

I put my hand on my forehead. The skin against my palm was wet. "How long have I been asleep?"

Sam sighed. "A little over an hour. I was really starting to worry."

"An hour?" I shot up and threw the coverings off me. "What have I done? I need to get back home. My father's in danger. Persephone—" I tried to stand up. My legs wobbled. They were still weak from my episode.

Damn this voice and damn these legs. Why had I wanted something the gods didn't see fit to give me already? If I hadn't been so selfish, I'd have been celebrating my eighteenth birthday with my father. Everything would be like it was before.

"Aurianna? Sit down, I don't want you to fall."

Images of what could be happening to Father peppered me one after the other; Persephone stabbing him with Oceanus's sword; red fire erupting from the ring of Phorcys, turning him to ash; an army of creatures from the Seawood Forest overrunning the kingdom, slaughtering everyone, eating Father alive.

I released all the weight from my legs and fell onto the bed. My hands shook. There wasn't enough air in the room for me to breathe. I choked water began to pour from my eyes.

"Aurianna. Breathe. Just breathe. Everything is going to be alright."

"It's not. It's not going to be okay, Sam. You don't know what's happening! You don't know who I am."

Sam's expression changed. He raised his eyebrows and a small smile spread across his face. He reached up and wiped a tear that fell on my cheek.

"I spoke to my Father while you were asleep. He told me who you are. Father has been telling me wild bedtime stories about Poseidon and his underwater kingdom since I was a child."

His words only served to panic me more, and my breaths came even faster.

Sam squeezed my hand. "The stories always fascinated me. But as I grew older, the dedication and passion behind his study began to worry me. He became obsessed, ordering books about the gods and goddesses of the sea and the underworld from every corner of the world. He'd scrutinize and dissect them until all hours of the night." Sam shook his head and looked up at the ceiling. "Whenever I'd ask him about it, he'd make light of it, told me not to worry, and encourage me to leave him alone. I always thought him a bit odd because it seemed like he really believed them, like he was convinced they were true." He sighed and adjusted his weight in the chair. "I even wondered if his heartbreak over losing my mother had driven him mad."

He rubbed his forehead with his other hand, then slid it down his face. His eyes flashed with something I hadn't yet seen in them. Sadness.

"Then one day after I'd just turned twelve, he sat Johanna and me down and told us in detail about what really happened to our mother. He explained he'd been approached by the queen of the underworld just after I was born. He said her name was Persephone." My heart did a flip as Sam continued. "She told him a heart-rending story of how the god of the sea, Poseidon, had overrun all the kingdoms in the ocean, including hers. She cried over how he'd murdered her love, Hades, and she asked for my father's help to defeat him."

His hand dampened and gripped it harder, just tight enough to make it uncomfortable. Drawn through morbid curiosity to his explanation, I let him squeeze and listened.

"The king across the sea had been warring with our kingdom's ships, threatening to overtake our kingdom since my grandfather had been on the throne. Persephone made a vow to my father that if he helped her defeat Poseidon, she would protect and save our kingdom."

The color drained from Sam's face and his hand grew cool. "My father had no idea who or what he was dealing with, and in desperation he struck a deal with Persephone. After he signed the contract, she told him he needed to procure five mythic hallows, one from each of the oceans, and together they would give her the magic she needed to assist him. When my father found out about what they were and what it would take to get them, he refused." The grip on my hand grew tighter. I wanted to pull away, but I sensed he found comfort in it, so I tightened my own grip to relieve some of the pressure. He closed his eyes but continued to speak. "Upon his refusal, she kidnapped my mother and hid her in a prison on an invisible island. She told Father that when he returned, and they defeated Poseidon, she would set my mother free."

The mythic hallows? That's where they came from? I thought Father won them in the oceanic wars. Persephone lied to me. More guilt spilled into my gut. I'd been deceived, played. I don't know why I was surprised but I felt betrayed. By her and my own stupidity.

Sam opened his eyes and I could see pain in them. "It took him five years to find the hallows. I wasn't even a year old when my mother was taken from me and he left on his quest. When he returned, he found Persephone and gave her the five magical objects." Sam let go of my hand and ran both of his hands through his hair. He slid forward on his chair, his shoulders slumping. "They gathered all his ships and armies together, and with the mythic hallows built cannons powerful enough to penetrate the water. They forged large wood and metal catapults that would launch enormous shards of sharp rock deep into the sea. But that only angered Poseidon."

Sam narrowed his eyes and the pain faded as the gleam of fiery rage ignited. "Father's ships were brutally attacked by large sea creatures, some as large as his ships."

Father sent his army of whales? No wonder they lost the battle.

"Full of pride and ignorance, Persephone tried to use the magic of the hallows to build devices to trap the creatures but failed to understand their strength and intelligence. Most of Father's armada was sunk within the week."

Sam grabbed both my hands and hung his head. "My father returned, three-quarters of his men dead, barely alive himself. Persephone was so angry with my father's defeat that she brought my mother back from the island and tortured her in front of him. He begged Persephone for mercy, for my mother's life, and eventually Persephone struck another deal with my father to save her. She convinced him the only way he could defeat Poseidon was to break him. To take the thing that was most precious to him and destroy it."

My mother.

"His only daughter."

But he didn't kill me. He killed my mother.

My mouth felt dry. I didn't understand. Sam looked up at me and set his jaw. Then went on.

"My father would never kill an innocent. Especially a child, not even to save his beloved wife. Desperate, he decided he would try to make a deal with Poseidon instead. Trick the goddess of the underworld into believing Poseidon had surrendered after he threatened to take you, not only save my mother but also to make Persephone pay."

If Persephone wanted me, how did I survive and not my mother?

"Then why did my mother die?" I shakily asked. Another lump formed in my throat.

"When my father tried to approach Poseidon in peace, he attacked. All but four of Father's soldiers were killed in the fray, but those few that remained fought to get Poseidon's attention. With one last desperate attempt to survive, they launched the largest, most powerful weapon they had—the claw of

Archimedes." Sam raised his arm and swiped it downward with a quick movement. "The weapon drove into the ocean with inhuman speed, hurtling toward Poseidon's army. Poseidon raised his triton to stop the claw, infusing it with a focused surge of energy, splitting it into hundreds of spiraling spears. He raced through the barrage but couldn't stop them all. Several plunged into the castle and in her attempt to shield you, your mother was killed."

Confusion blurred my thoughts for a moment, then realization came flooding in. I let go of Sam's hands and covered my mouth. It was like someone had reached in, taken hold of my stomach, and clenched it between their fists to the point of tearing. Father said the humans killed mother. He never told me she died saving me. I had no recollection of the barrage.

Sam's face blurred. My limbs were light for a moment, then sunk into the bed as if made of solid stone. Sam reached for me and I fell against his chest. He stroked my hair as I buried my face in his shirt.

"Upon learning of your mother's death, Poseidon rose to the surface and captured my father. He begged for his life and pleaded with Poseidon to help him save my mother, he even offered the five mythic hallows. Poseidon took them, but instead of helping him, he used my father to find Persephone. He told him once they found her, they'd both be dead. But when Poseidon and my father finally caught up with Persephone, she mocked them both." Sam's heart beat faster and his chest rose and fell with a shorter, faster rhythm against my cheek. "He learned then that my mother had died from the injuries she sustained during her torture. Persephone had been using him and lying to him the entire time."

I sat up and our eyes met. Pain pulsed inside the pools of green gold staring back at me and we connected on a level neither one of us wanted but longed for. Contradicting feelings swept back and forth, competing for attention inside me: love, relief, anger, sorrow. Sam cupped my cheek with his palm and the weight of his hand began to calm the storm of turmoil raging inside me.

"Seeing my father's grief now equal to his own, he let my father go. Poseidon took Persephone though Hades's Hole and disappeared. Wanting to avenge my mother, my father has searched the last sixteen years for the lore that would help him find Persephone and kill her. He'd begun to give up, thinking it was impossible to find her until he saw you and realized who you were."

A deep kind voice echoed behind me. "So, young lady, you and I have more in common than you think. How about we help each other."

King Alistair stood in the doorway, his light blue eyes reflecting the same pain as Sam's did. I rubbed my hand across my chest and it stopped just above my heart. In one night and day my entire life had shattered, each piece falling to the floor to shatter again and create more questions.

The first hour of my human day brought life-changing and miraculous transformation that filled me with joy I'd never known. This last one had introduced crushing truth and pain that threatened to suffocate me in sorrow.

The king stood, Sam stared, both awaiting my answer, but I had nothing to give, no way to help now I was human.

"I want to, I really do. But Persephone tricked me. I was born mute. I'd never spoken a single word before today. She made me a deal. My voice for five pieces from my father's treasury. She made them sound unimportant, like they were just treasure." I hung my head in shame before looking back unto Sam's eyes. "I only found four of them, but I gave them to her to pay for my voice. I realize now I handed over the hallows to her in exchange. After she gave me my voice, she claimed she need vengeance against my father and turned on me. She made me human and sent me to the surface. I thought I had time. The crown of Medusa was still missing, but it looks like it didn't take her long to find it."

I twisted the fabric of my dress between my shaking fingers. "I can't do anything to help you now. By the looks of it, Persephone already started her war against my father."

King Alistair walked toward me, one arm behind his back, a sly smile carving into his cheeks. "You said you gave her four of the hallows."

I narrowed my eyes, confused and nodded.

"Yes. I couldn't find Medusa's crown. She was pretty angry about that. But the other four seemed powerful enough. At least they had enough power to give me my voice, turn me human, and begin her attack."

The king stopped next to Sam.

"When I was captured by your father, he held me prisoner for a short time in a cave that butted up against the ocean. It was encircled by the water, with only a small footage of land. He assigned his most loyal guard to watch me, even though it would have been impossible to escape.

Over the weeks I was there, I got to know this merman. At first, he refused to speak to me. But I can be very persuasive."

His most loyal guard? Bastian?

King Alistair looked at Sam and winked. Sam laughed and nodded.

"I spoke of Sam's mother, her kindness and beauty. I told him of our children, Sam and Johanna, and explained in great detail about our predicament with the neighboring kingdom and how my desperation to save my people led to my foolish alliance with Persephone."

The king shook his head and closed his eyes, clearly regretful for the choices that led up to the tragedy.

"Although he never freed me, the guard listened and took it all in. After your father found out about Persephone murdering both my wife and his, he did take pity on me and released me on two conditions. The first, that I would make an oath never to go against him or his kingdom again and that I would research all I could about Persephone's power, so we could work together to defeat her. The second, that I would check in with his guard every new moon, so he could be assured of my allegiance to our pact."

The king stepped into the room. "For years I met with the guard, Bastian and we grew a bond of friendship. I shared all the information I was able to glean so he could relay it back to Poseidon."

He smiled and the softness in his eyes convinced me he spoke the truth.

"I searched for years and years, and during my last trip to Greece a few weeks ago, I discovered the only way to destroy her was for the mythic hallows to be freely given over to her and to use a bolt of Zeus's lightning to strike her when all five were in contact with her body."

I focused on the hand behind the king's back wondering what he could be holding. Sam looked up at his father in awe, clearly hearing about this for the first time.

"When your father imprisoned Persephone in the Seawood Forest, he took the hallows from her, thinking he was taking the power from her. So, when I told his guard that was how we could defeat her, he told Poseidon. Your father ordered his guard to bring the hallows to me and that he would visit his brother Zeus after his daughter's birthday coronation to get the bolt of lightning. He said he wanted to his daughter to have her coming of age celebration and one more day of innocence before he had to tell her he was going to war."

I hung my head and squeezed my eyes shut as tight as I could.

So that was what Bastian was doing down in the treasury that night. That was why he said my coronation was going to be hard on him. And I interrupted him and stole the rest of the hallows. *Oh, Father. I ruined it all. Had I not been so selfish, so reckless, you could've had her. But I didn't know. I didn't know.*

Sam put his hand on my shoulder, and the calmness it gave me made me feel even more guilty and torn. I covered my face with my hands.

What a mess. How could this have happened? How could the most horrible thing I've ever done and the most wonderful thing that's ever happened to me come to me all at once with the same decision?

"Don't despair, Aurianna. All is not lost."

The king's words pierced me, and a flood of cool relief washed the hot pain searing my heart. I let my hands fall from my face and peered up. Resting in the palm of King Alistair's hand was a stone crown.

"Last night, Bastian brought me this and told me he only had time to look for one of them. He promised that he'd return on the morrow with the others. He'd heard someone coming and panicked."

Medusa's Crown!

I sucked in a breath, grabbed the crown, and shouted with high-pitched laughter. The king looked at Sam and he shrugged his shoulders.

"Bastian was talking about me! I was sneaking into the treasury to get the hallows for Persephone. I saw him coming out of the treasury, and he acted like I'd caught him doing something. And from the sounds of it, I did."

I rolled with laughter and hugged the crown to my chest. The shaking of my lungs dislodged all the anguish and tension swirling there moments before.

"Don't you see? We can do this now. As soon as Father gets the bolt of lightning from Zeus and you give Persephone the crown, she's as good as dead."

A loud boom sounded outside, and I jumped nearly dropping the crown. King Alistair ran to the glass opening and Sam jumped up from the chair. I followed him, grabbing onto his shirt. Spurts of flame and multicolored water shot up from the sea in spires. The ground beneath us rumbled and the glass shook.

"Father!"

CHAPTER 12

"What's going on down there?" the king gasped.

"Persephone," I answered.

Sam turned to the king. "Father, we need to help."

The king nodded. "I'll call out the armada. You secure Aurianna and we'll set sail with the tide."

Secure Aurianna? Do they think I'm just going to stand here and do nothing?

I folded my arms across my chest. "I'm not going to be secured anywhere. This is my fault, and I won't have you going off fighting a fight I started without me. My father's life and the lives of my people are at stake because of what I did. I'm coming with you."

Sam looked at his father, and the king set his jaw and shook his head. Sam reached for my hand, but I pulled it away. His eyes lit up with an over-bright fever.

"Aurianna, you've only been human for a day. You haven't even explored all your new body can do. You would . . . you could get hurt yourself and get others hurt."

I pushed past him and stared into King Alistair's face. My heart pounded in my ears.

"I can help you. We'll just have to figure it out. If you leave me here, I'll just find a way out there and get myself killed anyway. So, you better take me now."

"We're coming too," said a familiar voice. I peeked past the king and saw Johanna stomping down the hall with Colin. Her eyes were bright red, and it looked like she'd been crying too.

"We heard the whole thing, and we're ready to fight. We're going to take down the woman who tortured and killed my mother."

Sam pushed past me and his father with his arm outstretched. "No, you two are getting married next week. What if something happened to one or the both of you?"

Colin threw his head back, then looked at Same. "Do you really think I'd let you go and reap all the glory of saving our kingdom and the sea?" Colin raised an eyebrow and smirked. "C'mon, we've been on a lot of adventures, even some you never knew about." He gestured to King Alistair, who frowned. "Sam, you know if we worked together, we could take this sea witch out, even if she is the goddess of the underworld."

Colin punched Sam's shoulder. Johanna walked to me and extended her hand. I took it.

"Father, we're all going."

King Alistair sighed, then reached over with his palm outstretched toward me. "The crown, please." I handed it to him, and he gripped it and closed his eyes. "I started this many years ago and I must finish it. Even if it doesn't bring back your mother, I finally have a chance to make things right, so Persephone can't hurt anyone anymore."

"You won't be alone, Father." Sam put his hand on the king's shoulder, and King Alistair looked at all of us. I could see fear in his proud eyes.

"With Medusa's crown, there's hope," I said. "All we need is Zeus's lightning. I just hope my father was somehow able to get it."

CHAPTER 13

We followed King Alistair down the shore and reached a bay where dozens of ships rocked back and forth in the water. There were lines of men standing on the shore, their eyes darting back and forth, watching the eruptions coming from the middle of the sea.

"Your majesty." A tall man with ruffled hair and clothes approached us. "The last time I saw something like this was when I was a child during the sea war."

"And I fear there is another upon us," said King Alistair. He turned and shouted to the crowd. "Pull the anchors, men, and get ready. We're joining the fight."

The sailors scattered, each running toward their ship. I watched them and prayed to Athena she would protect us all. I had no idea what was happening below, but it didn't look good. I wondered what chance we had to fight from the surface, but I hoped I could trust Sam's father to know what to do.

A shorter man approached, this one dressed in an ornate blue-and-white uniform. He saluted the king.

"Set sail and wait for my signal," Alistair ordered.

"Yes, my king." The uniformed man headed to the ship down the line while we boarded the closest one to us.

Sam took the wheel of the ship, and we headed into dark horizon. Colin, Johanna, and I were hugging the side of the ship, peering down into the water. The dim light made the colors flashing back and forth under the water much more intense. Colin tapped his fingers on the wood. Johanna kept biting her lip and tugging at her long hair.

No one spoke.

I kept silent as well, visions of the destruction that must be happening to my kingdom haunted my every thought. My knees knocked together. I had to keep gulping for air because I was holding my breath until my head swam.

King Alistair approached us and put his hand on Colin's shoulder. He jumped, startling both Johanna and me.

"Drop the port anchor, Colin. We stop here."

Colin ran to the other side of the ship.

"Father, what's happening?" Johanna asked, then bit off the tip of her fingernail.

"Poseidon and Bastian knew that someday this would happen. They knew Persephone would find a way to escape the Seawood Forest and she'd be after them and me, so they put a safety plan in place."

King Alistair reached inside his pocket and drew out a large dolphin-shaped diamond.

"This will signal Poseidon to our location, and when we get his signal back, we can fire."

The king dropped the dolphin in the water. A burst of blue light exploded and remained glowing. A large glittering dolphin jumped into the air, then dove deep into water. Alistair then reached inside his jacket and pulled out Medusa's crown.

"May I?" I asked, and he handed it to me. I peered down at the stone jewels and intricately carved designs and wondered what power it held.

"As soon as we get your father's signal back—"

King Alistair's sentence stopped short and Sam's voice rang out behind me in a panicked scream.

"Aurianna, no!"

A stinging pain gripped my waist. I looked down just long enough to see a large tentacle wrapping around me, then I flew from the ship's deck and plunged into the water.

Kraken.

Sound muted. I thrashed to free myself from the monster's grip, but it grew even tighter. Lights flashed before me, blinding me. The crown slipped from my grip. A burning heat coated me from head to toe. My legs grew stiff and locked at the knee. I whipped my head from side to side as shooting pain pulsed up from my toes, clawing into the flesh of my calves and thighs.

Darkness threatened to consume me, squeeze the last bit of air from my lungs, then the water gurgling in my ears stopped. The sides of my neck pinched tight and liquid flowed inside my mouth. It poured down my throat, melting into my chest, and the dizziness in my head dispersed. I kicked out and felt the water swirl powerfully around me. My fingertips met the smooth scales of my tail and my heart sunk.

A snide voice reverberated in the water around me. "Welcome back, Princess."

I blinked until the image before me cleared. Persephone stood on the ocean floor, white-eyed, a wide toothy smile carving an ugly hole in her pretty gold face. Her hair floated in every direction, pulsing with beads of purple light, the shield of Proteus peeking out over her shoulder.

"I see you found yourself some friends."

My eyes shot down to her hand to see the ring of Phorcys glowing red on her finger. They moved across the golden belt of Heracles hugging her waist and the sword of Oceanus hugging her hip. The kraken who had grabbed me from the ship towered behind her awaiting her next order.

"I see you were able to procure the crown after all. Now that Poseidon is imprisoned, I have no one to worry about." She moved closer, her eyes on the ocean floor under me. I looked down to see the crown of Medusa lying upside down in the sand. I reached down and retrieved it, remembering what King Alistair said. I must give it to her of my own free will.

"Now be a good girl, let's not have any fuss." She held her hand out, an arrogant gleam in her eyes. I met her stare and placed it in her palm.

"Pretty thing, isn't it." She bit her lip and placed Medusa's crown on her head. The moment it touched down, her eyes ignited with silver light that traveled across her face and permeated her golden skin turning it white. Her hair floated upward, engulfed in silver flame. The mythic hallows burned with fiery illumination. The kraken slinked backward and disappeared as if frightened of her presence, but I smiled. The sight was terrible, yes, but the hallows were together now. All I needed was Zeus's lightning.

I darted to the right to escape and she lifted her hand. A purple spark flew from Phorcys's ring and struck me in the chest. Crippling pain ripped through me, and I hurtled backward, spinning out of control. I crashed to the ocean floor, and paralysis began spreading outward from my core. I couldn't move my arms or my fins.

"Oh look, your idiot human is trying to play hero. He's plunged in to save you." Persephone cackled. "Poor soul. He has no idea what he's up against. I told you earlier. There are no heroes in this story."

Panic shot into my gut as I saw Sam diving at us with a sharp metal spear.

I tried to scream out to tell him to stop, but I was too late. I watched helpless as Persephone raised her hand. The ring glowed purple. Just before the spark released, Sam hurled the spear at Persephone. She had to jump aside to avoid it and a violet spike flew past him barely missing him.

"You fool!" She screeched. Sam turned around to swim back to the surface and Persephone pulled Oceanus's sword from her hip.

"You want to play?" she said and launched the sword at Sam. The tip of it drove home, slicing a large gash in Sam's leg before turning around and returning to Persephone's open hand.

Crimson flowers poured from the wound as Sam struggled and kicked to reach the surface.

"I take you a piece at a time until you drown."

I launched toward her, but the kraken emerged from its hiding place, it's beady black eyes watching me. I stopped short knowing it could crush me with one squeeze. My eyes darted between Persephone and Sam. There was nothing I could do. I was as useless as a net full of dead fish with it guarding me.

Persephone pulled her hand back to launch the sword again, but the ground beneath us rumbled and split in front of her. She teetered, then tumbled backward, the sword falling from her hand. Sam kept swimming and I prayed to Athena he'd reach the surface and get help.

I looked behind her to see where the miracle had come from and met the most beautiful and welcome sight I'd ever seen. My father emerged from the cloudy water, bloody and bruised, a handful of soldiers, including Bastian, at his side. In his hand, a silver bolt of lightning crackled.

"Pick up your sword, Persephone. Let's finish this."

Persephone rose, the silver glow from her skin pulsing brighter than before, leaving the sword on the ground.

"Put down the bolt, Poseidon."

"Never. This ends right now."

"Fine. I don't need the sword, Poseidon. I have this." She tapped the crown on her head.

Persephone took the crown off, pressed Phorcys's ring into the stone jewel in the center, and the stone façade faded. She placed it on her head and the interweaving spires of the crown writhed and squirmed like snakes.

"Shield your eyes, men," Father shouted. "One look at the crown will turn you to stone."

The men covered their eyes and I watched in horror as she stalked them one by one, piercing them with the burning spark from Phorcys' ring. When their eyes opened in response to the pain, they tried to fight but once they'd met the snake's glare, their bodies stiffened into stone. One by one they froze, leaving only my father and Bastian, both helpless without their vision. Persephone picked up the sword and with a swift swipe across Bastian's abdomen, he fell to the ground at my father's feet. My father dropped the bolt and dropped to his knees.

"Bastian, no!" he screamed.

Persephone took off the crown and pressed the ring into the center jewel once more. The snakes bent and stiffened melting into sharp spires. The crown returned to stone.

"Open your eyes, Poseidon. I have turned the crown back to stone. I want you to be wide awake so when I cut your daughter's heart from her chest. I want you to see the light leave her eyes."

"Persephone, spare her. For the love of the Gods, I beg you," my father pleaded, his eyes opening.

"Spare her, like you spared my Hades?" she hissed. "I'm going to fillet her flesh from her bones."

A metal spear came flying at Persephone from above. This time it connected but merely bounced off Proteus's shield. Persephone screamed in surprise. I looked up to see Sam, his arm pulled back to launch another spear at the goddess.

Persephone turned her back on my father to face Sam. She raised her hand and released an enormous violet ray from Phorcys's ring right at Sam. A scream that had been building in my chest rose up my throat and broke free. I looked at my Father and he stared at me wide-eyed, shocked at having heard my voice. I shot him a pleading look and he nodded. He reached down, retrieved the lightning bolt, and thrust it at her back.

Vivid red, purple, and blue sparks erupted from her ring as the bolt pierced the shield on her back and exited out of her chest.

Time stopped.

White lightning exploded from her eyes, fingertips, and toes. Persephone's body trembled with violent jerks, then she collapsed into a thousand granules of black sand.

I vaulted into the water above me, searching for any sign of Sam, but he was gone.

Is he dead, did the spark kill him? Please. No. No.

"Aurianna, your voice. I heard you scream." My father swam up beside me.

"Yes, I'll tell you about that later. Right now I need your help." He blinked.

"Who was that human? Why was he helping us?" Father looked agitated and surprised.

"That human's name is Sam. He saved my life. I need your help, Father. We must find him. Come on. Please."

I shot up toward the surface and Father followed me. I could see the bottom of a large ship and prayed it was King Alistair's ship.

I needed it to be his ship.

I broke the surface and searched. "King Alistair. King Alistair. Can you hear me?"

"King Alistair?" Father repeated beside me.

A group of people peered over the edge of the hull. The king waved his arm.

"Where is Sam?" I yelled, the words choking in my throat.

Please tell me he got up here safe. Please tell me you've seen him.

Sam's face peered around the front of the ship. "Aurianna!"

"Sam!" My fin felt light. The breath in my lungs was stolen. He was alive. I swam to meet him, and we collided into each other's arms. His wet lips met mine and I gripped him close to me, beating my tail to keep him upright. He kissed me, roaming his lips over mine, then pulled away and held my face in his hands.

"I thought I lost you," we both said at the same time, then burst into laughter.

He pressed his lips against mine again so hard I had to fight to keep my head up. I returned the kiss, and he traced my lips, then pulled back and kissed my forehead, nose, and lips again.

"How's your leg?" I said, worried about the deep gash from Persephone's sword.

"I'll live," he said.

My father cleared his throat I realized he was still behind me. "Sorry, Father."

"Father, this is Sam. King Alistair's son."

Sam tipped his head and bowed. "It's a pleasure to meet you, Poseidon sir, uh, your majesty."

My father looked at Sam with piercing eyes, straight lipped for a long moment, then he smiled under his long white beard.

"Thank you for saving my daughter."

CHAPTER 14

"Sam, catch!" A rope smacked the water from the side of the ship, and I saw King Alistair holding onto the other end. Sam grabbed the rope to keep him afloat.

"I better get this leg wrapped up." He said and kissed my nose.

"Okay."

Sam hooked his arm around the rope and the king pulled him back onto the ship. We followed it back to shore. My heart beat heavy in my throat feeling my fin swim underneath me. I was a merwoman again. Sam was human. There wasn't really a happy ending that could be had. I mean, I was happy he was alive, and that Persephone was no longer a threat to his kingdom or mine. We'd both avenged our mother's deaths and lived. And I knew how he felt about me. It was clear by his reaction. He felt the same way I did.

I loved him, and he loved me.

But love wasn't going to be enough. We'd be able to see each other, even try to spend time together, but we could never have what my father and mother had, what his father and mother had.

Marriage and a family.

The king's armada docked, and I waited in the water with my father as King Alistair's ship unloaded. I watched them walk on their legs and remembered how it felt to have land under my feet instead of water beneath my tail.

Sam limped to shore as soon as he left the boat.

"Aurianna," he yelled and waved his arm.

I swam as close to the shore as I could, and he waded out to meet me. I put my arms around his neck. He laid his forehead on mine and we closed our eyes.

"Now what are we going to do?" he whispered.

"I don't know," I said.

"Aurianna, I know it's too soon, and I shouldn't say this, but . . . I love you. I can't imagine my life without you now."

I reached around his neck and hugged him tight.

"I'll come to the shore every day," he pressed on. "We can still be together." He caressed my wet hair.

"Sam, I can't let you do that. You've given me so many things to remember, I'll always be grateful to you for that."

Sam pulled away and took my face in his hands. "Don't say that. I can do it and I will. Every day, I'll be here."

"Aurianna?" my father's voice rang out behind me.

I closed my eyes. I knew what his tone meant. He wanted me to say goodbye.

"Aurianna, can you give Sam and me a few minutes? I'd like to talk to him privately."

My eyes sprung back open. "But, Father—"

"Please, Aurianna."

I let go of Sam, kissed him once passionately, then swam away without another word.

"Aurianna. I'll see you tomorrow, right?"

I looked back at Sam. Warm liquid filled my eyes. I didn't know what to say to him. I had no idea what my father was going to do or say. I would see him tomorrow even if Father forbade it. I'd find a way. But deep down I knew it would be prolonging the inevitable. Human and mermaid. Neither one of us fitting into each other's worlds. Only living halfway. Even if my father didn't forbid it, the odds of it working were insurmountable.

I barely had enough energy to keep from sinking. All feeling left my arms and fins. I put my hand over my mouth and let myself descend into the water toward our kingdom, wondering what it would look like after the battle with Persephone. So much had been gained but so much had been lost. A heavy price paid on so many accounts.

I reached my castle and, to my relief, found much of it intact, including my bedroom. I swam inside and looked around. All my journals and writing tablets had fallen in heaps on the floor. There were a few cracks in the walls, and many of my trinkets lay in disarray on the floor. I spotted the music box my father gave me yesterday and realized, it was still my birthday. Surprise overwhelmed me. I leaned down and retrieved the gift, then sat on my bed and opened it. The miniature glowing figures of my parents rose once again and began to spin around the room, unknowing, unaware of the day's events. My mother's sweet melodious voice filled the silence.

> When your heart found mine, true love came to be
> Two souls so divine, joined under the sea
> I'll always have you, you'll always have me
> Together forever, my beloved you'll be

Pride swelled with the pain in my heart. My mother's death had been avenged today, and the people of my kingdom were forever safe from Persephone and the mythic hallows. My father was safe. Sam was safe. We were all okay.

My chest heaved, and a cry broke from my quivering lips. I buried my face in my hands. We were all okay, but I wasn't really. The only person I'd ever connected with, who had seen me as more than just a silent princess to feel sorry for was gone. I'd never dance like my parents, never find another who could love me like Sam could.

I let the music box play over and over again and spent the next hour cleaning up my bedroom, restacking my memoirs, and wondering what I was going to do to keep myself from breaking in half. Yesterday, all I wanted was my voice. I thought having my voice would make everything else perfect. Nothing else would matter. Now I had my voice, I would've given it up in a second to be with Sam.

After my room was clean I settled on my bed and watched the dancing figures twirl and glide through every corner of my room to keep my mind occupied as I waited for Father to return.

"Your father tells me it's your birthday."

I bolted up at the sound of the impossibly familiar voice. I whipped my head toward the door and found Sam floating in my doorway, a strong blue fin swaying back and forth under him, his white shirt undulating in the water, barely covering his bare chest.

"Sam, what are you . . . how are you . . . ?"

"Your father could see there was something special between us. Out of his love for you and respect for my father, he offered me a choice. He asked me if I wanted to become one of you, and, of course, I didn't hesitate."

I looked at him. Seeing him like this was so surreal, it was hard for my eyes to believe it. "Sam, what about your life? Johanna and Colin, your father, the kingdom?"

Sam shrugged and winked at me. "I told them about my choice, and they fully supported me. Colin told me that I'd have to teach him how to swim with the dolphins. Johanna made me promise to bring her lots of pearls. Father . . . well, he just wants us to be happy."

He swam inside my room and noticed the tiny figures dancing around my room. He smiled a wide-toothed grin that made me laugh and reached his hand out. I placed my hand in his and he kissed the top of it.

"Now, birthday girl, how about a dance?"

THE END

ABOUT THE AUTHOR

Angela Brimhall grew up trying to decide whether she liked romance or horror novels best. She graduated college with a BS degree in health, but decided she'd much rather experience the drama of life through her characters. She received an MFA in English and creative writing from Southern New Hampshire University and is a member of the Sigma Tau Delta English Honors Society, Romance Writers of America and Horror Writers Association. She lives in the heart of a city between two mountains with her husband, son and four dogs where spired castles dot every hill and fairy tales really do come true.

www.authorangelabrimhall.com

AFTERWORD

We hope you enjoyed Fractured See! We would love to have you leave a review on your favorite retailer!

Keep in touch with us and get updates about the next Fairy Tale Ink installment at www.FairyTaleInkBooks.com.

Made in the USA
Middletown, DE
17 December 2020